PREY FOR REVENGE

PETER ROCHE

ArrowGate

Published by Arrow Gate Publishing Ltd

London

20 19 18 17 15 16 15 14 13 12

Arrow Gate Publishing's titles may be purchased in bulk for educational, business, fundraising, or sales promotional use. For information, please email info@arrowgatepublishing.com

A CIP catalogue record for this book is available from the British Library
ISBN 978-1-913142-48-3
eBook 978-1-913142-47-6

www.arrowgatepublishing.com

Arrow Gate Publishing Ltd Reg. No. 8376606
Arrow Gate Publishing 85, Great Portland Street, London W1W 7LT

Cover Art Design By Nikol Paldanova
Book Cover Design By Hannah Wong

EU GPSR Authorised Representative LOGOS EUROPE, 9 rue Nicolas Poussin, 1700, LA ROCHELLE, France
Email: contact@logoseurope.eu

For My Son Toby James

Revenge is a kind of wild justice, which the more man's nature runs to, the more ought law to weed it out. For as for the wrong, it doth but offend the law; but the revenge of that wrong, putteth the law out of office.

—Sir Francis Bacon, 'OF REVENGE' Circa 1625

• PROLOGUE •

Six Years Prior

"We are the Pilgrims"
(James Elroy Flecker's: The Golden Journey to Samarkand)

The self-proclaimed Saifullah, *sword of Allah*, Asif Badawi, stood proudly on a rocky ridge and surveyed the barren landscape far below in the pre-dawn haze that heralded the blistering arrival of the sun. It was a perilous place – alive with hostile actors of every colour and creed.

A region governed by warlords and tribal elders, where money, drugs, guns, and religious persecution dictated power. Often referred to as The Badlands, it lies near the turbulent borders of Iran, Afghanistan, and Pakistan, areas where many individuals from each country faced severe oppression under an anti-Western religious theocracy.

Iran is recognised internationally as the largest state sponsor of terrorism. Afghanistan is a totalitarian emirate controlled by the Taliban, while Pakistan offers a haven to terrorists of various groups. Badawi, despite limited combat experience, was a clever and strategic thinker, skilled in deception. Now, it was time for revenge. His beloved uncle, Adeem Badawi, had been killed two weeks earlier, along with twelve members of his tribal family, at an Iranian-funded sniper training school less than fifty kilometres north. From childhood, Adeem had been like a surrogate father to Asif. His own father, an extremist, kept him at a distance, and they were estranged for many years – compounded by the fact that Asif's mother was killed by a car bomb intended for his father in Beirut years earlier – fostering in Asif a deep hatred of the West and making him uneasy around his father.

The sole survivor, Abu Zayed al-Zarqawi, a close friend of Asif since their childhood days, told him that he only avoided his own death by covering himself in the blood of his comrades and pretending to be dead among the over 200 killed, all decimated by hellfire rockets in cold blood without warning at the time of dawn prayer salat al-fajr. – *Subhanallah,* praise and thanks to Allah – the one and only. The most glorious. Now, revenge – فَعَاقِبُواْ بِمِثْلِ مَا عُوقِبْتُم بِهِ *punish them with the like of that with which you were afflicted.* Asif noted the exact timing of the brutal attack. It was no accident that it happened during this holy prayer time. He raised his hands to the sky in prayer to Allah, pleading for Satan's forces to be overcome.

A joint team of SEAL and SAS Special Forces was then deployed on the ground to carry out cleanup operations, comprising a brutal group of ruthless professional killers. In a calculated act of retribution, Asif had sent his second-in-command, Syed Ayad, two days prior, to establish a fake camp with five of his men in a valley ravine beneath the towering rocky terrain. Following instructions, Syed Ayad subtly spread rumours among their tribal contacts that Abdulaziz Badawi, Asif's father, would be present at the camp, indicating an imminent important meeting.

Asif also meticulously prepared scripted dialogues for his people to broadcast on their radios, fully aware that these communications would likely be intercepted and relayed to American and British forces nearby. Recognising that such information would be invaluable to them – especially since his father was a notorious terrorist financier and high on their Kill List- he was confident that American surveillance satellites would detect the camp, prompting a special forces team to be deployed to attack.

He'd positioned his three Iranian-trained snipers in strategic vantage points high above the encampment the previous night, under cloudy skies and a faint crescent moon. The low light was meant to conceal their deployment. However, he made two misjudgements. Firstly, his snipers would later face a rising sun, making target acquisition harder. Secondly, their telescopic scopes would likely reflect the rising fiery sun, revealing their position.

Friendly tribal sources had indicated that American SEAL teams were heavily involved in the North, so the likely deployment would be the British Special Air Service. However, he didn't care either way. He was prepared – Death never offers a second chance. To support his snipers, over forty of his men were hidden among the rocks and crevices around the camp, ready to execute a brutal and successful ambush.

He leaned back, satisfied, and waited for everything to unfold. A carefully planned ambuscade – in Hebrew אָרַב, meaning to lie in wait. Little did he realise that this trap would eventually lead to his own downfall years later.

He didn't have to wait long. Using his binoculars, he watched the Desert Camo AH-64E Apache Attack Helicopter fly very low and fast towards his position in the early morning desert haze. They had fallen for the trap. He had to admit the pilot was clever enough to ensure his approach, about a kilometre away, was over rocky terrain, avoiding the usual sand clouds produced by the rotor blades' downdraft. Hovering just about a metre above the rocky, barren ground, it deployed its special forces team. They wore no insignia that clearly identified them as members of the British Special Air Service.

He counted an eight-man SAS squad dressed in full desert combat gear, wearing body armour and armed with H&K 33s. He noted that two of them also carried L96A1 sniper rifles, which he knew were among the finest in the world. He should know, as his Iranian-trained snipers use the same rifle. Chambered to fire the 7.62x51mm NATO cartridge from a 10-round detachable magazine, it is a lethal long-range weapon. He recalled that some military units nicknamed it the Green Meanie.

Asif hurriedly and surreptitiously ran to advise his men, unaware that the team had shrunk to six from the original eight. The two British snipers had already moved ahead to higher ground to secure their well-hidden Snipers Nest. This was a costly mistake due to Asif's arrogance in assuming his numerical advantage and the placement of his snipers would ensure his success.

The remaining six SAS soldiers deployed, immediately running in a wide fan formation toward the target zone as their boots hit the harsh, unforgiving rocky terrain, while their vehicle disappeared into the mid-morning haze. This process took less than three minutes. Unaware, they were being closely watched by Asif Badawi from his concealed vantage point.

Well ahead of their comrades-in-arms, Sergeant Angus McGregor and Captain Peter Meer, both the designated snipers in the team, covered the 1-kilometre distance to their pre-selected location and embedded themselves in under eight minutes. Carefully placing their 25-pound full Bergen rucksacks in Multicam MTP beside them on the steep rocky outcrop overlooking the encampment. They set up 20 yards apart, checked their rifles, and scanned the zone through their Schmidt & Bender 6x12 telescopic sights. The choice of optimum positions had been discussed and decided the night before, using American satellite imagery.

"Looks pretty quiet, mate," Angus said.

"Too bloody quiet, if you ask me," replied Capt. Peter Meer, turning his scope back to the camp and his team below. "I see six. They're wearing Ghutra's, so it's hard to tell if our target is there. One is pouring from an Ibrik, so I guess they're enjoying Arak, a strong-flavoured liquor for their sins."

“There are large stacks of AK-47s lying around the camp. What do we do now?”

Angus asked, eager to proceed.

“We wait."

"Yeah, I've heard that before. At least we’re not buried up to our heads in snow or stuck in worse conditions for hours," Angus chuckled as he checked his rifle.

Capt. Meer conducted another sweep of his team’s positions and flicked on his comms.

"Okay, boys, it’s looking good so far. Stand by, wait for my ‘Go’."

"Affirmative, boss,” responded each member of the team.

Suddenly, the glass of a scope flashed high above the encampment, alerting Meer. "Watch out, Angus, sniper up to your 10 o’clock, I’ll take him," warned Meer.

Simultaneously, a round shattered a rock inches from Meer’s face. So close to his ear that he felt the shockwave. Shards of rock badly shredded the right side of his face. Having lost its momentum, the round bounced harmlessly off his GS Mark 7 helmet. Captain Meer instinctively reached up with his right hand to check the integrity of his tactical comms headset and found it undamaged. Ignoring the pain and the blood pouring from the lacerations, Captain Meer calmly took down the sniper with a clean, measured shot.

“Must’ve been 700 metres plus, mate – nice one,” said Angus, having taken out another scope flash at his 12 o’clock at a similar distance as his fellow sniper took out yet another.

"We've been set up, Angus, like ducks in a row. Go, boys, we've got your six."

Commanded Capt. Meer and his team hurriedly advanced towards the encampment.

Both British snipers, having located and eliminated Asif's snipers, focused their attention and weapons on the increasing number of hostiles emerging from their well-hidden positions in the jagged fractures and wide clefts characteristic of the desert rocky landscape. Meer's team charged forward, taking down many of the terrorists who appeared out of nowhere. In Captain Meer's experience, this was rapidly becoming, tactically, a bloody mess and an untenable situation as more of Asif's reserves streamed into the firefight from their rocky hideouts – flooding the Kill Zone with relentless, indiscriminate fire from their blazing AK 47's.

"So much for Intel mate, this's turning into an almighty clusterfuck," said Angus, grim-faced but simultaneously impressed that so many hostiles had been taken out with no casualties to the team.

"Disengage – Fall back. Fall back now!" Meer commanded his team over comms.

"We'll cover your six. Go."

"Affirmative, boss."

The team retreated from the kill zone to regroup at the designated Evac Point, awaiting further instructions. During the intense firefight, Asif was devastated to see over twenty of his men, including his snipers, eliminated. He signalled his remaining forces to move forward. However, more of his ragtag group fell, unable to keep up with the SAS's unmatched speed and agility, which are renowned in combat for their high level of fitness.

But then, suddenly, the SAS team had vanished. Confused, Asif pondered what his next move should be. It was then that he saw the bodies of his beloved three younger brothers lying dead. He fell to the ground in despair and laid his hands lovingly on his lost family members, crying out, *"Inna lillahi wa inna ilayhi raji'un".* Surely, to Allah we belong, and to Him we will all return. Each had suffered a clean, single fatal headshot that could only have been achieved, at that distance, by the precision shot of an exceptional sniper.

Six hundred yards away, the sniper in question, Capt. Peter Meer was reloading. Without a desert wind, the smell of gunpowder and death filled the air like a choking fog that refused to disperse, but Meer had been there before; death was in the air. He didn't see Asif Badawi charging up the hill on his blind side until it was too late. Captain Peter Meer, 22 SAS, Sabre Squadron, lay in the rocky sand now, mortally wounded.

In his final moments, his heart was heavy with grief as he gazed at the body of his long-time mate, Angus, now only an arm's length away. They had met when both were serving in the Parachute Regiment and, after three years, decided to submit their papers for the SAS. However, they didn't truly bond until they had successfully completed the gruelling and perilous 'Endurance' phase of training in the Brecon Beacons, known as the Fan Dance – a demanding 15-mile trek carrying a 35lb Bergen and weapon over the mountains. Angus was not only his closest friend for more than a decade, but he had also been his Best Man on that joyful day, some years earlier.

He couldn't see any obvious wounds, which briefly filled him with hope. He struggled to reach across and gently turn his old friend over. A round had grazed his forehead at the hairline. It might have been survivable, ironically, if it hadn't been for his helmet. As it was, the bullet must have ricocheted around inside with devastating effect. A tragic coincidence, but either way, the bullet had Angus's name on it. An old saying never openly discussed, but everyone knew that if it's your time, that's it. At least his passing would have been instant. He closed the eyes that stared back at him and kissed his friend's forehead in respect and comradeship. His only wish now was that they would lie side by side at the SAS Cemetery in St. Martin's Church Yard, Hereford—home to their fallen comrades.

Now, the desert sun had turned the entire area into a blazing inferno. As a highly skilled expert in the art of killing, he was well aware that he was on the brink of death. He'd been hit directly in the chest and left leg by a sustained burst from Asif's AK-47. In a sudden and unexpected charge up the hill, the target caught him off guard, despite the higher-cut helmet's enhanced peripheral vision. His body armour had absorbed the impact to his chest, but his left leg was severely wounded, and at six hundred rounds a minute, it was barely holding together, and he was bleeding out quickly.

He leaned against a rock with a grim, bitter smile at his fate, knowing he had taken nine of the bad guys with him. He understood that intelligence was often imperfect – he knew that –

but this time, the desk warriors had outdone themselves. He was assigned to eliminate Abdulaziz Badawi, yet the intelligence suggested a small cell of six extremists. Instead, his team was ambushed by over forty enemies. As his team retreated under his command from the brutal, one-sided firefight, he and Angus held their ground to facilitate the withdrawal. Tragically, Angus paid the ultimate price in the bloodbath. The deadly exchange lasted only a few minutes, but the outcome was final.

And now his field dressings were fighting a losing battle. He reckoned he'd only got moments of his life left before he joined his mate, Angus. Placing his pistol in his left hand, he managed to reach into his kit to get his wallet with the picture of his wife and children. Tears streamed down his bloodied face as he turned it over and read, *'Come home safe, my darling, we love you, Cathy and the children'*. Cathy had been his soulmate from day one – never complaining, always there to welcome him home, mission after mission. It was, of course, against all the rules to carry personal stuff into combat, but then, like Angus, he'd been a rule breaker all his life too and as a result had lost 'rank' many times throughout his military career. However, they'd both found their niche with the SAS, who had noted and rewarded their particular skill sets. But that mistake would have serious repercussions for his family down the line, though he wasn't to know that.

In the midst of death, his last image was Cathy and his children running toward him, smiling happily, arms outstretched as he finally faded into eternal darkness. Asif looked down at the bodies of the men who had killed his three younger brothers and spat in their faces, his only satisfaction being that it had been his own weapon that had taken them out. He had charged in an uncontrollable rage at the two embedded snipers, an act on any battlefield that would have been praised as courage and heroism, and he thanked Allah for his survival. He snatched the soldier's crumpled ID and bloodstained family photograph from his grip. As he stared at the image, he viciously kicked the lifeless body of Captain Peter Meer and raised his arms to plead with Allah, the supreme creator, for revenge – an eye for an eye. He'd find them and kill them, Allah willing – it would not end here. And indeed, it turned out it didn't. Little did he know that his chosen path would lead to his own entrapment a few years later.

Time was slipping away swiftly, and he realised the SAS would, predictably, call in air support to eliminate his remaining men. Although he trained them well, they couldn't match their skill levels, and he lost the day despite having the advantage of numbers. Now that the element of surprise had disappeared, it was time to retreat. He slung his cherished Russian-made AK47 over his shoulder – its barrel still too hot to touch – and signalled to his remaining men to follow. He felt humiliated by how few of them were left.

Then, as feared, the menacing Apache Attack helicopter reappeared moments later, blazing in relentlessly with full force. He took cover in a deep rock crevice for protection. The gunner chose to use his M230 30mm cannon rather than his Hydra-70 2.75-inch rockets or Hellfire missiles – the only weapons required to eliminate the remaining terrorists desperately fleeing.

The pilot of the Apache Attack helicopter swept back to the designated Evac-Point – devastated to see the bodies of Captain Peter Meer and Sergeant Angus McGregor, as the SAS team respectfully carried their remains onboard.

As Asif lay safely beneath the rocky overhang, with heavy calibre rounds pounding the rocks and sand around him, he reflected on the irrevocable changes to his life and mindset since his mother was killed when he was thirteen years old – the only woman he had ever loved. His appetite for killing was paramount – killing was a pleasure to savour, just as relationships with women. He was surprised to find tears washing the sand from his face, the first since her death. The helicopter roared away overhead, having completed its task. Hesitantly, he stepped out of hiding and was horrified to see his men decimated, a carnage he couldn't ignore. As the sole survivor, he escaped into the mountains' safety. Over the years, Asif had learned the strength patience could offer. He planned to survive, fight again, and someday enjoy a bitter revenge.

Qur'an: *'Whoso fighteth in the way of Allah, be he slain or be victorious, on him we shall bestow a vast reward.'*

• CHAPTER 1 •

The full moon illuminated the room and the Painter's body with a cold, white light. He lay on the bed – the rumpled silk sheets arousing a sense of desire as he stirred impatiently, waiting for his friends to arrive. He wasn't a painter yet, but, unknown to him, he was destined to become one very soon.

He looked down at the lithe body that had satisfied so many women, both willing and unwilling, with no attachment ever involved. All dead now. In fact, he couldn't remember how many he'd murdered over the years. Those he did recall had left him with happy memories hidden in the dark shadows of his mind. But he'd never taken any gratification in the kills. Not at all – it was always the natural outcome of every encounter – typical and without doubt. But now, only two remained to be dealt with. As to the method of their despatch, he would wait.

No doubt his friends would show him the path to take with that decision.

As he waited, he reflected on the enormous success of his latest book, 'Thanatos' – the Greek god of death, written under a pseudonym. He appreciated the anonymity it provided. Over fifty million copies had been sold worldwide in forty different languages. The main character was dear to him, as had been the case with all his bestsellers. His hero's inclination for murder was simply an extension of his own appetite. He found it amusing that, despite his success as a writer, no reader knew his true identity. Even his literary agent and publisher had never met him. He never appeared at book signings, and his picture never featured on any of his books. Surprisingly, this anonymity had actually increased his sales, much to his agent's astonishment. Over the years, fans looked for any clue to the author's identity but found nothing, which only intensified their desire for more of his work.

The Painter, to be, had never experienced the fantasy called love; he only knew of a lust that had to be sated at all costs. It wasn't that he hated women – only an ingrained mistrust – perhaps worsened by the fact that his mother had abused him as a child. Later, in his troubled mind, he decided to return to her. Payback – his first kill. Yes, some had declared their love for him – fools and liars as they were. They had only enjoyed his body for their own selfish pleasure, just as he had enjoyed theirs, until their inevitable downfall at his hand. His appetite for domination was only surpassed by his desire to kill, but then he had never been indiscriminate in his choice of victims. The criteria are simple: the younger the better, within reason.

The Painter had to admit that there were times when navigating the line between what's real and what wasn't became blurred, but his belief in his friend's guidance never diminished. It had never ceased to fascinate him how his mind was able to portray and display, so vividly and perfectly, the images of his fictional murderers for him to enjoy.

But there had been one woman he had allowed to linger too long in his life. She had not only ticked all his boxes from the start but was also the exception in that he spared her life because her skills were unmatched, especially with her twin sister in the mix – he had enjoyed their wantonness, but today their fate was to be decided. True, only one had broken the cardinal rule of infidelity, but the other had been complicit in the unforgivable deceit. And so, both had to be fatally punished.

He reached for a second glass of sacramental wine; the touch of irony it presented did not escape him. He had taken the wine from the cellar of a disgraced Jesuit paedophile years ago. That act of killing him had felt so justified, so sweet, and well-deserved. Little did that loathsome priest realise what a true blessing the wine would become. It was almost like a heaven-sent moment, or perhaps, from the other place, literally.

His only true friends were so easily summoned to do his bidding, offer their counsel, and attend to his special needs – just a glass or two was enough. The conduit for their presence. Over the years, they stayed longer with their host, always eager to please. Each, created by him on the page, each revered by his readers. Now, they slowly evolve and morph into the delightful liberators of madness they have become. Ephemeral entities cavorting uninhibited in the space provided by their master. His invitation is always welcome, releasing them from the torment of waiting to be called from the dark corners of his mind for their direction and guidance. The result is all that matters.

And now, at last, they appeared. Their fleeting arms reached out in supplication. He was always euphoric to see the deliciously ruthless macabre spirits of his murderers materialise before him, paying homage. No victims, of course. They were of no consequence to them or their revered host. Nobody cheated death in their world. Slowly, the images began to dissolve. Their work complete. It was time for them to leave the harsh moonlight behind. In his mind, their departure always caused a fleeting moment of loss, but then there was always the next time for him to savour the unfailing clarity they brought to his thinking. He thankfully drank the remnants of the deeply purple wine, savouring its exquisite taste in a gesture of farewell and in salute to them for their guidance – he raised his glass, grateful as always. Decisions had been made.

For old times' sake, the women's deaths would be swift. There would be some pain, of course, but not too much, as his friends had counselled. The Painter was initially surprised by their uncharacteristic clemency, but then he reflected that it was only fair concerning both women. After all, both had eagerly played their roles in his satisfaction. It wasn't that he was sentimental – far from it. Sentiment was an emotion foreign to him, but for one of the women to use him and then discard him for another had been a fatal mistake in the game they played, and she would pay the ultimate price, as would her twin.

But the demise of the illicit lover would be deliciously slow – but not just yet. His friends had wisely advised that it would be too soon... But in the matter of the lover's death, he'd been destined to become an artist. How satisfyingly inventive they were. He'd never have imagined such a delightful and unique method of dispatch without them. Yes, his ego had been irrevocably wounded. That was true. But now it was time for retribution at last — but only the women for now. As for the lover, he couldn't wait to start his debut as an artist, but patience was necessary. The delay itself added an irresistible touch of spice. The anticipation of that was all-consuming.

Happy now with the last sip of wine spent, The Painter was ready to kill – it had been too long since the last.

CHAPTER 2

As he waited for the women to regain full consciousness, The Painter relaxed in his study, relishing the flavour of his oval cigarette while sipping and enjoying a glass or two of Louis Roederer Crystal Brut-1947, one of his many preferred selections from his well-stocked cellar.

Content, at his antique 19th-century oak, ornate, engraved leather-top writing desk, he considered the two women now handcuffed to the heavy oak chairs before him. It amused him that the padded handcuffs were now playing a different game in securing their hands and feet instead of the usual bedposts. The effects of the liquid ecstasy that he'd added to their champagne earlier were beginning to wear off, gradually. It hadn't been difficult to carry them from the bedroom – they were, after all, as skinny as hell – which was always his preference.

On his desk lay a matched pair of rare English flintlock duelling pistols by Wogdon & Barton, London, circa 1795. Each featured 10-inch octagonal barrels in .54 calibre smoothbore, with signed top flats. They had engraved and sighted tangs, gold-filled touch holes, signed and bolted locks, and engraved trigger guards with pineapple finials, all fitted with full walnut stocks. Beside them was their decorative inlaid mahogany case, his pride and joy. A welcoming and inspired method of dispatch, suggested by his friends. Helen woke first, incredulous as she took in the scene. He watched her eyes shift from confusion to wariness, then to wide-eyed fear. The Painter could not have wished for more. Melissa stirred, now fully awake too, and her reactions followed the same progression.

"Do I have your full attention, ladies?"

"What the hell is going on? Have you gone crazy?" said Helen.

"Far from it, my dear. I have a special and unique surprise! And here they are, one for each of you."

He picked up the pistols, enjoying the feel and perfect balance in his hands. The sensation of gripping the checkered butt also brought him sensual pleasure.

"You see, they are identical, just like you two, but are certainly more trustworthy. If you get my drift," he smiled. "Beautiful, aren't they, don't you think? But wait, there's more. They're not loaded yet. I thought I'd share with you how that's done; it's quite a complex and interesting process. And I've got all the original tools right here," he said smoothly, patting the mahogany-inlaid case affectionately.

Melissa started moaning and crying uncontrollably; she had always been the gentler-natured of the two.

"Do please try to concentrate as this part is, almost, the most fun. First, we half-cock the pistol using the ramrod to ensure the barrel is clear. We don't want any mishaps, do we? Then, just the right amount from the powder flask down the barrel."

He held up the 54-calibre lead ball between his fingers to show them.

"Can you imagine the force of impact at about a thousand feet per second, eh? Not bad for two-hundred-year-old pistols. But I digress. First, we place it in the wad and ram it down the barrel. I like to give the wad a bit of a lick first – not sure why, but it personalises it in some way for me. And finally, we need a little powder in the pan for the flint to ignite, and we're ready to go. Oh, then, we just fully cock it, and it's ready. You like things fully cocked, don't you, Helen?"

He repeated the process with the other pistol and reverently laid both on his ornate leather-topped desk.

"I... I've always been faithful to you... I..."

"Such welcome news, Melissa, but I wonder, is it conceivable that you are implying your sister hasn't been?"

"Leave her alone, you piece of low life, this is between you and me. Leave her out of it," screamed Helen.

"Too late for that, I'm afraid."

"So, what *do* you want, you perverted bastard?"

"Perversion hasn't seemed to have troubled you in the past, my dear Helen. However, I've had you both, and that was mostly fun, but now it's farewell time, I'm afraid. In fact, it's well overdue. I just have two simple questions. But only for you, dear Helen. First, who gave you those beautiful emerald earrings that you insist on wearing so often?"

"I told you before, it was my mother."

"Oh dear. Wrong answer."

The Painter raised the pistol slowly and methodically, took careful aim. His left hand was supporting the long barrel, and he pulled the trigger. In the time it took between the flash and the bang, he was delighted to see a flicker of hope in Melissa's eyes that maybe this was just another game after all, but then the .54 calibre lead ball did its work. She'd been so eager to please, so charmingly submissive. He had satisfied his wish that her death would be deservedly quick. Helen screamed hysterically as she watched her twin slump forward.

"That's one of the amusing aspects of these flintlocks. I've heard that time slows when one is staring down the barrel, waiting for death, but flintlocks involve a dramatic delay between pulling the trigger and it actually firing. Lost for words? So, why don't you just calm down? It was quick and painless. Can't you be grateful for that?"

"Nick, it was Nick. It was just a little present. It meant nothing," she managed to stammer. Her words became increasingly jumbled and incoherent as her sister now slumped dead beside her.

"That's better. But sadly, it's a bit too late for Melissa. So, to the second and final question, how long have you been sleeping with him?"

"No, no, I swear he was only a friend. Please...please believe me," her words jumbled with disbelief and shock.

"It seems you forgot about the camera, my dear. You know how much I enjoy watching the replays of our games. But it's movement-activated, and my goodness, you two were impressively active. Always quite a turn on, really, but I wasn't so taken by watching you and good old Nicky baby hard at it and, unforgivably, in *my* bed."

Helen struggled to speak. Her lips moved without sound – her eyes pleading.

"I'm truly sorry. I... I wasn't thinking – it was just innocent fun, I swear..."

"Wrong answer." Fear overwhelmed her, and she sagged forward, unconscious.

The Painter, growing increasingly bored with the game, decided to complete the kill. He carefully reloaded and aimed the pistol at the centre of her chest and released the charge – yes, it had been a quick death for her too. Satisfied, The Painter removed the handcuffs, amused that once cleaned, they would be returned to the bedside table from which they came, to await further adventures. As he loaded the bodies into his Land Rover and drove them to the Estate, his only regret was that his ancient oak chairs would need attention to remove the bloodstains.

He could have, of course, offered them to the Club as live prey for the Summer Hunt, but it wasn't summer yet, and this kill had been far too personal to share with the club members.

The Painter gripped each of his prized pistols reverently in turn and carefully cleaned them. A methodical process that brought a sense of calm and deepened his overwhelming contentment.

• CHAPTER 3 •

de Vere – Abu Dhabi

The ferocity of the early-morning sun was losing its battle to penetrate the sophisticated air conditioning in his palatial offices, which were designed to mitigate the region's climate. Nevertheless, Captain Marcus de Vere, the CEO and owner of de Vere Security, preferred to sit outside comfortably in his favourite rattan chair, savouring his first cigarette and coffee of the day on the terrace of his office. Adaptable to most climates, except for his dislike of extreme cold, he'd only invested in air conditioning because it was standard in the region and he had his clients' comfort to consider. When arriving in Abu Dhabi, it always pleased him to leave the air-conditioned climate of his corporate jet and be hit by the oven-like heat. It made him feel welcome. Desert temperatures, at least during daylight hours, had been his mainstay for many years, first during his active service with the Special Air Service, then in his time with E Squadron missions. The heat had always made him feel at home and never failed to welcome him. He was glad to be back, albeit only for a few days.

He was briefly distracted when his PA, Penny, brought him another cup of coffee. As she approached with a smile, he thought about how lucky he was to have found her. Now in her early sixties and only about ten years older than him, he rarely thought about ageing – it's in his DNA not to. She, however, made a striking impression: slim, elegant, and fluent in four languages, including Arabic and various local dialects, which was extremely useful given their location. She was familiar with all the protocols necessary for living and working in the Arab world, a crucial skill. Having worked with him for several years, she was widowed from a distinguished SAS officer, making her the perfect assistant. She ran his offices with disciplined efficiency, blending that with charm and discretion that endeared her to everyone, especially his clients.

After several years, he discovered his ideal niche in running his own successful security firm. At its core, it provided, among other services, effective executive protection, with armed bodyguards available at home and during overseas assignments. All his team members were exclusively former Special Air Service and Special Boat Service personnel.

The former was established in 1941 by Colonel David Sterling, with its motto 'Who Dares Wins', a phrase that has become globally renowned over the years. The latter was formed in 1943 by Major Roger 'Jumbo' Courtney, with the motto 'By Strength and Guile', which may be less familiar to the general public. The Special Boat Service is recognised worldwide as the elite sub-unit of the Royal Marine Commandos.

Sixty per cent of his income was derived from the immensely wealthy business entities within the UAE. He pondered the history for a moment. In 1971, the UAE became a federation of six emirates: Abu Dhabi, Dubai, Sharjah, Ajman, Umm Al-Quwain, and Fujairah. The seventh emirate, Ras Al Khaimah, joined the federation in 1972. The capital city, Abu Dhabi, was the largest and wealthiest of the seven emirates, and it was where he had decided, some time ago, to establish his prestigious UAE Office. Over the years, he secured an extensive armoury and three Ribs in their Boat Shed, providing unlimited supplies of equipment to cover all eventualities faced by his company in the region.

His clients demanded high levels of security, and ex-SAS and SBS personnel were very high on their wish list, which suited Marcus very well, as all but one of his people were. All his operatives were highly skilled and had all served their country with honour. Two of his ex-SAS team members were women, bringing valuable expertise and a necessary element of balance to his regional operations. His source of such operatives came from The Regiment, The Royal Marines, and The Parachute Regiment, which continuously supplied personnel regularly. In his view, they deserved the monetary rewards that came with serving their country so faithfully during their careers. The few former Special Boat Service operatives on his payroll were a highly valued asset to many of his clients, who owned super yachts in the region – always attractive targets for those inclined to cause harm or theft of these expensive assets of the wealthy. For several years, his company held the security contracts for many marinas and the main harbour, and they were, of course, managed by his SBS personnel.

The British Security Services maintained close ties with the region, and he and his team occasionally contributed to their successes in certain covert operations that attracted little or no publicity or local recognition. Many lives had been saved without the general public ever knowing, which was typical given the nature of his past operations. Recognition of sensitive and successful missions never made the headlines. In the security world, anywhere in the globe, those who intend harm need only succeed once for it to matter. Conversely, international security forces are scrutinised and criticised immediately if they falter, even though 99% of the time, they keep everyone safe from threats that critics are unaware that they had indeed been thwarted.

Penny broke his reverie. He looked down at his empty coffee cup, not noticing her earlier delivery.

"Good morning, Marcus," she said with a smile as she carefully refilled his cup, which sat on the ornate wrought iron table beside him. This table was one of many scattered across the attractive terrace.

"I have Major Carr from MI6 on the secure line. Will you answer, or should I tell him you'll call back?"

"No, no, thanks, Penny, I'll take it. Please patch him through here."

They had begun their friendship during their fifteen years of service with The Regiment and had experienced many challenging missions together. Later, Major Freddy Carr was headhunted by British Military Intelligence, MI6.

Marcus had taken a sabbatical from service for a while. Why, he didn't know. But then, some months later, MI6 invited him to join the elite SAS E Squadron. An honour and privilege he could not, for a moment, refuse. His experience in E Squadron involved conducting clandestine operations for the SIS in countries worldwide. He formed alliances with various factions within foreign nations and gathered intelligence from a wide range of sources. He operated in many hostile regions, and these relationships and experiences became crucial when the September 11th terrorist attacks occurred. His extensive involvement was a learning curve he would never forget.

But then he moved on, applying all he had learnt to the private sector. He founded de Vere Security as owner and CEO, with offices in his native Kent and in Abu Dhabi. He had never looked back or regretted that decision.

His phone buzzed.

"Freddy, good to hear from you – it's been a while. What's up?"

"Abdalla al-Battal's up," said Major Freddy Carr.

"That bugger. Please tell me he's dead and it was a painful demise."

"Not yet, mate, but that's where you come in," said Major Freddy Carr, in a sombre tone.

The mention of the extremist's name caused Marcus to shudder, remembering his close friend and his family's massacre. It had always been clear to Marcus that the man had been an unwavering patriot and a dedicated soldier committed to eradicating threats from those wishing harm to the West across the Globe. Off duty, he was a caring husband and a loving father to his beautiful child. Many years earlier, they met during an exchange program between an American SEAL Team and the British SAS at Hereford. Marcus waited, expectantly, to hear Freddy's words – in the hope that he would have the opportunity to exact his revenge.

Marcus mused for a moment on his attendance at the Navy SEAL Amphibious Base (NAB) in Coronado, California, and the moving burial service at the Sacred Heart Church nearby. He noted that the care and warmth of the SEAL family towards their fallen mirrored that of the Regiment.

"I'm right in remembering that one of al-Battal's fanatics took out a SEAL teammate

of yours, along with a bunch of innocent tourists, some time ago in Tunisia – right?"

"Affirmative. His name was Todd Miller, a Lieutenant Commander on R&R with his

wife and three-year-old daughter at the Riu Imperial Marhaba Hotel attack. Wrong place, wrong time – but his name, rank, and family were never published in the list of those massacred. So, the terrorists never knew the prize they'd taken out," replied Captain Marcus de Vere.

"Yeah, Tunisia used to be a safe place to relax and take a holiday – sadly, it's no longer, and its proximity to the Libyan border doesn't help. Look, we know al-Battal is due to meet with Abdulaziz Badawi, the terrorist financier, at his home in Abu Dhabi in about three weeks or so. Flying in on his private jet out of Qatar. My source will confirm as soon as he has the exact ETA details," said Major Freddy Carr.

"How trustworthy is the source?"

"100 per cent plus. My man's on Badawi's staff and bears a grudge against his lord and master. And with a wife and four kids, he needs the money."

"What's al-Battal doing in Qatar, as if I couldn't figure that out?"

"Our contacts there advise that he's meeting with Hamas leaders."

"As I thought. Sounds ominous."

"Yeah, and that's not even the half of it. Anyway, here's what we've got so far. My asset advises that Badawi's been preparing one of his yachts, the al-Malik, for sea – as we speak."

"Why?"

"Well, my fellow M.I.6 Operatives and I believe it's all about money – lots of it – and we suspect Abdalla al-Battal will use the yacht to transport it."

"Where?"

"We have several potential scenarios here. Although it may be money earmarked solely for weapons, our asset confirms that Badawi has been amassing a large sum of cash over the past few months, well above normal. So, the worst-case scenario is that they are planning to purchase a weapon of mass destruction, either from Iran or North Korea."

"Bloody hell, do your people have a potential target?"

"If the worst scenario pans out, then we think Israel. Some kind of dirty bomb or, in their words, 'a holy bomb' is likely," said Major Carr gravely. "We're keeping Mossad, the American and British Government security services in the loop."

"So, potential Armageddon then. From the Hebrew right? 'Hill of Megiddo'."

Major Carr grimly warned, "Imagine this: with Israel under such threat, or on the brink of obliteration, the Americans would have to intervene in force, leading to a full-scale Middle East war. Iran, along with Hezbollah, Hamas, and the other Iranian proxy extremists in the region, would create the worst possible scenario. And that's where your role begins," he said.

"Why doesn't your people just take him out there?"

"Two reasons: first, he's surrounded by a tough security shield which isn't insurmountable, but to avoid too much international scrutiny and the risk of provoking local unrest, we'd prefer his demise to be more...erm...off the radar, i.e., providing maximum deniability. Second, it's also about the money – we want that secured and destroyed along with the primary target."

"Got it. Let me guess, MI6, along with the other players, want my team to raid the al-Malik, take out Abdalla al-Battal, and blow the money away at the same time, right?"

"Affirmative, that's the preferred scenario. Look, we've known each other for far too long to beat around the bush, Marcus. With your Special Air Service background and your work with MI6 as an E Squadron operative for three years – The Best of The Best, right?"

"E Squadron, well that's a blast from the past – even the UK Government doesn't admit it exists," chuckled Marcus, recalling how long it took him to mentally adjust after leaving that elite unit.

"The fact is, you're on everyone's wish list in the business. You have all the right experience. And, of course, you're local with all the resources you need readily available. By the way, if the hit could be beyond the Marina, for example, offshore in the Persian Gulf, that would be preferable. Leaving the Marina to achieve a zero signature for everyone involved."

"Agreed, that makes sense. Anyway, have to see how it all plays out, but yeah – offshore would be the best and cleanest option," replied Marcus.

"It's workable, in our collective view – I mean, we're speaking here at the highest levels. You and your company's reputation are well-known to all parties involved. And as I mentioned, you're local, and your people are more than capable of pulling it off. The plus for you is that you can seek revenge, personally," said Major Freddy Carr, in a serious tone.

"So, no pressure then?" said Marcus.

"Right. But we'll discuss this further when we meet in the UK. By then, I'll have more precise intelligence. We have enough time to plan and bring your team in Abu Dhabi up to speed."

"Affirmative. I must admit I've been missing the action at the sharp end."

"You mean you'd lead the raid yourself?"

"Too right I will, matey – it's personal as you say, and revenge is a dish best served cold, eh. I look forward to seeing al-Battal up close soon, and we'll have a little last chat. Emphasis on the word 'last'," said Marcus grimly.

"Sounds good to me – who better and more fitting than you to take him out?"

"Thanks for the vote of confidence, cheers, Freddy."

"My pleasure, mate, stay safe."

• CHAPTER 4 •

Two Weeks Later

The Barn Owl hooted loudly, irritated at being disturbed early in the morning.

After a night of hunting, he needed rest, but since his sanctuary had been so rudely interrupted, he angrily flew through one of the many openings in the worn cedar roof to find shelter and tranquillity elsewhere.

The ramshackle old barn stood alone and forgotten, incongruously, in the middle of acres of farmland. The years of neglect had taken their toll. The oak frame and timbers had stoically kept it standing, and the weathered cedar tiled roof was still largely intact, allowing a few beams of sunlight to illuminate its contents. An old, faded blue Ford tractor rested in one corner, with both front tyres worn and deflated, as if resigned to its fate. It was so rusted now that any hope of revival had long disappeared.

An old horse-drawn plough nearby had suffered the same fate, its blades coated in blood-red rust. The walls displayed a collection of old leather harnesses tarnished by time, with an array of farming implements beneath them, leaning in surrender to their fate of abandonment – pitchforks, spades, and a corroded old scythe, all destined for the same future. The floor was strewn with rotting fodder and disintegrating small square bales of hay. No one had entered the forgotten building for many years... until now.

The rising sun was slowly triumphing in its effort to pierce the grimy, shattered glass windows. It might have been that or the effects of the drug wearing off, but in any case, Nick awoke, naked, disoriented, and in agonising pain. He couldn't move, and when he tried, the pain was intolerable. At last, bright sunlight quickly flooded his space. He rotated his head with great difficulty, and to his despair, he saw that his swollen hands were shackled by his wrists to a beam, his legs tied at the ankles and weighted down. The effect resembled a medieval rack. Desperately, he looked around as best he could – it seemed like he was in some kind of rundown barn. The pungent scent of aromatic tobacco filled his nostrils, making him want to cough, but he was unable to do so.

In considerable agony, he lifted his head once more, searching through the haze of smoke and could just discern the figure of a man sitting casually, directly in front of him, smoking. It was surreal. He squinted into the sunlight, but the face remained in shadow.

"Good morning, Nick. Welcome back. Good of you to, finally, join us," said The Painter as he turned to smile at his friend, lurking expectantly in the shadows behind him.

"Are you pleased to see me?"

Nick tried to place the voice but to no avail. Tried to understand. Tried to understand – the why.

"What the hell is happening? Where am I? Who are you?" Nick asked, his throat and mouth so parched that his croaking voice was almost indecipherable.

"So many questions. I'll do my best to answer each. First, I'm going to kill you – *eventually*. Second, I'll try to make the *why* clear – maybe you might remember these, eh?" He waved a pair of emerald drop earrings in front of Nick's eyes that sparkled, flashing a brilliant green in the morning sunlight.

Stunned, realisation suddenly dawned.

Turning to The Watcher, The Painter said, "Time for a little pink, I think. Poor Nicky needs some refreshment."

The Watcher placed three beautiful Waterford crystal glasses on the small, long-discarded, cracked oak table beside The Painter's chair and filled each to the brim. Grasping Nick's hair, The Painter pulled his head back and poured the wine into his mouth, causing Nick to splutter.

"You are so privileged – this's one of my favourites – a 2004 Grande Cuvée Rosé

Alexandra. In fact, Laurent-Perrier's flagship Rosé. I do hope you're impressed," said

The Painter, turning to his friend, The Watcher.

"Your good health, my friend," said The Painter in an extravagant toasting gesture.

"That hint on the nose of strawberries and redcurrants combined with candied fruits. I hope you agree," said The Painter, addressing Nick, sarcastically.

"Yes, indeed, a rare and cherished experience," agreed The Watcher, raising his glass in an appreciative toast.

"But let's not get too distracted from the matter at hand," said The Painter, turning back to Nick. "Rather an expensive gift, wasn't it? She'd told me that her mother had given them to her for her birthday. Another sweet, easy lie that passed through those sensual lips, but then again, she'd always lied about everything – did you find that? I suppose not."

"What have you done – where is she?" said Nick, struggling to speak. His mind in torment.

"Ah, enlightenment strikes at last. Well, she's long gone and resting with friends, my dear fellow. And I'm pleased to say that her and her sister's deaths were quick – only fair, don't you think, considering. By the way, did you have Melisa too? I mean, they were like two peas in a pod, but no, I'm sure you didn't. How remiss of you – you really slipped up there, my boy; you could've had two for the price of one."

Nick managed a struggling gasp, "What...the...!"

"You're so naïve. They both relished the sex with enthusiasm – you missed out on that, dear boy."

"Oh no. Please God no."

"Oh yes. Time to pray if you want, but perhaps it's too late now – maybe we'll find out if there's a Deity listening after all.

But I digress; I'm here to provide some entertainment, probably more for my sake than yours, but we'll see. I've been so admirably patient, don't you think? I mean, it's been weeks since those not-so-halcyon days, eh? And yet here we are at last. I can't tell you how much I've been looking forward to spending quality time with you... I mean, we never really sat down together to have a chat, but then again, we never had the chance to meet, did we? But of course, I remember now that you were rather busy elsewhere with Helen – do you recall those times, Nicky? Fond memories for you, I'm sure," said The Painter, suddenly distracted when he heard the voices of his *friends* in his mind, urging him forward to complete his task. He was pleased, of course, to listen to their encouraging words, but he felt momentarily concerned that they had spoken to him without being summoned. Could it be that he was not entirely in control of his private world? Complete power and dominance were of utmost importance to him, both in matters of killing and sex. But he let the thought go for now. He needed to focus his attention. Nick stared in anguish at the emeralds flashing in the sunlight before his eyes – he couldn't stop the tears from streaming down his face.

"Ah, now you remember, don't you? Well, you see, here's my dilemma, where shall we put them for you to enjoy once again, Nicky? Silly me, I know."

Nick screamed as each slowly pierced a nipple.

"You see, even I can be a bit of a romantic sometimes," said The Painter, relishing the moment.

"By the way. What *is* love, Nick? It's a fantasy, right? I mean, what's it like? – I'd really like to try to understand that conundrum. Now's your chance to elucidate; we've got a little time to discuss that, if you wish. I can't wait to know what that emotion would feel like."

Nick managed a rasping, "Screw you."

"Been there, done that. Well, now, it's lovely to have this first but sadly, final little chat with you, Nick, but tempus fugit and all that. By the way, did you know that I'm a bit of a painter, or at least I'm destined to be after this little engagement comes to its artistic conclusion? I've brought with me a very special brush – it was my father's. Although he was more of a cutter saving lives rather than me. Nevertheless, an artist too, in his own way. Well, you're going to be my canvas. And, where's the paint you're thinking of? Well, you've got all the paint I need, and it's a much-loved colour of mine."

Nick's head fell to his chest, exhausted in despair and agony.

"I admit this is my first painting – indeed, my debut into the art world if you like – but I promise that each stroke will be delicate and applied with deliciously perfect sweeping caresses – not too fast, not too deep. I want you to be with me all the way. Aren't you thrilled? And the plus for me is, please don't laugh, but the fact is that I don't even need to go to the trouble of thinking about where to hang your portrait when complete, seeing as, of course, you are already hanging nicely."

Nick tried to speak through the pain, but his throat was too dry.

"And look, here it is! Isn't it beautiful? So well-crafted." He waved the scalpel in front of Nick's face, the glass blade flashing in the sunlight.

"Oh, how thoughtless of me, I'm sorry. I nearly forgot. Happy birthday! Thirty-seven today, and what a coincidence! Can you guess why? Well, I'll explain, it's because my masterpiece will have exactly thirty-seven brush strokes, no more, no less. We'll celebrate your special day in style, together."

The Painter began to paint slowly, methodically, and with great care, his face a mask of serenity.

Nick tried again to speak, but his mind had shut down, literally frozen in horror. He felt the slight dragging sensation on his skin as the blade made its first slow, long incision. He screamed a silent scream at the indescribable pain that followed.

Torment consumed his mind and body. Time lost all meaning amid the fog of his suffering. He could see The Painter return to his chair, relaxing back with another cigarette to admire his work. Nodding repeatedly and smiling as if listening to some unseen entity.

"Hope you can still hear me, Nicky baby. We're nearly finished, just two more strokes to go, but please be patient. I need to sit down again and rest for a moment. I apologise for these interruptions, but this creative process is much more exhilarating and exhausting than I expected. Still, I believe my friends are pleased with our progress."

The pain was overwhelming, and with the severe loss of blood, he began to wish for death to come quickly. In his tormented mind, he hoped for 'a coup de grace', but it wasn't to be. A slow, relentless warm river of blood flowed down his trembling body – draining his life away little by little. He shook his head, or at least tried to. The last thing he heard in his life before the blackness came was high-pitched demonic laughter.

Angered that his subject was no longer with him, The Painter struck him savagely and repeatedly across the face, but received no response. "C'est la vie," he told himself, amused by the irony of the French phrase – how apt. He eagerly continued working on the final touches of his project.

“Damn it!” cried The Painter as his blade hit a rib, damaging the knife edge. As a result, the final two strokes were not perfect. His masterpiece was flawed.

The Watcher applauded from the shadows, feeling privileged to have been invited to witness such an exquisite kill.

“What’s wrong, my friend?” asked The Watcher.

“Not quite perfect but an engaging experience,” smiled The Painter.

“I was expecting you to remove the offending appendage,” said The Watcher.

“My dear friend, I am an artist, not a butcher!” said The Painter, smiling.

“What now?”

“I’m going to sign it, of course,” laughed The Painter, removing a silver lipstick case from his pocket and opened it.

“Lipstick, really?”

“Not any lipstick, my friend. A Dior Rouge no less. Helen’s favourite.”

He signed his name on Nick's back with a satisfied flourish, and it was done.

"A nice touch," said The Watcher with admiration as both men shook hands warmly.

CHAPTER 5

Doctor Cathy Meer looked out of the kitchen window at the birds enjoying a feeding frenzy at the large bird table that took pride of place in the centre of her garden. It had been a safe haven for them for many years. So friendly and unafraid, they would often land next to her on the garden furniture and take food from her hand.

She was delighted to see that Fred the woodpecker was finally back from his holidays, pecking happily at his favourite old pear tree, which she would leave there for him until it finally fell. She loved his pied black and white plumage and the distinctive red patch on his lower belly – so incredibly beautiful. It had always been a private, cherished joy for her whenever he visited.

The property, Willow Tree House, was a modest yet impressive Tudor-inspired, Grade II-listed, four-bedroom country house. Built in 1868 in a secluded location just outside the village of Cowden in Kent. After the tragic death of her parents in a car crash and being the only child, she returned to the family home. Mature oaks, ash, beech, sycamore, and fruit trees filled most of the one-acre garden, but her favourite spot ever since she was a toddler was just outside the kitchen window in the corner of the ancient brick-walled garden. A very special sanctuary, surrounded exclusively by several beautiful golden weeping willow trees, lay a natural spring that provided a small, shallow pool for her feathered friends to drink and bathe, which they did frequently.

She'd planned to turn it into a small swimming pool for her children to enjoy, but she hadn't got around to that yet. It was on her wish list, but given her workload, the list was taking longer and longer to come to fruition. Today, reality had hit home once again. It was the end of the school holidays, and she had to admit to herself that she dreaded the pain of getting the children up and going. She had a few moments before the inevitable chaos began and escaped to the terrace with her coffee to enjoy her secret vice of a cigarette or two.

"Come on, children, breakfast! It's time to rock and roll," she bellowed up the stairs.

Oblivious to the cries of displeasure, solely from Jenny, she waited for them to crash into the kitchen like a tornado, as usual. They were like chalk and cheese. Jenny was a seven-year-old bundle of boundless energy. George, on the other hand, was always relaxed, calm, and collected, very much like his father had been, and at only ten, he had the beginnings of the same broad shoulders.

The children rapidly finished their goat's yoghurt and fruit, to the point that anyone watching might assume they hadn't eaten in months. As they eagerly finished their breakfast, she slipped away to the sitting room. There was no particular reason for her move, but perhaps it was because she was looking at George; he was so much like his father. Her moments of reflection over the past six years or so, since Peter's death, were diminishing. It was only when something triggered those memories for some reason that she allowed her mind to recall them, even if only briefly. She rested her elbow on the mantelpiece and looked at Peter's picture holding the Sandhurst Sword of Honour. He had told her it was one of his proudest moments.

At quite an early age, she realised that, in the eyes of many, she was considered beautiful. But she never understood why so many young men shied away from her. It was only later that she realised that many men felt intimidated by her looks. Unable to relate due to their own insecurity or lack of self-confidence, they struggled to move beyond her appearance and seek to know her as a person.

Her life changed when she met Peter at a regimental dance. Although it might seem cliché, it was genuine love at first sight across a crowded room. They soon became inseparable soulmates. Since Peter's passing, she hasn't entered another relationship. Many tried to break down her emotional barriers over the years, but without success. She feels at peace with her children and cherishes her close friendship with her sister-in-law, Monica, who has become her confidant. She stepped into the hall, glanced at herself in the mirror, and muttered, 'Not too bad,' before tying her blonde hair into a bun. Since she was on call, she needed to be prepared.

George found his mum lost in her memories and gently placed his hand on her shoulder.

"Mum, we should go. Jenny will be late for school."

Her work mobile rang as she sped away from the house, a distraction she didn't need now as she navigated through the chaos of mothers on school runs and office workers with the Monday Blues. With her children in the car, she skipped the hands-free option to prevent them from overhearing anything inappropriate. As a Registered Home Office Forensic Pathologist for nearly fourteen years, she carefully shielded her children from the more sensitive and sometimes disturbing parts of her work. Cathy's children were the most important part of her life, and she was very happy when Monica became part of their lives too. As a working mum, Monica's help, warmth, and kindness had been a blessing, and the children loved her.

"Doctor Meer," she responded.

"Good morning, doctor. DCI Johnny Jordon from Maidstone Police here. I believe you are on call today, correct?"

"Yes, Inspector, how may I assist you?"

"We need you at Old Barn Farm, a few miles outside Edenbridge. There's been a murder with one victim. One of my team members is waiting for you there. Are you familiar with it?"

"Yes, it's practically on my doorstep. I'll be there in twenty."

"Mummy, you were talking on the phone while driving. If the police saw you, you would be in trouble," muttered Jenny, who was her children's clever clogs.

"Darling, I'm practically...erm...at least, almost the police," she laughed. She arrived at the school, gave her daughter a kiss, and a hug.

"Have a good day, darling. Probably Aunty Monica will pick you both up."

Soon after her brother's death, Monica moved to the village to help her with the Children, and the quiet village setting was perfect for her work as a successful children's writer.

George broke the spell...

"Don't worry, mum, I can walk from here," he said. She hugged him as well. No kiss, of course, he was, as he put it, a man now.

She quickly got into her Range Rover, contemplating the challenges that might await her at the crime scene. She knew that regardless of what lay ahead, her purpose was driven by the victims who couldn't speak for themselves; she spoke on their behalf. At her mortuary, she valued the intellectual challenge of uncovering the truth and firmly believed that her post-mortem reports would help bring the perpetrators to justice, giving voice to the victims and closure to their families. Each day in her work was unique – every crime scene brought new challenges, and that was exactly how she preferred it.

She pulled into the farm and was greeted by a uniformed police officer.

"Doctor Meer," she said, flashing her ID.

"Good morning, doctor. Everyone is at the crime scene. Follow the track over there; it's about a quarter of a mile, but go slowly because of the ploughed state of the fields," he said, pointing to a dirt track beside the farmhouse. She quickly checked the list of attendees, signed in, and then hurried back to her car, eager to face the challenges that the crime scene ahead would bring.

The team stood outside a dilapidated barn. Cathy shook out a Gauloise and lit it just as a familiar figure strolled towards her.

"Bloody hell, is that you, Tim? What on earth are you doing here?" she laughed.

"I could ask you the same question. Anyway, nice to see you again too, Cathy, after all these years," he grinned. "I see your language has become a tad more colourful since our days at Oxford. DS Tim Riley, at your service. I got transferred here from the Met a few months ago. I'm the SIO at the scene."

"Well, I'm Doctor Cathy Meer at your service, the Home Office Forensic Pathologist on call for this one. So, I'll take over now. Take me to it," smiled Cathy.

"Right, okay, follow me, but be warned, it's pretty grim in there, Cathy."

He led her into the dilapidated barn. The scene sent a noticeable shiver down her spine. Bodies were her business, after all, but she cringed internally at the coldly methodical brutality of what she saw. It was gruesome, yes, but the unsettling aspect lay in its simplicity. Not the usual savagery here, but a measured and controlled act of violence, almost ritualistic in a sense. She pulled herself together, put on her professional mask, and started to work. Apart from Tim, forensics stepped back to give her the space she needed, and they had been ready to finish up anyway.

Hanging from a beam was the body of a naked Caucasian male. His jaw hinged in a final scream. The body was covered in several bloody red slashes. Hands and feet were bound, and the latter, weighted down. Bizarrely, a pair of what seemed to be emerald drop earrings had been attached, one to each nipple. Cathy took her time.

There was much to consider, and as the professional, she had never thought about rushing anything. Tim stood patiently waiting, not wanting to risk disturbing her thought processes.

"Out of curiosity, do we have an ID for the victim yet?" Cathy asked, breaking the silence.

"Actually, the local uniform identified him as… well, I'm not sure. Ah yes, his name's Nick Parish," he said, consulting his notes. "An architect based in Maidstone. One of the local fox hunts called it in after they heard their pack barking frantically outside the barn doors earlier this morning. They looked through the broken windows, saw the carnage, and contacted us. Anyway, Cathy, what's your first impression of this?"

"Well, it's not typical for me to offer much comment at this early stage, but seeing as it's you, my first impression is that he died from multiple incised wounds. These cuts seem to have been very precise slashes, not too deep but enough to cause his eventual death. Certainly, his death would have been slow and agonising. This was not a murder committed with rage. On the contrary, in my opinion, the killers' actions were measured, controlled, careful, and surprisingly skillful. I mean, he didn't hit any major arteries, for example. I'll know more once I get him on the table. What's also interesting are the words painted on his back in what appears to be lipstick—that's a first for me. And the placement of the earrings, that's another bizarre aspect," said Cathy.

"Me too. We've collected samples of the lipstick and will test them. Hopefully, we might get some good results," said DS Tim Riley.

"Looks like some kind of signature?" said Cathy. "A bit blurred, but could be 'The Painter'. What do you think, Tim?"

"I agree that it appears recognisable, but what kind of mindset would the murderer need to have to commit such an act and then *sign* it?"

"Perhaps the perpetrator sees himself as some sort of surreal artist. Maybe that's why he left the body to be found so easily. Every cut was, in a sense, a work of such skill that his ego compelled him to sign it," said Cathy, contemplating thoughtfully.

"Time of death? What would you guess at this early stage?" said Tim, eager to gain some understanding of the timeline.

"Somewhere between three and four hours ago, roughly, if that helps. So, about 4 pm tomorrow at the mortuary?"

"Okay, Cathy, I'll be there. We can catch up afterwards?"

"Works for me, so many years to catch up on," she smiled. "See you tomorrow then." Suddenly, a reporter appeared out of nowhere, snapping photos quickly — catching both of them off guard.

“Any comment, Dr Meer?” they shouted.

“No comment,” said Cathy, surprised to have been recognised.

“Well, you’ll be on the front pages tomorrow, that’s for sure. My boss, DCI Jordon, tells me they’ve never seen such an appalling murder here before."

"So be it, Tim, what can we do?"

CHAPTER 6

Doctor Cathy Meer greeted DCI Johnny Jordon and DS Tim Riley as they entered the mortuary.

"Good afternoon, gentlemen."

"Good afternoon, doctor. I believe you're familiar with DS Riley. I'm DCI Jordon; we spoke recently. Because of the high-profile nature of this murder and the media frenzy it has caused, I thought I should be present. Unfortunately, you and Riley made the front pages of the local paper today, but that's just how it goes. I expect the Nationals will pick up on it next, given the circumstances. The media has always been good at sniffing out these stories, but what was most unsettling was the image of the body. Thankfully, it was a very blurry photo, and the fact that it was in black and white was an advantage, though it still clearly depicted a bloodstained hanging corpse."

"Yeah, where the hell did they get that from?" asked Cathy, looking dismayed.

"We think one of the fox hunters must have snapped it through the barn window in the confusion surrounding the discovery and subsequently sold it to the local rag, for a princely sum, no doubt, or so I heard," said Riley.

"It's a bugger, but too late now. Let's move on. So, what have we got, Dr Meer?" asked Jordon wearily.

"Well, inspector, as you can see, the feet and hands display considerable bruising and deep ligature marks, as expected from a body that had been hung by the wrists with the feet weighted down. There are also signs of perimortem facial trauma. I can only surmise that the murderer attempted to revive the victim to allow him to complete the torture while the subject was still alive. As I told Riley at the scene, the cause of death is multiple incised wounds, and I can now confirm that diagnosis as correct. Following my autopsy, I observed that there were precisely thirty-seven clean cuts, none involving major blood vessels, which requires a significant level of skill to achieve successfully. There are two wounds that don't quite match the level of precision seen in the others, but I'll address that later. They would cause bleeding, of course, but wouldn't have incapacitated or killed him quickly. It requires significant skill to inflict so many injuries without causing major damage. The victim could have survived for about half an hour or more. There are no indications of heart disease or other conditions that would have sped up his death beyond what's typical. The low number of flies and larvae suggests death occurred approximately 3 hours before discovery. I will have more information once I get the toxicology results, and then I will complete and submit my report."

"Do you have any idea whether the emerald earrings played a role in all this?" asked DS Riley.

"That aspect was a first for me, gentlemen," she replied, "but as far as his demise is concerned, they would have played no part. They were attached perimortem, and he would certainly have experienced considerable discomfort as his nipples were pierced, but apart from that, who knows the significance or the meaning for their use in the mind of the murderer? Maybe some bizarre or obscure ritual.

By the way, in my opinion, these seem to be Colombian Trapiche emeralds," Cathy added, "an exceedingly rare and costly type of emerald valued by gem collectors. These unusual stones are characterised by a six-pointed radial pattern of ray-like spokes of dark impurities. The pattern displayed resembles, if you like, the spokes of a cogwheel used in sugar mills in South America. Take a closer look." She passed him a tamper-proof evidence bag and a magnifying glass.

Tim scrutinised them and handed them to Jordon.

"You seem to know a lot about this stuff, then, doctor?" said DCI Jordon, fascinated.

"My mother was a collector of gemstones, and she passed that passion on to me. Either way, as far as you chaps are concerned, it shouldn't be a ball breaker to track down the jeweller who sold them, given their rarity."

Again, Tim had to smile inwardly at the language.

"Doctor, if the incised wounds you mention were so precise, why didn't his blood clot? And based on what you've suggested, could the instrument have been a surgical scalpel?" asked DCI Jordon.

"Well, on the first point, subject to the toxicology report, I wouldn't be surprised to find that some low molecular weight heparin was introduced into the equation. One can certainly bleed to death slowly and painfully from such surface injuries, but if we add some blood thinners into the mix, then the blood would flow for much longer. I would also not be surprised to find either elevated levels of alcohol or, more likely, a short-acting benzodiazepine drug like Midazolam or Rohypnol would do the trick to render the victim compliant so the murderer can haul him up and complete his work. However, as I mentioned, I'll need the toxicology report to confirm. Regarding the second point, that's an interesting question, inspector. Yes, I have no doubt a scalpel was used. But the cuts inflicted, as I've already said, were extremely fine, which led me to consider that an obsidian blade may have been used. Obsidian blades are still used today by some surgeons as scalpels. As well-crafted blades of this type have a cutting edge many times sharper than high-quality surgical scalpels, with the edge being only about 3 nanometres thick," said Cathy, matter-of-factly.

"What's...erm...an obsidian blade?" inquired Jordon, intrigued.

"It's a type of volcanic glass that allows for a much finer edge than conventional steel blades. It may also surprise you both to learn that this kind of blade was actually in use millions of years ago and, as I mentioned, is still used by some surgeons today."

"Who'd know," spurted Riley.

"So, are we dealing with a doctor here... um... doctor?" asked DCI Jordon.

"I believe that's your department, gentleman," Cathy replied, "but we are certainly examining a murderer with above-average knowledge of the human body and a good skill set. However, these blades can be fragile if used improperly, and I am pleased to say I found a fragment indicating the perpetrator had nicked the second sternal rib. This confirmed my earlier suspicion that such a blade was used."

Cathy handed them another evidence bag containing the fragment.

"And, if you look closely at the incisions here from the right shoulder to the hip and similarly from the left shoulder, you'll notice that they are not as fine as the others. Since the chip was along the edge of his blade, the step caused these less-than-perfect cuts. I believe, without doubt, that those were his last two incisions. He's clearly a perfectionist, so I would guess damaging his blade must have been a rather irksome moment for him, but especially useful for us," she grinned. "When and if the murder weapon becomes known in your investigation, it would provide the perfect match," concluded Dr Meer.

"That's potentially incredible news. I mean, how on earth did you find it, doctor? It's barely visible and translucent to boot," said Jordon with admiration.

"Well, after I identified the nick on the rib, I looked for the chance that a fragment might still be in the nearby tissue. The edge of this type of blade is very fine and can be fragile if not handled carefully. Fortunately, as I mentioned, I found the fragment in the surrounding tissue after quite a bit of probing," said Cathy.

"Murder – always a nasty business, but this one goes beyond the pale. I've got the Chief Constable Bob Brimley breathing down my neck for results. Anyway, doctor, really excellent work. Finding the fragment was a brilliant piece of detective work in discovering the type of weapon, but, sadly, the reality is that it's a long shot that we'll find it. I think the real focus will be on the emeralds, because of their rarity. So, Riley, your job is to locate the jeweller and find the purchaser. If it turns out to be Parish, then we have a good path to pursue. Either way, it's a tremendous potential lead."

"Yes, sir," said Riley, who appeared to be lost in thought.

"It's been a pleasure working with you, doctor," said DCI Jordon with a warm smile.

"Thank you, Inspector. My gut feeling is that this one has the potential attributes of a revenge killing – as your investigation progresses, perhaps we'll learn more about the motive."

Cathy signed off the evidence bags to Tim, and they all moved to her office.

"So, Tim, what's your take?" asked Cathy, noticing a subtle shift in Tim's body language during their discussion about the emeralds. She couldn't quite identify what it was, but she decided to dismiss it, thinking it might just be some rivalry between the two police officers.

"Well, Cathy, finding the fragment was excellent work, and as you mentioned, those rare pieces of jewellery should be relatively easy to trace back to the jeweller and then to the buyer. Given their rarity, that list will hopefully be quite short. Both factors will be crucial in the ongoing investigation," he replied cautiously.

"I agree, Riley. I'll leave this with you – start working on it as soon as you return to the station, and keep me updated on progress at all times, night or day," Jordon ordered brusquely.

"Yes, sir," responded Tim.

"Look, we've both got loads of paperwork to do, but what about dinner tomorrow to catch up on old times 'sake?" said Tim, changing the subject.

"I'm up for that, Tim. Where?" said Cathy, looking at Jordon, who seemed deep in thought.

"Do you enjoy Thai food?"

"Love it."

"Right, let's meet up in Ashford. I know an excellent restaurant, 'The Old School Thai', the food is just great, and I know the owner very well, although he's a little eccentric," smiled Tim.

"Okay, that works for me, why not. So, how is he a bit eccentric, then?"

"Wait, you'll see. Check out the bloke sitting at the bar when we get there."

"How'd you know *he'll* be there?"

"He's always there. So, see you tomorrow then, about seven?" smiled Tim.

"Look forward to it," said Cathy.

CHAPTER 7

de Vere's Office – Abu Dhabi

"Got Major Carr on the secure line, Marcus," said Penny.

Marcus reached for the phone, eager to find out what was going on.

"Good morning, Freddy. A tad early even for you, mate."

"I'm a 24/7 kind of guy – you know that. When are you back in Blighty?"

"Tomorrow evening."

"Okay, good. Anyway, GCHQ have passed us details of some intercepted terrorist chatter which might be of interest regarding the name Doctor Cathy Meer," said Major Carr.

"A name that doesn't immediately come to mind?" replied Marcus.

"Her late husband was one of yours," explained Major Freddy Carr.

"Of course, now I think about it, yes, Captain Peter Meer, 22 SAS, Sabre Squadron. Yeah, I knew him quite well. I was his instructor at the SAS Sniper School for a while – a natural. I also recall meeting a good mate of his...erm... Angus something."

"Sergeant Angus McGregor."

"Yeah, another exceptional shot, but Peter had the edge. If I recall correctly."

"Spot on – I see that increasing age has not dimmed the memory," chuckled the Major, good-heartedly.

"Ha bloody ha. They both got taken out in some black op, right? About five or six years ago," grunted Marcus. "I looked into it at the time, but it was all classified – even my usual sources came up empty."

"Interestingly, our people here have noted that her name has come up multiple times in terrorist chatter over the past few years, since Captain Meer's death, but we didn't realise the connection until now."

"And?"

"Well, one of the people in the intercepted conversation was called Saifullah."

"The Sword of Allah?"

"Affirmative. But here's the catch – wait for it – Saifullah is the code name for Asif Badawi.

"That bugger."

"I mean, we haven't got a full translation yet, but I thought I'd give you a heads-up – not sure what it all means at this point. I managed to retrieve the unredacted file on Captain Meer. It was a covert Black Op in a location where we weren't meant to be, as usual, but it turned out to be the mother of all clusterfucks. Flawed intel. The target was the terrorist Asif Badawi, son of the notorious terrorist financier Abdulaziz Badawi, as we all know. What a coincidence, considering our last chat. Anyway, Asif Badawi set a trap with, I must admit, impressive strategic skill. Both Angus and Peter were killed by Badawi. I spoke with some of Peter's team. Badawi escaped; in fact, he was the sole survivor after one of our helicopters went in to clear up after the firefight. Peter was credited with taking out Asif's three younger brothers, among others. Which ties in with the file on the operation," explained Freddy.

"So, what's going on now, over six years later?"

"Thanks to the intercept by GCHQ, we now believe that Asif might be seeking revenge on Peter's family."

"But how's that even possible? And why now? I mean, our people on active duty never carry any personal belongings or ID; it's completely against protocol. So how could Badawi and his people connect the dots?"

"We're not certain, Marcus, but based on Captain Meer's file, he had a history of being somewhat of a rule breaker. We believe it's plausible, and quite likely, that he possessed a picture of his wife and family, along with who knows what else. This is the only scenario that makes sense," said Major Freddy Carr.

"Well, okay, I suppose that's possible, but as I said, why now? I mean it's been, what, six or so years ago."

"The clincher is that Doctor Meer, a well-respected Home Office Forensic Pathologist, had her image plastered all over the local and national newspapers a few days ago, along with the fact that she's an army widow. So, for Asif, that would have ticked all his boxes. Over the years, we now believe that Badawi's people have been trying to locate her on his behalf and, sadly, have finally struck gold. You know what it's like with these people, 'an eye for an eye', revenge and all that," said Freddy solemnly.

"Why the press coverage?"

"She had completed the autopsy on a high-profile murder case, so it made headlines."

"So, she and her family are in clear and present danger," replied Marcus.

"Looks that way."

"Why isn't the bugger locked up somewhere or better still, under the ground by now...?"

"We've never been able to directly link him to anything that sticks."

"Yeah, you say that, but still, The Regiment and MI6 tried to eliminate him anyway, right?"

"Come on, mate, you know the answer to that one. Different rules apply when we're offshore and off the grid. Right?"

"True, but a pity he didn't go down. But his time will come, right?"

"No doubt about that. Anyway, our friend is now a respectable businessman with a luxury house in Abu Dhabi, not far from you."

"Yes, I am aware of him, but I've never met him personally. He tends to keep a low profile, but his father's situation is different. Abdulaziz Badawi is actually a client of ours. We hold contracts with other super yacht owners in the marina to protect their vessels. The marina and harbour are under our 24/7 security supervision," said Marcus.

"However, Abdulaziz Badawi remains a notorious figure who has so far avoided being detained for his suspected terrorist financing activities. And Asif also has a prestigious penthouse in Mayfair and, unbelievably, is a fully paid-up member of the Cavalry & Guards Club, and on bloody good terms with Sir Charles Billington no less," explained Major Carr.

"Unbelievable, but who is Billington anyway – I've never heard of him?"

"He keeps a low profile. He's the head of Section 12 at MI6. In my opinion, he's well past his prime. An opinion shared, I may add, by many of my team here who feel he's overdue for release to the green pastures of retirement, but having said that, I don't really know him that well, only in passing."

"Right. I have a feeling you guys are not joined at the hip, but what is Section 12?"

"Erm... well, I'll tell you what I know, and it's not much. Section 12 is, effectively, a one-man show, Billington. But the rumour is that he's running some informants and agents off the books for his eyes only, if you get my drift. And Asif Badawi, in my opinion, is a likely candidate to be one of them."

"So, it gets worse, off the grid then. So, you do think he might be tied up with our boy in some way?"

"I'm uncertain, but Asif appears to have some sort of unwarranted protection from above, though that's just my gut feeling. I'm not suggesting Sir Charles is working with him, but everything seems a bit suspicious to me. I've seen them dining together a few times at the Cavalry & Guards Club, but I avoided drawing attention to myself to avoid any repercussions. I did confront him about it once at the club, but he ignored me."

"Okay, so, what's the rest of it?"

"Well, Asif was taken in for questioning by the boys in blue last summer regarding a missing girl at a trendy nightclub in Knightsbridge, where she was last seen dancing with him. But nothing came of it, and he managed to walk away, even though three more girls went missing around the same time and from the same club – so, go figure that one."

"Did they ever turn up?"

"The missing girls? No. They all disappeared over that summer, but only in August – and what a coincidence that that's when Asif is usually in London. So, there you go."

"Alright, you're in London now, aren't you?"

"Affirmative."

"Okay, let me think – I suggest you contact a DCI Johnny Jordon down at Maidstone for me. He's someone I've worked with before, and he owes me a few favours. Ask him to liaise with Bob Brimley, the Chief Constable of Kent, a very old friend of mine, and see if they can organise some protection for Peter's family. When I get back, I'll see what I can do to help. As you know, MI5 reports that the current National Threat Level is Critical, and as a result, our security services are stretched to the limit. But you'd know more about that than me. In my view, Peter's part of the SAS family, and by definition, so is his wife and family. Look, I'll get in touch with Dr Meer when I get back and sort it out. I have all the resources needed and will deploy them without hesitation to protect one of our own," said Marcus, firmly.

"I know that. I'll work with Johnny Jordon and see if he can persuade Brimley to step up until you return," said Major Freddy Carr.

"I know Bob well. As I said, we've been friends on and off for some time. Confirm that I'll take over as soon as I'm back in Blighty," said Marcus de Vere.

• CHAPTER 8 •

One Year Before

Full of eager anticipation, three members of The Summer Hunt eagerly roamed the country roads looking for suitable prey, preferably young and definitely female. It was a warm, peaceful summer's day with just a few wispy clouds drifting high in an otherwise clear blue sky.

They'd been driving for just under an hour before they struck gold. Her tight blue jeans showcased her body perfectly. A hitchhiker was thumbing vigorously. She looked about seventeen, which perfectly matched their ideal profile. The country lane was deserted, too good to be true. But it was true, nonetheless. The driver pulled over a little further down the road and, in his depraved mind, enjoyed the view in his wing mirror as she ran to catch up. Her Rolling Stones T-shirt was bouncing nicely, hinting at what lay beneath. The other two men were waiting patiently in the back of the van.

Sara Grantsbury was no fool. She had secured a spot at Cambridge to study Molecular and Cellular Biochemistry, and was eager to meet her three girlfriends in Maidstone. They planned to organise their gap year, starting with a holiday in Cyprus before heading to the Austrian Alps to work as chalet hosts for the season.

She instinctively hesitated when the vehicle stopped for her. It was an old, battered grey van with dark-tinted rear windows. Cautiously, she approached and kept her distance to observe the driver. Seeing him clearly, she felt relieved to discover he was a well-dressed, attractive man in his fifties, articulate, with a warm, genuine smile. Feeling more at ease, she leaned into the open passenger window. Her first mistake.

"Good morning, where are you headed, my dear? Would you like a lift?" He had to smile to himself when he saw the words on her T-shirt... 'You can't always get what you want.'

How delightfully accurate. Well, they were definitely going to get what they wanted very soon.

"You're a fan of the Rolling Stones, I take it, looking at your T-shirt?"

"Oh yeah, definitely. I think Mick is fantastic. I've attended many of his gigs, and he's one of the top stage performers, full of energy. I adore him, even at his age. How about you?"

"Well, as you can see, I'm a bit older too, but I must admit I'm more of a Rod Stewart fan myself; my favourite is 'Hot Legs'. Great title, don't you think? Do you know it? I mean the one he did with the late Tina Turner – but a bit before your time, I believe," he smiled.

"Yeah, I'm with you on that. Anyway, I'm trying to get to Maidstone."

"No worries, I'm heading there too for a furniture auction and hoping to get lucky. That's why I'm using this crappy old van today. Chuck your rucksack in the back, the doors are unlocked, and then we can rock and roll, as you might say."

As she opened the back, she was immediately grabbed and didn't see the needle until it was too late. The sting was the last thing she felt. She never had a chance. Over the years, the men had played out this scenario so many times that there were no mistakes.

The driver pulled into the estate and parked the van in one of the many barns scattered around the main house. Now awake, Sara was roughly manhandled into the entrance of what appeared to be a large country house and thrown roughly to the floor of a ballroom-sized room. Bright sunlight shone, incongruously, through magnificent stained-glass windows. For a moment, she thought she was in a church. But then she realised the images were far too surreal for that. Patterns of blue, red, and purple colours flooded the huge room. Shaking with fear, she noted that the men surrounding her were drinking champagne, and it was then that she recognised the older man who had been so charming, but who now faced her with a malevolent smile that heightened her fear. On a long oak table lay three scary-looking crossbows.

"Welcome back, my dear, you're awake at last. I hope you enjoy the light display. Each window is a unique masterpiece. Custom-made for me."

"Look, please just let me go, I won't tell anyone, I promise. Please don't rape me," she pleaded desperately.

"Don't be silly, my dear. I have a promise for you: we'll be very gentle. We only wish to give you pleasure. So, let's begin," he whispered.

"I need to go to the loo first, please," she said, as her mind hurriedly processed the reality of her predicament.

"Good idea, why not, my dear, but there's no escape — all the doors are locked. Come back soon; we can't wait for your company."

She found, to her delight and peace of mind, that the window in the loo led directly to grassland and the tree line of a dense pine forest just within sprinting distance, escape. Although the window was small, she squeezed through it and climbed out, removing her hiking shoes to make running easier. She put all her energy into heading towards the tree line. She had been a school sprint champion. She paused for a moment to catch her breath and looked back in terror as she saw an old open-top Land Rover approaching her from the rear of the mansion.

"Go!" shouted the older man again, excited that the hunt had truly begun. The two men at the back of the jeep fired their military-grade crossbows just as she reached the edge of the tree line. Both hunters missed by a hair's breadth; the arrows embedded themselves in the trees right beside her as she plunged into the forest, unharmed.

Not so easy to be accurate in a moving vehicle, mused the older man.

"Damn it. Circle the wood, and we'll wait for her to break through," said the older man.

"But she'll be running again," complained The Watcher. As the new boy, he was unsure about the protocol but eager to succeed.

"What do you want? – Her standing still? It's The Summer Hunt. Act like a sporting hunter," shouted the Master of The Hunt, irritated by his friend's remark, notwithstanding the fact that this was his first time participating in a Summer Hunt – but that was no excuse.

Shafts of bright sunlight filtered through the dense canopy of trees here and there, offering her some guidance. But now, her feet were raw, badly torn by the carpet of pinecones on the forest floor, making it increasingly difficult to maintain her pace. Yet she was now so deep within the forest that her spirits lifted – they would have to pursue her on foot. Despite the agony of running with injured feet, she was confident she could reach safety.

She stopped to listen and catch her breath – hearing nothing, she felt a further glimmer of hope. It was then, to her delight, that she saw the green meadows beyond the trees and broke through to what she hoped was freedom, falling, thankfully, into the long, cool grass. She lay back, relieved, filling her lungs with the sweet-smelling fresh air and seeking to find the strength to complete her escape. Refreshed and with renewed energy, she was ready to run again and peered over the top of the long grass to see where she was – only to find the jeep a hundred or so yards away. Far enough – maybe. Sobbing in despair, she reached for and found the reserves of adrenaline that had sustained her thus far and sprinted away in desperation and defiance.

"Now for the kill!" cried The Master, grinning as he took careful aim. The first and second arrows missed, flying just inches past her. Somehow, she found the energy to keep swerving left and right. With her lungs bursting and her heart hammering against her chest, she ran back towards the relative safety of the forest – almost making it.

"We've got her," cried one of the men as he released his arrow. It found its mark, shattering her left shoulder blade, spinning her off balance. The older man waited a split second until her body turned, facing him. He aimed carefully, just below her right breast, and let loose his arrow. She was dead before her body hit the ground.

"Nice kill, sir," said one of his companions as he approached the body. "Just over 40 yards, great shot."

They threw her body into the jeep dispassionately and happily returned to the mansion, satisfied.

The older man turned to the others, "Take her to the mine shaft. She'll be happy there with all the rest of them and be careful to incinerate all her belongings." But then he hesitated, "Wait! On second thoughts, leave her T-shirt in my study and burn the rest."

Uncharacteristic of him to consider keeping a memento, but she had been unquestionably one of the best prey of all, in terms of the chase, albeit they had not enjoyed the satisfaction of her body. Nevertheless, he intended to have it framed as a souvenir and placed in his study to treasure. A mistake he would later regret.

She had done well, much better than some of the other quarry had. But in her panic, of course, she had headed in the wrong direction – just like all the others had. It was true that it had always been a calculated risk for the Club. Had they run to the main road, then it might have created a problem, but no one had ever done it. In his mind, that risk was simply an integral part of the thrill of it all. The older man mused, as Master of The Summer Hunt, he would savour this perfect memory.

His fellow companions had joined him in the study to discuss the sport. He reached for a bottle of one of his favourite champagnes, Bollinger La Grande Année Brut, and after giving it a twist or two in the ice bucket, he filled the beautiful Waterford fluted lead crystal glasses for them to toast their success. Having given his butler and staff the day off, as always when he and his friends enjoyed their sport, he'd have to go to the cellar himself to get another bottle, but he didn't mind that chore – he was more than satisfied.

"Well, gentlemen, it was a disappointing day on one level, but the hunt itself was indeed satisfactory," exclaimed the older man as they raised their glasses.

"I look forward to the next, may we be successful on *both* counts then?" smiled Asif Badawi.

CHAPTER 9

Present: The Old School Thai-Ashford

Cathy entered the car park feeling somewhat nervous about seeing Tim again socially after many years. She was aware that he had always had a crush on her, as shown by the way he looked at her back at the crime scene and mortuary, that familiar look in his eyes as he discreetly checked her out once more. Nonetheless, she decided to accept this reality. After all, many men had looked at her in the same way through the years; that was just life. However, she longed for more: a man who would see beyond her appearance and appreciate her for her intelligence as a professional woman, not merely as an object of desire.

Tim was leaning against his Inspector Morse-style Jaguar, smoking, and waiting. The evening was pleasantly warm, and he wondered what she would be wearing. He hoped it would be figure-hugging, and even in a bloody burka, her flashing green eyes would be enough to excite him.

Tim wasn't quite sure why, but he'd made an effort, wearing a light summer jacket with an open-necked blue shirt and slim-fitting cream jeans. As he saw her arriving, he reflected on how much he'd always desired her. At Oxford, everyone, including him, had tried asking her out, but without success. Some even speculated that she might prefer women to men, who knew? But that might explain her reluctance to accept a date. She was an absolute stunner, still slim, with long, flowing blond hair and green eyes that could melt your soul. Although she seemed unattainable at Oxford, she was very popular with everyone, and he enjoyed her company and quick wit, but he'd never stopped fancying her. After seeing her again, his feelings had reignited. But things had changed – he had changed.

He'd met quite a few pathologists in his time as a police officer, but he was truly gobsmacked when she arrived at the crime scene. She parked beside his Jaguar. Her slender figure slipped gracefully out of the car in true Joanna Lumley style. She wore a simple black dress and a silver silk shawl as she approached him, looking like a model strolling down a Paris catwalk. A stark contrast to the weather-beaten Barbour and torn jeans she had worn at the crime scene the day before. He felt his body respond, and he clenched his fists to suppress the feeling. She waved, bringing him back down to earth with a bump.

“Well, Tim, you look quite impressive. Anyone might think we’re on a date or that you were expecting someone else. Did I get the wrong evening?” she said with a slightly forced laugh.

“You don’t look so bad yourself, doctor,” he smiled, thinking about the chances of getting to know her a little more intimately.

“Do you mind if I have a quick puff before we go in?” asked Cathy. He shrugged his shoulders in compliance. She lit up thankfully, and he joined her with another.

“Look, before we get too social, I got the toxicology results a few hours ago,” she said with a quick frown.

“Good, go for it,” smiled Tim.

“Well, as I speculated at the mortuary, Midazolam was found in the victim’s blood. A short-acting benzodiazepine, which would have made him compliant, and, as I anticipated, there were also traces of low molecular weight heparin, which would account for the blood not coagulating, thus prolonging his eventual demise,” explained Cathy, drawing on her cigarette with great relish.

"Do you have it with you?”

“Yeah, it’s in the car. I sent a copy to the coroner and your boss by a secure courier.” Tim walked with her, collected the copy, and placed it on the passenger seat of his Jaguar.

“Nice motor, probably inspired by Morse," Cathy grinned.

“Guilty as charged. You’ve got it in one – she’s my baby. I’ve got an old friend who’s passionate about classic cars; he restored the body and engine for me and keeps it running as good as new.”

"My son George would love it, he collects vintage cars."

Tim's mouth fell open in surprise.

"He's ten, Tim! and saves his pocket money. He even goes to online model car auctions to bid for what he wants – it's a real passion."

"Good for him, let's go and eat," Tim said, smiling, eager to get started.

They were greeted warmly by a short, somewhat chubby gentleman.

"Tim, good to see you. Your usual table's ready."

"Cathy, let me introduce my dear friend Jamie," said Tim.

Cathy held out her hand to shake his. "I'm delighted to be here. Your restaurant comes highly recommended."

"You don't mean that this reprobate is responsible for giving me a decent critique?" said Jamie, laughing. "You know this chap was one of my best customers in Battersea back in the day before I relocated everything here, and I believe I can speak for both of us when I say we've never regretted it," he added, winking at Tim, who nodded in agreement.

They sat down at a comfortably sized round table and examined the menu and wine list. Cathy looked up at the bar and, to her amusement, saw a very lifelike mannequin dressed as a British Colonial Officer, wearing a pith helmet and resting his hand on what appeared to be the butt of an Adams revolver, which was certainly appropriate for the period, tucked into his holster.

Jamie looked over at her, "Ah, I see you've noticed Major Carruthers. He's my mentor, confidante, and, of course, my silent business partner. And even better, he never talks back; he listens. The perfect psychotherapist, in fact. Not like her indoors, i.e., *she who must be ob*eyed, if you remember 'Rumpole of the Bailey' TV series," he grinned.

"He's a splendid-looking chap, Jamie. I trust you have a deactivation certificate for that weaponry?" smiled Cathy.

"In his top pocket, bloody hell, Cathy, you're not the fuzz, are you?" said Jamie, laughing.

"No, but I know a little bit about firearms, and if that's an original piece, then it could be worth quite a lot to a collector," smiled Cathy.

"Okay, time for a little test for you then. Tell me something about it," said Jamie with a mischievous twinkle in his eye as he passed the revolver to her, "And if you get it right, then the first bottle's on the house," he grinned.

"Well, this is a very attractive example of a 5-shot percussion Beaumont Adams Model 1854. Take a look here at the crisply engraved tight foliate scrolls, which, as you will note, are also present on the lower rear of the frame, as well as on the trigger guard and but-cap," she said as she turned the elegant-looking piece over in her hands, delighted. "This really is a collector's piece, especially in its condition. If you've got the original case and all the full accessories to go with it, then you have a very desirable item of weaponry. Thank you so much for showing it to me. You should have it valued and insured, Jamie, if you haven't already done so," said Cathy appreciatively as she returned it to him.

"Thank you. You're spot on. I'll take your advice. I feel like I've just been a guest on an episode of the 'Antiques Road Show'. And, it's only cost me a bottle of wine," guffawed Jamie, giving Tim a knowing look.

"Talking of wine, let's get into the serious business of choosing one. Are you happy, Cathy, with a Gewürztraminer, as it complements this food well? And it's nice and expensive, which will please Jamie," said Tim, smiling.

Cathy nodded, and they ordered the wine and their meal.

"So, let's get down to the business of catching up. I know you've got a son called George, any more of them floating about?"

"Jenny, she's seven and an active volcano ready to erupt at any moment."

"And what does your husband do?"

"Erm...he was in the army. Killed in action some years ago."

"I'm sorry, Cathy."

"Well, now it's your turn to spill the beans."

"I'm married to Beth, a language teacher at Benenden School. We have five-year-old twin girls and live here in Ashford."

"Wow, what an impressive school. We used to play hockey against them."

"So, where were you then?"

"Roedean."

"Ah, well, you two should get on like a house on fire then."

"She applied for a job there a few months before we moved down from London and was lucky to get it. She loves it. I wanted to leave London as I have several good friends nearby. She was happy to escape the rat race, too, and when a post came up in Maidstone, I jumped at it, and neither of us has had any regrets about moving down," he said carefully. "We're lucky to have found a terrific live-in French au pair – so all's good on that front," he said, trying to push from his mind the rising gambling debts that haunted him – the risk of discovery by his wife was only a matter of time... he needed money – how to get it was another matter.

"So, where do you live now, and how do you manage the kids all on your own?" he asked.

"Cowden, I'm very fortunate too, as my sister-in-law, Monica, lives in the same village and is utterly indispensable. I'm on call for one week, then have a week off. Tomorrow marks the start of my break, so it's perfect timing for this evening," smiled Cathy. "Anyway, it all works out well. But having said that, as you know, my job often involves quite a lot of travelling. I mean, I cover Kent, of course, and then there's Buckinghamshire, East Sussex, Hampshire, Oxfordshire, Berkshire, Surrey, West Sussex, and even the Isle of Wight. In fact, I was there just a few weeks ago, when some bright spark in the local police noticed that the husband, a serious suspect and not the sharpest tool in the box, had just built a new terrace, and lo and behold, underneath was the body of his missing wife!" laughed Cathy.

"So, how is your investigation of *The Painter* coming along?"

"Well, I...erm...haven't actually got it underway yet," said Tim.

"What?"

"I've been too busy with some personal stuff," said Tim, again thinking about his rising gambling debts.

"But all you needed to get started was to send the photographs of the emeralds to jewellers – I mean, that's the best potential lead you've got. Find the seller, and if Parish was the buyer, that opens everything up, right? You know, girlfriends' lovers, etc.," said Cathy, stunned by his inaction.

"Anyway, Jordon's under pressure to deliver results, leaving me to handle the nitty-gritty."

"That would be the norm, wouldn't it? I mean, it's a high-profile case, and he's the senior officer, right?"

"True. Not sure how to handle the scalpel business yet," said Tim, attempting to make conversation while his mind was preoccupied with more pressing personal issues.

"What's going on with you? The priority has to be the emeralds, right? So, the sooner you get on with that, the better. The scalpel's a long shot at best. I was delighted to have discovered the fragment, of course, and therefore identified the weapon. But there's only a snowdrop in hell's chance of finding a match; I mean, all the murderer had to do was chuck it into the river – end of story. Either way, I'll check with my medical friends about suppliers of obsidian blades and get back to you," said Cathy, beginning to wonder what was going on with Tim's reluctance to move forward.

"Look, Cathy, I'm the detective here, so why don't you stay out of it?" Tim said, scowling.

“Right. Works for me. Good luck," said Cathy, mystified and concerned, but she considered it was no longer her business; she’d done her part.

• CHAPTER 10 •

After dropping the kids off at school, Cathy stepped into her local newsagent's only to discover that her face was once again plastered all over the local and national newspapers. This time, however, it displayed a picture of her in a gown, probably taken at some regimental ball years ago – she looked sadly at Peter beside her. Even though it was a bit blurry, memories of happier times with her husband floated through her mind. She was thirty-six when that picture was taken. How time flies, she mused sadly. She went home and sat on her terrace with a cup of coffee and a cigarette to read it through again. Watching Fred pecking away at his favourite old pear tree made her feel better, as always.

She thought, 'Where the hell did they dig out that picture?' As she pondered, her private number rang, making her jump...

"Caroline, what a surprise. Great to hear from you! How have you been? It's been a while. You've been a bit of a stranger," said Cathy.

"I'm well, thanks – just saw the papers only to find that my best friend's front-page news and now a celebrity to boot," Caroline laughed.

"Seems so. God only knows where they found that picture – it could have been worse. I mean, I could have been standing in a ditch over a body somewhere, collecting maggots or something. Sadly, that's what pathologists find themselves having to do sometimes, as you know."

Caroline had been her closest friend in the past. They attended Roedean together, and by chance, their careers had followed a similar path. She was a forensic clinical psychiatrist and often called upon to assist the police as a profiler. They used to enjoy 'off the record' chats about cases, but for some reason, unknown to her, Caroline had gone off the grid, and they hadn't seen each other for quite a few years now. They looked so alike that many thought they were sisters or even twins, something that had always amused them both.

"Look, let's meet up when you're free, Cathy?"

"This is my week off. Are you up for dinner at mine tonight?"

"I'll be there, what time?" said Caroline without hesitation.

"Great, so come round about seven, and you can say hello to Jenny and George before they go to bed. And as you know, George loves your classic E-Type, that is, if you don't mind him crawling all over it once again. He won't be able to resist," chuckled Cathy.

"It's a deal, see you then, and George is welcome, as always, to crawl all over it to his heart's content, but now that he's older, I hope he doesn't start the bloody engine and drive off down the road," laughed Caroline.

• CHAPTER 11 •

Monica had popped in, and she and Cathy were chatting in the kitchen while Monica helped prepare dinner for Caroline. The children were enjoying watching TV. The distinctive melody of her work phone announced the arrival of a voice message, breaking the spell. She dropped her tea towel and reached for it, somewhat irritated by the interruption.

"Good evening, Doctor Meer. It's DCI Johnny Jordon. If it's convenient, could you please ring me back? Thank you." Cathy sighed at the distraction and poured herself a bourbon to compensate before considering his request, wondering what the hell could be so important to disturb her during her evening off.

She rang back.

"Good evening, Inspector. How can I help you?" she asked, trying to sound polite and friendly, though she didn't feel like it.

"Doctor Meer, I'm sorry to bother you, but would you mind popping in tomorrow? I just have one or two more questions concerning your PM report."

"Can't it wait? It's my week off, and I've sent the Post-Mortem and toxicology report to you by secure carrier. Didn't you receive it?" Cathy asked, irritation creeping into her voice.

"Ah, sorry for troubling you. It hasn't reached me yet. I'll check it out. Thanks. I'll get back to you, Doctor." And with that, he hung up.

"Shit, what's going on?" she said to Monica, who was refilling her glass with yet another bourbon. Cathy sat back, exhausted and feeling a little tipsy, which was unusual for her, but she reminded herself she was on her break, after all.

"What?"

"Oh, sorry, no worries, Monica, just stuff. I just get tired of my downtime being interrupted. I think I should let it go – I'll be honest, I get exasperated when people waste my time, especially now when I'm trying to relax."

"Come on, Cathy, have another drink, and it will all go away," Monica smiled as she refilled her glass.

"Easy, I feel a bit tipsy already," said Cathy wearily.

There was a gentle knock on the kitchen door, and George sauntered in.

"Sorry to disturb mum. I'm going up to my room to do some research before dinner. There's a new 1st edition model car that I heard about at school today that's up for auction, and I want to check it out."

"Okay, darling, guess what — Aunty Caroline's coming for dinner soon, so if you could round up Jenny and be back pretty sharpish. Then we can all tuck in."

"Wow! Aunty C's coming. Does she still have the E-Type, mummy? I can't wait! And what's on the menu?"

"Yes, to the first question and as for the second, you'll just have to wait and see, darling," smiled Cathy warmly.

Monica hugged her and took the last sip of her whisky as she left. She could walk to her cottage easily; it was just down the road. The hardest part to navigate was Cathy's driveway, especially after a glass or two.

Caroline's timing was impeccable. The food was nearly ready on the table, and the children were all sitting expectantly and unusually peacefully at the kitchen table. The heavy serpent-shaped door knocker, its sound echoing around the house, announced Caroline's arrival as they hugged each other at the grand oak door entrance. Taking her hand in hers, she led Caroline to the kitchen and poured her a large glass of rosé, her favourite tipple.

"Hi kids, it's been a while, but here I am in the flesh at last – just cleaned the motor, George, if you want to take a quick shufty."

"Go for it, George, but dinner will be on the table soon," laughed Cathy, beginning to feel a little more intoxicated but increasingly more relaxed.

"That's so cool, thanks, Aunty C," said George, delightedly.

George sat in the car, running his hands over the controls and gazing lovingly at the long, classic aerodynamic bonnet. He knew that the definitive shape was designed by Malcolm Sayer, an aircraft engineer, in 1961, and even the famous Enzo Ferrari considered it the most beautiful car in the world. Every time George sat in the car, he felt wonder. Now, he wished he could start up the 265bhp, 3.8-litre engine beneath the bonnet and hear the roar of its power. *'One day I will have one of these,'* he dreamed, leaning back into his own private ecstasy as he breathed in the rich leather smell. He was in car heaven.

"I'd forgotten your skills in the kitchen. Great meal, as always, Cathy."

"Well, I've got Monica to help, too. Please help yourself to more plonk while I take the children up to their cells," grinned Cathy.

The evening was warm, and Caroline stepped out onto the terrace to enjoy her drink and have a smoke. She was in the same boat as her closest friend regarding this vice, but even as another doctor, she was guilty of ignoring all the advice not to.

Cathy joined her a little later.

"So, they're down?" asked Caroline.

"Yeah, George was tired after rugby today, and Jenny, well, she fell asleep as soon as her head hit the pillow – very out of character.

But just maybe that fluffy Pooh Bear you gave her did the magic," laughed Cathy.

"Be grateful for small mercies, my dear."

"I'm going to pour myself another bourbon. How about you?" said Cathy.

"Never say no to the pink stuff, as you know, but this time, I'll take the bourbon to run with you," smiled Caroline.

Cathy poured two fingers of Bourbon and joined her with a rather overly generous portion too – thinking she shouldn't – as she was already feeling even more woozy...

"It's been quite a bloody day, Caroline."

"In my professional opinion, doctor, I think we should put it all to one side for the day and relax," said Caroline with a twinkle in her eye.

"Good idea, but let's go out for another smoke before it gets too cold."

They sat in silence for a while, lost in their own thoughts, and watched the sun set. Then, they went back inside. They happily relaxed together on the sofa. They hadn't been so physically close since boarding school, and Cathy felt warm and at ease inside for the first time in ages, and feeling comfortable inside for the first time in a long time, but maybe that was the bourbon talking.

"Do you think about Peter much these days, Cathy? I remember the wedding well."

"Yes, you were the bridesmaid but never the bride. We've never really talked about you. I mean, you've never mentioned anything about your love life in all the years I've known you, apart from that unpleasant encounter you had back in the day. Have you ever been in love?" smiled Cathy warmly.

"I've loved someone for years, Cathy, but I haven't talked about it. The right moment to discuss it with you has never come. That's me, in a nutshell, but you didn't answer my question about you and Peter."

"Truth is, Caroline, that our relationship all happened so quickly, and then I spent years worrying whether he would survive the missions in which he was deployed. The reality was that we didn't spend that much time together at all. I think the longest was about two or three uninterrupted weeks a year. You know, in a way, he was a member of a club that I didn't really belong to and never, in reality, ever could. First, a prestigious private school, university, Sandhurst, then the Paras and subsequently the Special Air Service. I never really did have a chance, now that I think about it," said Cathy, suddenly feeling the burden of opening up and the effect of too much Bourbon.

"You never mentioned that part of your life before. It must have been difficult for you all those years."

"Let's just relax, Caroline. I'm so happy that you're here." She couldn't stem the flow of tears that came.

"It'll sort itself out," said Caroline kindly, wiping Cathy's tears away. She reached out with her hand and gently ran her fingers through Cathy's hair, drawing her closer. She found her mouth and kissed her softly.

Cathy felt as if she were in a dream and tried to move away, but found herself swaying uncontrollably.

"Did ... did you just kiss me?

"I want to stay with you tonight, Cathy."

"No way, Caroline, that's really not a good idea, and what just happened – should never have happened," said Cathy, sobering up briefly.

Again, she tried to stand but, decidedly drunk, now collapsed into Caroline's outstretched arms.

"Come on, Cathy, I'll take you to bed – you need to sleep this off."

"No, Caroline. I want you to leave. Leave now, please," she said forcefully as she staggered to the front door and, essentially, shoved her out into the driveway. "And don't come back."

"I'll have my revenge for this," cried Caroline, as she jumped into her car, slamming the door in frustration.

Exhausted and shocked, Cathy listened to the throaty sound of the car roaring off.

"Good riddance," she said to herself as she made her way upstairs to her bedroom, still a bit wobbly, and fell, thankfully, into bed, hugging her pillow and wishing for sleep to come.

As soon as Caroline hit the open road, she pressed her foot down. Since her early 20s, she had been confused about her sexuality. The one or two encounters she had with men had ended badly, and it was only when she met a girl of a similar age at her tennis club that she experienced something new and unexpected. She allowed herself to be seduced and, as a result, enjoyed an intimacy that had previously been unknown to her.

Now, consumed by the anger of rejection, she'd find a way to exact her revenge.

• CHAPTER 12 •

Cathy, still shaken from the previous evening, reached for some Aspirin to clear her head. Thankfully, the children finally burst into the kitchen, breaking the memories that had been consuming her mind, and sat down to cereal and fresh raspberries for breakfast. George couldn't stop talking about the sound of Caroline's E-Type and explaining in detail all the complexities of the engine. Jenny just pouted in indifference, as usual.

Cathy pushed everything out of her mind and simply listened to him, once again impressed by his knowledge. She reflected on how much she loved her very special children and thanked God that they had not heard Caroline's noisy departure earlier that morning.

"Will Aunty C be back again soon, mummy? I want to show her the new 1st Edition model E-Type I've ordered, and it'll be the same colour as hers."

"She's going away for a while, George, so I don't know, okay?"

"Alright, that's fine."

"Come on, you two, get your kit together. We're off to school, and Mummy needs to get back home quickly. I've got loads of paperwork to catch up on."

Her work phone buzzed – much to her annoyance...

"Good morning, Doctor. It's DCI Johnny Jordon. I'm really sorry to bother you again. I know it's your week off, but there's been another murder, and I understand the body was found hanging from a tree in Spencer Wood with multiple slashes. I'm heading there now and wondered if you could have a quick look, in case the modus operandi is the same as Parish's. Doctor Paul Granger is on call and will meet us there. Do you think that's a problem? I mean, two pathologists at the same crime scene. And do you happen to know each other?"

"I've known Paul for years. He's an excellent pathologist and highly respected; he won't mind me taking a quick look. No problem, inspector. I'll be there as soon as I can."

"Do you know the wood?"

"Oh yes, I know it like the back of my hand, see you there," said Cathy, grateful to have something else to focus on.

Cathy had always loved ancient forests, and Spencer Wood definitely met that criterion. As a young girl, she spent every spare moment there wandering with her father, searching for rare species of trees, flowers, plants, fungi, and, of course, birds. It was her father who had instilled in her a passion for wildlife, especially birds. She also remembered that it was during one of these expeditions that she unexpectedly became famous at just eleven years old. She had not only discovered an example of the extremely rare 'Ghost Orchid', probably the rarest plant in Great Britain, but it was also in flower. This event occurs only roughly every 30 years. Her discovery caused a sensation among Britain's botanists, and even the Natural History Museum paid homage to the plant and to her for finding it.

Cathy's musing was interrupted by her arrival at the crime scene.

"Hey Cathy, good to see you, long time," said Paul, shaking her hand warmly. "I'll take you to the scene, DCI Jordon's waiting. It's about two hundred metres in."

It wasn't difficult to navigate through. A rough trail, which she assumed was a fire break, made it easy for them. The muddy track had long been churned up by tractors and jeeps, so little or no chance, in her opinion, for the police to note anything worthwhile there. But she guessed that the murderer must have used a vehicle to get the victim in here and, being virtually in the middle of nowhere, would have also been an advantage.

"Morning, inspector."

"Good morning, doctor. Thank you very much for your time. By the way, I clarified my remaining questions about the Parish murder after receiving the Toxicology Report from you," said Jordon.

"No problem. So, shall we get on with it?"

As she and Paul approached the body, everyone moved to one side. She took it all in very carefully. Her eyes swept the scene with the same intensity as always – first impressions were everything, and she'd held that belief repeatedly at crime scenes. A naked woman, around thirty years old, had been tied by her wrists and was hanging forward from the branch of a mature oak. The floor of the wood below her was saturated with blood, which was not too surprising given that she appeared to have been literally hacked to death; it was like an abattoir on a bad day.

As Cathy moved back slightly to gain a different perspective, she observed that the rivers of blood had been indiscriminate in their flow. Beautiful honeysuckle and dazzling bluebells had all fallen victim to its invasion of their space, finally pooling around a cluster of deadly nightshade, which somehow seemed a fitting end to its journey – from life to death. The irony did not escape her as she noted that the tree was a red oak, known for its flaming-coloured lobes; however, this autumn had arrived early, and its lower spiky leaves had suffered considerable arterial blood spray.

"What are your first impressions, Doctor Meer?" asked Jordon eagerly.

"That's a question for Doctor Granger, inspector."

"It's okay, Cathy," said Paul graciously, unmoved by being sidetracked by the inspector.

"Given the state of rigor mortis, I'd say the time of death was around 03:00 in the early hours. Last night was a full moon, bright enough for him to do his work. The weapon was probably a large, very sharp blade, perhaps even a machete, but of course, Paul needs to get her on the table. There's no doubt in my mind that this was an act of pure, uncontrollable butchery in every sense of the word. I can categorically state, Inspector, that this is not the work of our boy. The skill set isn't there, nothing even approaching the finesse of the first, so we're looking at another player," said Cathy, matter-of-factly.

"I concur, Cathy. Thanks for coming. It was good to work with you again," said Paul.

"Any other comments, Doctor Meer, before you...erm... leave?"

"No inspector. It's Dr Granger's crime scene. I'm just an invited guest, remember?"

"Er, right. Sorry, I didn't mean to overstep the mark, doctor."

"It's okay, I understand, Inspector," replied Cathy.

"So, Doctor Granger, what are your initial thoughts?"

"Well, she'd have died very quickly as major arteries have been severed and she'd have bled out rapidly. I'll get her on the table A-SAP and let you know, inspector, once I've had a good peek," said Paul, giving Cathy a wink.

"I hope you catch your killer, inspector – nasty business," said Cathy, prepared to leave.

"Good to see you again, take care, Cathy," said Dr Paul Granger, with respect.

He'd always admired her expertise and agreed with the reputation she had, always, rightly earned from her fellow pathologists.

"You too, Paul. Good luck."

"I'll be off then. Just out of interest, inspector, do you have an ID? A habit of mine to ask?"

"Her name was Mary, a well-known local prostitute. We've actually got a suspect in custody and witnesses who claim to have seen him with her at the local pub on numerous occasions. Maybe he was inspired by Parish's murder. Who knows, but we don't have any motive yet other than that he was seen leaving the pub with her, visibly intoxicated. Maybe he murdered her out of jealousy. You know, her being a prostitute and what that could mean," said Inspector Jordon, dispassionately.

"That's pretty fast work," commented Cathy, on her way to leave the scene.

"Yeah, well, we received an anonymous tip unexpectedly early this morning, and when we went to the suspect's flat, it was like an Aladdin's cave. Newspaper cuttings were plastered all over his bedroom wall, including a picture of DS Riley and you, along with a load of other interesting and potentially incriminating items, which we are working on as we speak. I mean, even I can see that he wasn't capable of the first murder, which was a completely different kettle of fish. However, inexplicably, we found the weapon for the first murder hidden away, and it's a perfect match to the fragment you found during your post-mortem. We'll go through the motions on that, but it was certainly 'a plant' to throw us off the scent and cause confusion. But we've got him pretty well cornered on this – her bloodstains on the seat of his jeep, and he hasn't disposed of his blood-soaked clothes yet."

"Well, I'm pleased, as I said, that it's not our boy. I need a drink. How about you, Inspector?" said Cathy, trying to mend the bridges in her mind regarding how irritated she'd been with him lately.

Jordon's phone suddenly buzzed, and Cathy watched intently as she saw his face grow increasingly concerned. The fact that his eyes were fixed on her, while he spoke to whoever was calling, heightened her anxiety about what was happening now.

"I'm sorry, doctor, this is going to take a while, but it seems to concern you. I'll catch up with you as soon as I can."

"Okay, I'll be in The Pale Horse. You must know it, it's just down the road, and I need a drink anyway."

• CHAPTER 13 •

The Pale Horse was a charmingly old-fashioned village pub with heavy oak beams and a genuine, friendly atmosphere. She'd always liked the owner. He'd consistently been a sincere and warm host, jovial with everyone, and not fazed by her admittedly infrequent visits, unlike the usual plastic smile and insincerity some landlords displayed.

"Good morning, doctor, good to see you again. What can I offer you?"

"I'm in need of a good white Burgundy," she replied hopefully.

"Got just the thing for you, doctor, from my private collection, a Coche-Dury Genervrières, Meursault Premier Cru," he said with a smile as he disappeared for a moment and returned with the bottle of wine that he displayed with pride before her.

He pulled the cork with an experienced flourish and poured her a generous glass. She sipped and winked her appreciation, delighted. It certainly hit the spot, and she made her way out to have a puff in the pub's garden. Moments later, Jordon appeared, grasping a pint. She'd always prided herself on her ability to read people, but with Jordon, there was something else going on. She had, during her career, worked with many police officers of his rank and status, but he didn't seem to fit the mould, and her feminine intuition had begun to kick in that all was not what it seemed.

But she couldn't quite put her finger on why. Yes, he'd irritated her by ringing the night before – an evening she'd rather forget. Nevertheless, she pushed her concerns aside.

"Okay, inspector, hit me with it," she said, impatiently.

"Well, doctor, I'm not quite sure how or where to begin."

"Try the beginning."

"Well, the call I just received unexpectedly was from Major Freddy Carr of MI6, who advised that you and your family may be in danger. Major Carr has asked me to inform you on behalf of Captain Marcus de Vere of de Vere Security. You may know they have an office here in Maidstone, Abu Dhabi, and elsewhere."

"No, why should I? I don't know him or his company. What threat? What are you talking about?"

"I'm very sorry, Doctor Meer, but he advised that GCHQ, part of our security services, has intercepted chatter concerning what they believe to be a possible threat to you and your family. He has also informed Special Branch and MI5 as part of standard protocol, and, as you may know from your experience as a pathologist, the link between these security agencies is quite close."

"Chatter. What on earth does that bloody mean?"

"It means known terrorists have mentioned your name in intercepted communications, and it would seem that, as I said, there is a potential threat."

"But how's that even possible?"

"Major Carr is sending me a copy of the file. You know that your husband was a top sniper in the Regiment. Something of a legend, apparently."

"Look, you don't need to tell me about my husband. Can you get to the bloody point?" said Cathy impatiently.

"The Major examined the file on the mission, which was truly an off-the-radar Black Op to capture or eliminate a terrorist named Asif Badawi. Poor intelligence led to a scenario where our men walked straight into a carefully planned ambush, and in the ensuing firefight, unfortunately, Peter was killed along with his fellow sniper, Angus McGregor."

"AND?"

"Sorry, the surviving members of Peter's team explained that Captain Meer had killed three of Asif's younger brothers before Asif himself charged, apparently like a suicidal maniac, and by some fluke, managed to get the drop on both Peter and his mate Angus and kill them."

Cathy sat back, stunned. She'd never heard this information before. The Regiment had remained tight-lipped about the circumstances of her husband's death, and in some small way, it made her feel better to finally learn the truth.

"But how does this bastard Badawi know who I am?" said Cathy, now somewhat less belligerent.

"Good question. The Major's best guess is that Peter must have had a picture of you, the family, and other private items on him. Of course, if he did, then that would have been against protocol for a soldier to carry into a combat zone."

"Peter was always a rule breaker, inspector, and, to be honest, I think the Major's assessment is probably right. It's the only thing that makes sense from what you are saying. Oh dear. But then, again, it doesn't explain the how of it all," Cathy said, sadly.

"Don't forget, doctor, your picture has been on the front page after that high-profile murder at the barn. We think his people, or he, saw it in the bloody newspapers. I mean, they gave everything except your telephone number and address."

"So, what to do now?" said Cathy, feeling a lot less antagonistic now.

"Special Branch has deployed a plainclothes officer at the school and two at your home very discreetly, 24/7, instigated by Bob Brimley, the Chief Constable of Kent. Who I understand is a close friend of Captain de Vere and is, as I say, authorising this interim protection until such time that de Vere Security can deploy their people."

"Thank you, but why aren't our security services able to protect me until this threat is resolved?"

"Frankly, it's a matter of available manpower. Our security resources are currently stretched to their limit. The UK is under what is called 'a critical threat' regarding other terrorist activities and potential actions at home."

"I'm sorry, but this is a lot of information for me to process."

"Understood. Have you heard of 'de Vere Security' in Maidstone?"

"As I said – no."

"I've met the CEO, Captain Marcus de Vere, in the past, and I understand that he will be returning from an overseas trip tomorrow and will contact you. He has offered to deploy his own considerable resources to mitigate and control this threat to you and your family. Major Carr assured me that Captain de Vere will, certainly, deal with all of this upon his return and has asked me to make you aware that de Vere Security have stepped up. Who, by the way, are held in very high regard by the powers that be."

"Please thank your colleagues, inspector, for the police protection, and could you also convey my thanks to Major Carr. Please ask him to inform Captain de Vere that I look forward to hearing from him and, no doubt, my eventual meeting with him."

"Of course, and I apologise for being the one to bring this distressing news to you and your family, Doctor Meer."

• CHAPTER 14 •

The Painter settled back in his grand oak-panelled library and study, relaxing in a comfortable leather-backed swivel chair while sipping a glass of white Burgundy. He had decided he didn't want to drink his sacramental wine today; it wasn't necessary. Alcohol, the demon drink, as some say, was true for him, but not now, as he had no wish to invite the shadows lurking in his mind, waiting. Although they were always welcome, now he had much to contemplate, and they would, unwittingly, be a distraction.

He reached once more for his copy of 'The Times' newspaper to examine the picture of Dr Meer and DS Riley, who were investigating Parish's death. From all accounts, she was a clever woman, and he hoped she hadn't uncovered any further evidence that could threaten him. A reliable source and close associate had indicated that the doctor had found a fragment of his scalpel. That wasn't an issue that worried or unsettled him in the slightest; no way it could lead back to him. All he had to do was toss it into a river, no problem. However, what did concern him was the risk that the jewellery he'd implanted on Parish might come back to haunt him. Glancing at the small, ornate carriage clock on his leather-topped desk, he pushed the matter from his mind for now. It was almost time for luncheon. His lurking friends in his thoughts weren't going to be able to help him with his concerns about the meddlesome doctor, at least not for the moment. When and if her time came to deal with her permanently, they were more than capable of suggesting satisfying solutions for his revenge on her irritating involvement.

His father had been a renowned surgeon in the past, and The Painter had inherited his collection of books and other interesting items – he had already considered destroying his father's collection of rare, fine obsidian blades – just in case. He turned the blade over in his hands – the murder weapon. To relax, he gladly opened the box of Chaliapin cigarettes on his desk and lit one, savouring the look and flavour of the oval-shaped cigarette. The paper had a hint of antique yellow and contained a very exclusive blend of Turkish tobaccos that arrived in boxes of twenty-five every week or so. He had been smoking these since his late twenties, introduced to them by his father. As he enjoyed this rare indulgence, he recalled the amusing story he was told at a dinner party many years earlier in Knightsbridge about the origin of the cigarette.

The Painter was rarely amused by anything unless it concerned the misfortune of others, but on that occasion, he had

had to smile. One of the guests at the dinner party was a partner of a prestigious London maker of bespoke cigarettes whose firm had been commissioned in the 1930s to provide a mixture of Turkish tobaccos by the famous Russian opera star Feodor Ivanovich Chaliapin, who requested that they craft a blend that would not affect his throat unduly. Which they did, it seems, to Chaliapin's satisfaction.

But the amusing twist was that he had learnt from his dinner partner that evening that the London supplier had added a trace of opium to the mix to achieve that result. Of course, these days, that was no longer in the blend, but he thought how amused his father would have been if he had known he had been unwittingly a drug addict for years. The amount of opium was, in reality, insignificant but perhaps enough to soothe the throat of the famous singer. Even so, he was quite sure that his father would have laughed about it, especially considering his role and standing in medical circles as a renowned surgeon in his day.

While he sat, he began to reflect on his action, once again, regarding the delightful payback he'd enacted upon Parish. A development he hadn't been pleased to hear, but now, nonetheless, he had decided that rather than dispose of the damaged blade, which, of course, would have been so easy, he would put it to some nefarious use. He had recently become aware of a local reprobate believed to be responsible for at least two murders locally, but who had evaded arrest so far due to a lack of evidence. The idea was to make this individual the perfect patsy and confuse the police at the same time.

He had followed the potential pawn in the game to his flat and waited until he left for the pub, which he knew he would do from previous observation. He slipped on his surgical gloves and picked the lock with a set of picks that some trash had gifted him years earlier, but he had to admit they had been quite helpful over the years. The lock was not sophisticated, and he quickly gained entry. Once inside, he quickly looked around. The flat was reasonably sized, open plan, and furnished expensively. In the well-equipped kitchen, he found an envelope addressed to Mr Roger Mayne, confirming he was in the right place, the target's home. There were only three other doors, one to the bathroom, full of marble and upmarket fittings; a second to a guest bedroom; and a third, which he opened and froze in place. His mouth dropped open in astonishment and delight.

The enormity of the potentially damning evidence before him was staggering. One wall was completely covered with newspaper clippings. He examined them more closely and recognised the picture of both the pathologist bitch and DS Riley, who were, of course, dealing with the unfortunate death of Parish. But then, on top of that, he was pleasantly stunned to see clippings covering at least three unsolved murders, each full of all the grisly details. His patsy's trophy wall, he hoped. Not only had The Painter struck gold in his desire to shake things up, but this was the motherlode of all gold mines, right there for anyone to see. All conveniently displayed. Once the police saw all of this, they would salivate in a frenzy of excitement. Of course, he knew they wouldn't take down his patsy for the Parish murder, as he was clearly too unskilled for that, and certainly not the sharpest tool in the box to have, in his obviously distorted mind, blatantly displayed this montage of supposed evidence. But there was definitely enough here to put Roger the Dodger away for good. It seemed long overdue to take this nutter off the streets. He took out his cherished but damaged obsidian blade and hid it. The perfect way to dispose of it and create confusion and problems in the minds of the police, an amusing prospect, to say the least.

He decided he would call them from a public phone to tip them off anonymously about Roger the Dodger. He didn't care whether he was guilty of anything or not, but after everything he had seen in the flat, he was pretty sure that good old Roger was well overdue and ready to be taken down; The Painter had his civil duty to perform, after all.

But the one thing that troubled him more than anything else, being the perfectionist he was, was that he had made a potentially grave error in embellishing Parish's body with the damn earrings. At the time, he had been so overwhelmingly consumed with the need to make a statement that he had, uncharacteristically, not thought through all the possible ramifications of that lapse in care. Yes, of course, the boys in blue would now, presumably, be well on their way to finding the jeweller who sold the emeralds to Parish, and with Parish being amicably divorced, the police would be examining Parish's girlfriends for any link that could lead them to a person of interest, God forbid, Helen. And then, ultimately, him.

How could he have been so insanely careless, he reflected, as it would, in their eyes, give him a motive should they trace them back to Helen. Who was, certainly, a girlfriend if not the main one, but he would have to deal with it when and if it came up. But perhaps he was being overly concerned. After all, he'd been interviewed by the police at the time of her disappearance, and he'd employed a private detective to try and locate her – an effective ruse on his part – with no results, of course. But noted by the police at the time...

Yesterday, he jumped into his car and drove away from the area to find a public telephone box where he could make his anonymous call to the police. As he drove, he turned on the news and learned that another murder had been committed, purportedly similar to his work, which really irritated him; it didn't matter who was responsible. It was the audacity of someone thinking they could even remotely match his skills. But then, as he considered the development, he was fairly certain that Roger the Dodger would foot the bill for that one, and good riddance.

• CHAPTER 15 •

The blue flag of the Cavalry and Guards Club fluttered in the light summer breeze as Asif Badawi passed through the doors of the Grade 1 listed building. He knew a little about its history: in 1975, the Guards Club, founded in 1810, vacated its premises around the corner on Charles Street and merged with the Cavalry Club, a successful union that had lasted more than 40 years.

As he walked through the elegant entrance of the Club, he returned the nods of recognition from the porter and reception staff – he was well-known here and enjoyed it. He was actually a member of two London Clubs, but his palatial Mayfair apartment was just a stone's throw away, making it perfectly convenient, and he spent most of his downtime here when in town unless he was enjoying interesting weekends in the Kent countryside at a friend's estate.

He headed towards the covered smoking terrace next to Geoffrey's Bar and the Garden Room. The large doors of the Conservatory opened into an enclosed courtyard with a green 'living wall' at the far end.

He sat happily, having been served a bottle of his favourite Puligny-Montrachet, a wine produced in the commune of Puligny-Montrachet in Côte de Beaune, Burgundy. He had only recently returned to London and felt immediately at home as he entered the club. He studied the luncheon menu, which had been courteously presented to him, as always, by the restaurant manager John, dressed in the club's signature style of pinstripe trousers and a black jacket. His appetite began to increase as he examined the fare on offer. He lit a Romeo y Julieta to complete his satisfaction. He was, of course, dressed appropriately in an Armani suit, a white shirt, and a regimental Light Dragoons silk tie, knotted to perfection. John returned with perfect timing to take his order. Asif chose the Crab & Prawn Drumkilbo with Crab Mayonnaise and was somewhat amused to see that it had been a favourite dish of Queen Elizabeth, the late Queen Mother, before selecting a Dover Sole for the next course. John removed the presentation plates with the Club crest before the first course and, with practised subtlety, moved away in a manner that suited the mood and culture of the club.

The waiters in blue waistcoats, white shirts, and gold ties hovered unobtrusively in the background while he enjoyed his starter. He sat back, sipping his wine and puffing on his cigar contentedly. Unlike many Arabs, he had no qualms about enjoying his cigar between courses, unlike his fellow diners. After a while, he nodded to a waiter, and moments later, by the magic of perfect timing that excelled there, he received the fish, which was then expertly boned at the table by the waiter without delay, leaving the fish fillet at a perfect temperature.

Having satisfied his appetite with thanks to the chef responsible, via John, he looked around and noticed nearby was Sir Charles Billington, head of Section 12 MI6. Feeling instinctively that he was being watched, Sir Charles looked up and, after a moment, nodded in recognition – Asif returned the gesture. He smiled inwardly at the irony of it all. Unknown to his father and his associates, he had made a pact with Sir Charles a few months earlier to provide information on terrorist groups' plans and activities, which suited him because he only revealed details of opposing tribes with whom he and his family had had centuries of conflict. He was happy to see them taken down as a result of his intelligence. A sweet revenge. He had been paid handsomely with money he didn't need, and used it to play Texas Hold'em at many of the city's poker clubs, discovering to his satisfaction that he was very good at the game, despite never having been a gambler in any true sense. It really was a win-win scenario for him.

But what they all failed to realise, including his father, was that all he wanted in life was to indulge his sexual desires and his craving to kill – it was a hunger he had embraced ever since a CIA black ops team had assassinated his mother. She had been the only woman he'd ever loved. They had taken her away in a single fatal strike when he was in his teens – his father had been the intended target, but by some twist of fate, his father survived – and he had never forgiven him or America for that. He was only thirteen at the time, but that event ingrained a mindset within him that had never faltered. Revenge at any expense was the only outcome he sought; it didn't matter who it was for – every death was justified in his eyes and only heightened his desire to kill.

But here he was, actually in bed with a representative of Satan himself, albeit America's close ally. Still, close enough to relish the proximity. The head of Section 12, MI6, the UK's Secret Intelligence Service, is primarily responsible for the covert overseas collection and analysis of human intelligence in support of national security, along with GCHQ. Naturally, by many in the Security Services, he would be seen as a terrorist or at least a person of interest, just as his father was. If only they knew the rest of it, he mused.

The West had terms that suited them, and he pondered the incredulity of their perception of the Arab world. When they approved the incumbent tribe in power, they called them 'tribal leaders', but when they disapproved of them, they called them 'warlords'—much like the Irish problem many years earlier... He sat back and gestured to one of the blue waistcoated waiters to bring his Cognac, which the club kept exclusively for him in their cellars. It was a Henri IV Dudognon Heritage Grande Champagne Cognac, aged over 100 years from the family business Maison Dudognon, founded in 1776. It never ceased to please him to see the sterling platinum bottle arrive; a bottle dipped in 24-karat gold and adorned with allegedly 6,500 certified brilliant-cut diamonds, though he'd never had the time or inclination to count them all. Weighing nearly 18 pounds, it was a bit of a handful, and each time he indulged in its magical contents, he experienced joy—an emotion he rarely felt. The spectacle of its arrival always drew attention from those nearby, which pleased him. He made a mental note to remember never to forget to take it home with him one day, as soon as he'd savoured the very last drop. It had been an unexpected and enormously extravagant gift from his father, costing around 2 million dollars a bottle. A drop in the ocean to his father, with whom he had been estranged for several years. Nonetheless, he regarded the gesture as perhaps an attempt at 'let's make it up'. But so far, that had not come to pass. From Asif's point of view, there was little hope of reconciliation, given his father's ongoing support and funding of international terrorism, which made it hard for him to maintain a low profile and be recognised as a successful businessman in his own right. It was his fate, and nothing could be done about it now; he had lived in his father's shadow for so long, just accept it, he mused.

Taking another sip of cognac, he envisioned the magnificent piece of art eventually taking pride of place in his penthouse down the road – adding even more flair.

He noticed that Sir Charles was engrossed in a conversation which, sadly, he could not overhear. For a brief moment, it unsettled him, but he quickly remembered that he had survived so far by living his life with a heightened sense of security. Therefore, even the smallest thing could sometimes trigger his defences.

A little while later, perhaps merely by chance, which he didn't truly believe in, two well-dressed gentlemen joined Sir Charles's table, and from their bearing, Asif was certain they were military or former military.

But what unsettled him slightly was that Sir Charles's companions, after chatting for a while among themselves, turned their heads towards him, giving him a once-over – but never mind, it probably meant nothing. Asif was not easily rattled and relaxed back in his comfortable chair to enjoy his cigar and brandy. After all, he and Sir Charles had an arrangement that suited them both, but Asif knew all too well, instinctively, that this did not mean the other players in the game might not be privy to it – he recognised it was a dangerous world.

He was a master of counter-surveillance techniques, and all his communications with his contacts were constantly updated using the latest encryption technology. But of course, aside from that, he had always been cautious regarding his actions here in the heart of the enemy territory. There had also been the issue of the four missing girls from Clouds Night Club in Knightsbridge, which had briefly drawn police attention. It was a club he frequented regularly while in London, and the police had interviewed him about their disappearances, which had coincided with his visit last summer. He had been seen dancing with one of them. He knew he was attractive to women, the younger, the better, and he had exploited this fact.

It had become quite simple to take each of them to his apartment over time for a night of intimacy, then in the morning slip a sleeping drug into their coffee and take them to his friend's country estate to participate in The Summer Hunt. Like his old friend and fellow huntsman, he took pleasure not only in the conquest but also in the kill itself – but all had gladly accepted this fact. The anticipation of the chase heightened the pleasure, which was carefully orchestrated before the Hunt itself. Again, he reflected on how very cautious and patient he had been over the past few years in that particular activity. But now he realised he would need to be even more cautious and allow more time to pass before he was tempted again to continue that delightful and rewarding pastime. With his growing relationship with Sir Charles, he understood that his profile had risen a notch or two and that he could not risk any unwelcome attention.

Fortunately, those investigations had dispersed fairly quickly. He pondered whether the police might have been encouraged to retreat under Section 12, given that he was valued in their eyes like gold dust unless they had concrete evidence against him. He believed this was a reasonable assumption, but they hadn't yet managed to link him to anything suspicious. He also suspected that the Special Branch was unaware of his connection with MI6. However, it was unthinkable that the British Security Services would overlook his activities involving the discreet disposal of young women he had drugged and provided for the Summer Hunt over the years. Therefore, he remained ever vigilant.

To anyone observing, they would not notice the nearly indiscernible frown that now appeared on Asif's face as he reflected once again on the newspaper cutting he had received at his apartment just a few hours before lunch from his No. 2, Syed Ayad. It depicted a man and a woman involved in a high-profile murder case in Kent. He knew the county well since he had shot there during the pheasant season from time to time, although he hated the inclement weather that season brought. But the Summer Hunts had more than compensated for that and remained one of his greatest joys in life, even though that pastime was currently on hold for the foreseeable future. He had always spent only July and August in London, but even then, he often felt cold and was happy to return home to the comfort of Abu Dhabi's climate.

But he could not and never would refuse the invitation to join his old friend at his estate, where the gamekeeper had always managed to please with high and fast low birds to test his skills. In fact, he had decided to visit his old friend that very afternoon and had telephoned him to check if it was convenient, which it was.

He decided to drive down in his silver Porsche 911. An apt number, he thought with a small smile – to mark the heroic actions of the Wahhabi terrorist group Al-Qaeda on that significant date many years ago – so many killed in one strike. He could have used his chauffeur-driven black S-class Mercedes, but he felt it was a bit ostentatious for a social visit.

But now, thinking once more about the newspaper clipping, the woman's face did seem to fit, undoubtedly, the woman he sought for his revenge. He reached into his pocket and withdrew the ultra-slim seal skin wallet, grasping the blood-stained image that he'd kept there for more than six years. He stared closely – alkaliba (الكلبة), he muttered. A dangerous slip that was entirely out of character for him to use his native language here and to employ Arab slang, but even more so, his expletive drew the attention of those at Sir Charles's table.

One of the military types turned towards him, his face deeply tanned, no doubt, Asif thought from prolonged exposure to the desert sun, and he gradually wagged an admonishing finger at him with a wry smile.

Asif acknowledged the gesture by raising his brandy glass in salute, smiling. It was a dangerous world.

Asif gave John a subtle wave...

"Yes, Sir?" whispered John.

"The chap with Sir Charles. He looks vaguely familiar to me, but I can't quite place the name."

"Ah, that would be Major Carr, sir. An...erm...unexpected guest today, I believe."

"Oh yes, I remember now. I'll swing by to say hello on my way out." Which, of course, he had no intention of doing.

"Actually, sir, if I may?" John bends down to whisper.

"What?"

"Well, it may not be the best time, sir, as they seem to be in a rather heated discussion, if you get my drift."

"Thank you, John. Another time, perhaps," he wondered what all that was about, hoping he was not the subject of discussion.

Over the years, his finely honed survival instincts had matured, and now they triggered suspicion that Carr was a threat. He returned to the issue at hand. The picture in the clipping bore a strong resemblance to the one in his wallet. The name fit, and the article mentioned she was the widow of a British army officer. Therefore, he was convinced it was her – wife of the SAS soldier he'd killed so many years before. He silently prayed to Allah that it was she. Equally important to his desire to kill was his craving to violate her, and if she was who he hoped, then indeed he would seek to have both – what a sweet revenge.

He'd sent a double-encrypted message to Syed to investigate further. He'd have to wait. But patience was one of his undeniable strengths, along with the fact that he'd never failed in repaying a family debt or any other debt, for that matter. He nodded his thanks to John and left to walk to his apartment, deep in thought about what, if anything, untoward had happened at the club, and decided there was nothing for him to fret over. So, he focused on what to pack in his overnight bag for the weekend in the Kent countryside and eagerly jumped into his silver Porsche.

• CHAPTER 16 •

Marcus sat on the upper terrace of Little Manor, contemplating how to approach his conversation with Doctor Meer, whom he was supposed to call that morning. He decided to ring his friend Bob Brimley, the Chief Constable of Kent, first.

"Bob, it's been a while – how are things?"

"All good, Marcus, but I'm not happy with the slow progress on that ghastly Parish murder case."

"Yeah, well, it's become quite high profile, but what's the problem? I mean, you've got Jordon on it and his sidekick...er..."

"DS Tim Riley."

"Don't know him, but surely Jordon's on top of it, right?"

"Riley's the new boy. Transferred from the MET, at his request, a couple of months ago. I haven't got the measure of the man yet – anyway, what's on your mind?"

"Well, I'm just about to ring Dr Cathy Meer and wanted to run through my thoughts with you first, Bob."

"Ah, yes. Well, firstly, thanks for stepping up. As you probably know from Freddy, our security services are overwhelmed to breaking point with numerous active terrorist threats in the country. Between you and me, there's no way we could provide the security cover for her and her family. I mean, it would demand 24/7 protection not only for her but also for the children."

"So, you're okay with me deploying my team on your territory?" asked Marcus.

"No problem. Try not to kill anyone," chuckled the Chief Constable of Kent. "I've got enough on my plate already."

"It's a deal, and thanks, Bob. I'll keep you in the loop. Oh, I nearly forgot, with everything going on – you *are* coming tonight, right?"

"What? Where?"

"Emily rang your secretary a few weeks ago to invite you and the kids to my house. I'm having a small birthday party."

"Blast. I'm so sorry, Marcus, I completely forgot – we'll be there."

"Not to worry, see you later, take care," said Marcus, hanging up.

Monica had taken the children to school, and Cathy was taking the time to enjoy her coffee and a puff on the garden terrace. As always, it was comforting to see Fred pecking away at the old pear tree. Her relaxing break was interrupted by her work phone buzzing, and she wondered who would be calling her on her week off.

"Am I speaking to Dr Meer?"

"Yes, speaking," she answered irritably once again at being disturbed during her downtime.

"Sorry to bother you, Doctor Meer. My name's Captain Marcus de Vere. I understand DCI Jordon has been in touch with you regarding the potential security issues concerning you and your family."

"Ah, yes. Thank you for calling, Captain. As you can imagine, my life has been turned upside down upon hearing about this... erm... potential threat," said Cathy, relieved to hear his calm and reassuring voice.

"I would like to meet with you as soon as possible to discuss the entire issue. When would be convenient for you?"

"Well, it's Friday, and I'm on call again next Monday, so I'm unsure what's best to suggest."

"Look, I know it's short notice, but is it possible for you to come to my house tomorrow? The fact is, I'm hosting a birthday party, but it doesn't start until after 6ish. If you can come around 2 pm, we'll have plenty of time to go through the issues, and I can explain my plans to mitigate the threat to you and your children. To be honest, from my assessment of the risks involved, it's better to meet sooner rather than later."

"So, it's more than just a potential threat then?"

"Yes, I'm sorry to say, in my opinion, it's serious, Doctor Meer, but I don't want to alarm you. So, are you available at 2 pm tomorrow?"

"Yeah, that works for me – thank you. Would it be alright if I bring my friend Monica Summers and my children?"

"Monica Summers? Good grief, it's a small world indeed. I know Monica. We met a couple of years ago at one of her children's book signings. She is a fantastic writer and knows where I live. There will also be a few kids running around to keep your children entertained."

"Great, that's truly perfect. I look forward to meeting you then, and thank you so much."

"No problem, bye for now, and don't worry, we'll sort it out."

Monica returned and joined Cathy outside for a coffee and a smoke, listening to her news with growing interest.

"Captain de Vere mentioned that he'd met you?"

"Yeah, at a book signing. You were on call, if I remember, so you didn't have the pleasure!"

"Pleasure?"

"He's not only a successful businessman but bloody attractive as well."

"Married?"

"No."

"So, Monica, are you interested?"

"Are you kidding. I'm almost old enough to be his mother."

"Come off it. You're a stunning woman."

"Cathy, give me a break. I enjoy being with my books. I met Emily there, who's his PA, and she's really nice. She filled me in a bit about him."

"Do tell. I mean, he does sound a little too good to be true," said Cathy."

"Well, he spent 17 years with The Regiment and then worked as an MI6 operative for a while under E Squadron, which is, or was, very off the radar. All I heard were rumours – no idea what they actually do – something like James Bond stuff. Anyway, he then started his own company, de Vere Security, with an office in Abu Dhabi, and his head office is here in Maidstone. Emily and I got on straight away, and she confided in me that, in her opinion, he hadn't wanted to commit to anyone over the years because of the risky life he'd led in the Special Air Service. But gradually, over time, he's begun to relax and has had a few female companions, but none that seemed to work out – so that's all I know. But how is it that he wants to meet with you? What's going on?"

Cathy explained everything about the threat to her and her children.

"Dear Cathy, poor you. Why didn't you tell me earlier?"

"I wasn't ready to share it and burden you with it all," she said with a shrug.

"Okay, so we're going on Saturday with the children?"

"Absolutely," Cathy replied, "as you can imagine, this entire situation is keeping me awake at night, and I need the risks to the children, and me, explained and clarified in my mind. Captain de Vere is setting aside a few hours to explain the measures he intends to put in place to protect us."

"To be honest, Cathy, I don't think that you could be in better hands," Monica said sincerely. "Let's get going."

• CHAPTER 17 •

After driving through the scenic Kent countryside, guided by Monica's directions, they finally reached the gates of Little Manor, Lingfield, Surrey. Before them, magnificent wrought iron gates came into view, an opening in the seemingly endless eight-foot-high ancient brick walls surrounding the estate. Cathy was captivated by the beautifully crafted wrought iron scenes depicting fox and deer hunting. She edged the car forward slightly so Monica could announce their arrival via the state-of-the-art intercom. A small camera swivelled in their direction, and almost immediately, the impressive gates slowly swung open.

Cathy drove up the seemingly endless winding driveway through a series of small, well-maintained woods one after another. Suddenly, a pair of massive, striking Irish Wolfhounds burst through the trees to join them on the drive; it was almost as if they had decided to escort her to the house. In fact, Cathy was beginning to wonder when and if she would finally see it. Then, there it was in all its splendour, a grand mansion nestled amidst exquisitely designed, mature landscaped gardens.

"This is called Little Manor!" exclaimed Cathy, laughing, as she took in the grandeur and size of the manor house before her. She looked at Monica for her opinion.

"Well, what did you expect? A suburban semi?" shrugged Monica, smiling.

"Not a bloody mansion of this size," laughed Cathy.

As she parked in the carriage drive at the house's entrance, she couldn't help but notice that the man who greeted them had a Glock 19 strapped to his belt, a weapon she knew all too well. In fact, it was one of her two preferred pistols when she was a competitive shooter – the other being her SIG P226. Unknown to most of her friends, she had been a top marksman at a renowned London pistol club and had collected numerous trophies for her achievements in competitions, not only against other clubs but also in surpassing skilled police firearms units and military teams. The only challenge to her dominance on the pistol range was the rare yet welcome covert visits from Special Air Service teams, who consistently outperformed her and the club's 'A' team without fail – every damn single time. To make it even more embarrassing, they seemed capable of doing so with any type of pistol or revolver – she had openly laughed once when she saw one of their team carry in a battered old leather kit bag filled with such old and obscure firearms that she would never have believed they could be effective or accurate compared to her trusty SIG Sauer. And yet, she recalled, that on that occasion one or two of the SAS lads relinquished their SIGS – good-humouredly, to demonstrate, for fun, their prowess with these seemingly doubtful weapons with devastating results which, of course, just rubbed more salt into her wounds.

Mr Glock 19 stepped forward. “Good afternoon, ma’am, you must be Doctor Meer. And good to see you again, too, Monica, it’s been a while,” he said with a welcoming smile. “Captain de Vere’s polishing his Fat Boy at the moment in one of the barns. I’ll take you to him. By the way, the name is Joe.”

“Hi Joe, A fat boy? Who’s that then? Seems a little unkind to whoever the poor fellow is,” laughed Cathy.

“Guess you’re not a Harley Davidson devotee, doctor.”

“So, it seems,” chortled Cathy. “So, lead me to enlightenment.”

As she passed the barn outbuildings to the main house, she noticed that they weren’t actual barns at all but beautifully converted stables with Cotswold stone blocks and lovely handmade clay roof tiles.

“Wow is that old van still running?” she asked, looking at a dilapidated grey vehicle poking its battered nose out of one of the stables – it seems like it’s on its last legs,” smiled Cathy.

“Ah, yes, it has sentimental value for Marcus. His father used it to move furniture back in the day. But no, it’s fully functional. In fact, he still uses it to pick up interesting items at auctions from time to time– one of his passions. And, while we’re at it, take in another well-loved relic,” as he pointed out a battered, decrepit old open-topped Land Rover Defender in an adjoining stable.

Both are circa late 70s. And believe it or not, that's still a go-er as well," smiled Joe.

"How big is the estate?"

"About 1,500 acres, ma'am," replied Joe.

Hearing their voices, Marcus stepped out from one of the stables, cloth in hand. Behind him, a gleaming black and white Harley Davidson lay.

"Just finished, you must be Doctor Meer," said Captain Marcus de Vere, smiling warmly as he wiped his hands clean. "Welcome."

"It's beautiful, Captain de Vere. It's like a piece of art, a sculpture in metal even. Boys and their toys, eh?"

"Exactly, I just got back from a ride, but most of the fun, apart from the mind-blowing sound of the engine, is keeping it sparkling – it helps me relax – but please call me Marcus."

"Cathy." She took in the tanned, very fit-looking gentleman, who appeared to be in his mid-to-late 50s, with enormously broad shoulders, as he approached. He walked with a fluid energy like a leopard's and reached over to give Monica a warm hug. For the first time since her husband's death, she felt a twinge of attraction which she, at once, tried hard to dispel from her mind. Many men had pursued her relentlessly over the years, but none had even come close to penetrating her defences...until, perhaps, now.

"I see you've met Monty and Churchill," said Marcus, stroking the two hounds affectionately. Their tails wagged furiously as they leapt up to hug him. Marcus's obvious love for them, and their love for him, moved her.

"Well, they've escorted and protected us all the way to your front door with relentless and boundless energy. Great names, by the way. And the gates, I have to say, are something to behold."

"Well, they clearly recognise important guests when they see them," laughed Captain Marcus de Vere, as he inwardly warmed to her.

"I'm pleased you liked the gates – they were designed by my late father, who paid close attention to every detail he worked on. Monica, it's good to see you again. And these must be your children, Cathy. Please introduce me to everyone," Marcus said with a friendly smile, captivated by her sparkling emerald, green eyes.

"Well, this is George and Jenny." The children stepped forward, and Marcus shook their hands before turning to Cathy, his face breaking into a broad grin. "Delighted to meet you all, especially you, Cathy. We have much to discuss. Thank you for coming on such short notice," Marcus said, trying to hide how drawn he was to this undeniably beautiful woman – like most men would be, he mused. But looks were not the be-all and end-all; far more important to him was the mind behind the beauty. He had learned of her renowned professionalism as a respected forensic pathologist, and he only wished that this first encounter had taken place under better circumstances. His regret was that the reality of the news he'd have to deliver later would be distressing – nevertheless, his gut feeling was that she would not be easily fazed by it.

"I'm pleased to meet you, too, Marcus, at last. This is quite an impressive pad you've got here for just one person," said Cathy, smiling, mischievously, with a wink to Monica.

"Ah, I see it's possible that Monica's been sharing all my secrets with you, eh?"

"Well, perhaps just a little background," grinned Cathy, embarrassed, hoping that her inward blushing had not reached her cheeks.

"Welcome to my family home. I inherited it some years ago, following my parents' passing," explained Marcus, a hint of sadness flickering across his face momentarily.

His thoughts briefly drifted to the past; he had long ignored any romantic interest from the many women he had encountered over the years. He still struggled to understand why, but perhaps after years of risking his life, he didn't want others who might care about him to endure the pain of waiting to see if he would return from his missions with the Regiment.

"George and Jenny, come with me. I have some friends you'd like to meet," Marcus said warmly. He took each of their hands and led them into the gardens to meet the other children. Their reactions were mutual delight upon meeting, and they immediately began playing hide-and-seek together.

"Try the maze, it's fun!" Marcus shouted after them, but they were all too busy socialising and having fun to hear him.

Cathy and Monica followed Marcus into the magnificent great hall, and Cathy was instantly struck by the impressive sweeping staircase that lay before them. “Time for a little bubbly, I think,” announced Marcus as his butler appeared out of nowhere with three fluted glasses brimming with pink champagne, offered on an exquisite antique silver platter.

“May I introduce Henry, ex-Corporal of Horse with the Blues and Royals. He keeps me on the straight and narrow, another treasure I inherited with the house,” laughed Marcus, unintentionally causing Henry some embarrassment and slight discomfort at the announcement.

Cathy and Monica happily clinked their glasses with Marcus’s in a thankful salute.

“My father used to say, ‘that a woman who says no to champagne, says no to life,’” he smiled. “And so, to life,” he chuckled, as he raised his glass.

“To life,” they replied.

“Forgive me, Monica. I have some very important matters to discuss with Cathy. Could I deploy you to the gardens to watch over the children? It will take quite some time, I’m afraid. But if you need anything, please call Henry.”

“No problem, good to see you again too. Cathy has told me what’s going on,” said Monica, her face full of concern.

“Don’t look so worried, Monica, we’ll get it sorted. Cathy, come with me. We’ll go out onto the upper terrace where we can talk in private – we’ve plenty of time before the hordes arrive.”

They ascended the staircase and stepped out onto a spacious, impressive balcony adorned with beautifully ornate white wrought-iron tables and chairs, then sat down.

"Do you mind if I smoke, Marcus? As a doctor, I should know better, of course, but..."

"One of my vices too," he smiled, tapping out one of his own from a soft pack of Camels.

"By the way, I must mention before we begin that I noticed your chap outside was armed with a Glock 19. Are you expecting some sort of trouble?" she asked, drawing on the French tobacco.

"Very observant of you, no one else has noticed that before! Ah, well, in my line of work, it's better to be safe than sorry. Having one or two armed fellows around is quite normal these days. In security, you never really know what might happen next, so it's best to be prepared for anything. Anyway, how is it that you seem to be so familiar with the Austrian 9mm weapon then?"

"I used to shoot quite a bit competitively, but that was some time ago. I like the Glock 19 and have used it frequently, but I favoured the SIG Sauer P226 for competitions," announced Cathy matter-of-factly. "My club consistently outperformed other clubs, police special firearm units, and the army. We did quite well, really, apart from the SAS teams that used to pop in from time to time, covertly, in the sense that they came in for fun, but we closed the club's entrance on those rare but welcome visits to respect their need for confidentiality. I found out early on, much to my dismay, that I never had much of a chance with those guys, even though I was usually on top form," smiled Cathy.

"Well, I spent seventeen happy years with the Regiment before I went native and opened de Vere Security. I have an indoor pistol range here that my father built out of his passion for the discipline, and he was a pretty good shot, too. So, you're welcome any time. In fact, let's do it next week sometime if you're free," said Marcus, surprised and impressed by her experience. The offer was made in the hope that he'd soon get the chance to see her again, and it seemed like a reasonable suggestion.

"Let's chat about that later, can we? I'm rather keen to get to the point," said Cathy impatiently, and she waited for Marcus to continue.

"Understood. Firstly, Cathy, please forgive me for intruding on your private life. Secondly, I know what's going on with you. And I empathise," said Marcus, with undisguised candour.

"Yes, I understand."

"An old chum of mine, Major Freddy Carr, MI6, has explained to me in detail the potential threat to you and your family. And I'm afraid it could turn out to be more than potential; in fact, it looks serious."

"Okay," she said, resigning herself to what was to come.

"Let me outline what we know. As you are aware from DCI Jordon, your husband was killed in action by Asif Badawi. His team was ambushed, and Peter and his best mate, Angus McGregor, sadly, didn't survive. I met Peter while I was running the SAS sniper school in the past. He was an exceptional sniper and was highly respected by his fellow soldiers. I didn't know him well, but I liked everything about him – his skills, attitude, and, frankly, his warm personality. As Jordon may have told you, we are now certain that Peter must have had his ID Pack and a photograph of you and your family on him. This would, of course, have been against protocol to carry into a combat zone. We believe that, as a result, Asif Badawi, because of your recent media exposure, has you in his sights for revenge. He's not only a killer but a dangerous sexual predator as well. This means that you and your family are in considerable danger."

"Why isn't this bugger in the ground or at least locked away in some distant cell – never to see the light again?"

Marcus smiled inwardly at the language, but was impressed by her straightforward candour and strength.

"Our onshore security services would prefer nothing more, but he has been very cautious to maintain a low profile regarding his terrorist activities, so they lack any solid grounds. According to reports, he is now seen as a successful businessman."

"So why did the Regiment and MI6 try to eliminate him?"

"Good question, Cathy. The SAS and MI6 work closely together on matters like this, but in practice, different rules sometimes apply when we operate outside the UK mainland. It was a need-to-know Black Op. If we had been successful, Badawi would indeed be under the ground, and no one would have known any different. That's just how it works. Sadly, this time everything went wrong entirely due to flawed intel."

"Okay, I understand. But we're not up to our knees in sand, I mean, we're not in some godforsaken desert now. So, what happens next?" said Cathy.

"Now, I'm going to protect you. The reality is that our security forces here at home, including Special Branch, MI5, and MI6, are quite stretched on the ground with numerous active threats to handle, and as a result, have limited resources to deploy to safeguard you and your family."

"Yes, I've been told all about that and more... And?"

Look, we know Asif's currently at his Mayfair penthouse. By the way, Badawi owns a house in Abu Dhabi not far from my offices, and I'll be returning there soon. My team will carry out a forensic search of his property, safe, and other belongings to see what we can learn that might help us better understand his plans. Anyway, before you arrived, I spoke with Gibbs. He's one of my top surveillance experts. He's ex-SAS, in his early sixties, very fit and sharp. He lives in Chelsea, which is ideal since Badawi's apartment is just a short distance away. As of two hours ago, he's been tracking Asif's every movement, around the clock. He's not licensed to carry a weapon, but, in his role, he doesn't need one. I've also briefed him fully on you and your family and told him that The Twins will be watching you and your children's six 24/7. They know each other well and are a formidable team together.

"My six?"

"Protecting your back."

"Understood, and 'The Twins'?"

"I'll explain about them in a moment."

"Okay."

Marcus buzzed Emily.

"Emily, could you please connect Carter to the secure line and patch him through?"

"On it."

"Just so you know, Cathy, Carter, and his girlfriend Anna are the best surveillance and protection team I've ever had. In the security community, they're called 'The Twins' and have saved my life and many others before."

His phone buzzed.

"Carter, how are you, mate, and Anna? I'm putting you on speaker. Is that okay? As I've got the subject with me."

"It's all good, boss. How can we help you?"

Marcus explained everything in minute detail, including addresses, Cathy's children's school timetable, and Gibbs's role.

"We're on it, sir. Good to hear Gibbs is in play. I'll ring him later."

"Thanks, Carter. Doctor Meer, as I said, is with me now at Little Manor, so we're all good from a security standpoint. This is a 24/7 operation starting right now and continuing until further notice. And report to me directly. I'm away for a bit in Abu Dhabi. If anything breaks and you can't reach me, ring Penny. She'll track me down, and I'll swing back to you as soon as I can. Okay?"

"Affirmative, see you soon. Actually, as it happens, I'm on my way now – ETA about one hour, okay?"

"Good, see you then. Thanks, mate," replied Captain de Vere.

"Will they be armed, Marcus?" asked Cathy, beginning to feel more at ease in the zone and more confident as a result.

"Yes, of course."

"Good."

"I'll advise Major Carr, and he'll bring the other security services up to speed as to the new security arrangements and be assured, Cathy, that my people will look after you and your family, but you won't see them unless something happens. So, please don't worry, they'll have you and the children covered."

"Thank you, Marcus. I already feel much safer. I don't quite know how to thank you. But please don't misunderstand me when I ask why you are helping me so much?"

"I understand, and it's a fair question, Cathy. Peter was with the Regiment. He was one of our own, and as his wife, you and your children are one of us too; we are a family. And we care about our family," said Marcus.

"Thank you again, Marcus," said Cathy, feeling both relieved and more at peace with the whole scenario.

"Look, why not stay for the party? I understand that after all this, you're probably not in the party mood, but it might help you take your mind off things. I mean, The Twins will be here within the hour to chat with my security team so everyone's on the same page, and Carter will introduce himself to you, right?"

"Right."

"The children seem to be happy out there," he said, gazing across the gardens.

"Absolutely, let's go for it," she said, gulping some more wine and lighting another cigarette.

"Great, I think my guests are starting to arrive. So, please excuse me for a moment while I mingle with my lads outside and greet my incoming guests. My boys know Carter very well; there's a lot of mutual respect there. So, we'll know as soon as he appears."

As he glided away, she reflected on the electricity she had felt flow between them when they shook hands and wondered if he had felt the same. Cathy mused once more on the fact that she had not looked at any other man since Peter's death... until now.

Cathy moved down to the expansive garden patio, decorated with the same ornate white wrought iron furniture that adorned the upper balcony, to watch her children having fun. Henry appeared beside her almost magically, the quintessential Jeeves, offering her another glass of bubbly, which she gladly accepted. Now, determined to enjoy herself, she was pleased to see Monica and the children coming to join her.

"Christ, Henry's like Jeeves," whispered Cathy to Monica.

"Yeah – the classic English butler. Who created that character, anyway? It's on the tip of my tongue," replied Monica.

"That would be Sir Pelham Grenville Woodhouse KBE," replied Henry in response, with a rare smile, as he smoothly swept past with more champagne.

Henry and Monica exchanged a grin before she refocused on Cathy.

"Well, Cathy, let's hear it," said Monica with a mischievous smile.

"Hear what, exactly?"

"Are you kidding? You know bloody well," giggled Monica with a wink.

"Okay, okay. He seems like a nice chap. Almost too good to be true," said Cathy, trying to sound disinterested.

"A *nice* chap! Oh, yes! Come on, Cathy, I know you."

"Okay, I like him. Actually, I like him a lot, and he's been excellent at explaining the details and protocol involved in creating a protective barrier around me and the children."

"He's that kind of bloke, Cathy. He's what it says on the tin – so, just follow your feminine intuition – that's what keeps us girls on the straight and narrow. Come on, let's go and enjoy the party."

"That's what he said I should do," smiled Cathy.

"So, what are we waiting for? Party time!" laughed Monica.

Outside, a mustard-coloured Mini Cooper S Countryman pulled up as Marcus and his home security team were chatting. A broad-shouldered, very fit-looking man in his fifties stepped out. His square-jawed face broke into a rare smile as Marcus strode forward to greet him.

"Carter, you son of a gun, bloody good to see you, mate. Where's Anna?"

"Probably in a gym somewhere or at a pistol range, she never stops," grinned Carter.

"What's this? We must be paying you too much," chortled Marcus, admiring his car.

"Yeah, I needed to step up a bit in the motor department. As you can see, it's a Mini Cooper S Countryman."

"What's it got under the bonnet?"

"Lots," smiled Carter. "Horsepower 301hp. And, can you believe it, 0 to 60 in 4.4 seconds. And the storage space at the back is great, you know, for those extra bits of kit that you need me to carry around when things get a bit hairy," smiled Carter proudly.

"Good choice, mate, and thanks for being up for this."

"I'm there for you – any time, boss, 24/7."

"We're having a bit of a do here right now, mate. Have a chat with the lads, and I'll introduce you to the subject shortly. By the way, she's a first-class pistol shot, which might come in handy down the line."

"So, I heard from Joe. Okay if I wander about a bit? I'd like to take a look at the kids," smiled Carter.

"Take your time – you know Henry, so let him know what you need in the food and drink department."

"Affirmative. Oh, by the way, I've got a little trinket from Anna, along with Penny, Emily, Freddy, and all the boys here and in Abu Dhabi."

Carter walked to his car and returned with a small mahogany box, surprising Marcus.

"Happy birthday, mate, from all of us," Carter said, displaying another rare grin.

"Come on, spill it, Carter, how'd you know?"

He laughed and handed him the case, saying, "After more than twenty years – what on earth are you talking about, boss?"

"Oh, my goodness, this is truly stunning. I don't know what to say," Marcus exclaimed joyfully as he opened the case, revealing a silver-plated, intricately engraved Walther PPK with antique pearl grips.

"It's a one-off commission – unique, mate. As I said, it's from all the boys and girls."

Both men embraced, symbolising a bond of mutual respect forged over twenty years or more, stretching back to Sandhurst and truly cemented during their missions together with the Regiment. Lifetime bonds that, perhaps, only comrades-in-arms can appreciate.

At that moment, Cathy stepped out of the house, and Marcus called out to her.

"Cathy, I want you to meet Captain Carter. I'll leave you both to talk," Marcus said, feeling pleased that everything was falling into place.

Carter moved forward to shake her hand. "Delighted to meet you, ma'am. I will explain how things will work. Unfortunately, Anna isn't here today, but it doesn't matter. The reality is that from this moment on, you will not see either of us unless necessary, but be assured we will always be nearby, 24/7 – 365, with you and your children."

"What should I call you?" Cathy asked with a gentle smile.

"Just call me Carter, ma'am. Look, I have a very important piece of jewellery for you and ask that you please wear it at all times until this is all over, but note it's not waterproof, so take care on that score."

Carter gave her an intricately designed Victorian-style gold spinning locket and chain.

"Wow, Carter, this is a really stunning piece. But why are you giving it to me?"

"It's actually a discreet panic button – all you need to do is hold the locket between your thumb and forefinger and press both sides firmly at the same time. It has a range of about 600 yards, and either Anna or I will never be further away from you than that."

"Gosh, I feel like Whitney Houston in The Bodyguard," Cathy laughed as she adjusted the pendant around her neck with Carter's help.

"Yeah, well, this is for real and I'm definitely not Kevin Costner," said Carter with another, rare and wry smile. "So, please give it a try now."

Cathy did and heard a series of blips from a device that looked like a pager on Carter's belt.

"But wouldn't it activate both yours and...erm...Anna's?"

"No, whichever one of us is monitoring you, then the other switches away from that secure frequency, but we keep our head comms open to avoid any missteps. We don't want to alarm your children by giving them a similar device, so whichever of us is guarding them will always have eyes on both George and Jenny."

"I understand. Thank you, Carter."

"No problem, ma'am."

• CHAPTER 18 •

Cathy returned to the party feeling completely reassured by the professionalism of everyone involved in safeguarding her and her family. She observed Monica as she embraced an elegant, lively-looking woman who rested one hand on a silver-topped ebony cane and skillfully balanced her glass of champagne in the other. Even from a distance, she could see the woman's generous smile and sparkling eyes that complemented the glittering diamond bracelet she wore.

"Who's that?" Cathy asked as Monica joined her.

"She's Marcus's great aunt, and she's a breath of fresh air – you wouldn't believe it, but she's in her early nineties. Come on, I'll introduce you," said Monica, taking Cathy by the arm.

"Agatha, I'd love you to meet Doctor Cathy Meer, a friend of Marcus," said Monica with a grin.

"My dear, it's a pleasure. I'm so glad to hear you are a friend of his. Now, there's a man, for sure, who needs a good woman as a friend, but I've not had the pleasure of seeing you before, my dear. Have you both only just met?" chuckled the old lady with a discernible twinkle in her eye.

"Erm... yes... he's helping me with something," said Cathy, feeling a little awkward with Agatha's directness.

"Put your faith in him, my dear. He's an exceptional man, and I've known him since he was knee-high to a grasshopper, and even back then, he was very special to me. I might add, nothing has changed in that department – so, if you get the chance, make sure you look after him!"

"Er... erm... of course," Cathy replied, feeling embarrassed and uncertain of what to say next. "Off you go, then, my dear. Enjoy the party," Agatha said with a mischievous smile, giving Monica a subtle nod before she moved away to mingle with other guests.

"My God, she's a tour de force," said Cathy, smiling at Monica.

Marcus observed the many guests arriving and noted the Chief Constable of Kent's arrival with his two young children. Bob Brimley's wife had died two years earlier in a fatal car crash and had taken an extended leave to recover from it.

"Bob, glad you could make it. Good to see you. It's been a while," said Marcus, shaking his hand warmly. "Off you go, kids. It's all happening in the garden," said Marcus, pointing to the other children playing around the extensive and impressive maze. The maze had been designed by his close friend, Adrian Fisher, internationally recognised as the world's leading maze designer, having created award-winning mazes in 36 countries across six continents.

Bob Brimley looked around the mélange of people, "Don't think I recognise anybody apart from Joe outside," said Bob Brimley.

"Well, never mind, enjoy yourself. If you need anything, just ask Henry," smiled Marcus. Cathy and Monica happily received a top-up from Henry as they gazed around the impressive drawing room.

"Come on, Cathy, let's go and do some more mingling. Bloody hell, take a look at the bloke in the corner – he seems to have his eye on you," said Monica with a wink.

"Christ, two attractive-looking men. Twice in one day, it's too much," laughed Cathy, relaxing into party mode now, determined to put her anxiety about the threat to her and her family on the back burner.

"Come on, it's time for you to leave the convent phase of the past few years and get out there, Cathy."

In the corner of the drawing room, a strikingly handsome man with a bronzed complexion stood, openly gazing at both of them through his blue-tinted glasses. He was dressed in an elegantly tailored, lightweight cream silk suit, paired with a dark blue open-necked shirt, and was sipping his champagne nonchalantly.

"Oh shit, he's coming over," said Cathy, unsure how she felt about his undeniable interest in her. "I mean, he looks like a tanned version of George bloody Clooney, for Christ's sake."

"Yeah, and it looks like he's only got eyes for you, Cathy – stand your ground, girl."

As he casually sauntered over, it was true that, with his salt-and-pepper hair, he resembled the famous American film star she admired. His body language conveyed effortless charm, radiating self-confidence in every gesture and movement.

"Good evening, ladies. Forgive me for intruding, but you look charmingly familiar to me. If you don't mind me asking – have we met before?" he said, looking directly at Cathy. He removed his tinted glasses and tucked them into the top pocket of his impeccably tailored suit. Cathy watched as his hazel eyes swept rapidly and unabashedly over her figure. She felt like a schoolgirl and hoped she wasn't blushing under his gaze. Instinctively, she moved her silk scarf to cover her breasts. Ignoring her outstretched hand, he placed his hand on her shoulder, holding it there a beat too long. She could feel the heat of his palm seeping through her silk shirt. She offered her politest, most professional smile and took a small step back.

"Ah, yes, wait a minute, now I remember you're... erm... Doctor Meer, am I right? Your face was all over the newspapers recently regarding that nasty barn murder case."

"That's right, I was the Home Office Forensic Pathologist on call that day, but as you will appreciate, I'm not at liberty to discuss any details of that case," said Cathy, trying her best to conceal her negative response to his overwhelming charm offensive.

"No, of course you can't, silly me. But I suppose I didn't really ask you anything except to confirm you are Dr Meer. That's the cost of fame, my dear, when your face appears in tabloids. And who might this be?" His smile was charismatic. Internally, he felt attracted to Cathy's slender figure, blonde hair, and green eyes. What did her eyes conceal or promise? He wondered.

"Ah, may I introduce Monica, one of my dearest old friends. I'm afraid I didn't catch your name," said Cathy, relieved to be free of his intense scrutiny at last.

"Surrounded by stunning women. I've never felt safer. It's Ben, Ben Malone."

"Looks as if you've been in warmer climes," said Cathy, hoping her question might discourage a further personal comment.

"Ah, yes. I've spent an enjoyable month or so with my brother. He owns a tea and sugar cane plantation in the Indian Ocean – the beautiful island of Mauritius."

"Oh yes, I know it. I was there about ten years ago or so. We stayed at the Le Saint Geran hotel – it was great," replied Cathy.

"We?"

"My husband, Peter."

"Is he here? I'd love to meet him."

"Sadly, he was killed in action some years ago."

"Military, then. I'm very sorry to hear that," he said smoothly, his gaze holding Cathy's, "Yes, Le Saint Geran was, I believe, opened in 1975 by...erm...a Mr Sol Kerzner, a South African entrepreneur. So, about seven years after the island gained independence from the British in 1968. A beautiful hotel and still highly rated among travel connoisseurs."

"And did you stay at your brother's estate?" asked Cathy, now fully in control of her earlier confused state of mind concerning how to handle this man's unwelcome attention.

"Er, no, I was fortunate enough to stay at his villa in St. Aubin-sur-Mer. It was truly magnificent and enjoyable – but nevertheless, it's good to be home again."

And with a slight bow, he simply melted away without another word.

"He's a bit over the top in the charisma department, don't you think?" said Cathy.

"I agree, but he did seem sincere and genuine – I liked him – it's not his fault that he's an excessively good-looking man," said Monica, laughing.

"Can't see another soul that I know here, do you?" said Monica, looking around. Also relieved a bit too at Mr Charm's departure.

Marcus interrupted their musings to introduce Bob Brimley.

"Cathy, Monica, may I introduce the Chief Constable of Kent, Bob Brimley," said Marcus.

"Pleasure to meet you, Chief Constable. And thank you for arranging protection for my family and me," said Cathy, feeling, for some inexplicable reason, uncomfortable. She'd always listened to her intuition, and there was something about his demeanour that she found disturbing.

"My pleasure, Doctor Meer, and in the matter of your and your family's security, you couldn't be in safer hands," said Brimley, placing his hand on Marcus's shoulder.

"By the way, very impressed by your results regarding your recent case involving the murder of...erm...Nick Parish," said the Chief Constable, his eyes boring into hers.

"Indeed – an unfortunate and unique case. I have to say the circumstances and method of dispatch were a first for me," said Cathy.

"Well, I'm sure we'll catch the perpetrator in the fullness of time," said Bob Brimley, "I've my best people on it," moving away.

Jeeves appeared, as usual, from nowhere.

"Ladies and gentlemen, please accept the menu offered at the table and enjoy."

Cathy and Monica approached to take a look, and their mouths dropped open as they scanned the fare on offer.

**

Soufflé Suissesse
Cheese Soufflé Cooked on Double Cream

◊

Gambas Rouge Grillée, Mouli, Shiso Vert et Algues Braisées
BBQ & Glazed Red Prawn, Dashi Broth, Mouli, Braised Kombu & Green Shiso

◊

Dorade Poêlée, Coulis de Tomate et Moutarde, Salade de Tomates
Seared Gilt Head Bream, Tomato & Dijon Mustard Sauce, Tomato & Onion Salad

◊

Agnolotti aux Petits Pois, Ragoût de Girolles et Madère
Fresh Pasta filled with Green Peas, Ragout of Girolles & Madeira

◊

Pigeon Rôti, Salade Sucrine Braisée et Farce à Gratin, Oignon Roscoff et Jus de Pigeon
Roast Squab Pigeon, Stuffed Gem Lettuce with Liver Farce, Roscoff Onion & Pigeon Jus

◊

Plateau de Fromages Affinés
Selection of French & British Farmhouse Cheeses

◊

'Cheesecake' et Sorbet aux Fraises, 'Pimms' et Menthe
Cheesecake, Strawberry Compote, Diplomat Cream and Strawberry Sorbet
◊
Café et Petits Fours

**

"My God, is this for real? I feel like I'm in the Le Gavroche restaurant on Upper Brook Street," laughed Monica.

"Looks like we're in for a real treat," guffawed Cathy as she perused the decadent over-the-top fare on offer and translated it for Monica.

Marcus walked over to both of them, "Don't worry about the menu; Henry likes to get a touch extravagant from time to time, and he's certainly excelled himself in that department today by inviting a friend into the inner sanctum of his kitchen. In fact, a rather famous London chef to boot."

"Not Le Gavroche, by any chance?" laughed Cathy.

"You got it in one. We're honoured. As you know, it's my birthday, and all this is Henry's generous gift to me, so I'm really to blame for all the excessiveness," he laughed. "But to be honest, I've never been very keen on celebrating birthdays, especially as the years go by – but Henry's always there regardless of how much I try to dissuade him from spoiling me," said Marcus with a look of genuine warmth.

"I was just chatting with one of your guests, Marcus. A bit of a charm merchant to say the least."

"Ah, you must mean Ben Malone."

"So, who's he then when he's at home?"

"Truthfully, I haven't the faintest idea. I met him at a Rough Shoot last weekend and discovered that he lives just down the lane at Frog Hall. I thought it was only neighbourly to invite him today. Actually, after the shoot, he came here for a while to try some skeet. I've got a pretty good setup. You may know that the sport was developed in 1915 by William Foster, an American. My friends use the facility here quite often, but I mainly use it to warm up before the pheasant season. But I must say I was impressed with his skill. He handled everything thrown at him with style. I don't recall seeing any clay survive, and what was even more impressive was that he wasn't using an open choke barrel. Nice gun, though, a Boss Over and Under, exquisitely engraved."

"Oh yes, I believe I'm correct in saying that they're London's oldest gunmaker and, if memory serves me right, a family-owned business established in...erm...1812?"

"Spot on, Cathy. You certainly know your guns."

"Well, my father inherited his Boss from his father, and now I'm the proud beneficiary. Oh dear, now I think about it, it's probably still lying in his Gun Room, neglected, which I should do something about."

"You should. Anyway, enough about our mysterious and aloof new friend and guns," said Marcus, keen to change the subject.

Cathy found herself sitting opposite Marcus, Monica, and his enchanting aunt Agatha. The latter, having just given her a wicked smile and wink, though she was unsure what that meant. Next to her was Ben on her left, and on her right was the mother of the children who had been playing with George and Jenny, all now sitting comfortably in peace, surprisingly, at their own little table nearby, bedecked with fish and chips, much to their apparent delight. Even Jenny seemed to be less volcanic as she dived into her chips.

"So, doctor, I gather from our earlier conversation that your time is spent talking to the dead, as it were?" said Ben, attempting to engage with this newfound femme fatale.

"On the contrary, they speak to me; that's the whole point," replied Cathy.

"Interesting. I imagine your work, then, to be much like that of a detective in that respect – I mean, in the sense of searching for answers regarding their demise," he said.

"You're right, that's exactly what I aim to achieve. To be honest, I enjoy the intellectual journey of seeking the truth – they can't speak for themselves, so I try to do just that, for them," said Cathy. "And may I ask what you do then?"

"Oh, nothing particularly interesting, I'm afraid, but I do enjoy collecting intriguing books and occasionally come across an odd first edition or two in my quest."

Cathy deliberately paused the conversation to engage with the woman on her right.

"Hi, my name's Cathy. Our children seemed to hit it off from the very beginning, like a house on fire today," she laughed, pleased, for some reason, to have had the chance to step away from talking to Ben for a little while.

"Sally. Yes, I'm so pleased about that too. I'm divorced, and my au pair's away for a few days, so I had no one to look after them. I was a bit concerned about bringing them, as they often seem reluctant to meet new friends; I'm not sure why, but I'm glad we came, and they are really enjoying it. I didn't want to refuse Marcus's kind invitation anyway; we've been friends for some years."

A tap on her arm made Cathy turn back to Ben. "I've just had a thought, Dr Meer. Do you speak French?"

"Yes, fluently, why?" she asked, curious about what was coming next.

"Well, you asked me earlier what I do. Allow me to elaborate. Among other things, I enjoy collecting books, as I mentioned, but I also sell them afterwards. Occasionally, I come across first editions of literary works, and it occurs to me that you might be interested in one I recently found that could be relevant to you in connection with your line of work, namely crime," said Ben.

"Really, what is it?" said Cathy, her interest piqued.

"Traité de Criminalistique' volume 7, by Dr Edmond Locard, who you may know was a French criminologist. Born, I believe, around 1877, he was a pioneer in forensic science who became known, I think, as the 'Sherlock Holmes of France'. It was he who formulated the fundamental principle of forensic science, namely, 'every contact leaves a trace.' Not that I'm particularly interested in that field, but it could nonetheless be a worthwhile investment for me, as a potential asset in future trading opportunities. I'm quite busy for the next week or two, but I'd be happy to lend it to you sometime."

"Thank you, Ben. That does sound like an enticing read. I must have overlooked that one during my studies. I'd love to read it, thank you."

"Delighted, when I get back, I'll contact you through Marcus," said Ben, smiling warmly. Once again, having finished his meal, he swept away without another word.

Dinner was over, and Cathy joined Monica for a smoke and a glass of wine as they watched the children playing in the grounds once again. Marcus joined them.

"Hi, he's a bit of a recluse, you know," said Marcus.

"Who?" asked Cathy.

"Ben. I noticed that he seemed besotted with you, Cathy."

"Well, he was interesting though a bit OTT in the charm department, I thought."

"Well, I don't really know him at all, as I mentioned before and to all accounts, he keeps to himself and stays away from social events, as I understand it. But enough of that, did you enjoy yourselves?"

"Absolutely," cried both women.

Henry appeared and refilled everyone's glass.

"To life," toasted Marcus once more. "The children seem more than happy; let's pop up to the upper terrace, have a goodnight puff, and enjoy our nightcap."

"Good idea."

"Can I try one of your French cigarettes, Cathy?"

Cathy shook one out for him.

"Oh gosh, they're strong," he spluttered as the women grinned at his sudden discomfort.

As they stepped onto the terrace, they saw Ben smoking alone. When he saw them, he turned and, to Cathy's dismay, appeared to be staring at her breasts. However, she didn't blame him for that; it was typical that some immature and arrogant men could not resist a covert glance, given the chance. She was unaware that the slight breeze on the terrace had drawn attention to her hardened nipples; she had always preferred going sans bra, as it simply felt more comfortable for her.

Ben rested his hand on Marcus's shoulder and graciously thanked him for his hospitality, smiling warmly at Cathy and Monica as he left. Moments later, the roar of a powerful engine interrupted their conversation, causing them to glance down to the carriage driveway.

"What the hell's that?" exclaimed Cathy as the tyres of a powerful, space-age-looking sports car bit into the surface of the drive, sending a spray of white chips everywhere.

"Bloody hell, that's a Bugatti Chiron, excuse my French," remarked Marcus with his eyes fixed on the magnificent car.

"So, what's that then when it's at home? It does look pretty spectacular," said Cathy, fascinated.

"The Chiron is one of the fastest, most powerful, and exclusive production supercars in Bugatti's history. 1,500 horsepower is ready to unleash under that bonnet, with acceleration capabilities worthy of a bullet train," Marcus explained enthusiastically.

"So, a tad expensive, I guess?" smiled Monica.

"Well, put it this way, you wouldn't get much change back from around 3 million dollars! I suppose our reclusive neighbour has a bob or two in his pocket. A little step up from the battered old Land Rover he turned up in for the shoot the other day."

"If he lives just down the road, I guess he'll be home and out of his silk charm suit before I can even take another drag on my smoke," laughed Cathy.

"Interesting, I must say, and quite intriguing. That's an awful lot of motor car by anyone's standards. I think I'm starting to feel a twinge of curiosity stirring in my bones. I'll ask my people to give him a discreet once-over... I really shouldn't, but I can't resist having a little poke around," said Marcus with a discernible twinkle in his eye.

"Actually, he wants to lend me a book," said Cathy, shrugging her shoulders.

"What's that then, the Kama Sutra? That's a bit of Indian Sanskrit to get the blood flowing."

"Very funny. It's a French book about forensic science."

"Surprise, surprise. As I mentioned earlier, he did seem quite taken with you."

"Jealous?"

"Should I be?" grinned Marcus.

"He's charming and interesting, but definitely *not* my type."

"Really, why?"

"As I said, a tad over the top in the charm department and call it feminine intuition, if you like, but I found him just a touch creepy."

"So, who else interested you?"

"Your aunt Agatha. What a genuinely great lady. I felt an instant empathy," laughed Cathy.

"She's very special to me, but beware has always been a passionate matchmaker – she never stopped talking about you throughout dinner – asking questions I couldn't answer," said Marcus, mischievously. "Look, changing the subject, I've got an idea. When and if Ben invites you over to pick up this treasure trove of forensic science, why don't we all go together? It might be interesting to take a look around Frog Hall. What do you think?"

"So, you can protect me?" grinned Cathy.

"That as well," Marcus laughed. "But don't forget that Carter will be lurking in the grounds to cover our six," smiled Marcus. "Anyway, I'm so glad that the party worked out in helping you to relax a bit, considering the news I had to impart."

"Our six? What's that mean? And who's Carter?" Asked Monica.

"Means he will watch our backs – keep us safe," grinned Marcus.

"And Carter's actually my Kevin Costner," said Cathy, winking at Marcus.

Monica tilted her shoulders in a noncomprehending shrug.

"Anyway, I want to say, Cathy, that it was lovely to meet you and the children, and I am really looking forward to seeing you again soon. Can we aim, if you'll forgive the pun, for a Wednesday evening for our shoot? But I'll need to brush up on my skills in the meantime," he chuckled.

"I'll let you know, Marcus, but I'm up for a shoot."

Marcus gave her a goodbye peck on her cheek. As he did, she felt herself blush and hoped he hadn't noticed, feeling embarrassed by the electric tingle that ran through her body once again – she wasn't sure what was happening to her.

• CHAPTER 19 •

Captain de Vere's secure line buzzed, and he examined the displayed ID.

"Gibbs, what's up?"

"Just followed Badawi down to Kent. He's entering Chiddington Hall as we speak," replied Gibbs.

"Interesting. Sir James Chiddington's estate. So, a new player in the game then?"

"Looks like it. I looked through my binoculars, and from Sir James's warm reception of Badawi, it seems they are joined at the hip. I'll keep in touch."

"Okay, well done and thanks for the update. Don't know what that all means for now, but good to know," Marcus said thoughtfully as he hung up.

Asif Badawi found the large gates of Chiddington Hall invitingly open as he powered up the winding carriage drive in his Porsche 911, enjoying the sound of his tyres crunching through the deep, white chipped gravel as he approached the manor house. Sir James had told him that the property had been in the family for more than 300 years.

Sir James was waiting to greet him beneath the grand oak porch of the house, supported by enormous trunks hewn from the same tree. Asif had been told that history on his first visit here all those years ago.

They embraced warmly. It never ceased to amuse Asif that the landed gentry always seemed able to carry off their titles and status, still wearing, as he was now, just an old tweed jacket with tattered elbows patched with leather and a pair of scruffy-looking jeans, but rescued by a regimental scarf he instantly recognised as a rather worn Household Division Guards' silk scarf – at least that made up for his otherwise scruffy, relaxed appearance.

"Good to see you, Asif. You're looking fit and well, and your motor, by the way, seems to have done a good job in ploughing up my drive for reasons I'm unsure of, as I've actually no wish to plant anything there," exclaimed Sir James good-humouredly.

"Ah, sorry about that – I got a little bit carried away," laughed Asif.

"Come in, let's go to my study and see what refreshments we can offer you as a reward for your efforts in trying to destroy my drive, old boy. Actually, I was thinking about you the other day, just before you rang, recalling that week I spent on your boat in Abu Dhabi. I enjoyed it immensely and the rather attractive company you provided for my entertainment. So very delightfully young and so very willing," said Sir James with a lascivious smile.

"The fact is, Sir James, that it's not my boat at all; if you recall, I did mention that to you at the time, that it belongs to my father," Asif said brusquely. "But I'm pleased that you enjoyed your stay. We'll do it again sometime, anything to get away from your bloody winter, eh?"

"Yes, I meant to ask you about that. I never got around to meeting your father."

"Well, we live...erm...separate and different lives. I don't see him much unless it's a family matter, and that doesn't come up very often, seeing as I'm the only family he has apart from his harem, which seems to be supplied with a never-ending stream of willing young women to satisfy his insatiable appetite. So, what's new?" said Asif, wishing to change the subject.

They walked through the grand hall with its chessboard flooring to Sir James's study.

"So, take a look around. Is there anything that strikes you as different since your last visit?"

Asif scanned the impressive oak-panelled room.

"Actually, I can't see...erm...wait a moment. That framed T-shirt definitely rings a happy bell, and you've signed it – I notice! Or rather, not you but the man himself, *Mick*?"

"Just a little forgery on my part, I must, regrettably, admit. But I think it simply adds a touch of...erm...panache, don't you agree?"

"A nice touch."

"Couldn't resist it, such great lyrics after all, and how appropriate for the day if you recall?"

"Indeed, but sadly, we didn't get to know her a little better before the hunt, eh?" sighed Asif.

"Agreed, it's entirely my fault as host and Master of the Hunt that we did not enjoy the usual preliminaries before the hunt itself. We'll make up for the loss next time, my boy. Be assured of that," grinned Sir James.

An almost indistinguishable tap on the door manifested itself in the form of Charles, Sir James's butler.

"Good afternoon, may we offer you something after your arduous journey, sir?" said Charles, addressing his question to Asif.

"It's a warm summer's day, Asif. May I suggest a bottle of Perrier-Jouet Blason Rosé?" smiled Sir James.

"Actually, I haven't had the pleasure."

"Forgive me, Sir James—may I introduce its attributes to your guest?"

"Certainly, go ahead."

"A marriage, sir, of the floral freshness of Chardonnay with the fruitiness of Pinot Noir, combining the essence of strawberries, raspberries, and blackberries with a hint of exotic pomegranate," said Charles with a satisfied flourish.

"How could I possibly resist after that introduction. Sounds irresistible," said Asif, winking at his host.

"Bring it out to the garden terrace, please, Charles."

They relaxed on the terrace, overlooking the landscaped gardens extending to the tree line. Asif raised his glass of rosé to catch the sunlight.

"Beautiful colour," he remarked.

"Indeed. It's new to my cellar – that's the way we like things, isn't it?"

"Definitely," said Asif, smiling in agreement.

They drank a toast to each other's health.

Asif noticed two wooden posts standing about 20 metres into the gardens...

"A new addition, I see, to the splendour of your lawn – some examples of minimalist sculpture. Tate Gallery, perhaps?"

"Don't be silly – target practice, my dear chap," smiled Sir James and called out for his butler, who arrived promptly.

"Pop down to the Gun Room, Charles, and bring up a couple of crossbows—there's a good fellow," instructed Sir James.

Charles placed the dangerous-looking weapons on a nearby wrought iron table along with a handful of arrows and disappeared rapidly, having never really come to terms with them. Yes, game shooting had been part of his life growing up. But he just didn't feel comfortable, for some reason, in handling these dreadful-looking weapons.

"So, Asif, let's see if your eye is in form today, the targets are exactly six inches wide," he grinned.

Asif loaded his bow and took careful aim at the post on his left. The arrow flew true and embedded itself in the Beechwood post, just slightly off-centre.

"Not bad, but of course, a moving target would have been preferable to test your skills."

Sir James went next and achieved a similar result. They played for a while before becoming bored with the simplicity and the lack of moving prey, then returned to enjoy some wine and a cigarette.

"Talking of moving targets, is the Summer Hunt on this year or has it been cancelled?" said Asif, cautiously.

"Postponed for now, I'm afraid. You see, since the recent high-profile murder hereabouts, the Fuzz have been swarming all over the countryside like bees to honey."

"Fuzz? I seemed to have missed that word somewhere in my rather expensive education!" laughed Asif.

"Ah, the Fuzz refers in the vernacular to describe our boys and girls in blue, but in this case, the boys and girls involved are mostly in suits, i.e., detectives," smiled Sir James. "It's such a high-profile case in the area, so I thought it prudent to pause our...erm...games for a while. What do you think?"

"Seems a sensible move, Sir James."

"Connected to that, I've always meant to ask you about the mine shaft on your estate, where our prey find their final resting place. I mean, it's well concealed, but how deep is it?"

"Deep enough, don't you remember? I mean, you helped us put the last guest of The Hunt there," laughed Sir James.

"That's true... erm... if you'll forgive me, I have an interest in the... erm... local case you just mentioned. I saw a picture in the National Press depicting the pathologist... erm... a Dr Meer, I understand," said Asif, choosing his words carefully.

"Yes, that's right. In what context are you interested?"

"It's a personal matter; do you know her?"

"No, but you'll meet her quite soon. As the new local celebrity, she's one of the guests I've invited to a drinks gathering I host around this time every year. You know, for the mayor, local business bigwigs, and a few other celebrities who live nearby. It's very informal but usually interesting. It's in two weeks' time. How does that suit? Are you free?" said Sir James.

"Perfect," said Asif rather brusquely. "I take it that the occasion will require formal dress, and how many usually attend?"

"Actually, no, it's all quite a casual affair. I don't think your Light Dragoons full dress uniform would fit in, and it might be a bit too conspicuous for the occasion. It's rarely a big event, perhaps thirty or so, give or take, but it keeps the locals happy and gives me and them the chance to...erm...reach out if anyone feels inclined," smiled Sir James.

"I understand. I'll dress to fit in then with the crowd," said Asif, returning a smile.

Their conversation was interrupted by the roar of a powerful motorbike approaching. A moment later, Charles stepped out of the house...

"I'm sorry to disturb Sir James, but a gentleman has arrived seeking the attention of your guest; he says it's rather urgent," he said graciously.

"Bring him around to the side of the house, Charles," said Sir James, gesturing towards Asif with his arms in a look of confusion.

A figure in a snug blue leather biker outfit appeared, removing his helmet as he drew near.

"Syed. What are you doing here?" Asif asked, clearly upset by the sudden interruption.

"I'm very sorry, sir, but I needed to speak with you in private." Asif shrugged an apology to Sir James and walked further into the grounds, lighting a cigarette.

"Okay, what is it, Syed? You have my attention, and it'd better be good."

"It's Abdalla al-Battal, sir."

"And?"

"Well, sir, I've heard he will be visiting your father in the coming week."

"So what? That's my father's business," retorted Asif impatiently.

"I'm sorry, sir. I thought you might like to know."

"Well, I don't. You could just have picked up the phone to tell me that, get back to London!"

What atrocities Abdallah al-Battal and his father might be planning didn't concern him; he didn't care about their schemes. Asif set it aside for now and allowed himself to relax. He'd been thrilled with the drinks party invitation and the bonus of meeting the SAS bitch; he couldn't wait.

"It seems I'm needed in London, Sir James. Thank you so much for your hospitality, and I look forward to seeing you again in two weeks."

Sir James saw him to his car and noticed that Asif's departure was much more relaxed than his arrival. Asif returned his wave.

• CHAPTER 20 •

Cathy had to admit she was genuinely looking forward to seeing Marcus again, although her feelings were somewhat confusing. The chance to compete in shooting again was too tempting to resist, and she wondered how much her skills might have declined after nearly two years away. But, knowing how competitive men can be, even with friends, she was pretty sure she would face a challenge and definitely did not want to be found lacking.

Monica had kindly offered to look after the children and walked with her to the heavy, ancient oak entrance door of her home.

"Best of luck, Cathy."

"For what exactly?" smiled Cathy.

"With the shooting, of course, what else?" said Monica with a twinkle in her eye.

"Yeah, I believe you," Cathy said with a brief laugh.

"I have to say, I noticed that you and Marcus seemed to...erm...get along well. The two of you were interacting quite positively," laughed Monica.

"Take it easy and give me a break. Everything has its time and place, doesn't it?"

"Right. But remember to keep your legs crossed," Monica laughed as she hugged Cathy.

"You're incorrigible, Monica," said Cathy as Monica waved goodbye.

Cathy realised she was driving faster than usual. She wasn't entirely sure why, but she needed to calm her racing heart, filled with anticipation at the thought of seeing Marcus again. She wondered if the Twins were nearby but soon convinced herself they must be. I mean, that was the deal, right – and she trusted Marcus completely on that matter. Eventually, she noticed in her rear-view mirror a mustard-coloured Mini Cooper falling significantly behind – probably Carter.

The gates of Little Manor swung open as she approached, and she was once again greeted by Mr Glock 19, who guided her towards the house.

"Welcome, Doctor Meer. By the way, I heard you were coming to the range this evening, so I rang an old chum of mine who shoots at your club. And, boy, oh boy, he said you were one hell of a shot, and just between you and me, ma'am, when Captain de Vere heard that, well, he's been busy on the range for the last hour or so," laughed Joe with a wink.

Cathy smiled and said, "I'm looking forward to some practice too, Joe."

"Not sure about practice doctor; I think the boss is heading into serious competitive mode, if you ask me," laughed Joe. "I'll probably join you guys later."

"Thanks, consider me warned. So, what exactly do you do for him then?"

"I look after him," said Joe, tapping his Glock.

"Does he need looking after?"

"We all do, ma'am," Joe said with a twinkle in his eye.

As always, Henry materialised out of nowhere.

"Good evening, Dr Meer. Captain de Vere is waiting for you on the range. I'll escort you down, if I may," Henry said politely.

Cathy was guided down a magnificent, wide wrought iron spiral staircase to a steel door with a security entry pad. Henry obliged by entering the required code, and the door swung open to reveal a state-of-the-art 30 metre pistol range with four firing lanes. Marcus turned from his firing position, removed the magazine from his pistol, quickly opened the slide lock to render the pistol safe, then laid it down carefully.

"Cathy, it's great to see you. Hope you've not had any bodies to deal with so far this week?" he laughed.

"All's good so far, but the night is still young."

He led her to a table beneath an impressive display of various weapons on a gun rack.

"So, as you can see, I've got your preferred armaments. A 15-round capacity SIG Sauer P226 and a Glock 19, both 9mm."

Cathy picked up the SIG, and it felt good in her hands after not handling one for a while.

“This’s a great set-up you’ve got down here,” said Cathy enthusiastically.

“Yeah, it’s pretty awesome, isn’t it? I upgraded it all a couple of years ago. It has a bespoke airflow system that maintains a steady supply of fresh, clean air into the range while simultaneously drawing air downrange, ensuring that all debris particles and powder smoke are pulled away from the shooter the very instant the trigger is pulled. It keeps the firing point supplied with fresh air while effectively drawing and extracting harmful by-products. And, as you can see, we’ve got the latest man-size snap targets set up,” said Marcus with a hint of pride in his voice.

Cathy glanced at the armoury safe with an appreciative look. “You’re pretty well stocked!”

“You should check out our armoury in Abu Dhabi,” chuckled Marcus. "Alright, Cathy, I’ve initially set the engagement distance to 5 metres, then we’ll increase it to 10 and then 15. Does that work for you?"

“Sure, bring it on.”

“Okay, let’s see what you’ve got,” smiled Marcus.

Cathy picked up the SIG and took her time pressing the web of her right hand hard into the top of the comfortable grip between her thumb and index finger. As a right-handed person, she wrapped her left hand around it, keeping her right thumb out of the way. She exhaled slowly and released twelve rapid shots.

Marcus fiddled with the range computer and pressed the target recall button.

"Wow, for a civilian, that's impressive shooting, Cathy. Nice tight six-shot group in the heart kill zone. Just two head shots clipping, but again a nice tight group of four in the head kill zone. Like riding a bicycle, eh?"

"Let's go again, Marcus," Cathy said, smiling as she firmly inserted another 15-round magazine. The SIG was a great pistol, but she was slightly off, so she cleared her mind for the next 12 shots.

Marcus set up another clean target for her in the neighbouring lane, similar to the previous one, but waited for her to finish first. As she prepared to shoot, he picked up and loaded his Glock 19 for a change. Like Cathy, his weapon of choice was the SIG P226, but he preferred the SIG .357 round when in a close combat scenario. Cathy's target returned with no mistakes, six rounds in a tight group within both kill zones.

"Bloody hell, you're a dangerous lady," exclaimed Marcus, impressed. He then aimed his pistol in response and fired nine tight rounds into each kill zone.

"Hey, that's impressive, Marcus, but I counted 16 shots?"

"Yeah, I had one in the spout and reloaded the mag. A little surprise, historically, that I worked out for any bad guy counting."

"So, a combat thing, right?"

"Yeah, I suppose so. Always handy to keep a card up the sleeve," grinned Marcus.

"That's a new twist for me," laughed Cathy, starting to enjoy the challenge after a long break from competitive shooting.

“Okay, real competition time now, if you’re up for it, Marcus,” laughed Cathy, hoping to pile the pressure on.

“Why not? I’ll buzz Joe to come down and join us. I’d like him to enjoy the pressure too,” said Marcus, turning to the intercom nearby.

Joe appeared, unholstered, and cleared his Glock 19, placing it facing downrange in the next lane.

"Alright, boys and girls, we’ll raise the stakes, okay?” said Marcus.

“Affirmative,” exclaimed Joe with a wry grin.

“Right, four consecutive targets, eight rounds, two on each of the snap targets, but the programme provides completely random timing, so be aware, Cathy. And they really do snap fast,” said Marcus as he punched in the target commands into the range computer. “And to make it a tad more interesting, we’ll go for the Mossad discipline, i.e., a double tap to each kill zone on each target, so that’s eight rounds for each player, not so easy with snap targets,” said Marcus. His respect for the HaMossad leModiʿin uleTafkidim Meyuḥadim, the national intelligence agency of Israel, was high up there on his list, and he’d trained with them while with the Regiment some years before on an exchange programme.

“So, it’s two Glock 19s against my SIG Sauer, then, no problem,” snorted Cathy, with a dry smile.

Joe asked, “What’s your take on both weapons, ma’am? I’d be interested to hear, since you are a civilian after all – albeit with your undisputed skills.”

“Well, an interesting question and, as a civilian, I would favour the SIG P226,” said Cathy with a smile. “I like the comfort of the hold, and after the first shot, it settles to about a three-pound pull, which suits me. As we all know, it was the pistol that the US Navy SEALs adopted as their primary sidearm, along with the Glock these days. I like the Glock 19; it has a really nice grip texture, but I find the trigger a bit too... erm... crunchy, gritty, and long, and the trigger pull is a little heavy for me at around eight pounds,” she added smoothly.

“Well said,” said Joe with an appreciative look.

They took their positions – targets now at 10 metres. The snap targets were indeed very rapid. Cathy felt a sense of déjà vu once more. She was being outshot by the two ex-SAS marksmen. Just two of her rounds missed, though they grazed the kill zone, which in a standard competition would have been considered a kill, but not with these guys; their skill level was simply on a different level entirely.

"Doctor, I have to say that was phenomenal shooting. I average about fifty rounds a day to stay sharp. You’re quite a dangerous lady,” Joe said, nodding respectfully as he waved goodbye to both.

“Can I smoke down here, Marcus?”

“With the air conditioning system, we could probably start a Bar-B-Q without any problems,” he laughed, lighting one of his own.

“Actually, I have a new toy if you're interested in taking on a new challenge with a few more rounds.”

“Sure, bring it on.”

Marcus tinkered with the range computer.

"Okay, so with this setup, the target isn't just a snap type; it also moves at running speed in random directions," said Marcus mischievously. 'It's designed for single shooters and includes a surprise. Are you ready? No pressure," Marcus grinned.

"Always up and ready for anything," said Cathy, with a grin.

"That's good to know," laughed Marcus.

Marcus pressed the Range Command, which not only caused their individual targets to dance in all directions but also created a distraction with flashing lights and the deafening sound effects of gunfire.

Cathy, with a fully loaded magazine, scored 13 out of 15 hits in the kill zone, all in tight groups. Marcus followed with a flawless 100% kill rate.

"Marcus, that was really impressive," Cathy said, clearly admiring him.

"No, Cathy, you're truly something. I definitely wouldn't want to be on the wrong side of you," Marcus laughed.

"I'll share a little secret. As far as I'm concerned, you'll never be on the wrong side of me. In fact, quite the opposite," Cathy said with a grin, unintentionally blushing at the same time.

"Let's have a drink on the terrace," he said, taking her hand in his.

She didn't notice Marcus slipping the SIG P226 and several magazines into his jacket pocket. With perfect timing, Henry appeared on the terrace with a bottle of white Burgundy, pouring the wine into elegant Waterford crystal glasses and carefully placing the bottle in an ice bucket on an ornate wrought-iron stand beside their table.

"Do you have time to have lunch, Cathy?"

"Yes. Monica is picking up the children from school, and I just need to return in time to give them their dinner."

"That's excellent. Henry, could you please put something together for us?"

"Certainly, Captain. Shall we say an hour?"

"Perfect, thank you, Henry."

They sat in the pleasantly warm sunshine, toasted each other, and enjoyed a smoke. Both welcomed the relaxation after the intense competition, which they both knew was precisely that.

Marcus instinctively reached into his pocket and took out the SIG, following safety protocols by dropping the magazine and clearing the slide. He then placed it on the wrought iron table along with three full 9mm magazines, sliding them across to Cathy, much to her surprise.

"Look, Cathy, I've made a decision. I'd like you to be armed."

"But that's illegal without a permit to carry, isn't it?"

"Absolutely right, but let's just ignore that minor detail for now," Marcus said with a smile. "The likelihood of needing to use it is very low thanks to the security measures I've put in place for you and the children. But if the situation becomes serious, try to avoid killing anyone. That could complicate the cleanup, especially since we're on British soil. And, if things do go tits-up, which I doubt will happen, Major Carr will handle it all," Marcus added with a smile.

"Okay," said Cathy, loading a mag and placing the weapon and the two spare magazines in her bag.

"I mean, after our shoot, I have unwavering confidence in your prowess and your innate safety protocols regarding the use of such weapons," said Marcus.

"To be honest, Marcus. I'm more than happy to accept it. Thanks," she added with a grateful smile.

Marcus's mobile buzzed with the tone indicating the incoming call was marked as a secure line.

"Freddy, good to hear from you. Were your ears burning? I was just mentioning your name. I'm sitting on the terrace at Little Manor with Doctor Cathy Meer. We've just been on the range, and who, by the way, is one of the very best civilian shots I've ever seen. I'm going to put us on speaker. I mean, Cathy's up there with everything. Okay?"

"No problem. Glad to hear that, Cathy's prepared for any eventuality in the future, Marcus. But for now, I'm calling to confirm that the hit on Abdalla al-Battal is proceeding. His meeting with Abdulaziz Badawi is scheduled for six days from now. So, it's best that you get to Abu Dhabi as soon as possible and coordinate with your team."

"Affirmative, Freddy. I'll be there in the morning."

"I suppose the Twins are properly in position, then?" asked Major Freddy Carr.

"Yeah, no problems there. I've got one of my surveillance specialists, Gibbs, monitoring Asif Badawi. So, Cathy and the children have 24/7 cover, and she's armed. Any problem with that for you?"

"From what you just told me, I'm all good on that score. See you. But just remind her to try not to kill anyone – unless necessary," said Major Carr with a chuckle.

"I hear you," said Cathy.

"Okay, Freddy, I'll contact my team as soon as possible. I'll be in touch," Marcus said before hanging up.

"Will Abu Dhabi be dangerous?" asked Cathy anxiously.

"Walk in the park, Cathy, don't worry. I've got a highly trained and experienced team at the top of their game to look after me. So, as I said, no need for concern. But I'm sorry, we'll have to postpone lunch today. I'll be back in a few days, and then we can relax. One of the important elements of this trip, as Asif Badawi is here, is to conduct a forensic search of his house in Abu Dhabi to determine whether there's anything there that reflects on his planned actions here. I mean, anything we can find in his house, particularly in his safe, may well help us to identify his plans concerning you and your family and indeed what else he might be up to."

They stood, and Marcus moved to kiss her on the cheek, but Cathy quickly adjusted and pressed her lips fully to his. They embraced, and she made her way to her car, trembling with electricity but feeling safe as she touched the beautiful pendant around her neck and the reassuring weight of the SIG in her bag. Leaving Marcus wondering about what had just happened.

Recovering, Marcus buzzed Emily – all business now.

"Emily, could you please organise our team to prepare the company jet for Abu Dhabi – wheels up at 18:00 tonight."

"On it. Shall I pack for you?"

"Thanks, Emily. No need, I'm a big boy now. I'll manage it somehow," laughed Marcus.

• CHAPTER 21 •

Marcus's private jet arrived earlier than planned at Al Minhad Air Base because of strong tailwinds. The facility was shared with the UAE and the RAF. His Challenger 350, lacking any company logo, an intentional choice he made years ago to stay under the radar, was suitable for discreet arrivals worldwide. Although not flashy, it was well-suited to his frequent Middle Eastern visits and other travel. The jet could reach speeds up to 541 mph, fly at 43,000 feet, and cover 3,200 nautical miles. Its luxurious interior was designed to satisfy wealthy Arab clients needing a discreet and comfortable ride. What he particularly appreciated was the low cabin noise, thanks to its sound-absorbing system. As arranged, his friend, Group Captain Jamie Mallory of No. 2 Squadron RAF, was there to meet him.

Jamie's squadron was among the top units—an elite parachute-trained team skilled at deploying to seize airfields and control refuelling stations nearly anywhere globally. Marcus had previously collaborated with him during a hijacking incident in Ghana and was impressed by their role within the Special Forces Support Group (SFSG).

"Marcus, bloody good to see you, mate. Glad to note you're still standing and looking fit and well. Is this a business trip, or are you up to some cloak-and-dagger stuff again – if you get my drift?" said Jamie.

"Do please remind me, Jamie, what's your security clearance level again? After all this time, I'm not sure you have enough of that level to even talk to me these days," chuckled Marcus.

"After more than twenty years of putting up with all your bullshit and knowing you far too well, you should really piss off, dear boy," he grinned.

"Well, to be honest, it's a bit of both, but mum's the word. So, are you going to give me a lift into town or what?" said Marcus, happy to meet his old chum once again. It had been a while.

"Got the old jeep ready and raring to go, mate."

Marcus reflected on how much he enjoyed these trips to town with Jamie. The journey lasted just over an hour but was mainly spent exchanging local knowledge and gossip, and Jamie's understanding of the region was encyclopaedic, a source of information he highly respected.

"So, what are you up to these days? I thought you were going out to pasture for Christ's sake, and yet here you are."

"I'm currently 'flying a desk', and yes, I actually have two more months. We're selling our apartment in Abu Dhabi and moving back to the UK by the end of the year."

"Who's been running the stud farm?"

"Harry, my brother and his wife. Lucy and I can't wait to get back; she wants to start a pony sanctuary there. I'll be happy to leave the game behind. I'm getting a bit too old for this stuff. Married yet, Marcus? Although I think I'd have heard about the impossibility of that by now, if you had," laughed Jamie.

"No, but lately someone quite remarkable has entered my life."

"Bout time if you ask me," chuckled Jamie.

"She's got two kids, and I understand they love riding, so maybe we'll come knocking on your door one of these days."

"You're welcome any time. I mean, my humble dwelling isn't far down the road from your extravagant mansion," grinned Jamie.

"By the way, I have a serious question for you: what do you know about a bugger named Abdalla al-Battal?"

"Ah, the quintessential face of evil. I've received quite a lot of feedback on this piece of low life over the years, Marcus. His filthy fingerprints are on the slaughter of thousands of innocent men, women, and children across the globe. Never-ending atrocities. If your visit concerns him, then I've heard rumours that he might be arriving any day now."

"Right. Okay, Jamie. I'll give you a ring when I'm finished, and maybe we could meet up for a drink or two? And I'll fill you in."

"Affirmative. I'll hold you to that – see you and good luck with whatever it is you're up to this time," grinned Jamie as he pulled up outside de Vere's security offices.

Sitting comfortably on the terrace of his office, leaning back on his favourite rattan chair, he picked up his pair of Zeus 20x40 binoculars. He swept the Marina below, with its eclectic mix of super yachts, down to the colourful traditional Arabic Dhow. He couldn't find what he was looking for, and then he finally located the super yacht 'al-Malik' anchored in the Persian Gulf just outside the marina. It was an imposing and elegant piece of kit, long and sleek in its configuration, looking like it had been designed in a wind tunnel, which perhaps it had, owned by Abdulaziz Badawi, an extraordinarily wealthy and powerful Arab and a known terrorist sympathiser and financier, albeit that the British or American security services had yet to link him directly to anything to take him down.

A flash of light off metal caught his attention, and he focused his binoculars on what he was pretty sure was a chrome-plated AK-47 being carried into a forward deck cabin. So, it looked like they're all geared up for something, he thought.

True, the boat was listed as being on charter, but since Badawi owned the charter company, that was academic. Marcus examined the specifications of the boat Penny had provided. It was a 34.4-metre yacht built by Salvagni Architetti from Rome, with polished ebony throughout and matte whitened oak with natural bamboo flooring. The living space and the independent dining area featured a table by Saarinen and chairs by Mies van der Rohe, which clearly indicated real money, and the kitchen, not described as a galley but by Boffi, whoever they were, was probably not cheap either.

Powered by a water jet propulsion system and six gas turbine engines, which allowed a top speed of 60 knots—relatively damn quick, thought Marcus. The captain's cabin and two crew cabins are located in the bow. A crew of five, including the captain, makes it quite a notable vessel to be floating around in. He noted that the lower deck was exclusively the domain of Abdulaziz Badawi; along with his luxury suite, there were two more VIP suites, all with en-suite bathrooms.

He reflected a little more on the spec and realised that, yes, this was a super yacht by most people's standards, but Badawi could certainly afford more. No, this was more about the yacht's speed. Ultimately, there were just three cabins for guests, including Badawi, though all were luxurious. This was a boat designed to get the bad guys somewhere quickly, while still appearing like a charter vessel. He glanced at his Rolex Submariner watch and noticed he had half an hour before his blokes arrived; undoubtedly, Penny would be floating back to remind him of this at any moment. He liked the watch because it was not ostentatious, unlike many others from the same brand. His father had given it to him on his 30th birthday, almost that long ago now, explaining at the time that it was just in case he ever unexpectedly fell into some water, he'd be up to speed with the time of day. Marcus had found his father's sense of humour amusing, especially since the watch was rated for 200 metres underwater, and what particularly amused Marcus was that, at the time, he was undergoing additional training with the Special Boat Service without his father knowing.

His father had been an exceptional man and a powerful force in his life. An unquestionable inspiration as he grew up. He loved and respected him dearly. It was true that he had been a hard act to follow, a man who received the rare honour of the Victoria Cross (VC), the highest and most prestigious military award. Yet, always so humble, he instilled in his son the need to follow his own path and trust his instincts, not allowing anyone to sway him from his chosen course. Advice, Marcus had never wavered from the very start. And yes, here comes Penny, breaking the spell of memories Marcus was enjoying.

"Marcus, I've placed copies of the mission brief, the boat's detailed drawings, and the target's profile on the boardroom table for your meeting at 10.00. Coffee's brewing and should be ready by then. By the way, I also passed the materials to them last night so they'd all have a heads-up," she said.

"Well done, and I'm sure the coffee will surpass all expectations, thanks, Penny," Marcus acknowledged, giving her a satisfied wink.

He started reflecting on the four of his former SBS personnel he was due to meet. Buster and Georgie, he'd known on and off for years, having been on many joint SAS/SBS missions in the past. Like all his men, he did not doubt that his back was always going to be covered, wherever they were. Harry had joined the company at the outset along with his mate Tits. A nickname that the latter had been given by his mates during his time with the Paras. Tits's parents, inexplicably, had given the poor bloke the first name Vivian, which had been a bit of a burden for him as he grew up. He considered, quite reasonably, that it was more of a girl's name – but he had taken on the tag graciously ever since, and so there it was.

Marcus sat at the boardroom table, taking in the elegantly dressed team before him in their lightweight, tailored linen suits. In fact, they were so well-tailored that he began to wonder if he was paying them too much, to his amusement. Penny sat in, as always, ready to take notes and respond to any requests that arose.

With their body shapes and mannerisms, any of them could easily be mistaken for high-end security personnel outside any prestigious nightclub in the world. He enjoyed their company and relished the calmness, self-confidence, and professionalism they always exuded, filling any room with it. He recognised that quality, as did his clients.

He contemplated their eagerness to hear what mission he was about to give them a heads-up on, albeit that with Penny's foresight, they'd already had notice of it and time to contemplate. The loyalty and skill set of these and his other personnel had made his international security company one of the most prized and sought-after in the security business worldwide.

"Good morning, gentlemen. Firstly, I'd like to thank you guys for my surprise birthday gift. It really hit the spot," said Marcus with a wry smile.

"Well, boss, we were in a bit of a quandary as to what to get for a chap who has everything," laughed Buster.

"Carter sent us a picture of what he'd chosen for you on behalf of all the boys and girls in the company. A truly iconic piece of kit – I mean, a Walther PPK – just such a brilliant idea. How fitting to give you that James Bond moment, every time you pick it up," added Georgie. This caused a ripple of laughter around the table.

"Okay, let's get down to business. Thanks to...erm...Moneypenny, you've all had time to read through and consider the mission." causing another ripple of laughter and a grin from Penny.

"Actually, before we get to the mission brief, I want to quickly discuss Badawi's son, Asif, who's causing a bit of an unwelcome commotion back home at the moment. Buster, I want you to take a covert look at his house here and see if there's anything worthwhile. And when I say look, it's an understatement. I mean, I want a forensic search through every bloody thing with a fine-tooth comb. Penny has advised that, as far as she knows, he's got a pretty large combination safe, and I have no doubt there are lots of goodies inside to find."

"You mean breaking in, boss?"

"Good heavens, nothing so imprudent. We are... erm... just going to visit. Penny says that entry is by an electronic keypad at the front door, and we have the kit to deal with that, right?"

"Yes, boss. It's a very high-tech, state-of-the-art piece of kit that Freddy Carr dropped in a few weeks ago. It will handle the entry point, the alarm system, and deal with entry to the safe, so all's good. Unlikely, Asif's security systems would be able to defeat it. And I'll ensure no trace of entry is left, boss. Are we expecting his...erm...return?"

"Not if I can help it."

"That bad, eh?"

"Yeah, his time's overdue to be taken out, but as tricky as we all know it is to do that on British soil without causing waves, I'm working on it."

"Got it, boss."

"Anyway, after the mission, go in and report back to Penny ASAP with anything of interest. Okay?"

"Affirmative. So, what's he up to, boss?"

"Well, it's not related to our mission here, and as I said, I'm dealing with it. So, back to the mission at hand. Buster and Georgie, can you give us an update following your 72-hour surveillance of the suspects before we proceed?"

"Yeah, well, the al-Malik was tied up for a bit in the Marina to let his nibs, Abdulaziz Badawi, have easier access. He left the yacht yesterday morning and hasn't returned, which is a good thing. We think he met our target, Abdallah al-Battal, for lunch at his house, but it's hard to be sure, 'cos the Mercedes had blacked-out windows, and all we saw was our guy being dropped off on his own last evening at the boat. His people were seen carrying a load of suitcases, but we had no trouble identifying him."

"Good work, both of you. I mean from MI6 and UAE sources, he's a very nasty piece of work, as you all know very well, responsible for countless acts of international terrorism," said Marcus.

"Anyway, boss, interestingly, the crew and chef went ashore shortly after docking and were soon replaced by a ragtag bunch. By the way, I've got pictures of all of them and ran them through. And, without exception, they're all on the hot list, and with no civilians to worry about on board, I suppose we'll take them all out at your discretion, of course, boss. Then they cast off and anchored about half a kilometre out. Tits met up with the captain in the yacht club bar before all that activity started unfolding, Tits?" asked Buster, nodding to his mate.

"Yeah, I casually...erm...bumped into him at the club bar, boss, and we started chatting. He was already nearly two sheets to the wind when I found him. But he did seem to be a pretty straight-up guy, ex-navy, and didn't have access to the yacht apart from the helm and his cabin stuffed into the bow, and I believed him. He described his role a bit like a pilot waiting for his boss to ring him to fly his private jet somewhere. Anyway, he was told to piss off until contacted, so I don't think he's involved in all this. But he did mention he had the impression they were gearing up to move off fairly soon. By then, he was pretty well into his cups, and his speech was getting a bit slurred, so I can't be certain. Either way, it's unlikely they'll get underway again till first light at least."

"Okay, thanks, Tits. That helps a lot. So, you've all read the brief that MI6 has prepared in liaison with and copied to Mossad and our friends at Langley. Be in no doubt that if the mission goes tits up, they'll all drop it like a hot potato. But the hit has been fully sanctioned by our political masters, nevertheless."

"Yeah, boss, but why us? Why now?" Buster asked.

"It's the 'D' word again, and the fact that we're in position and have all the right people and kit we need to tackle it," Marcus replied.

"Deniability, yeah, of course – I remember that word all too well. What a surprise," said Buster, laughing.

"And the now is that our boy's here, as you know."

"What about the clean-up boss?"

"Good question, Buster. MI6's yacht, Black Fox, anchored earlier this morning in the Persian Gulf about half a klick out of the Marina under the Emirates flag. It's the only other vessel besides the al-Malik just outside the marina."

Marcus pondered the luck that both yachts were outside the marina, the preferred location for the upcoming raid.

"Didn't realise we had one," said Buster, surprised by the never-ending MI6 kit that seemed to always be available.

"By the way, the skipper is one Captain Jack Sparrow," said Captain Marcus de Vere, with a wry smile.

At this, raucous laughter erupted around the table.

"You can't be serious?" cried Buster.

"Well, there you go. I'm just passing on the words of our esteemed mate Major Freddy Carr. Anyway," Marcus smiled, "actual ownership details have been lost in a maze of shell companies, all of which absorb costs unknowingly paid by the British taxpayer. MI6's assets are numerous, ranging from boats like this to planes, safe houses around the world, businesses, and more. Any searches of these companies would reveal the directors and such, but try ringing any of them, and you'd be lucky to get further than that. Anyway, Black Fox has an extra crew ready to take over the al-Malik once we're done and dusted, and then it'll be lost...erm...permanently—somewhere if you get my drift. It's a pretty quick vessel, powered by four

Caterpillar diesel engines, capable of reaching 58 knots. I understand from MI6 that there's also a team of three SBS lads on board, but we don't want to draw attention to the boat. So, keep clear of it on contact until we've finished. After the show's over, they'll pick it up, sail off, and blow it up somewhere. If, by chance, an unforeseen threat emerges during our operation, their proximity could be helpful. Understood?"

Nods of agreement all round.

"Okay, so to recap what you've already read, the primary target is Abdalla al-Battal. He's known as The Ghost. He never stays in the same place for more than a day. Recently, he was in Qatar and met with Hamas. We understand he's here to collect a significant amount of cash from Badawi, probably the suitcases you noted being taken on board. The most concerning scenario, according to the authorities, is that the money will fund the purchase of a dirty bomb, a very likely target being Israel. They consider it a holy bomb, in their view. Our colleagues in the CIA and Mossad are hopeful that our mission will be... erm... successful and meet their expectations. In essence, yes, we are to eliminate Abdalla al-Battal but ensure the cash is destroyed, which is the primary role of the Black Fox team."

Serious head nodding around the table as the team realised the grave possibilities.

"Basic arithmetic indicates five other hostiles, i.e., the crew. So, six bad guys in total.

This's how we'll play it," said Marcus.

"So, you're definitely coming with us, boss?" asked Tits.

"Yeah, it's personal. One of our targets' acolytes killed a dear friend of mine. A retired high-ranking US Navy SEAL officer, along with his wife and three-year-old daughter, while he was holidaying in Tunisia some time ago," said Marcus grimly.

"The beach massacre, right?" said Tits.

"Affirmative. So, it's payback time for me. And he's all mine – got it"

"As they say, the only easy day was yesterday, and I suppose the Yanks will be pleased with him going down as well," said Tits.

"Armoury at 02:30 hours and gear up. We don't want to attract any undue attention from our friends below decks during our little escapade. Then we'll move to the boat shed," said Marcus.

Which was an understatement for one of the most secure private moorings in town. Only Marcus's and Penny's thumbprints could gain entry through the Kevlar-armoured door. The 'garage door' itself, also armour plated, led out to their private jetty and the waters of the Marina. Unwelcome diver's access was virtually impossible, as thick titanium rods had been sunk to seal off that possibility. The Boat Shed contained three rigid-hull inflatable boats powered by twin 75hp Yamaha outboards, with two ribs in ready status 24/7 and the third as a spare.

"At 03:00 hours, Tits will move out on his Rib to align with our standard marine security protocol and cruise around doing his thing. At 03:15 hours, a local reprobate, but highly skilled in all things electrical, has been generously paid by our local MI6 contact to turn off the marina and harbour lights for precisely eight minutes - that's the longest he can manage for some technical reason - but it should suffice. That's my cue to activate the second Rib, which I will command and steer out to the al-Malik's port side. Tits will activate the wide-scan searchlight on his Rib and make his way to pass our target, creating a distraction for anyone on deck and reassuring our wealthy clients that we're doing our job regarding the super yachts anchored in and beyond the marina. As it happens, only the Black Fox is out there with the al-Malik at present, which suits us – no prying eyes around. The other yachts have, conveniently, up-anchored last night. Simultaneously, I'll power up the second Rib and go in stealth mode. The gunwale's a bit high off the water, so we'll take the boarding ladder with us since speed is critical. Tits' motor noise should mask our approach. I'll come in swiftly on the port side, as I said, while Tits will circle back to the marina on the starboard side once we're in position. Tits, let me know how many hostiles are visible on deck and don't forget to wave friendly at anyone you see as you pass by. Two priorities – One: Buster, you're first to take out anyone on deck or in the forward cabins. We'll get the lowdown from Tits' comm on anyone else who might be catching the night air, as well as our AK 47 guy, and then stay on deck; we don't want any surprise guests joining the party. Two: Meanwhile, Harry, your job is to cut communications so our Head Boy doesn't get wise to what we're doing. Before you discreetly destroy the computers – download everything, I mean everything, along with any files and data you find there. Meanwhile, Georgie and I will take out the primary target and the remaining culprits below decks. Okay?" asked Marcus.

"What if our friends get a bit too excited and fire off a few?" asked Buster.

"What day is it again today?" asked Marcus, much to the astonishment of those around the table.

Silence fell as the four special forces operatives exchanged bewildered glances at the question.

"Of course, it's Eid Al Adha for the next three days. The night sky will be constantly illuminated with nice, loud, and colourful explosions to blend in with our contribution to the festivities," said Tits, grinning. "Nice one, Boss."

"Correct, and ironically, this is translated as 'festival of the slaughter,' " Marcus noted, amusing the team.

"The other advantage is that the forecast looks promising, with heavy cloud cover, so the moon should be tucked away for a while, meaning not too much light, hopefully. So, are we good?" asked Marcus.

Everyone nodded.

"Okay, see you all at 03:00 hours, with your kit, i.e., full body armour, SIG P226's, and our suppressed H&K 53s with four spare mags each, just in case it gets a bit too hairy."

Marcus didn't hesitate in choosing the latter from their armoury. The weapon's short barrel did result in a lower muzzle velocity and, therefore, a shorter effective range compared to the H&K 33, but they would be up close and personal for this one. It was chambered for NATO 5.56mm x 45mm rounds, and at ten rounds per second, it was highly effective for close-quarters combat and would more than handle the situation. Even with a suppressor, the weapon still produced sound when fired.

"So, with the H&K 33's, I don't need to remind you that short, effective bursts are the name of the game. No need to go gung-ho, right?"

"Got it, boss – as if any of us would. Note you've decided to carry the SIG Sauer P226 .375 to the party. Nice, with a big punch," said Buster, smiling, taking in the SIG 375 rounds that Marcus was loading.

Captain Marcus de Vere smiled in response as he strapped the weapon in a shoulder holster rig under his left arm. A bit of kit that he preferred to use rather than carry on his hip.

"Yeah, some .375 Magnum rounds should be enough for our mate al-Battal – a bit more up close and personal than just spraying him with an H&K."

The team gave their approval and understanding with a nod.

"Good luck, mates, and keep your heads down. Oh, and you'd better lose the suits before we start. Don't want extra dry-cleaning bills, right?" said Marcus, causing another ripple of laughter around the table.

CHAPTER 22

03.00 Hours

Marcus sat with his SBS team in the 2nd Rib, resting at the boatshed entrance, ready to power up. Its nose rose and fell following the wake from Tits leaving to conduct his marina and harbour security patrol. Marcus's team wore matching all-black night combat gear, body armour, and tactical ballistic goggles, but Marcus kept his eyes uncovered.

"Comm check, Tits."

"All good, boss."

Marcus glanced at the glowing dial of his Rolex Submariner, noticing it was four minutes until the scheduled kick-off. As per his agreement with the MI6 contact, he sent a secure, coded message to the captain of the Black Fox, confirming everything was a go in exactly four minutes. He reviewed the conditions and decided they couldn't be more favourable. As expected, the crescent moon was obscured by thick clouds. In the distance, the al-Malik was displaying only an anchor light, leaving most of its forward deck in shadow and remaining stationary – ideal for their plans. To enhance the cover, occasional fireworks lit up the dark sky with loud bangs, which he found pretty amusing. Marcus chuckled to himself, thinking that some of the fireworks might have been launched by drunken expatriates still partying early in the morning. Unaware of them, their celebrations were actually helping to mask the sound of another party about to begin.

Tits was sweeping around the marina exactly as per standard protocol – everything was as it should be to any observer. At exactly 03:15 hours, the lights went down all across the Marina and Harbour. Tits deployed his powerful searchlight, sweeping the marina before gradually making his way towards the starboard side of the al-Malik. As he passed, he could just about see the chrome-plated AK47 flashing in the light of a spectacular starburst from a firework descending to earth, accompanied by several more welcome explosions – the timing was perfect. In the split seconds, Tits clearly saw one hostile on the forward deck smoking, his weapon slung over his shoulder. Tits's wave was returned. Moving on to circle the Black Fox and then back to the al-Malik on its starboard side, his actions fell exactly in line with normal protocol and the brief. He contacted Marcus on his comms to bring him up to speed as he prepared to pass the al-Malik once more. The 2nd Rib, commanded by Marcus, made its slow approach, causing only slight displacement of the calm waters of the Persian Gulf towards the port side of the al-Malik.

“Confirmed. There's just one nasty still on deck, boss—smoking and looking relaxed. He's your earlier boy, I reckon, cos he’s got a chrome-plated AK47 slung over his shoulder,” confirmed Tits on his comm.

“Affirmative. We’re approaching rapidly now, ETA one minute to port side, so prepare to surge past. As soon as you pass, we’ll board it. If he gets fidgety, take him out, but he shouldn’t be able to tell our engine noise from yours, but you never know,” said Marcus calmly. Marcus’s team secured an anchor magnet and silently threw the rubber-hooked ladder onto the gunwale; they were on deck in seconds.

“Hold,” whispered Marcus to his team as Buster was up and running, ducking and weaving towards the forward deck. A skill set finely tuned over numerous such scenarios over the years. His sweeping scrutiny, tactical and well-rehearsed, took in everything to his left and ahead, alert to any threat. His rubber-soled shoes made no sound, and with the moon still hidden behind clouds, that suited him perfectly. The shooter, driven by some instinct for self-preservation, raised his AK-47 towards the shadows, but his reflexes were far too slow as his chest was literally torn apart by the twenty or so rounds fired in less than two seconds from Buster’s lethal weapon, and he was thrown back, mortally wounded. The rapid chatter from the gun was not loud enough to alert those below decks. In his death throes, the terrorist’s weapon fell overboard into the calm waters of the Persian Gulf.

‘Good riddance,’ thought Buster. It was like taking candy from a baby.

With virtually no real military training, it was a walk in the park to take these sorts of buggers out, but nevertheless, nothing was ever taken for granted – that's what kept you alive. All in what seemed like one movement after the kill, he'd instantly checked the forward cabins again for hostiles and then carefully swept all the upper decks from bow to stern.

"All clean, boss. Bunkering down now," said Buster.

"Copy that," replied Marcus. Pleased that Buster was securely in position to guard their six in case any unwelcome guests appeared – an unlikely event, but still an important scenario to prepare for. Harry carefully and silently opened the door to the communication centre, much to the disbelief of the heavily bearded Arab busily working at the keyboard before him. The Arab's wide-eyed stare fixed on the barrel of Harry's weapon, and the realisation that he was about to die was unmistakably visible in his eyes. He didn't have time to even consider reaching for the Iranian-made Raa'd 9mm Polymer pistol beside his desk before he was blown away. His face and body showed shock as the rounds hit their target. Harry quickly examined the layout of the communication systems. They were sophisticated, as expected. Without hesitation, he dismantled them and set about connecting his tech kit to the computers to begin downloading all the data stored there. While that procedure was running, he began thoroughly checking all the drawers and cupboards, stuffing as much paperwork as he could find into his waterproof satchel while his kit continued downloading files. As soon as he received confirmation that the download was complete, he took action to permanently disable the computers. He had no idea that shutting down the communication system had triggered a silent alarm at Badawi's residence – a fact that would have repercussions later.

Marcus and Georgie positioned themselves outside two of the three VIP suites. Marcus chose to sling his H&K 53 over his shoulder, preferring to use his pistol instead.

Marcus whispered into his comms, "Georgie – on three we'll rock and roll. One - two – three, go."

They kicked open the doors of the two suites simultaneously. Marcus, at once, struck gold by finding himself face to face with the target, an astonished, unarmed Abdallah al-Battal, who immediately raised his hands high in submission with a wry smile on his bearded face, and commanded his associate in the room to do likewise in rapid Arabic. However, al-Battal's comrade, ignoring his leader's order, tried to react by diving for the 9mm GSH-18 lying on a nearby desk – the favoured weapon of the Russian Spetsnaz Special Forces. A fatal mistake on his part – being completely outclassed by the skill and speed of the ex-SAS leader. Marcus fired a double-tap into his chest – the devastating impact of the two SIG .357 rounds pushing his shattered body far back into the rear of the room.

In the split second that followed, Marcus's peripheral vision noticed that al-Battal had shifted position very subtly towards the Russian pistol still untouched on the desk behind him. His arms remained raised in surrender.

"Don't even think about it. Back up slowly, my friend," smiled Captain Marcus de Vere as he reached for the pistol with his left hand and slipped it into his waterproof satchel – a tasty souvenir. Abdalla al-Battal looked into Marcus's steel blue eyes and appeared unfazed by his predicament.

"A SAS team, I presume?" he smiled confidently, ignoring the blood-soaked body of his fallen comrade – the white dishdasha now vividly red.

"Actually, you have the pleasure of the SAS and the SBS visiting you this evening, Mr al-Battal. We didn't receive an invitation, but there are some parties we just can't resist crashing," Marcus grinned.

"You British are too soft and pampered to kill an old man in cold blood, eh?" snarled al-Battal.

"Do you want to kneel or stand?" said Marcus, ignoring the old man's words.

"Do you have any idea of the unbelievable riches I could give you? You could have more money than you can imagine. You'd never have to work again for your weak and treacherous government. Untraceable funds, in any currency you desire, deposited anywhere on the planet at your wish. Nobody would ever know. You'd be a very wealthy man, my friend," he sneered.

"It's not about money, it never could be," said Marcus, grimly.

Abdallah al-Battal examined the man before him more closely – his self-confidence gradually waning, ebbing away second by second.

"Please show mercy to an old man. I am eighty-five," Abdulla al-Battal begged, extending his arms in plea.

“It’s your time, and it’s long overdue. To send you off, I’ve loaded SIG .357 rounds," said Captain Marcus de Vere, waving his pistol slowly. "Just for you, at 1425 fps, it won’t take long.”

“You SAS, piece of shit.”

“The Bullet always tells the truth, my friend. All glory to Allah, right? They say revenge is a dish best served cold. Well, here’s a first-class, one-way ticket to your mythical Paradise,” Marcus said, with satisfaction. The blinding muzzle flash illuminated the kill as he released three rounds in a tight group into the terrorist’s chest, shattering al-Battal’s breastbone and shredding his heart.

The whole exchange took less than thirty seconds.

Georgie’s suite contained twelve Louis Vuitton luggage cases stuffed with Swiss Francs – all apparently in 1,000 note denominations, the highest Swiss currency notes. After leaving them, he went to the third and final VIP suite and kicked open the door – turning off the deafening rock music as he burst in. He heard the shower running at full blast and found two young Arabs in explicit positions, both naked.

“Hello boys, try sucking on this,” he said, pointing the barrel of his H&K 53 weapon and firing two short bursts, smashing the shower glass to smithereens and nearly splitting their bodies in half. Remarkably, the water was still running, so he let it continue, literally a clean kill. He smiled to himself. He then reported two bad guys down on his comms to Marcus.

Marcus, Georgie, and Harry exchanged nods outside the suites.

“Help me bring out the cash, mates – there’s loads of it,” George said.

Marcus and Harry helped George carry the heavy cases out of the suite.

“Crikey, there must be millions of dollars per case,” said Marcus, astonished. “And, literally, encased in the world’s most expensive luggage. Guess that’s appropriate, considering."

“Yeah, 60 million dollars could buy some pretty terrible things," Harry said. “Destroying it will create a big hole in al-Battal’s and Badawi’s cash flow.”

“Too right. Okay, lads, turn over the cabins for anything else of interest. Leave no drawer, cupboard, shelf, or whatever untouched. All hands on deck – 60 seconds tops.”

On deck, Buster kept sweeping the water with his binoculars for anything incoming.

“Boss, do you read me?” Buster asked calmly over his comm.

“Affirmative. What’s happening?”

“Speed boat approaching quickly. I’m under fire – I count six bad guys...I...."

A firework burst caused a distinctive flash from the glass of his binoculars, revealing his position, and he took rounds to his chest. It was no problem for his body armour, but one tore through his right upper shoulder, knocking him back hard onto the deck

“Damn it! Can’t hear you, Buster. Are you alright?" said Marcus, finding it hard to hear over the noise of the firefight and the other fireworks in play.

“I’m down, boss,” said Buster, groaning in pain as he rolled for cover behind the gunwale.

“Hang in there, old friend. We’re coming up,” said Marcus and sent a flash message to the Black Fox – with a status update.

Within twenty-five seconds, a rib was launched from the Black Fox, and the three SBS soldiers aboard the MI6 vessel leapt into the water, prepared the rib's engine, and surged forward at maximum speed to engage the approaching speedboat, unleashing a deadly barrage of fire at the same time. The speedboat had no chance of success, being caught in an effective crossfire from both the Black Fox’s rib and the al-Malik. Tits had held back in his rib during the firefight, recognising he was not in the right position to be effective. Georgie, Harry, and Marcus lay down a burst of fire along with the Black Fox team, decimating the hostiles.

Marcus checked on Buster, quickly establishing that the round had passed through the muscle of his upper arm.

“Don’t worry, mate, you’re going to live, but no tennis for a while,” said Marcus with a chuckle of relief as he pulled a field dressing from his pack to stem the flow of blood. The Black Fox team and Tits went about the business of finding and collecting the bodies of Abdalla al-Battal’s men and those of, they assumed, Abdulaziz Badawi’s men. It was a priority to leave no trace of what had transpired here. It was over.

“Okay, Tits, get back to the marina and do your stuff – all’s good,” said Marcus as Tits powered back to continue with their normal security protocols.

The three-man team from the Black Fox pulled up alongside the al-Malik and dumped the bodies on deck to join the others who'd met the same fate.

"We've got a bonus boss," Harry said with delight, turning over one of the bodies.

"Well, well, if it isn't Badawi himself," grinned Marcus. "Two birds with one stone, eh?"

"That'll teach him not to go out and play at night," laughed Georgie.

"The gates of Paradise are going to have a long, happy queue tonight," snorted Marcus, as he introduced his team to the lads from the Black Fox. Marcus turned his attention to the broad-shouldered leader standing before him. "Thanks to you and your team – nice work. What's your name?"

"Oh, you can call me Blake, boss. It's been a pleasure," said the former Royal Marine.

Both teams gathered around Buster. Blake knelt beside him and gently ruffled his hair and said, "That'll teach you to keep your bloody head down next time." This broke the spell and made Buster and the others break into a grin.

"There are twelve cases of cash below that require urgent attention," said Marcus.

"Yeah, we were briefed on that. Those will meet the same fate as the boat – don't worry."

"So, over to you guys, and thanks. Find somewhere nice and deep for these chaps, and their money, right?" said Marcus, addressing the Black Fox SBS team leader.

"Affirmative," said Blake with a wry grin.

As Marcus and his team returned to the marina, the reserve crew of the Black Fox had already taken control of the al-Malik and were heading through the Strait of Hormuz, destination the deeper waters of the Gulf of Oman.

The entire raid and firefight lasted precisely twelve minutes and eighteen seconds, with no fatal casualties.

"What do you have there, Harry? Looks like a Raa'd," said Marcus, noticing him holding a pistol.

"Yeah, spot on, boss – a little memento I picked up from one of our departed friends. Iranians – they'll sell their poison to anyone with the cash."

"Got a souvenir too," said Marcus with a grin as he waved the Spetsnaz pistol in the air. Well done, everyone. Just one more thing: Tits, I want you to take over from Buster and conduct a forensic search of Asif's house, right?

"Yes, boss. I'll handle it after I finish my patrol, alright?"

"No, clean up and get on it now, and have everything to me at Aquarius tonight. You can have a kip after that," smiled Marcus. "Download his computer and then destroy it. Collect any paperwork – all of it, and bring it too. "I'm meeting with Penny for dinner before I go back to Blighty."

"Consider it done, boss," said Tits.

"Anyway, well done lads," said Marcus, grinning, joining the group's high-five celebration. And he left them cleaning their weapons and stashing their gear away – tomorrow was another day.

Harry, as commanded, took over their normal marine security patrol protocol until sunrise. All was calm.

Buster was in good spirits as his wound was cleaned and re-bandaged – the SAS and SBS, not only trained in combat but also effective field medics.

• CHAPTER 23 •

Back at his office, Marcus showered, changed in one of the company's apartments, and headed to the agreed-upon meeting point at the British Embassy on Khalid bin Al Waleed Street to deliver the proceeds of their incursion, which he believed would be sent by diplomatic bag on the next flight to London. As he approached, he observed a tall, lanky, very well-dressed gentleman casually leaning against an embassy silver-grey Mercedes with diplomatic plates, smoking a cigarette held in a short black lacquered Dunhill holder. He was wearing a double-breasted blazer, and Marcus noted, with an inward smile, the black tie with light blue stripes, flagging him as a member of the exclusive Old Etonian Club, along with a pair of lightweight cavalry twill trousers that contributed to his quintessential Englishman appearance.

Marcus estimated him to be in his mid to late seventies, and from his bearing, he was ex-military.

"Good morning, Captain de Vere. I have this for you," he said in a rather plummy voice, handing him an unopened envelope with the embassy's red seal conspicuously affixed to the back in red wax, leaving Marcus to break it open and read – which he did, discovering an embedded picture of the chap opposite and signed by the Ambassador, thanking Marcus for his services to King and Country.

"And who am I speaking to?" Marcus inquired politely, dismissing the superficial chatter of the man, whom Marcus had perceived from the beginning as dangerous, despite his apparent age and the different circumstances.

"I...erm...just heard from Sparrow that, apart from a few hairy moments, all's well. Sorry to hear that one of your boys took a bit of a clip. Trust he's okay. I have to say, we're all delighted that Badawi was taken out as well. That was well overdue – a nice and very welcome surprise bonus. Along with, of course, the demise of the cash, which I understand was encased in some rather fashionable luggage. Sparrow has confirmed that all received a formal burial at sea with full military honours. Along with a bit of a bang," chuckled the MI6 contact with a twinkle in his eye. "The powers that be in London and elsewhere are incredibly happy that the...erm...party went without any local or international awareness."

"Erm... right. Yeah, well, my lad Buster's fine, thanks. Just a flesh wound. He'll live."

"Good show all round, old boy. If I'd got a hat, I'd whip it off right now, in a flash," he said, ignoring the question about his identity.

Marcus noted the almost indiscernible bulge in the immaculately tailored blazer.

"Are you carrying?"

"Yes. Tricky times, don't you know."

Marcus handed him the aluminium case filled with all the goodies, for which he got a cheeky half salute.

"Not that it matters to you, but we've had a slight change of plans for this baby," he said, patting the case. "We believe your treasure trove might just be that, and London and our friends have decided not to follow the old diplomatic bag route this time if the stuff is genuinely very hot. So, I'm about to jump into my motor and fly to London to deliver it personally to our chums there. Our RAF chaps at Al Minhad Air Base, south of Dubai, which we share with the local friends, as you're probably aware, have kindly agreed to take me into their care. It's only about 170 klicks from here, and they've got a flight leaving in approximately," he reached into his jacket and produced an ornate-looking gold fob watch. As he flipped it open, Marcus noticed a deeply engraved symbol on the cover which he did not recognise.

"So, I... erm... leave in two hours with one of their scuffers to hold my hand and keep me safe and cosy."

"Scuffers?"

"RAF police, dear boy. What's happened to one's education in everyday slang these days? I mean, the country must be going downhill, eh? By the way, have you been a good boy regarding what's in the case?"

"I have no idea what you mean."

"Captain de Vere, please don't be coy. I mean, have you taken a peek, or even worse, are there any bloody copies?"

"Of course not," lied Marcus.

He didn't mention that, of course, he'd taken copies of everything, both digital data and paper records. After all, he and his team had risked their lives to obtain this information, not to mention taking down some very dangerous individuals along the way. The computer data would, of course, be heavily encrypted, and he would have to leave that to MI6's expertise, but he'd give it to his IT guy to have a go at cracking it back at Maidstone. As for the paper documents, Penny would handle the translation. Either way, he planned to take it all back with him on the company's jet later that evening; he'd be the only passenger, so security wasn't an issue. Since he was well known at Brize Norton in the private arrival area, he didn't see it as a problem before reaching the sanctuary of his UK office.

"Alright, so that's it, impressed?" asked the embassy's MI6 intermediary.

"Very," smiled Marcus.

"Just wanted to mention, on departing Captain de Vere, that you and your organisation are held in very high regard across all key areas. I suspect our paths will cross again, and if so, hopefully, we'll have more time to chat more freely without time constraints for a bit more of...erm...chit chat."

And at that, he opened the door of his limo, threw the case onto the passenger seat, and powered off with a relaxed wave out of the driver's window. Leaving Marcus wondering who the hell he was, he then thought that if anyone would know, it'd be

Penny, whom he'd invited to an early dinner since this was his last day and he was looking forward to visiting one of his favourite restaurants with her. However, his priority now was to get some serious shut-eye, and like most special forces people, he'd only need to put his head on the pillow to achieve that goal.

• CHAPTER 24 •

Captain Marcus de Vere sat on the terrace of Aquarius, an award-winning seafood restaurant with stunning views over the marina and the Abu Dhabi skyline, enjoying a cigarette with a glass of Mount Gay Eclipse rum, which he had always adored for its spicy, floral, banana, and vanilla flavours, as he waited for Penny to appear.

As he sat back enjoying his rum, he reflected on the recent hit. Even in his extensive experience of combat scenarios, it had to rank highly on the list as one of the cleanest ops he'd ever undertaken, even with the surprise visit by Abdulaziz Badawi in the mix, but that intervention was a rather large cherry on the cake. He'd been happy to take the lead in the operation – it'd been a while since he'd experienced the unique buzz and adrenaline rush that only direct combat provides, and the fact that he personally took out Abdalla al-Battal added to his satisfaction. He'd received an encrypted message of thanks from none other than the CIA Director and the head of Mossad's security services – so, all was good in his world.

Dreaming about your earlier jaunt this morning?" said Penny warmly as she silently approached, waking Marcus back from his reverie.

"Hello Penny, you're looking decidedly delicious. What can I get you?"

"Oh, let me think. Yes, I'll have a Lychee Martina," she said to the hovering waiter.

"Not familiar with that one. I mean, I know what a lychee is, but...?" grinned Marcus, beginning to feel much more relaxed now following his recent activities. The adrenaline rush was now beginning to fade – the epinephrine hormone had long since dissipated from his system.

"Let me broaden your knowledge of all things drinkable, Marcus. It's a Ketel One Vodka, lychee liqueur, lime, and orange bitters," she explained matter-of-factly, and as if by magic, it appeared before her just moments later. The service was impeccable, as always."

"Look, Penny, there are a couple of other things I'd like to ask before we settle in to enjoy their renowned fare here. First, what do you know of the late Abdulaziz Badawi's remaining son, Asif? I've asked one of our people, you know, Tits, of course."

"Need you ask – love that tag," smiled Penny.

"Well, I've deployed him to conduct a full search of Asif Badawi's house and safe, and he's joining us later with, I hope, a load of useful stuff I can use," said Marcus.

"Okay, makes sense. What's Badawi up to?"

"I'll explain later – so, back to the man himself, what can you tell me?"

"He's very wealthy, for starters, as we all know. Good-looking, suave, and well-educated. Charterhouse, Cambridge, Sandhurst, and then a spell with the Light Dragoons. Born in the UK, he holds a British passport and spends most of his time here doing God knows what, but he usually slips back to the UK in July, August, or both. Like most Arabs, he prefers August. He lives in Mayfair and is a member of the Cavalry and Guards Club, moving in the upper echelons of society both there and here. And he is now playing the successful businessman – does that do it for you?" smiled Penny, taking a sip of her cocktail with relish.

"Yeah, but I already know most of that. What I'd really like to hear is your opinion of him on a personal level, based on what you've gathered from the times you've crossed paths. I mean, your ears are always close to the ground, and your instincts are usually spot on," Marcus said with a twinkle in his eye.

"He's a nasty piece of work, that's for sure. Anyway, to answer your question, I know for certain he was a person of interest a year ago with the Abu Dhabi Police Force."

"Really, what was that all about then?" Marcus asked, his interest suddenly piqued.

"Well, he was interviewed regarding the disappearance of two teenage girls with whom he was seen dancing at a disco, and, by the way, they were never seen again. A mate of mine on the force said they didn't have enough evidence to detain him. All circumstantial, unfortunately. Then I heard, just recently, from the same source that there was another case where a sixteen-year-old girl was allegedly raped by him, but then she mysteriously dropped her claim. My mate's pretty sure she was paid off. She and her family moved up the coast and bought an expensive beach house.

Raising eyebrows considering they were a pretty poor family, but there you go. A bastard, as I said, anyway you care to look at it."

"Interesting stuff, Penny. But I think his day's coming soon, though."

"Do tell."

"No, can't do. Mum's the word at the moment, I'm afraid. But he's not coming back here any time soon if I've got anything to do with it."

"Happy to hear," said Penny, wishing to get more info on that piece of news. But, knowing Marcus, it would be like extracting blood from a stone until he was ready to share. However, she knew she'd get into that loop soon enough.

"Anyway, how's my plane? Is it good for wheels-up at 22:00 hours?"

"Marcus, you're teasing me again."

"Sorry, couldn't miss the chance to try and rattle you a bit, but, of course, it didn't work, as usual. You're far too well-organised and far beyond just being up to speed," he laughed.

"And so, what was the other thing, as I'm beginning to get a tad hungry?"

"It was about this chap I met earlier this morning to pass over the loot."

"What did he look like?"

"Mid-seventies, maybe older, slim, very well dressed, sporting an old Etonian's club tie, plus he was carrying."

Penny was visibly engrossed in thought for a moment or two. "It must have been Colonel Charlie Dankworth. Did he have a rather plummy accent and wear a double-breasted blazer and look pretty fit for his age?"

"Yeah, you're spot on."

"So, it's him then, he always wears one. He's actually in his late seventies now, at least. And he's just the sort of bloke that the Ambassador and MI6 would task for the handover."

"So, what's his story then?"

"An interesting one, actually. I've had dinner with him here a couple of times. He knew my father very well. They were at school together. But even more interestingly for you perhaps is that his father worked with David Sterling in 1941 to help form the early version of the Regiment and then in 1943 with George Jellcoe to form the SBS."

"So, what was he up to back in the day when he got going?" said Marcus, impressed.

"Well, after Oxford, he was headhunted by our British Security Services and operated in some quite dangerous places. His reputation is legendary, or so I heard from friends who knew him better than I did, and then later he worked for 'Maximus' until he retired with honours, medals, and all the rest of it."

"What's Maximus? I've never heard of it, and I'm in the business," said Marcus, visibly intrigued.

"Well, it was all very hush-hush at the time and perhaps still is now, but Maximus was, back in the day, a covert black ops department run by MI6"

"So, what was his role there?"

"He was an assassin."

"That explains everything! I sensed something when I met him: beneath that mask of bonhomie lay a complex and dangerous man if you were on the wrong side of the fence, as it were."

"True, anyway, I do know he has a country estate tucked away somewhere in the Gloucestershire countryside, and rumours suggest that foreign undesirables who want to become desirable to the British Security Services are entertained there and...erm...processed. Suspected terrorists are also...erm...interviewed there, off the grid, or at least that's what I've heard. So, he has a pretty full agenda one way or another."

"Bloody hell, Penny, you're a treasure trove of information."

"Yeah, that's exactly why you hired me, right? Remember?"

"Let's order," said Marcus, waving at a waiter nearby. His mind feels a little overloaded with so much information. They both chose the Chinese Wild Mushroom Soup for starters, and Penny opted for Charcoal-Grilled Chilean Seabass in honey, while Marcus chose the Charcoal-Grilled Canadian Lobster and the Five-Spice Butter Sauce to go with it.

They both felt like they were in culinary heaven, and why not? They'd both served their country well over the years and deserved the occasional treat. Marcus ordered a bottle of Louis Jadot, Grand Cru Batard-Montrachet white Burgundy, but he engaged the waiter emphatically, making a serious request that the bottle be buried deep in an ice bucket, receiving a nod of delight and approval from Penny. He remembered the last time he ordered a bottle of this here, celebrating with one or two of his ex-SAS colleagues in gratitude for their success in a high-profile kidnapping case in Dubai. The wine was too warm to drink, which, given its pedigree and price, was unforgivable, and he had to send it back, quite annoyed at the time. They raised their glasses in a toast, both eager for the flavours of bold, ripe apples, peaches, and the creamy oak to hit their palates. As Marcus savoured the aroma and taste, he looked at Penny with almost fatherly affection. What a blessing she'd been since she joined his team.

"Oh, by the way, Penny, I've met someone."

"Really? About bloody time. Who is she?"

"Cathy. She's a registered Home Office Forensic Pathologist and is beginning to turn my life around more than I ever thought possible. You'll meet her, eventually, of course."

"Wild horses couldn't keep me away. So, how long has this little, if not major, covert liaison been going on?" grinned Penny happily.

"Long enough, Penny, for me to catch myself thinking about her most of the time. Cognac to finish? Are you up for that?" laughed Marcus as they drained the last of the wine. "By the way, I didn't want to go into details earlier, but suffice it to say that Asif's involved in a threat to Cathy and her family. She has two children, a boy of ten and a girl of seven. Great kids. So, as I said, if my boy gives you anything of interest, get it to me quickly; any tidbit could help."

"Christ, I'm sorry to hear that, Marcus."

"It's under control. Give Emily a buzz; she'll fill you in. I just don't want to talk about it anymore. I just want to relax."

Marcus turned to a waiter. "Two cognacs, please, L'Esprit de Courvoisier, if you have it?"

Marcus reached for a Cohiba, and they settled back to enjoy the cognac. Penny reached for one of her rare cigarettes; she'd tried to keep it down to around five a day, but it didn't always end up like that, especially today as she was beginning to feel decidedly but happily pissed, and she liked to smoke when she was drinking... She looked across at Marcus while he was distracted by a passing Harley-Davidson. She knew he had a gleaming white-and-black 'Fat Boy' in his garage at home, and when not riding it, he was cleaning and polishing it, *'boys' toys,'* she thought. But as she looked at his handsome, leathery face, which spoke of many years of working and fighting in deserts and jungles all over the globe, mostly covertly, she wondered what Cathy would be like and couldn't wait to meet her. She felt that she must be really something to have caught his eye. In her opinion, that's exactly what Marcus needed: a strong woman to look after and care for him.

"There's something I've always meant to ask you," said Penny, her voice beginning to sound a little slurred.

"I can't wait. And there I was thinking that you must know all there was to know about me and all my secrets – go for it," he laughed.

"I was wondering why you formed the Company? I mean, didn't you have enough action and risk in your life up to that point? And that op this morning was so potentially dangerous, it could have all gone tits up. I mean, why not settle into civilian life?"

"It's a good question, Penny. The truth is that many military skills aren't easily transferable to civilian life. We can all respect someone who hikes 40 miles with a backpack full of gear and still shoots accurately at the end, especially when they and their team are in danger. However, most businesses don't have much use for that skill set. There's also the issue of managing the relative lack of structure and organisational chaos in civilian settings. Someone once told me that when you leave that 'Club', as it were, it can quickly become a slippery slope into personal chaos, and I didn't want to risk that. Anyway, I'm very happy with what I do now. So, I made the right choice for me, and that's all there is to it. Does that answer your question? Or do you have any other in-depth psychological questions for me, doctor?" laughed Marcus.

"That makes sense to me, Marcus; it's in your DNA after all," Penny smiled.

"And as you know, I only employ ex-SAS and SBS boys and girls, and that's not just because it's good for business but also because they can earn proper money to prepare for their eventual retirement. Sadly, in my opinion, our government doesn't do enough for veterans who've made so many personal sacrifices and risked their lives repeatedly to keep our country safe. I mean, some of them end up on the bloody streets, for Christ's sake, I don't want that to happen to any of my people."

"That's very true, Marcus."

"And just before I step down from my soapbox, you know that these people run each of our offices, some of whom are well into their late sixties and still thriving and delivering real value. So there we have it, 'speakers' corner is done for the day," chuckled Marcus.

At that moment, Tits arrived, appearing pleased yet exhausted.

"What have you got, Tits?" Marcus asked, observing the slim briefcase he was holding. Penny, as usual, couldn't help but smile internally at the nickname and nodded a greeting to him.

"Well, boss, I don't know what's going on in London with our friend Badawi, but his computer was quite the treasure trove – for example, there's a list of eight of his cohorts active there, albeit under the radar. Just codenames so far, but MI6 and GCHQ will, no doubt, check the 'Chatter Box' to see any links," said Tits, passing the goodies.

"Good job," Marcus said, smiling. "Anything else?"

"Some paper stuff in Arabic, which I guess Penny will run through. I was using precision Nitrile gloves throughout the search, and so if there's any DNA signature on anything of interest, then it wouldn't be contaminated," said Tits.

"Just one more thing. I suppose you've kept a copy of the computer stuff?

"Yes, boss."

"Good, send it to Major Carr. It'll give him a heads-up before I meet with him," said Marcus, pleased.

"On it, boss."

"Brandy, Tits?"

"Bring it on, boss."

Marcus waved at a nearby waiter.

Tits finished the brandy and left, eager to get some sleep.

Marcus and Penny, now fully sated, said their goodbyes with a warm hug. Marcus returned to his apartment in the office to pack for his flight and enjoy a quick nap. It had been a busy but fruitful few days, and he was looking forward to returning to Cathy and his Maidstone office.

• CHAPTER 25 •

Marcus arrived back safely at RAF Brize Norton with his mobile in hand. Even before his jet finished taxiing, he was eager to make the call he had been trying to get through to Cathy, but her number was engaged.

Captain Marcus de Vere sat at his desk, flipping through the mail and messages that Emily had efficiently arranged in neat piles for his attention earlier that morning, alongside a fresh pot of Sumatra Mandheling coffee. An Indonesian favourite of his, with intense flavours of dark chocolate. Sumatra's rich soil and tropical climate give it its distinctive taste.

Nothing exciting caught his eye, so he stepped outside to enjoy a cigarette and a coffee to relax on the covered terrace – the only access to which was from his office and was not overlooked, which suited him just fine. It was a pleasantly warm morning with a light, refreshing breeze.

He'd been disappointed that the stuff Penny had translated from the Abu Dhabi raid hadn't met his expectations – there was nothing juicy in it. His IT chap reported that he was unable to decipher the computer material. That wasn't too surprising, considering he wasn't a proper codebreaker, but it was worth a try. He was overdue to give Freddy a ring, and he was a bit surprised he hadn't heard from him yet. Since he got back, Cathy had been on his mind, and he was thinking about her when his phone buzzed.

Yes, Emily, what's up?

"I've got Doctor Meer on the line, sir."

"Oh, good, put her through, please."

"Cathy darling, so good to hear your voice. I'm home and really looking forward to seeing you. How are you and the children?"

"We're all good, Marcus. I'm so glad to hear your voice as well. Sleep peacefully, sending you a kiss," Cathy said with heartfelt sincerity and warmth.

"Do you have time to join me for lunch tomorrow? I can fill you in then. Sorry, it's such short notice."

"Love to, where?"

"Little Manor, say around noon? I'll get Henry to prepare one of his masterpieces."

"Sounds good to me. Monica can watch the kids for an hour or two and see you then. She has her latest book to read to them and to show the work of a new illustrator she recently discovered, who is fantastic."

The next day at noon, Joe welcomed her, whom she now understood was Marcus's bodyguard. Which was not surprising, given his shooting prowess on the range. Smiling, he waved her into the house. To find Marcus striding towards her, arms outstretched. Uncertain how to respond, as her whole body trembled with a mixture of desire and the pleasure of seeing him in one piece. He hadn't fooled her when he'd left for Abu Dhabi. She'd sensed he was going on a mission, but he'd not wanted to alarm her. And she'd spent the last few days in fear of losing him. So, she fell into his arms and kissed him passionately – she just couldn't help herself.

"I'm so happy to see that you are safe and well, darling. I bet whatever you were up to over there that it wasn't a walk in the park, as you said last time we met."

"Water under the bridge, Cathy. Come on, let's go in. Also got some useful stuff on Badawi, but want to speak with Freddy Carr first before filling you in."

"Sounds hopeful. Let's catch up with that later, as you say. I'd love to see a little more of your house," said Cathy, her green eyes flashing signals that Marcus was unable, successfully, to decipher.

"I'd like that," said Marcus, shifting a little uncomfortably on his feet.

Cathy sensed his body language as positive in the sense that she, like him, was approaching a moment they'd been waiting for, ever since they'd met.

"Actually, I want, more than anything else, to see where the master of Little Manor rests his head when all about him are losing theirs."

Her body is now visibly trembling with anticipation. They ran up the sweeping staircase like a couple of teenagers.

"So, this is the master suite, impressive and wow, what a bathroom. Fit for a king," said Cathy, slowly undressing. Her uninhibited actions took Marcus by surprise.

"You mean a queen. Cathy, you're unbelievably beautiful; it's incredible. Erm...Cathy, I... I... erm... I'm a bit out of practice..." spluttered Marcus as he hurriedly undressed.

"Join the club," Cathy said softly as she carefully guided his naked body back onto the king-sized bed and sat astride him. Their bodies merged in a heat and intensity neither had felt before.

Marcus's mobile buzzed and vibrated on the ornate bedside table, breaking the spell of the moment. He reluctantly reached for it, picked it up, and accidentally pressed the speaker button as Henry's voice filled the room.

"Erm...er...Henry?"

"Indeed, sir. I apologise for bothering you, but lunch is ready. If it's not convenient, I can put it away," said Henry, sensing that the timing might not be ideal."

"We'll be there in a jiffy, thanks, Henry," said Marcus, switching off his phone and gazing into Cathy's green eyes to see them wet with tears.

"That was so beautiful, my darling Marcus."

Marcus kissed away her tears, and they both couldn't help laughing at each other.

"He knows what just went down. I feel like a kid who's just got caught with his finger in the cookie jar," said Marcus, laughing.

"Well, Captain, I have a confession to make."

"Now seems to be as good a time as any," smiled Marcus, pulling her body even closer.

"Well, I can confirm that you can sweep my chimney anytime, anyplace."

"I'm falling in love with you, Cathy, but you do know that I'm... erm... twenty-something years older than..."

"I know. So, you'll need to look after me when I'm older," Cathy said, pressing her moist lips to his. "Let's have lunch. I suddenly feel very hungry."

After lunch, they headed up to the upper terrace and enjoyed the bubbly that Henry had thoughtfully provided.

Marcus's mobile buzzed and vibrated on the ornate wrought iron table beside him.

"Hi Emily, what's up?"

"I've got Major Freddy Carr on the secure line, sir – shall I put him through?"

"Sure," Marcus waited for the new enigma-esque technology to activate, which had recently been upgraded to meet the latest state-of-the-art security standards.

"Hello Freddy, how are you? You must be psychic, I was just about to call you," said Marcus, lying.

"Bloody good show in Abu Dhabi. We're still evaluating all the goodies you passed to our chap there. Glad you made it out. I was sorry to hear about one of your team taking a clip, but I understand he's well on the mend. And what can I say, Abdulaziz Badawi is also in the bag, a very acceptable plus to the mission, plus the cash, of course, which was blown up along with the al-Malik," said Major Carr with a serious tone. "We got footage today from Sparrow confirming everything on film, no conceivable comeback on that operation. No evidence can ever be found. It's all clean."

"Good to hear. Did you get the stuff from Tits?" Marcus asked.

"Affirmative. Good work, and it helps," said Major Carr.

"Good to hear," said Marcus.

"Okay, we'll address that once we have the rest under control," Major Carr said.

The silence was so prolonged that Carr wondered if he'd lost the connection. "Are you still there, Marcus?"

"Sorry, I've been thinking about Chiddington – he might be connected."

"Why, how come you think that?"

"My chap Gibbs, as you know, has a 24/7 surveillance on Badawi and followed him down to Kent. It seems he visited Sir James Chiddington recently, which, of course, implicates him as a player. I mean, anything's possible, right? I'll update my mate Bob Brimley – Chief Constable of Kent now, and no doubt he'll be in touch with you. What's noteworthy is that Chiddington's hosting a drinks party in a day or two, to which Dr Meer is invited, and, no doubt, Badawi will be there too. So, we'll have them both at the same event!" said Marcus.

"Interesting, but let's keep most of this on a 'need to know' basis. Not sure who to trust these days regarding our boys in blue, Marcus. There have been some rumours floating around recently from my colleagues here and from our contacts within MI5 that there's a possible bad guy in the mix. By all means, chat to your chum Brimley about the latest on Badawi's likely involvement with the missing girl, but let's keep any developments on Doctor Meer to ourselves. You've got all that under tight control, so no need to involve anyone else in the police or, indeed, the Special Branch," said Major Freddy Carr, carefully.

"Fair enough. By the way, I wanted to discuss your chap I met in Abu Dhabi – Penny filled me in on some of his background, and I've got an idea brewing that might work, but I'd like to speak to him."

"No problem. I'll ask him to give you a buzz," said Major Carr, sounding intrigued.

"I've got Cathy Meer with me. I'll put us on speaker, alright?"

"No problem."

"Good morning, Major, good to talk, and thank you for your involvement in all of this. I got a rather posh-looking envelope in the mail this morning, with a red seal and an impressive-looking crest on it, but I was in a bit of a rush to leave the house, so I haven't got round to opening it yet," she said, winking at Marcus. "But I've got it here," Cathy added, reaching past the reassuring bulk of the SIG in her bag to retrieve it. “Yes, it’s an invitation from Sir James Chiddington for this Saturday.”

“So, there we have it. Not much notice, but maybe an opportunity to figure out a way to entrap this bugger, Asif. Reason why I’d like to chat to Dankworth – think he might be just the chap to run with what I’ve got in mind,” said Marcus.

“Good to talk with you, Dr Meer. I wonder, Marcus, if you’d be free early evening today, because by then I’ll have more feedback on the stuff you provided from the Abu Dhabi show and the Badawi intel," said Freddy Carr.

"Sure, good idea,” said Marcus, looking at Cathy, who nodded in agreement.

"Right. Let’s meet up at The Pale Horse, say around 6ish?"

“A deal, see you then,” said Freddy, signing off.

"Cathy, are you really good with me going?”

No problem, darling. I’ve got the children to sort out, and by the time I get back, they and Monica will be pleased to see me and sharing dinner. Carter’s covering my six, right?” smiled Cathy, giving him a warm kiss.

"Affirmative,” Marcus responded.

• CHAPTER 26 •

Captain Marcus de Vere relaxed in the garden, sipping his favourite Mount Gay Eclipse rum, which the friendly landlord of The Pale Horse had specifically reserved for him. The Pale Horse epitomised an ideal English country inn, with mossy slate tiles, roses decorating the porch, and a quaint garden subtly decorated with understated parasols. Marcus was waiting for Major Freddy Carr, MI6, to join him. It didn't take long. He watched his longtime friend and former SAS colleague, who later became his MI6 chief while serving with E Squadron, approach confidently. Freddy's broad shoulders moved smoothly as he carried a pint of Black Knight, a top-quality local brew.

"Freddy, good to see you. Look, I'll get straight to it. I've spent some time considering how best to bring down our friend Asif Badawi. As I told you, Doctor Cathy Meer has received an invitation from Sir James Chiddington to one of his exclusive drinks parties at Chiddington Hall this Saturday, and I'm fairly sure Badawi's on the guest list. It made me consider some sort of scenario whereby we might be able to entrap him, down the line," said Marcus, fervently.

"Okay, what's on your mind? But remember, we're on the UK mainland – we can't appear to be engaging in any obvious dodgy entrapment caper by the authorities. That said, I'm listening carefully," replied Major Carr.

"I understand, but hear me out. I have an idea if everything works out. When I was in Abu Dhabi, I gave all the jewels to Dankworth, as you know. At least, that's who Penny believed it was, since he wasn't very open about his name, if you catch my meaning. Do you know him well?" smiled Marcus.

"Bloody hell, yes, I know him very well, he's one of a kind, a legend, and yes, Penny was spot on, as usual – he was the guy deployed to pick up the loot from you and personally hand it over to me. He's getting on a bit, as you might have noticed, but he's still razor-sharp and definitely dangerous to those who... erm... stray from an unacceptable path, shall we say," chuckled Freddy.

"Understood from Penny that he's got a place down in Gloucestershire, and I'd like to reach out?"

"No problem. I'll have him contact you. What's on your mind? I know for a fact that he's back at his estate now. He's been running a covert operation there for us for some years, as Penny probably mentioned. He owns the property, which has been in his family for generations. However, we approached him quite a while ago now to undertake various scenarios for us on an ongoing basis. With his impeccable background and experience in all things black, it was a no-brainer. And so, with off-the-books taxpayer funding, we set up the property to meet our security requirements," advised Major Freddy Carr.

"Perfect. So, it's off the grid then?" Marcus grinned.

"Way, way off. But before we get to all that, I want to fill you in on the enormous value of the treasure chest you handed over to Dankworth."

"Fire away then," said Marcus, eager to discover the potential value of the goodies he had obtained in the Abu Dhabi raid.

"Well, you and your team did a bloody good job over there, and some of the computer material was really hot. The biggest bombshell in the package was, thanks to you and your lads, complete specifics on a threat to the PM. We've got a timeline, date, and detailed plans for a major hit on Chequers," said Major Carr, enthusiastically.

"Bloody hell!" said Marcus, incredulous. Pondering the PM's retreat that has provided fresh air and open space for sitting prime ministers since 1917, when it was gifted to the nation by Conservative minister Sir Arthur Lee and his American heiress wife, Ruth. He had spent some time there in the past, on occasion, working with the MET's Protection Command and knew it reasonably well. It is a 10-bedroom country house with a putting green, a heated indoor swimming pool in the Orangery, and 1,500 acres of lawns.

"Yeah, we'll get Him out, of course, but it's an audacious plan, and if we hadn't known about it, all hell would have broken loose. I mean, can you imagine our PM being taken out? It's unthinkable. We're preparing a warm welcome for them, and there'll be no survivors, at least, as far as I'm concerned, just between you and me, if you catch my drift. Plus, there's a bunch of other high-profile stuff, so Marcus, the country thanks you and your team. And, as you probably know, the CIA, Mossad, and others are all in on the outcome in Abu Dhabi. Also, of course, all the right people here in government know where we got this intelligence. So, well done again, mate."

"Thanks, Freddy. I must say I'm stunned to hear of the threat to our PM. Look, getting back to the present issue, there's going to be a drinks party at Chiddington Hall – a large estate nearby from me, this Saturday, it's owned by Sir James Chiddington but the thing is that my surveillance guy, As I mentioned the other day my chap Gibbs's been tailing Badawi and found that he'd visited Sir James recently and that seems to confirm that he's in the game along with Badawi. With those players in mind, I've an idea brewing. Did you manage to get through to the Colonel?"

"Affirmative, Marcus. He said he'd get to you ASAP," said Major Freddy Carr.

"Great. So, any updates on the information Tits sent you?"

"Well, he did an excellent job. Emily sent me all the files, plus a few tapes and DVDs, which will undergo the usual forensic examination and DNA testing to determine whether there are any connections to the threat to Doctor Meer. Meanwhile, we're reviewing, alongside GCHQ, the list of Badawi's contacts. You mentioned that Gibbs is monitoring Badawi constantly, so we'll see what he discovers as we progress," concluded Major Freddy Carr.

Back at his home office, Marcus sat at his desk, reviewing the latest developments from his company's international and domestic activities when his phone buzzed, causing him to jump uncharacteristically.

"Yes, Emily?"

"A Colonel Charlie Dankworth is asking for you on the secure line. Should I connect him?"

Marcus sat upright, surprised by the promptness of the response to his request.

"Yes, please," said Marcus, lighting a cigarette as he waited, then stepped out onto the terrace to sit in his favourite rattan chair. The weather was much too warm to resist.

"Colonel, thanks for calling," said Marcus, pleased that the enigmatic colonel had responded so promptly.

"Our mutual friend advised me that you'd reached out. So, how can I be of assistance?" said the plummy voice that Marcus remembered so well from their encounter outside the British Embassy in Abu Dhabi.

Marcus explained in detail his conversation with Major Freddy Carr and the latest news that Asif Badawi was very likely to be a guest at Chiddington's drinks party this coming Saturday and that Doctor Cathy Meer had received an invitation which she would accept.

"Interesting, so what do you have in mind, Marcus?" said the Colonel, using his first name to soften the engagement, recalling he had been a tad distant during their first meeting.

"My idea is that, since all the players will be there, I thought perhaps we could come up with a plan to trap Badawi later, as he is our main threat concerning Doctor Cathy Meer and her family," said Marcus, cautiously.

"Reasonable, so expand on that," said the Colonel, sounding genuinely captivated.

"Look, I'm just putting this out there, but if you consider coming to join the party, you could pose as a relative of Cathy's, perhaps her uncle, and invite her and the children to your estate next Saturday at a moment when Asif is nearby or ideally when he's speaking to her, to register your invitation. I mean, we now know for certain, as I said, that he's our boy, and I'm quite sure he'll be using all his charm to get what he can from her. Cathy's fully on board and can feed him whatever he wants to hear. Then we can set a trap for him if he's tempted. Let's face it, the scenario would be irresistible for him. After all, in his mind, it would be a simple walk in the park to take out a helpless woman with two small children and, with respect, only an ageing relative to deal with," said Marcus, carefully.

There was a long silence, and Marcus wondered if the Colonel had gone off the line or if he'd gone too far with the age comment. Then...

"I like it. I must say I really like it. I'll be Uncle Charlie for the day, why not? Anything to finally bring this bugger down? Why don't we meet up that morning before the party starts? And we can put everything together and give Dr Meer a bit of coaching at the same time on the entrapment business," offered the Colonel.

"May I ask two questions?" Marcus asked.

"Fire away."

"Well, I know from Major Carr that your property has...erm...various activities going on at any one time, but do you have a safe room?"

"No. Not a safe room but a completely self-sufficient, fully secure three-bedroomed apartment underground with every facility you can imagine," chuckled Colonel Charlie Dankworth.

"Perfect, I can't wait to see it. Second question, would your facility be free of...erm...guests? Or is the time frame impractical? It's not much notice, but if we're going to play, then the next weekend suits for the invite. I understand from Freddy that you can be a little busy down there from time to time."

"That's true, Marcus," chuckled the Colonel. "But the timing isn't an issue. I'll ensure no extra guests are around to cause trouble. We want to avoid any collateral damage if things get heated. I have enough flexibility to pause activities here if needed, and I'm fully authorised under my agreement with MI6 to invite anyone I choose at any time – so that's settled," replied Colonel Charlie Dankworth. "However, your suggestion could be seen as potential entrapment by some. While I'm glad to see Badawi face justice and everyone gets what they deserve, we must also demonstrate to the authorities that we're operating within the rules when everything unfolds. Remember, we're on UK soil, so it's best to avoid creating issues. Understood?"

"I understand. Freddy implied that. So?"

"So, once we've got Badawi in play, meaning he takes the bait, Major Carr will need to formally inform Special Branch, the Chief Constable of Gloucestershire, and MI5 of the threat. I've read Badawi's file, and let's face it. If Badawi plays to our tune, he's no fool and will recognise a potential trap or at least be prepared for the likelihood of one. He'll come fully armed with a team – just to be sure. It's simply in his nature, judging by his profile. So, it could get a little hairy. Got it?"

"Got it. Glad to hear you're on board, Colonel," Marcus said with a relieved sigh. "Freddy told me it's quite likely that Badawi has a team here in the UK that's currently under their radar. But as soon as they surface, they'll be on it."

There was a brief pause, then Markus asked, "So, it's a go then, Colonel. See you at Little Manor at, say, 09:00 hours on Saturday?"

"Affirmative. Our second date then. It seems our relationship is becoming serious. Looking forward to it. Sounds like fun. What would you prefer, chocolates or flowers? I'm a bit out of practice in the dating department," said the Colonel, chuckling as he hung up.

"Emily, could you put Dr Meer on the secure line, please?"

"Hi Marcus, good to hear from you. What was that funny sound I heard for a few seconds while I was waiting for you?"

"Oh, I've updated our communication systems, so what you heard was just the new secure line tech-stuff kicking in, darling. All my offices, including this one, have now been upgraded using advanced Electronic Bug Sweep equipment every morning, and the use of an improved state-of-the-art secure line just tops that all off."

"That sounds a little paranoid," laughed Cathy.

"Far from it. On the contrary, our offices around the world handle, on a daily basis, a multitude of highly sensitive material – people's lives and identities are often at risk, and they rely on us to keep them and their loved ones safe from malicious eavesdroppers and those who wish them harm. Not forgetting issues of national security here in the UK, as well as concerns affecting the safety and well-being of allied states," said Marcus, his tone serious.

"Sorry, I wasn't thinking. I can understand all the cloak-and-dagger stuff with the phone, etc.," said Cathy, hiding her growing feelings of trepidation now that she had increasingly begun to fully grasp the world of risk that Marcus lived with and needed to navigate 24/7.

Marcus slowly and carefully detailed his plan to trap Asif and updated her on his discussions with Colonel Charlie Dankworth and Major Freddy Carr. The line went silent for such a long time that he nearly thought he had lost her as well, and he was about to ask Emily to reconnect when she finally came back online.

"I understand, Marcus, that I'm essentially the bait here, and I'm ready and willing for that and feel without any doubt that it's time to bite the bullet. However, I'll probably need a bit of advice on what I should say or how to respond to this bastard, as we now know he's our boy," said Cathy, using the parlance she'd grown accustomed to. But she felt a little more apprehensive than her tone suggested.

"Yes, I agree with you. But this is a credible opportunity to finally pin this chap down, if he takes the bait. I can tell you now, without any doubt, that if this works, you and your children will be completely safe. There's a secure room at the Colonel's property, and we'll have all angles covered and enough firepower if it comes to a firefight. And while we're on that subject, I want to say that should that eventuality come to pass, I can assure you of one thing, off the record, and that is that Asif will not be walking away! At least not as far as Freddy and I are concerned. Look, Cathy, the reality right now is to focus on our priority, that is, to get our act together and do our job at the drinks party, and I'll be there with you all the way because, for all intents and purposes, I'll be your partner for the day. The Colonel and Major Carr will meet us at my home that morning at 09.00 hours, to run through everything." Marcus said reassuringly.

"I understand, I'm on board. Can't wait to start sailing," said Cathy, hanging up.

• CHAPTER 27 •

At Cathy's request, Monica had taken the children to London Zoo for the day shortly after breakfast. If she had wondered why Cathy wasn't coming, she hadn't questioned it, and Cathy hadn't said anything, not wanting to alarm her at this stage.

Doctor Cathy Meer, Captain Marcus de Vere, Major Freddy Carr, and Colonel Charlie Dankworth sat conspiratorially on one of the balconies overlooking the gardens at Little Manor, enjoying coffee and a smoke. They relaxed slightly before getting to the nitty-gritty of planning the proposed entrapment. Much to Marcus's amusement, the Colonel was in his usual outfit plus the tie; the only difference being that today, since their first meeting, he'd added a pair of very English tan Barbour chukka boots.

"Well, Cathy, it's a pleasure to finally meet you. Marcus has told me all about you, and I must say I'm impressed for many reasons. So, do I seem like a decent uncle to you?" said the Colonel with a comforting smile.

"Absolutely, Colonel, but what should I call you later?" Cathy asked, her eyes fixed intently on the colonel.

"Uncle Charlie, of course – what else? Okay, let's get to it. We now know for sure that Asif is our man. Think of this as a stage play, with Chiddington's drinks party as the setting and us as actors playing our parts. No pressure, Cathy, but you're the star and will be in the spotlight. Your role is vital – so, as I mentioned – no pressure," the Colonel said with a smile. "Asif now believes you are the widow of the SAS soldier who killed his three brothers, and I'm sure he wants to see you face-to-face for closure. If we were outside the UK, he'd likely have made his move already, but so would we, and he'd be dust. But since we're on our home turf, we'll use that to our advantage. The only thing that matters now is that we all play our part on Chiddington's stage to try and suck Badawi in. On the face of it, I can't see any reason why he should be suspicious of us," the Colonel added with a steely glint in his eyes.

"I understand," Cathy said, growing more confident and engaging more fully with her role.

"What we don't know is what part Sir James plays in this game and whether he's even a player, other than being the catalyst, if you like – we assume he's unaware of Asif's plan to kill you. We don't think Sir James would leave himself open to anything untoward happening in front of so many people. And we're certain that Asif won't intend to kill you there. It, obviously, wouldn't make any sense for him to consider that as an option. He wants to eliminate you and your family, Cathy, without witnesses. And we are giving him the perfect opportunity to do just that at no risk to you and the children," explained Colonel Charlie Dankworth.

"Okay, so how do we play it?" Cathy asked, gradually embracing her new role and her uncle, even as he openly discussed the murder of her and her children.

"I think he's going to try to worm his way into our conversation, probably introduced by Sir James to get things started. You'll be paired with Marcus for the event, so it's very likely he'll try to establish who he is early on, and you'll introduce him by his full name as a friend. There's no point in hiding Marcus's identity. Plus, it's quite likely that Asif might recognise him anyway. I mean, it's a pretty small world in Abu Dhabi. If not, he'll certainly know of de Vere Security since they're a well-known and respected security firm, responsible for, among other things, the marina's security, where his father, a client of de Vere Security, keeps his yacht. That, I think, should spark a conversation, especially since his father's super yacht, the al-Malik, went...erm...missing recently," said the Colonel with a wry smile to Marcus. "I don't know anything about a missing yacht," said Cathy.

"Forget about it. It's not relevant to our conversation today. Sorry, it just slipped out," said the Colonel.

"Alright, what should I watch out for?" Cathy asked cautiously.

"Look, the key is to come across as friendly and relaxed. He's attractive and used to attracting women, and he's known to be a sexual predator. Please don't exaggerate, but it's fine to show you find him interesting, play to his vanity a little. Just don't overdo it. He's on a fishing trip, so expect questions about your husband's job or why he's not with you, or if he's on business trips, etc. Avoid revealing that he was KIA or similar too soon; Asif will suspect something. Talk about trivial things and let him take the lead. He'll try to gather information, but be reserved if he asks about your husband's fate. Don't give details too readily, or he might think you're too eager to share private info. Asif isn't naive, but he'll subtly find ways to get what he wants using charm or other tricks. That's all I can advise. We'll adapt as we go. Whatever happens, you're clearly not in danger; we have you protected," said the Colonel as he headed to the driveway. "Carter and Anna will be nearby, ready if anything goes wrong, but it won't, Cathy. Stay strong," added the Colonel, regretful that he mentioned possible risks.

"Colonel, one thing I must emphasise is that if the consequences of our actions here and the intelligence from Marcus's team monitoring him confirm that Badawi is a clear and imminent threat to Dr Meer and her family, then I would need to put on my official hat and report it to the Assistant Commissioner of Specialist Operations so they can take over with a team over the weekend of Cathy and the children's visit. Yes, the Sanctuary is a government-sanctioned location, even though it's off the grid. However, I believe it's reasonable to argue to the authorities, if necessary, that Cathy and the kids are weekend guests of the Colonel; after all, why not? That will be clear to anyone reviewing it later. And, as I mentioned, once your team has positive feedback indicating Asif's intention to respond aggressively, I will need to formalise it and arrange for the proper response team to be on site," said Major Freddy Carr.

"Understood, and I agree, Freddy," said the colonel.

As they wandered out to the driveway of Little Manor, the Colonel linked arms with Cathy, with a touch of affection and respect.

"Oh, by the way, my dear, I'd very much like to introduce you to my girlfriend. She's been a constant and faithful companion for over forty years, and as you can see, she's patiently waiting to take us to the event," as he opened the passenger door of his classic gunmetal grey Bentley.

"Oh my God, Colonel, this is simply stunning," as she sank into the plush, deep red leather. "I can see it's a Bentley, but what is it?"

"This, my dear, is a 1952 Mark 6 saloon, inline 6-cylinder, 4.5 litres of pure British heritage, enjoy. Jump in the back, Marcus," grinned the Colonel as the engine came to life with a delightful throaty rumble, quickly replaced by a satisfyingly eager roar as he put metal to metal. Cathy took in the beautiful walnut dash dotted with various dials. She had a photographic memory and took mental notes for George later, as the Colonel gave her a rundown on the specs while they made their way to the party.

"My son would love this, Colonel."

"Uncle Charlie to you, my dear, at least for the day. Don't forget our stage debut is about to begin now!"

Cathy, Marcus, and the Colonel arrived at Chiddington Hall to start their debut performance and were greeted warmly by

Sir James's butler, Charles. Cathy felt confident but, understandably, wary. He led them into a large drawing room that overlooked the landscaped gardens. It was a comfortably warm day, and the opulent French windows and doors were widely open. Marcus nodded to one or two guests he knew, and all three gladly accepted the champagne that Charles, graciously, had brought on a large, antique, heavy-looking solid silver salver with a thick cast border and feet.

"Please help yourselves to anything you wish; there's an assortment of salmon and cucumber sandwiches, along with a variety of cheeses, as you can see. The cooler has a selection of white and pink wines, and reds are on the wine rack - enjoy. I'm sure Sir James will be along shortly to welcome you personally." With that, he glided away, leaving the three to mentally prepare for their upcoming performances while they took in the splendour of their surroundings.

As they sampled the fare on offer, a tall, distinguished-looking gentleman in his sixties approached, whom Cathy assumed was Sir James. He was elegantly dressed, with a Household Division Guards silk scarf casually draped around his neck and shoulders over an impeccably tailored linen suit.

"Marcus, my dear chap, delighted you could make it. Perhaps you could introduce me to your entourage," said Sir James, taking in his two companions with undisguised interest. "Ah, but wait a moment, I recognise our new local celebrity, Dr Meer, I believe. You are more than welcome," he added with suffocating charm as he reached out to shake her hand.

"Pleased to meet you too, Sir James, and thank you very much for your kind, albeit unexpected, but welcome invitation," replied Cathy, slightly unsettled by his manner and the way his eyes seemed to devour her body in one sweep, with an obviously well-practised gesture. "And may I introduce my uncle Charlie, who's just here for the day. I hope you don't mind having an uninvited guest?"

"Of course, not, my dear, and where are you from... erm... Uncle... er... Charlie?'

"Oh, I have a little place in Gloucestershire. Popping back in the morning, as it happens. It's been a treat to see Cathy and the children again," replied the Colonel.

"I trust we're not a tad too early, Sir James, as there don't seem to be many guests floating about at the moment," enquired Marcus, changing the subject.

"Not too many yet. Early days, but a few are enjoying the clement weather outside on the grounds. Have no fear, you'll meet everyone as the mingling starts to pick up. So, Marcus, good to see you again. How's business? I'm sure you're taking every measure to keep us all safe and sound both here and elsewhere," said Sir James, with what seemed to Marcus a twinkle in his eye. What that meant, he was unsure.

"We try to do our best, as always, Sir James," said Marcus with a wry smile.

"I wonder, Dr Meer, if you'd like to take a quick peek around the house before it all gets too busy?"

"Thank you. I'd be delighted. I understand from Marcus that you've got quite an impressive library," said Cathy.

"Well, I wouldn't go as far as to say that, but you're most welcome. Please follow me, my dear," he said, leading her down a magnificent hall, its walls festooned with a variety of hunting and military prints, towards a pair of ancient oak doors.

As they entered, she was surprised by the size of it. The walls were lined with time- stained oak shelving, more than enough to support the collection of heavy tomes on display, many with extravagant leather bindings.

"The library also doubles as my study, as you can see," said Sir James, gesturing towards an antique bureau Plat Desk at the far end.

"My goodness, it's a fabulous piece with a very distinct French flavour, I think," said Cathy, awestruck by its splendour.

"Spot on. You have an excellent eye, my dear; it's French Empire 1930s," said Sir James, unable to hide his sense of pride. "And if you're interested, I've a few first editions over here that may amuse you. But if you wish to handle any, please use the gloves on the nearby table," he added, guiding her to a small section tucked away in a back corner of the library.

Cathy was, once again, awestruck as she noted some of the titles: 'In Our Time' – Ernest Hemingway. 'Pride and Prejudice' – Jane Austen. 'A Christmas Carol' – Charles Dickens. 'Casino Royale' – The Great Gatsby. The list of prestigious, extremely rare 1st editions seemed endless. Sir James walked up to her and took the Great Gatsby, 1st edition, out of his gloved hand.

"Take a look at this, my dear," he said as he tried not to stare at her too much. It's particularly interesting as he pointed out the typo on the dust jacket, as you can see it was originally printed as by 'Jay' Gatsby with the 'J' in lower case and the error had to be corrected in ink by hand, as you will note", Sir James added.

"Fascinating, I guess that sort of error adds considerable value to a collector?"

"Absolutely."

"Thank you, Sir James, for your time. I must say, I'm truly impressed," Cathy said sincerely. "Oh, what's this? I didn't expect that. Are you a fan?" she asked, pointing to the framed lyrics on a Rolling Stones T-shirt hanging near his desk.

"Oh, that," he laughed. "Couldn't resist it. I... erm... picked it up at Camden Market about a year ago. Loved the lyrics, you know, 'you can't always get what you want' etc. – so true, don't you think?" Sir James chuckled.

"I suppose so. Is that really Mick's signature in the corner? I mean that would, truly, make it another collector's piece, wouldn't it?" laughed Cathy, surprised to find something so out of place in the timeline and content of his study.

"Erm...no...I have to admit that was me – a forgivable forgery, at least in my mind. But I...erm...just thought it added a touch of je ne sais quoi to it, don't you think?" He smiled. "Well, I suppose we should return to the fray and mingle," said Sir James, clearly beginning to tire of the exchange.

Cathy, thankfully, returned to Marcus and the Colonel and found them outside on the terrace, chatting with a few guests. As they moved away to join her, they politely nodded their departure from the group. Cathy filled them in on her interesting tour of the library as they sauntered back to the drawing room to help themselves to more wine and snacks. Sir James suddenly appeared, accompanied by an imposing figure, tall, slim, and very fit-looking. His Arab face seemed carved from sandstone, with hard edges, an aquiline nose, and piercing, narrow eyes that gave him a somewhat feral aspect.

"And so it begins, curtains up," the colonel whispered quietly to both of them.

The hairs on the back of Cathy's neck rose as she tried to come to terms with the fact that the man approaching was the one who had killed her husband. Nonetheless, she composed herself but had to admit that to many women, he would indeed be attractive, or at least they would give him the benefit of their attention. As they drew near, she noticed his impeccably tailored blazer bearing the regimental badge of the Light Dragoons, and she was well aware of their motto 'Viret in aeternum,' meaning 'It Flourishes Forever' – and she hoped that he himself wouldn't flourish for much longer.

"Dr Meer, may I introduce Mr Asif Badawi, a close and longstanding friend?" said Sir James in an overly polished tone.

She observed Ben Malone in the background; it wasn't unexpected since he was a prominent local figure.

"Delighted to meet you, Mr Badawi," said Cathy, smiling, wincing inwardly as he took her outstretched right hand and, instead of shaking it, grasped it gently and kissed it.

"And you, doctor. I recognised your face immediately – I'm sorry you had to endure the intrusive scrutiny from the local and national press about your involvement in that rather nasty murder...er...recently. That must have been quite an irritation for you," said Asif, trying to hide his growing sexual desire for her and his urge to kill.

"Par for the course in my business, I'm afraid, Mr Badawi," said Cathy, now fully immersed as the leading player in this increasingly complicated stage debut.

"Indeed, I believe I recognise one of your companions – Captain de Vere, if I'm not mistaken. Isn't it? We haven't met before, as far as I recall, but of course I've seen you around in Abu Dhabi from time to time," he said cautiously. His accent was as British as the Colonel's, but without the bonhomie.

"Yes, Abu Dhabi is such a small world that's more than likely, although I don't visit there often. I've got some competent people running the show there. My company, as you probably know, deals with, among other things, the security of various marina's and the harbour," replied Marcus, carefully.

"Yes, I do know. Interestingly, the name of your company came up just the other day in connection with one of my father's yachts. It apparently left without notifying the marina's authorities of its departure, as per protocol," said Asif, his narrow eyes fixing intently on Marcus.

"Really, how so?" asked Marcus carefully.

"Apparently, it just up-anchored and left, as I said, without notification. Along with my father, presumably; at least, that's what I heard from his household staff, as he seems to have vanished too," replied Asif, his eyes once again boring into Marcus's.

Marcus feigned deep thought. "Yes, come to think of it, I do recall a report from my people on that, but my chaps patrol the marina and harbour twenty-four seven, so if they'd seen anything untoward, it would've been dealt with on the spot. So, what actually happened then? As I said, I've had no indication of anything unusual from my people," said Marcus.

"I have no idea either, but as I said, its departure did not follow normal protocol. So, it's a bit of a mystery, but it's none of my business anyway. You see, my father and I don't chat too often these days since we rarely see eye to eye, but I'm sure he's looking into it, wherever he might be. It can't have been hijacked or something, or your security people would have been on top of that, right?"

"Of course. I'm sure the reason for its departure will become clear in the fullness of time," said Marcus. Hoping that was the end of it.

"To be honest, I really don't care either way. My father has unlimited resources. I mean, after all, he owns the largest yacht charter company in the region. And anyway, as I said, it's not really my concern. Perhaps it's as simple as him deciding to take a trip somewhere or other," said Asif, now making light of it.

"May I introduce my uncle, Charlie Dankworth, Mr Badawi. He's here just for the day to see me and the children, and I thought Sir James might not mind an extra mouth to feed," said Cathy, attempting to steer the conversation and shift the subject. Nearby, within earshot, Sir James waved his arms again in greeting towards the Colonel and Cathy, who both nodded in acknowledgement.

"So, what part of the country are you from exactly, sir?" said Asif, smiling warmly.

"I have a small place in the Gloucestershire countryside," replied the Colonel.

Beautiful county. Actually, I did have some friends living in Ampney St Mary a year or two ago, but sadly, they moved away. Do you know the village, Mr Dankworth?

"Of course, it's practically on my doorstep, a lovely village, probably only about half an hour or so from me. I live near Bibury, a lovely part of the world too," said the Colonel, beginning to sow the seeds.

Charles wandered by, offering refills.

"Ah, I remember this from last weekend, Charles," said Asif as he, in turn, offered up his empty glass.

"It's a Perrier-Jouet Blason Rosé, if I recall correctly, that I enjoyed during my last visit," said Asif, taking a satisfied sip.

"It is indeed, sir," said Charles, pleased.

"And Dr Meer, could you tell me your medical specialisation? I don't recall the press reports in detail, as I tend to avoid dwelling on murder cases. If I remember correctly, weren't you the pathologist involved in that gruesome barn murder? Is my memory accurate?" Asif asked.

"Correct, I was the registered Home Office Forensic Pathologist deployed, for my sins," replied Cathy, warming to the stage.

"Not too many sins, I trust, Dr Meer. And, so a detective of sorts then?" Asif asked, trying to engage and sound enthusiastic.

"I hadn't thought of it that way, but you're right. Each case is an intellectually demanding quest for truth, and once I have the victim before me, they communicate directly with me," Cathy said frankly.

"Interesting, and you, Mr Dankworth, from your bearing, it seems we might share a similar background. I suspect some military experience. Am I right?" asked Asif, trying not to appear too focused on his target. At this point, he was now fully convinced that she was the one he was seeking.

"Oh, well, I did dabble for a while, but that was... erm... centuries ago. And you? I see you're wearing the badge of the Light Dragoons," said the Colonel.

"Indeed, I spent a sojourn with them after graduating from Sandhurst," said Asif, patient as always.

Sir James strolled away, clearly eager to mingle with his other guests and nodded to signal his departure.

"Dr Meer, may I ask if you have children?"

"Oh yes, two. My daughter's seven and my son's ten."

"Charming, how joyful children can be. May I ask what they are doing this summer?"

"Going out for a spot of fresh air," Cathy replied, smiling at everyone and ignoring the question. Leaving the stage open for the Colonel and her need to have a puff and take a break, if only momentarily, from her starring role that was becoming a little overwhelming.

"Ah, I can answer that one," said the Colonel, stepping in to seize the welcome opportunity of Cathy's timely departure. "Actually, I've invited my niece and her children to my estate,

The Sanctuary, in Gloucestershire next weekend, as it happens. To cheer them all up. They love it there," said the Colonel, hopefully cementing the bait.

"Sounds like some spa or wellness centre. I hope it works for them," replied Asif, fishing.

"Oh, silly me, no, no, it's the name of my house, and I've got a few ponies for the children to ride, so, as I said, they love it there. Cathy's workload has been quite exhausting lately, so it will be a welcome rest and change of scene for her as well. Anyway, Mr Badawi, how is it you know Sir James so well?" said the Colonel, deftly changing the subject, delighted by Cathy's actions, leaving the stage open for him.

"Oh, I've had the pleasure of shooting here many times over the years during the season, but I have to say that I'm a bit shy of the cold at that time of year, not my cup of tea at all. But I must say that Will, his gamekeeper, is excellent and makes up for the inclement weather by providing a great variety of fast, high, and low birds to test my skills. I don't know how he manages it so consistently, but he does, every single time, and when I'm in London during the summer months, I never miss the chance to pop down to see Sir James, a close friend for many years. He always has some entertainment up his sleeve, and I'm always happy to get out of town for a bit," said Asif, hiding his excitement that all was going so well.

His work complete, Asif Badawi nodded his thanks and stepped outside to smoke, reflecting on the overwhelming success of his mission. He then sent a text to Syed Ayad, commanding him to locate 'The Sanctuary' in Bibury and to dispatch a drone immediately to photograph the house and grounds in detail, and to ensure that the images were on his desk first thing in the morning. He would kill her, of course, but not before taking her first. Seeing her in the flesh had intensified his lust for her, and then he planned to eliminate the children along with the upper-class fool of an uncle for good measure. But then, on reflection, had it all been too easy? Was he being set up? As always, he avoided taking things at face value, even though everything seemed secure at the moment. However, caution and meticulous planning remained essential. That focus had kept him alive over the years. Once he had scrutinised the surveillance images, he would plan his attack. After all, he had eight experienced fighters trained in Iran at his disposal. It always surprised him how porous the UK security environment was for people like him, given the context. He had the resources. He would know in the morning if it was a go or not.

If everything looked good, he'd launch a fully armed assault on the property, eliminate the old man, and then have his way with Dr Meer before taking her and her children down. Patience had always been crucial, and he would wait for the images. Cathy and Asif passed each other at the French doors of the drawing room as she returned. Cathy smiled and nodded in response to his similar gesture.

"Well done, Cathy. The perfect leading lady, you deserve an Oscar for your timing and performance – bravo. What a nice twist to leave at that moment," said the Colonel. "I do believe he's taken the bait." They stepped out into the sunshine to have a cigarette and mingle with the increasing number of guests.

“Badawi and Sir James seem very close, and even Ben Malone appears to know them well, but I suppose that’s not surprising,” said Marcus to the Colonel.

“Not our place to play or consider it right now, old boy. We have more urgent matters to attend to than their display of friendliness and its potential importance. One thing at a time, right? I think we should leave,” said the Colonel with a wink.

“Agreed,” Marcus said, taking Cathy’s arm as they waved thank you to Sir James.

As they jumped out of the car at Little Manor, Cathy reached out to give the Colonel a peck on the cheek. “Thanks for everything, but I really need to get home and prepare dinner for the children. They’ll be back from their day out soon. Oh, and thank you so much for the ride, Colonel. I’ll be giving my son George a full report of your car; he’ll be over the moon.”

The Colonel, pausing briefly, reached into the glove compartment and pulled out a photograph. ”If he’s so keen on this kind of motor, perhaps he’d like this,” said the Colonel as he handed her a picture of the car and a copy of its original manual.

“Wow, this is just great; he’ll be over the moon,” said Cathy, slipping into her Range Rover but not before giving Marcus a passionate kiss.

The Colonel raised an eyebrow at Marcus as Cathy drove off.

“Come on, Colonel, with all due respect, it’s the 21st century, and Cathy is a truly exceptional person, highly intelligent, strong-willed, and one of the most straightforward and feminine women I've ever met," said Marcus.

"Well, forgive an old soldier for being used to his ways when it comes to public displays of affection," replied the Colonel, embarrassed to reveal his old-fashioned thinking.

"Do you mind if I ask whether you ever took the plunge yourself?"

"Good God, man, there's no time for that kind of distraction. I was too busy dealing with those threatening our country, along with a few other tough encounters along the way. Do you understand? For Queen, now King, and Country, and all that," said the Colonel, hoping the conversation was over.

"So, who takes care of you?"

"Ah, that would be Katja. She's been with me for twenty-five years as my housekeeper and friend, and to top it all, she's an excellent Cordon Bleu chef as well. So, I've really got it in spades. She speaks five languages fluently. She and her late husband worked for Polish Intelligence until he was taken out, which she believes was by some obscure Nazi team; then she teamed up with MI6, working as an interpreter and translator until she retired. She keeps me on the straight and narrow and, much like your Penny, she's indispensable in helping me keep the show on the road. But you'll meet her next weekend, and even at nearly seventy, she's quite handy with that pistol designed by our friend Nikolay Fyodorovich Makarov," grinned the Colonel.

"9.27 calibre, I believe, from memory," said Marcus, warming to the sound of this lady.

"Yeah, and she keeps the bloody thing under her mattress. Takes it out every week or so for practice and cleaning. I suppose old habits die hard, but the funny thing is she's never told me from whom she... erm... liberated it, but I'm pretty sure he didn't live long enough to tell the tale!"

"Can't wait to meet her. Do you have a range down there?"

"Of course, I've got a bloody range. It's not a Butlins holiday camp for Christ's sake," laughed the Colonel, "but I suspect we'll be having some live practice before that weekend's out."

"So, what's your opinion on today, Colonel?" asked Marcus.

"Well, if he smelt a rat, I didn't see it. But he's a tricky chap to read, and either way, he's too canny to move in without a fully equipped team. I suspect he'll use a drone to take pictures of the estate's layout, to confirm, of course, that it's only poor old Uncle Charlie, Cathy and the children floating about."

"Assuming they'll be monitoring her progress. I'll have a quick word with our MI6 contacts to ensure we keep a discreet watch on her."

"Not necessary. Don't forget, Colonel, I've got The Twins watching her six, as Major Carr is fully aware."

"Ah, yes, of course. Carter and Anna. First class team, so I've heard."

"And I've also got Gibbs, another member of my team, monitoring Asif's movements 24/7, so we have his call on that."

"Good to hear."

"By the way, I'd really like to have one of my ex-SAS snipers at this party. What do you think?" asked Marcus, hopefully.

"I imagine you're referring to Anna. Her skills are well known to me, but it's unlikely they'll be sanctioned, old boy. If it comes to it, the security services would insist on a serving soldier taking that role. You know protocol and all that, and anyway, this is Blighty after all, not some hellhole in a remote sandy wasteland," grinned the Colonel, back to his old self again.

"Yeah, I suppose so. Anyway, I'll dwell on it all and give Freddy a ring once Gibbs's confirmed it looks like Badawi's taken the bait and has a team assembled. Thanks again for your help today, and I'll keep you in the loop, but I'm sure, in the meantime, you'll be having a chat with Freddy as well," said Marcus as he waved goodbye to the Colonel, roaring off in his gunmetal grey Bentley back to his Sanctuary.

• CHAPTER 28 •

Cathy gave no more thought to Badawi and focused on preparing dinner for the children. There was a roast lemon chicken and potatoes in the oven, nearly ready. She had just finished setting the table when the children burst through the door, perfect timing. After greeting everyone with hugs, she stepped back to listen to their stories about the day, which had gone very well. Looking lovingly at her children, she hoped they did not see anything in her behaviour or attitude that would reveal the deep distress and concern flooding her mind. Not for a moment since hearing that her family was in clear and present danger did she think of herself – George and Jenny were her life, and she was determined to protect them, whatever it took.

"George, I have something for you," Cathy said, reaching into her handbag for the picture of the Colonel's car. Her fingers brushed the cool, reassuring metal of the Sig as she did so.

“This is really awesome, Mum. Gosh, I can’t quite believe it. It’s a Bentley Mark 6, but I’ll need to check it out. Thanks, Mum,” said George, eager to get to his computer upstairs. Cathy wouldn’t be surprised to hear that he’d have the complete history and specifications from the manual memorised within the hour and be searching for a diecast model for his collection.

“I’m not done yet, George. Here’s a copy of the manual.”

“Oh, wow, that’s brilliant," said George.

“No problem, take your sister upstairs and get ready for dinner. I'll be back in twenty minutes. Does that work for you guys?" laughed Cathy, winking at Monica, who had just sat down after helping with dinner. The children nodded in agreement and disappeared.

"Monica, let’s pop outside to satisfy our vices,” chuckled Cathy as she mixed the dark spiced rum with ice for both of them. Given recent events, she was careful not to overindulge.

“How was your day?" Monica asked eagerly, keen to discover what was truly happening.

“Promise to fill you in later. Let’s sit down for a bit,” said Cathy, raising her glass in a toast as she savoured the familiar crackling of the ice blending with the dark rum.

“And how are you and Marcus doing?" Monica asked with a grin.

“He’s exactly what’s on the tin as you said," Cathy said, with an embarrassed smile.

“Right,” said Monica, hugging her as they clinked glasses.

"I've got a little present for you!" Monica suddenly exclaimed, surprising Cathy.

"Oh, goody. I love presents! What is it?"

"Not yet. I promised the children we'd give it to you before dinner, but I couldn't resist telling you," she smiled.

"Typical, now I'm overwhelmed with curiosity and anticipation. That's so unfair, Monica," she laughed.

"Something from the zoo, then. Maybe a penguin? You know it's one of my favourite aquatic friends," said Cathy, grinning.

Monica chuckled and replied, "You'll just have to wait and see."

And, when are you going to tell me what's really going on?" Monica asked, feeling the rum start to hit the spot.

"When the monsters are finally asleep, as I mentioned, I promise I'll fill you in on everything," said Cathy.

George and Jenny emerged onto the terrace, interrupting the moment. Jenny, her excitement palpable, handed the wrapped gift to her mum.

"You'll love it, mummy."

"I finished it yesterday, Cathy, but since this morning was so rushed, we all agreed that now was the right time to give it to you," Monica said with a smile as Cathy held it. She guessed it was a picture by the feel of the frame, and everyone was watching her as she carefully unwrapped the 10" x 12" package.

"Oh my God, it's truly breathtaking," Cathy said, wiping away a tear of joy as she looked at the oil painting of Fred the

Great Spotted Woodpecker. The bird's black, white, and red feathers were rendered with stunning colours, as if illuminated by the early morning light, which was likely the case. She adored how Monica had depicted her favourite bird, painting its head tilted to one side as if giving a cheeky hello.

Cathy exclaimed happily, “I didn’t realise you are such a talented artist in addition to all your writing skills. Thank you so much, Monica darling. I really couldn’t have asked for a more talented and creative friend,” said Cathy.

She joyfully admired the lovely image of Fred, her fingertips gently brushing the textured surface of the oil painting. It truly moved her from the moment she saw it. As they all enjoyed their roast chicken, she looked at Monica, once again, so happy that they had formed such a close bond. It was a full moon and so warm that they both sat on the terrace to finish their white Burgundy, which had accompanied their dinner, and to enjoy a puff or two.

Cathy recounted everything that occurred at the drinks party and the scheme she had devised to trap Asif Badawi. Monica listened closely, her eyes wide with interest, as she absorbed the details of the plan. Despite the cold moonlight, the atmosphere and air stayed warm and tense, likely aided by the excellent wine, which seemed to help keep the warmth.

“Oh my God. Well, I’m coming with you. If you don’t agree, I’ll just follow you down there anyway, and that’s that," Monica declared stubbornly.

“No, you’re not," Cathy said softly. "I won't risk your life as well."

“And yet you’re taking the children! And without me!” said Monica, bluntly.

There was a long silence as Cathy reflected that this was, in fact, a quite reasonable rebuff.

“I understand your feelings. Honestly, I’d feel the same in your position. I will ask Marcus to notify the Colonel that he will have one more guest. If there’s any issue with that, he will let me know. Otherwise, I don’t see any reason why it should be a problem, Monica, so we’re all set. We plan to leave on Friday morning. The arrival time has been moved to 11:30, as requested by Marcus and the Colonel. They believe that any armed threat is now more likely to occur early Saturday morning. My role, as you might see it, begins after lunch. This is important because they expect a drone flyover of The Sanctuary in the afternoon, to observe that his targets are there and unaware of the threat against them. I’ll ring the schools to inform them that the children will be away on that day.”

Monica stayed silent as she began to process everything Cathy had shared. Cathy looked at her, begging her to trust that everything would be alright.

Cathy said confidently, taking Monica’s hands. "Clearly, say nothing to them. I will tell them on Thursday evening that we’re going on a weekend trip. After I inform George about the Bentley, he won’t be able to wait, and Jenny will have ponies to ride, giving both of them something to look forward to."

The two women embraced, then Monica headed down Cathy’s driveway towards her cherished cottage to reflect on the upcoming events. She, like Cathy, had no doubts that Marcus and the assembled team would be there to protect them. As she watched Monica walk away, Cathy burst into tears – she'd held her emotions in check when with others but now, alone, she allowed herself the relief to release the tension that had been building inside her.

• CHAPTER 29 •

07.00 The Sanctuary

The Tudor property was concealed behind two grand, electronically controlled wrought-iron gates decorated with intricate hunting scenes. Seeing them open invitingly, Marcus drove his Subaru Forester along the quarter-mile driveway to The Sanctuary. Unofficially and illegally, he carried a loaded SIG Sauer P226 with SIG .375 rounds; he wasn't sure about carrying, but he found it comforting, nonetheless.

He preferred this weapon over his usual Glock 19 today, holstered in a leather rig under his left arm, a long-standing habit, and carried two 10-round magazines in his back pockets. Wearing a light summer linen jacket, it was obvious to any trained eye, but he knew he'd address that when necessary. The house was situated on approximately twenty acres of meticulously landscaped grounds, with an ancient oak forest bordering the eastern edge. Upon arrival, Colonel Charlie Dankworth greeted him and directed him to park his car, along with others, in the various barns surrounding the house.

The Colonel said, "We don't want Badawi to notice our welcoming party, especially since he'll likely fly another drone over later today to assess the situation."

"Affirmative," replied Marcus as he manoeuvred his car, as instructed. The Colonel followed to padlock the barn, just as all the others had been, except for two.

One containing the Colonel's eight-seater Land Rover, which he'd soon be using to take the team for a thorough reconnaissance of the estate. It would then be left conveniently nearby in case it was needed for any pursuit that might arise later. The remaining open barn housed his pride and joy: the Bentley, with its classic gunmetal-grey nose peeking out in all its glory, waiting for everyone's appreciation.

Walking back to the main entrance of the house, where several people were huddled together, chatting among themselves. Marcus noted Major Freddy Carr waving him over to one side before introducing him to anyone.

"Marcus, I contacted the Assistant Commissioner of Specialist Operations last night to advise that a terrorist attack was imminent here and received a call back first thing this morning from the designated Ground Commander, Chief Inspector Johnny Brinkworth, who, by the way, I know from a few previous similar scenarios. He's a good bloke, and I gave him a full update on the people you've deployed. Brinkworth knows of you by reputation and is looking forward to meeting with you, and is delighted that your people have been deployed by you, but made it clear that you and your team are under his command. Apparently, he knows Carter very well – so it's all good. He and his team are waiting for us, and he'll be giving a Brief shortly on the applicable protocol for this operation," said Major Carr.

"Okay, Gibbs is keeping an eye on Badawi's progress and placed a tracker on their vehicle a few days ago, just in case he loses them," Marcus replied.

"Good to hear. I want to introduce... erm, let's call him Willy," said Major Carr.

Marcus scrutinised the young man, noting his fit appearance. The soldier was dressed in full camouflage combat gear, devoid of any insignia, suggesting he was a member of the Special Air Service. He carried an L96A1 sniper rifle slung over his shoulder and a SIG Sauer P320 .375 at his belt, at least, that was Marcus's impression. The soldier had been standing nearby, waiting patiently. As Marcus approached, he observed the soldier's relaxed stance and quiet confidence, which, to Marcus's trained eye, resembled those of his team in Abu Dhabi and throughout his active service. Marcus has always appreciated that the Regiment consistently produces men of the highest calibre.

"Willy, meet Captain Marcus de Vere," Major Freddy Carr introduced the soldier to Marcus. As Marcus observed him closely, he thought that this was the picture of a man not to be messed with at any level.

"Good morning, Captain. That's a name I've heard quite a few mates mention from time to time, boss," said the young man with respect and a slight grin. "I understand there was a bit of a fireworks party in Abu Dhabi recently," grinned the soldier.

"It's a small world," Marcus smiled.

"In our game, that's an affirmative," Willy replied.

"Hereford?" Marcus asked with a wry smile, looking at Freddy. While their exchanges continued, the group gathered at the entrance of the mansion waited patiently for the three men to join them.

"Yes, boss," said the SAS soldier now with a much broader grin, recognising Marcus immediately, for sure, as one of his own.

"How long have you been on site... er... Willy?" asked Marcus.

"18 minutes, more or less, boss," said Willy, checking the MX-10 watch on his left wrist, a Nite's bulletproof field watch issued as standard kit to UK SAS forces and officially NATO-certified.

"Right, so what have you been doing so far?"

"Sod all, boss – just waiting. That's our speciality, isn't it?" said the soldier, lighting a cigarette and offering his pack of Camels to anyone interested, both Captain de Vere and Major Freddy Carr accepted.

"Right. So, what do you know so far?"

"I received a full brief, including floor plans, aerial shots of the estate, and other details last night, along with the other team members, I believe. The operation has been fully approved, but I haven't yet met everyone involved," Willy said, gesturing toward the group near the house's main entrance.

"Good. So, what's your take on it all so far, soldier?" Marcus asked.

"If I were this Bad Boy boss, I'd come in the early hours, no question. And I'd bring in my boys through the wood."

"Why?"

"In my opinion, boss, daylight isn't an option. Based on what I've heard, he's a cautious strategist who wouldn't risk being caught in the open by crossfire from any welcoming party waiting for him and his crew. His initial drone sweep would have provided him with all the necessary intelligence to plan the attack. But on that front, he'll likely send another drone shortly to verify that everything appears legitimate and to visually confirm that his targets are present and unguarded."

"And? What happens next?" asked Marcus, impressed by the soldier's assessment so far.

"Well, as to the approach, I'd go straight for the woods, boss."

"Why?"

"Cover, access, and ease of withdrawal. It's quite a shallow wood used by the estate for rough shooting, so I would expect that the estate's gamekeepers' ground maintenance would clear it of any debris, making it easier for them, regardless of moonlight or whatever the weather forecast predicts. The tree line is only 1,000 yards from the east side of the house. And from the map, there's a rough dirt track behind the wood leading to the main road half a klic away. As I see it, this would be their entry and exit point."

"Copy that, well done, Willy. Why don't you take a walkabout and give it all another once over, and we'll all meet up later."

"Affirmative. Just two more things, boss, if I may, before I go for a jog around," replied Willy, happy to finally be doing something.

"Fire away," said Marcus.

"The security setup here is state-of-the-art, but there's no security camera coverage at the back of the woods or over the dirt track that leads down to a gate a klic down the road as I mentioned. I was wondering if it might be useful to consider installing a pressure plate inside the gate entrance. If the intruders do come in that way, which seems likely to me, they won't be driving with headlights blazing, and the Security Centre would get an alert upfront."

"First-class idea. I'll get the Colonel on that, Willy," said Major Freddy Carr, his words showing his respect for the young soldier.

"And the second point?"

"The dogs and ponies' boss?"

"Colonel Dankworth considered that, and his gamekeeper will take the hounds back to his cottage to prevent them from barking loudly when the party begins. He'll collect them this morning after finishing clearing up from the storm winds last night, and the Colonel's No.2, Katja, will take the ponies down to a paddock at the far end of the estate to keep them from getting spooked by any fireworks that might be set off later. So, we're all sorted. Appreciate your input, Willy. You can now go off on your jaunt, if you like," said Major Freddy Carr.

"Affirmative, I'll just check that with Brinkworth and be on my way," said Willy.

Freddy and Marcus began making their way back to the group waiting for them.

"The lad looks pretty handy and's got a head on his shoulders," said Marcus.

"SAS snipers, as you know, are an elite breed. Look at him, can't be more than twenty-something, and I'm told from a reliable source he's already got about thirteen confirmed kills in some pretty hairy locations that are best left unspoken," said the Major quietly.

"Impressive!" Marcus said, stealing another glance at the young soldier. They strolled in silence towards the awaiting group, and Marcus said softly, his voice barely above a whisper.

"Freddy, I have the report on Tits's visit to Badawi's house in Abu Dhabi, which I sent to you early this morning via Penny. You might not have had a chance to review it yet."

"No time yet, so spill the beans."

"Well, it's hot. Firstly, he was able to confirm from the contents of Badawi's safe that he already has eight fighters here, along with the necessary hardware and weaponry. We've only got code names so far, but at least we know possible numbers, and once GCHQ and your lot have those code names, they can follow up the chatter. You know, Freddy, it never ceases to surprise me, in reality, how porous the UK coastland actually is. I mean, we all know about the people traffickers and their boats and all that, but there's a multitude of other coastal spots where the bad guys can get in without a whisker of a risk of discovery. The other stuff is also interesting but not relevant to this operation," said Marcus.

"Don't leave me hanging, what's the other stuff then?"

"Okay. A treasure trove of intel about Asif's father's past activities. Looks like he had someone hack into his father's computers. Why? We can only speculate, but maybe he wanted a lever he could use against him. As you know, they are not singing from the same hymn sheet, and there was considerable tension lurking between them, but as I said, who knows. But that's academic now, considering his father's thankful demise. Anyway, the intel could greatly assist in clearing up a lot of unanswered questions that MI6 have concerning outstanding issues relating to past atrocities," said Marcus, in conclusion.

"That was a clever move on your part, mate. Re your other point, yeah, God knows who's walking our streets these days, and yet successive governments seem hesitant to introduce advanced ID cards, ones that can't be easily forged or copied. I suppose since they're in power for such short spells, they don't want to upset public opinion and risk losing votes over a measure that might be unpopular. You know, the Nanny State and all that fuss," said the Major.

"Not our play, Freddy, but I agree," Marcus said.

Freddy led Marcus to the group patiently waiting to engage and introduced him to the team. "Chief Inspector Johnny Brinkworth, the Ground Commander for this operation, Sergeant James Bradley from the Tactical Firearms Unit, my fellow officer Captain Justin Armitage from MI6, Inspector Jacky Forsyth of the Special Branch, and Major Simon Barker from MI5. The other five members of the protection team will be introduced after the briefing by the Ground Commander," Major Freddy Carr explained.

Everyone shook hands, pleased that the full introductions had been, finally, made and that they could now concentrate on the task at hand.

"As I informed Major Carr and Chief Inspector Brinkworth earlier today, I am reiterating this here for those who might have missed it to ensure clarity. I would like to introduce Colonel Katya Kaminska, a retired Polish Intelligence operative that represented their military counterintelligence department. Before her current role here, she served as an advisor and translator for our security services. Notably, she observed a drone making a slow, deliberate flyover yesterday. The drone appeared especially focused on the house, likely capturing detailed photographs as it hovered around each window before moving to survey the grounds. She assists me daily with our routine activities, some of which you may be aware of but are not relevant to today's proceedings. I now invite the Ground Commander, Chief Inspector Johnny Brinkworth, to speak," explained Colonel Charlie Dankworth.

"Okay, listen up. We expect Badawi to run a second drone over the property later today to confirm that his targets are indeed on the premises and are unprotected. The subjects: Doctor Meer and her two children will be on site at 11.30

hours. Before their arrival, we will deploy to the estate's Gun Room, where I will deliver a formal briefing on protocol and deployment at 12.00 hours. During this time, Katja will provide lunch. After the briefing, we will carry out a weapons check. To prevent unnecessary anxiety for the children, the entire team will stay in The Gun Room from 11.00 hours until their deployment. As you all know, Dr Meer and her family will be moved to The Safe Room as soon as it is deemed appropriate and will remain there until the operation is complete. I don't expect another flyover until sometime after lunch, but who knows. Either way, Doctor Meer and her children will be outside after lunch until that intervention is observed. Badawi will see what he expects to see, i.e., a mother playing with her children and Colonel Dankworth, aka the elderly uncle, wandering about harmlessly," smiled Chief Inspector Brinkworth, nodding at the Colonel.

"Any questions?"

"When is the recon?"

"Now. Colonel, if you could make ready, please?"

"Affirmative, Chief Inspector," the Colonel confirmed as he headed to fetch the eight-seater Land Rover.

"Just one more thing before we begin. I would like to mention that we have a civilian with us today. Most of you will either know him or have heard of him. Captain Marcus de Vere is the CEO and owner of de Vere Security. I have no hesitation in saying that he and his company have been held in high regard for many years by the British Security Services and, internationally, by similar organisations for their services to international security," said Chief Inspector Brinkworth in conclusion.

"Thank you, Chief Inspector. I want to provide a brief backstory as to why we are here today. I became involved with Doctor Meer and her family recently, when advised by Major Freddy Carr, MI6, that intelligence from GCHQ suggested a potential threat to her and her family by the terrorist Asif Badawi. Doctor Meer's husband, Captain Peter Meer, a renowned SAS sniper, killed Badawi's three brothers about six years ago. His associates eventually identified her as the possible wife with whom he sought revenge. At that time, there was no actionable protocol in place for our security services to respond, because the threat of a clear and present danger was not sufficiently credible to justify deploying their forces. It is understood by all of us that the UK is currently in 'Critical Alert' status, and so I took it upon myself to act. You will all understand that, as the wife of a fallen SAS officer, she and her family automatically became our family, and so I stepped up. Dr Meer, her family, and I were invited to spend a relaxing weekend at the invitation of Colonel Dankworth. It was an opportune moment, as his operations here were suspended for various reasons this weekend. We were looking forward to a peaceful break," Marcus said, staring at each man before continuing, "and so, as it turned out, it was pure coincidence that Badawi...erm...discovered that they would be here, unprotected."

He observed a sly wink and nod from Freddy Carr, recognising Marcus's fabricated story to conceal the fact that he, Marcus, and Dankworth had organised the trap.

"I understand and appreciate the background info, Captain de Vere, but for the sake of everyone here, what's the bottom line?" asked Chief Inspector Brinkworth.

The bottom line is that my man, Gibbs, is monitoring Badawi around the clock and has reported eight individuals, including Badawi, who were caught on camera with Major Carr's help yesterday, loading weapons into their SUV in the underground car park of Badawi's flat. M.I.5 and MI6 intercepted terrorist chatter indicating that Badawi was indeed planning to raid this property with, we believe, the intention of murdering Doctor Meer and her children, seeking revenge. At that moment, Major Carr informed the Commissioner of Specialist Operations. And this is where we stand now," said Marcus.

"So, you're saying Badawi and his team can't progress without Gibbs finding out?"

"Yes, that is correct. Gibbs's already covered that possibility thoroughly. There's no rear access to the building, and the fire escapes all lead down to the underground car park where Badawi's Black Toyota Land Cruiser 200 Series is parked. As I mentioned earlier, there's a Tracker in place – so all's good, said Marcus.

"Understood. Well done," Inspector Brinkworth said.

Just before Brinkworth's team set off on their recon, the Chief Inspector called Willy over.

Willy drew closer.

"So, Willy, how does it all look?" questioned Brinkworth.

"Had a good trot around, Chief Inspector. I see a farmhouse out of sight, just beyond the rise of the ground on the other side of the woods. There are no signs of life there, but it doesn't affect our plans. I believe the best entry for Badawi's team is through the farm gate a klic down the road, then across the track and into the woods, as I mentioned earlier to Captain de Vere and Major Carr," said Willy, lighting a smoke.

"And did they agree with your take on it?"

"Affirmative, Chief Inspector," said Willy, carefully, to the Ground Commander.

"As the designated SAS sniper, where in your experience would you set up?" asked Chief Inspector Brinkworth.

"The standalone oak tree east of the house has a wide canopy of branches and leaves, and, conveniently, it already features a well-concealed game shooting platform with an access ladder that can be easily pulled up to hide it. So, that would be my preferred position. With my night vision kit, if needed, I'd have a 180-degree view over the tree line and full sight of the entrance and the entire east side of the property," said the soldier, without hesitation.

"First-rate choice and, in my opinion, the only setup worthy of consideration, under the circumstances," concurred the Chief Inspector.

Marcus, Freddy, and the rest of the team nodded in agreement.

"One point I'd like to add. I've got my gamekeeper cleaning up after the storm winds last night, but he'll be heading back to his cottage in the village with my dogs once he's finished, which should be in about an hour or so. And don't worry about him blabbing about what's going on here. He's seen it all before, and as an ex-Para, he's one of us anyway," said the Colonel.

"Understood, no problem," replied the Ground Commander.

Marcus and Major Carr moved away from the group to chat.

"So, Marcus, I'd agreed with Dr Meer that she should arrive at 09.00 hours, but I've pushed that back to 11.30 hours to give them time to settle in and be ready for lunch. No point in her and the family coming earlier; we don't want to worry the children with our operation build-up. Right?"

"Right."

"I've advised Brinkworth of the new timeline, as you heard. You've got Gibbs covering Badawi's movements, so we'll know when he kicks off, and it takes an hour, at best, to get down here anyway, okay?" said Major Carr.

"Copy that," Marcus said.

"By the way, Brinkworth has asked me to pass on to you that you tell Carter to stand down once Cathy and the children are safely here. He doesn't want too many civilians wandering about, which, on the face of it, seems reasonable. I mean, if anything untoward were to happen, then it's his head that'll roll. The village pub's only a stone's throw away, so Carter can hold up there with Gibbs once he's peeled off from tracking Badawi down. And by the way, he's noted you're carrying," said Major Carr.

"Oh, dear, so am I going to be sent to the naughty corner then?" said Marcus with a grin.

"Not to worry, mate. He's willing to ignore that, as long as you don't kill anybody unless things reach breaking point, right?" chuckled Freddy Carr.

"Affirmative. It makes sense to me on all counts, Freddy. Don't envisage any fun and games until well after nightfall. In fact, early mornings are more likely. I'm with Willy on that score. So, after lunch, we'll get Cathy and the children outside to play for the rest of the afternoon to facilitate the appearance of normality. The expected Badawi drone, I've no doubt, will make its flyover then, as discussed to check things out and all they'll see is what they expect to see, i.e., the family riding ponies or whatever and the ageing uncle pottering about harmlessly," said Marcus.

"Yeah, I agree, that sounds good. And the kids will behave normally – as they have no reason not to. I mean, they won't have a clue that our team's here, ready and waiting in the Gun Room," replied Major Carr.

"A final point to all concerned – protocol states that we act as a protective force only in relation to the property and those within it. Therefore, you will use lethal force only as a last resort. Is that understood?" said the Ground Commander, Chief Inspector Johnny Brinkworth, as he strolled over to join the two men.

Captain Marcus de Vere and Major Freddy Carr nodded in understanding but still exchanged knowing looks at this optimistic, somewhat unrealistic dialogue, given the nature of their adversaries. Both men knew that if given the chance, they would take Badawi out.

• CHAPTER 30 •

Captain Marcus de Vere stood alongside Major Freddy Carr, briefly glancing at the sky to check for drones as Colonel Charlie Dankworth approached to join them.

"I'll show you around the house, Marcus," said the Colonel.

"Great, thanks, Colonel. I can't wait to see the safe room, or rather safe apartment, from what Freddy tells me," said Marcus, with enthusiasm.

"I'll leave that as the last point of the tour," chuckled the Colonel.

He led them into the impressive, spacious, and spectacular Georgian-style entrance hall, laid out with black and white checkerboard tiles, which led to a graceful, sweeping staircase – not unlike his own home entrance. Marcus had already noticed the small, windowless security centre on the left of the entrance doors. Off the hall were four sets of magnificent eight-panel oak doors, each leading to a separate room: the kitchen, dining, sitting, and drawing rooms, which exuded the style and elegance of bygone years.

"Not bad, eh? Most of it was in the early 19th Century," said the Colonel with undisguised pride as they ascended the ornate staircase to the first floor.

"There are five bedrooms in total; entry to three of them is via keypad."

The Colonel showed them the bedrooms, each complete with a bathroom and a living room.

"Those with key-pad entry are designated for guests seeking acceptance on the payroll of both MI5/MI6 as prospective informants and for others requiring interrogation to determine if they pose a threat to UK security."

"And what's in there?" asked Marcus as they were led past a highly secure door with a sliding viewing window.

"Ah, that's... um... an interview room," said the Colonel, moving on quickly.

"A euphemism for an Interrogation Room?" asked Marcus, but the Colonel ignored the question as they moved on.

At that moment, Katja appeared, showing interest in speaking with Marcus further after their earlier introduction.

"Good morning, Captain de Vere. I've been eager to speak with you. The Colonel has told me all about you and your recent trip to Abu Dhabi. Which led to a rather excellent outcome, I hear," she laughed.

"Good to meet and chat with you, too, Katja. You'll have to meet up with Emily, my PA, sometime; I'm sure you two would get on like a house on fire," he grinned.

“Katja, could you please confirm the setup of the Gun Room?" asked the Colonel.

“Affirmative, the team’s there and soaking up the atmosphere,” she replied with a grin.

“Copy that, Katja, well done, thanks,” replied the Colonel.

The Colonel led Marcus and Freddy Carr down a wide, ornate wrought-iron staircase to the Safe Room. Marcus was almost speechless as they passed through the Kevlar-armoured door, which had a bulletproof observation window that could be sealed from inside by a sliding shutter. Just as Freddy had told him, this wasn’t just a safe room; it was an apartment, entirely self-contained. This was, certainly, a first. He took in the spacious living room, featuring a state-of-the-art flat-screen TV with an eclectic collection of DVDS spread across several racks. A music centre and a kids' play console completed the entertainment setup. Besides all the controls, lay a satellite phone, and near the secure door was an intercom. In the centre of the large kitchen stood a beautiful, yellowed pine table and chairs, aged but charming. The rest was, again, state-of-the-art, with American-sized fridge and freezer units stacked with food and drinks that could withstand a prolonged siege, should it ever occur. A nearby cooler offered healthy, organic soft drinks along with a selection of white and pink wines. Next to it was a wine rack boasting an eclectic range of reds, enough to satisfy any discerning palate. They were then shown to three small bedrooms, each with an en-suite bathroom.

“So, what do you think?” the Colonel asked with a twinkle in his eye.

"It's absolutely incredible! I've never seen a safe room this large before, and so well equipped," said Marcus, clearly stunned.

"The reality is that this setup sometimes provides a safe haven for visiting diplomats, foreign leaders, and their families who are either under some threat or need to keep their visits to the UK discreet, if you understand what I mean. It is also used by MI5 and MI6 operatives and their families as a safe house if required for any reason."

"Interesting, that would certainly explain the extensive accommodations and facilities," said Marcus.

"Actually, that's not quite the end of the story," smiled the Colonel. "It's really entirely self-sufficient. I mean, for example, should the power go down, it has a standalone generator, solar-powered by rechargeable batteries good for seventy-two hours, not only powerful enough for this area but also for the entire property, which would kick in immediately should things go dark. And that bit of kit's located in one of my cellars, secured by an armoured biometric Kevlar door. Plus, the air conditioning here is fed with real air, not the recycled crap," explained the Colonel.

"Out of curiosity, how does all of that work?" Marcus asked, eager to understand more.

"There are two concealed ducts leading up from the grid panels visible above in the ceiling to a fake chimney that looks exactly like the other three operational ones above the main house. One duct extracts air and the other supplies fresh air into the safe room. The noise of the pumps, also hidden beneath the ceilings of the property, is suppressed," said the Colonel.

"Just one more question, Colonel. If everything goes awry, is there another exit from here?"

"Affirmative, I'll explain in a moment," he replied. "I'm sure that Dr Meer, her children, and Monica, who will of course remain out of view as far as the outside world is concerned, will have everything they need right here. And, as I've heard that both Doctor Meer and her friend Monica are inclined to enjoy a puff or two, there's a closed smoking room behind the utility area with an extraction fan linked to the main air conditioning system I mentioned earlier. But to answer your question regarding an alternative exit or escape route, if you will, it's here," said the Colonel as he pressed one of the many panels in the oak-panelled rear wall of the smoking area, exposing an underground passage," said the Colonel, enjoying the moment of surprise displayed on Captain de Vere's face at its revelation.

"And where does that lead to? A wellness centre, or what?" laughed Marcus.

To a camouflaged but operational game feeding station located south-west of the property near the main road. Completely undetectable. I understand from Brinkworth that he will position one of his tactical firearm units there, with two more stationed in the stables overlooking the east side of the house. His overall deployment plan will, no doubt, be detailed in his upcoming briefing. As we know, Willy's position has now been authorised," said the Colonel.

"All very impressive, Colonel," Marcus said.

"In our business, at the taxpayer's expense, we've had to. What goes on here is a vital part of our nation's well-being and security," said the Colonel, rather pleased to share, at least, a few of his secrets. But by no means all of them.

"Crikey, Colonel, I tip my hat to you. If you recall, you said the same to me in Abu Dhabi, which feels like a lifetime ago," laughed Marcus.

"If you remember, I also mentioned that I'd look forward to a more in-depth chit-chat. Well, that seems to have come to fruition, too," laughed the Colonel.

Marcus and Major Carr followed the Colonel back upstairs and onto the terrace balcony overlooking the landscaped gardens of the estate, where Katja had provided freshly brewed coffee for them. On their way, the Colonel showed them both the Security Centre, where multiple screens displayed images from every angle of the property via concealed surveillance cameras. Marcus noted that the entrance hall and first floor were also well covered.

Katja suddenly appeared, interrupting them to say the package was being delivered up the drive.

Carter, following instructions, saw Doctor Meer, Monica, and the children safely to the entrance of the manor house. He then returned to the village, but not before stepping out of his Mini Cooper to wish them good luck and to reassure Doctor Meer that he would be just down the road. Cathy expressed her gratitude, fondling the pendant around her neck but carefully avoiding squeezing it.

Cathy, Monica, and the children eagerly jumped out and ran up to the entrance. Once introductions were complete, the Colonel led the children to the spacious kitchen, where Katya's exceptional talent in preparing food delighted everyone, especially the children. Anxious to get their luggage out of sight, Katya quickly took it from the entrance and carried it down to the Safe Room, where she would later take them. Cathy, Monica, and the children then ventured out to explore and were delighted to see the stables, where two ponies were waiting, resting their heads on the stable doors and awaiting attention. Leaving them to wonder, the Colonel turned to George. "Let's go for a quick spin, George," said the Colonel to the delighted boy as they approached his classic Bentley.

The village was only a mile down the road, and he considered the trip a worthwhile risk for the boy to experience.

"Wow, this is awesome," grinned George as he gratefully slipped into the passenger seat. Delighted to smell the rich leather and watch the large circular dials embedded in the walnut dashboard register the activity of the powerful engine as it made its way down the drive. He was in seventh heaven. Waving to Jenny and his mother, they roared off. All the way to the village and back, George never stopped talking passionately about the car's history, engine specifications, etc., in such detail that the Colonel was genuinely impressed as he listened patiently. And as an overwhelming plus for George, he was allowed to sit on the Colonel's lap to steer the magnificent car, finally guiding himself up the winding drive back to the entrance of the property.

On arrival, George ran eagerly to his mother to describe his adventure. Everyone went back to the kitchen ready for lunch. Katja had prepared a feast of roast lamb and potatoes, with some chips for the children to dip into. As everyone enjoyed the food, she quietly slipped away to serve the same meal to the team waiting in the spacious Gun Room, where they all smiled appreciatively as they dug in with obvious relish.

As planned, after lunch, the children dashed outside to play and ride the ponies, which Katja oversaw as an accomplished horsewoman in her own right. Taking Cathy to one side, the Colonel explained the plan for the afternoon and reassured her that she and the children would be safe outside until further notice.

Major Freddy Carr, Captain Marcus de Vere, Colonel Charlie Dankworth, and Ground Commander Brinkworth were sitting and chatting on the terraced balcony, overlooking the grounds that stretched to the tree line. They were out of sight of the children, which was exactly their intention. The children remained unaware of the team's presence, remaining hidden until after dinner, when the women and children would be safely in the Safe Room.

• CHAPTER 31 •

Gun Room Briefing at 12.00 Hours

"Good afternoon, gentlemen. The children are completely unaware of our presence, and the package is secure. Due to the current situation, they are effectively bait for Badawi and his men. We could try to intercept Badawi's group before they arrive, but that's not practical. Without evidence of intent to harm, we can only charge them with possession of illegal firearms, which isn't enough to justify action. Therefore, we will proceed with our plans. I remind you, though, that we are on UK soil and must follow the law, which permits lethal force only when there's no alternative and it's reasonable. It's also crucial that we avoid any aggressive action unless our adversaries threaten us with weapons. We've assured the Chief Constable of Gloucestershire that we will adhere to engagement protocols to prevent Blue-on-Blue incidents and cooperate fully with the Criminal Investigative Team afterwards. Our main goal is to contain and arrest the suspects. As I mentioned earlier, no team member should engage unless the terrorists initiate contact. Stand down and observe until I give the order. If a lethal shot is necessary, it will be at my command only," said the Ground Commander.

"Is that clear?"

Everyone nodded in agreement.

Marcus and Major Carr temporarily moved away from the group under the pretext of having a smoke.

"Prisoners, forget that. If Asif arrives with his friends, I'll handle him myself if necessary," Marcus whispered to his old friend.

"Affirmative," Freddy replied with a grin. As it turned out, they didn't need to worry about that aspect.

"The only downside for Badawi, apart from us, is that the weather forecast predicts there will be a full moon with minimal cloud cover tonight, so it's bad for them but good for us," said Marcus, as they turned back to join the group.

Brinkworth stopped to listen to his communication device.

"Badawi's drone recently flew over and buzzed the grounds for a while, so all he would have seen is Doctor Meer and the kids playing with their uncle. This confirms the show can proceed," said Brinkworth, in a serious tone.

"Good to hear," Marcus said, unable to contain his eagerness for action at the forefront once more.

"Yes, it's a go. As you can see, each of you has a tactical comms kit laid out. We have a one-off, fully secure frequency, so there's no need to go through a complicated call-signature protocol. Keep your comms open at all times. Since no one has the same first name, we'll use those – it's easier and quicker. The truth is, these days, with so many whizz kids around with their radio sets, I'd rather not use last names or ranks, just in case. Agreed?"

All nodded in agreement once more.

"So, regarding the deployment strategy, I'm assigning one of my team members to the Feeding Station located to the west of the property. His call sign will be West 1. Another will be positioned at the stables on the east side, designated as East 2. We have a field medic on standby in case things go wrong; he will be stationed at the east back corner of the property with the call sign Medic 1. Sergeant James Bradley will take a position in the hall of the residence at the bottom of the staircase, while Captain Justin Armitage will be at the entrance to the kitchen. Major Freddy Carr will be situated in the corner of the TV room beside the French windows. Colonel Dankworth plans to set up the TV to play a movie on continuous replay throughout the evening, maintaining an appearance of normality for any observers. I believe he's arranged 'Live and Let Die' as suitable for the occasion, and to any observer, he will appear seated watching the film in a high-backed chair, which he won't actually be," said Brinkworth.

This elicited laughter from the gathered group.

"At the appropriate time, Katja will activate the bedroom lighting to signal the retirement of the children and, later, the adults, in case of any observation. Leaving the illusion of the Colonel sitting in the TV room as initial bait, if you like, watching the movie. The entrance porch and hall lights will remain on as usual. Perimeter lighting will dim at midnight, in accordance with the normal practice for this property. Are we all clear?" the commander asked.

"And what about you and everyone else?" asked Marcus.

"Okay. I'll handle the Security Centre, leveraging the estate's security cameras for real-time movement monitoring and command from there. Major Simon Barker will take the top of the staircase, while the Colonel and Katja will move around upstairs. Any other questions?"

"What about weapons?" asked Marcus.

"SIG MCX 5.56 x 45mm NATO weapons are ready on the table. All relevant personnel have received Glock 19 side arms. It's essential to wear body armour and ensure body cams are on and functioning throughout the operation. Real-time footage is crucial, as the Criminal Investigative Team will need all recordings after the event. We will also record all communication to support the CIT. If the situation becomes too dangerous, leave any casualties in place, including shell casings where they fall. Keep your weapons and body cams ready for post-event analysis. The medic will handle any treatable injuries on either side. Is everyone clear?" said Chief Inspector Johnny Brinkworth.

Everyone nodded in agreement.

"Okay, listen up. We'll deploy at 00:30 hours. Once we have intel from Captain de Vere's man, Gibbs, that Badawi's on the move, I'll give the alert. Always keep your comms open. So, stand down and check your kit. Captain de Vere, replace me in the Security Centre in two hours. Are we good?”

“No problem, commander, everything's fine," Marcus responded.

• CHAPTER 32 •

Caroline sat alone in the deserted garden of The Pale Horse Inn, feeling miserable while sipping rosé wine. She preferred solitude, neither needing nor desiring company. The warm early evening sunshine flooding the garden offered no comfort or relief from her growing depression. The bottle, now half full, rested in the ice bucket, but in her mind, it appeared half empty, reflecting her inner feelings. Her hatred for Cathy persisted, stubborn and unmoving, despite her efforts to let go. That woman had repeatedly torn out her heart and thrown it back at her. The sexual tension consumed her, fuelling thoughts of revenge, although she was unsure how to achieve it. She felt on the verge of breaking, and the wine only worsened her state.

Her first sexual experience happened at eighteen with an older man. Although consensual, it ended badly, leaving her feeling empty and violated. She then confided in a girlfriend, which led to a lesbian relationship, causing her to question her true sexual orientation. Was she bisexual or a lesbian? Her feelings for Cathy suggested a strong attraction to women.

Beginning to feel decidedly tipsy, she poured more wine – self-destruction seemed the best course. It was then that she couldn't help but notice the elegant, attractive-looking man emerge from the pub, dressed in a well-tailored cream linen suit, pausing for a long moment to stare at her with undisguised interest. To her alarm, he began to approach slowly, a half pint of local brew in his hand. His attentive gaze never faltered. But it was the way he moved that intrigued her; he was radiating confidence, charm, and something else she couldn't quite identify.

"Please forgive me, my dear, for intruding on your personal space, but you are almost identical to a lady I recently had the... er... pleasure of meeting. I must say that the... er... likeness is so remarkable that you might even be twins. Of course, that's highly unlikely. But please forgive me, as I said, it's not my intention to disturb you. It's just that I couldn't resist mentioning the unlikelihood of this coincidence once I saw you," he said, taken aback by his strong sense of immediate déjà vu.

"Really, and who was that then?" Caroline asked, now feeling quite upset and trying to figure out how to handle her growing discomfort and conflicting emotions during this surprising meeting.

"Do you mind if I join you for a moment or two? I assure you my intentions are completely honourable and friendly," he said, smiling charmingly and irresistibly as he took the chair opposite.

"Why not," said Caroline. "And who *is* this supposed twin of mine?"

"Well, her name's Doctor Cathy Meer, and as I mentioned, the similarity is uncanny. I don't know if that name means anything to you."

"Not anymore."

"Meaning?"

"Sorry, I do know her, but we are no longer friends. In fact, it's quite the opposite."

"Oh dear. I'm so sorry to hear that. She seemed such an interesting woman. But it's none of my business, of course, but I think it's always such a pity when we lose friends, don't you think? Do you mind if I ask what happened?"

"I prefer not to discuss it, especially not with a complete stranger, even if charming."

"Ben, Ben Malone," said The Painter, taking a sip of his beer and reaching into his pocket for his box of Chaliapin cigarettes. He observed that this version had much shorter blond hair and that her light summer jacket no longer concealed her upper chest, which highlighted her designer T-shirt perfectly.

"It's Caroline. I love the aroma. Are they Turkish? Can I try one?"

"Yes, of course," said The Painter, lighting one for her.

"So... um... Ben, what else do you do besides chatting up lonely, depressed women?" said Caroline, inhaling the aromatic tobacco with relish.

"Collecting and dealing rare books is one of my passions, for my sins."

“Do you mean books or sins?" Caroline asked, starting to relax.

“Oh, the latter’s much more interesting when given the opportunity.”

“May I ask what it is that you do?” asked The Painter smoothly.

“I‘m a forensic clinical psychologist," Caroline said.

“Ah, so both of you are doctors, interesting! What role does a Forensic Clinical Psychologist play in this context?"

“I mostly offer my expertise to the police in suspect profiling."

"What does that actually involve?" asked Ben, his interest growing.

“A profiler examines evidence to find patterns that connect different crime scenes, aiding in identifying the culprit,” said Caroline, straightforwardly. She began to sober up slightly.

“Interesting. I suppose that could be... um... stressful at times," he said, unable to stop himself from watching her chest rise and fall with her speech. "I don’t want to seem too intrusive, Caroline, but would you like to talk about what happened? I’m a good listener; it might help."

“I made a pass at her while she was drunk, and she threw me out – never wanting to see me again – she ferociously rejected me. I’d loved her since we were at school,” said Caroline, wiping away her tears and surprised that she’d opened up to a complete stranger.

“Oh dear, I’m very sorry. Are you attracted to women? Not that it matters either way.”

“Well, I’ve been a bit confused about that for many years. You see, I had a very bad intimate encounter with an older man when I was eighteen. He physically hurt me and left me feeling devastated and unfulfilled. It was a traumatic experience, and I turned to a girlfriend for a shoulder to cry on, which then led to something I actually enjoyed.”

“What happened then?” asked The Painter, increasingly intrigued to hear more.

“It was intense for a month or two, but then she became obsessed with me, which was overwhelming. I decided to walk away," Caroline said, wiping away a tear. "I can’t believe I’m sharing all this with you."

“Oh dear. Where does Doctor Meer fit into this now?”

“We’d been close friends since school. I always loved her, and later realised that my feelings had deepened from friendship to something more meaningful. I want to have an intimate relationship with her.”

“Which was not reciprocated? I presume. And from what you said earlier, that’s not likely to happen,” said The Painter.

"No, she never knew or at least never acknowledged it.”

“And then?”

“Well, recently I was at her house, and she got really drunk, so I kissed her. I couldn’t help myself. As I said, she threw me out. It was so unfair; I didn’t deserve the level of her vitriol, and I’m determined to get my revenge one way or another.”

A plan started to take shape in his mind; she might be the trigger he needed to carry out his revenge on Meer.

"Of course, I understand, Caroline. But if I may just say, and forgive me if I'm crossing a line, if Dr Meer has hurt you and caused you pain, then we are on the same page, literally. I've a bone to pick with her too, but we'll have a chat about that later. Perhaps we can work together to seek some recompense. Erm... by the way, I must say that this rosé you're drinking is, to put it mildly, utterly unacceptable by any reasonable standards."

"Really, what are you drinking?"

"Ah, it's Bishops Finger, a great Kentish masterpiece. Look, my home's not far from here, and I would be delighted to offer you a glass or two of Clos du Temple, a wine that will blow you away," he said charmingly.

"Ben, thank you, that's very kind of you, but I think I've had enough to drink and I'm not thinking clearly right now. I'm certainly not looking for a one-night stand, especially not now," said Caroline, becoming overwhelmed with emotional confusion but simultaneously knowing for sure that she was going to go with him wherever he wanted to take her. Why, she couldn't understand.

He reached across the table and gently took her hand. "Caroline, trust me, I have no hidden agenda; I just want to keep you safe and lift your spirits a bit. Come with me, and I vow to take care of you," he said, his voice filled with an irresistible charisma that enveloped her. She rose unsteadily, taking his hand as he led her out. He then turned to the landlord, placing what he considered enough money on the bar, and departed with his arm around her, softly holding her slender waist.

“What’s this? It looks like it can fly," said Caroline as she observed the sleek lines of the Bugatti, patiently waiting for its owner to unleash its power.

“Ah, my latest toy, and is this beautiful classic yours, my dear?” he said, as he ran one hand along the sleek body of the E-Type while still holding her slim waist with the other.

“Yes, it’s my baby,” Caroline said proudly, leaning into his lean body.

“Take me to that Clos du Temple, Ben, but I don’t think I’m in the right state to drive,” she smiled, deciding to relax and enjoy herself regardless. “Where did you say we’re going again?”

“To Frog Hall, my dear. You’ll love it,” said The Painter as he started up the Bugatti.

The powerful roar of its engine made Caroline’s body shudder as she was thrown back in the passenger seat by its force. Her mind was dizzy yet free of any reservations now. He carried her effortlessly over the threshold of Frog Hall, much to her surprise and delight. Her slender body wrapped around him, and the sensation of her full breasts pressing against his chest began to arouse him pleasantly. They then continued up the magnificent winding staircase and through the vast master bedroom suite onto the balcony terrace overlooking the grounds.

“My God, the view is stunning," Caroline said, sobering up as she gazed at the expansive estate. “What kind of deer are those?”

“Red deer, I permit the herd to roam freely and safely here. No hunting unless culling is necessary,” said The Painter as he set the ice bucket and wine on one of the ornate tables around the balcony. The Master-Suite featured a concealed cooler behind an oak panel, easily accessed by pressing the right panel, a toy he enjoyed using. He then returned with chilled Waterford fluted crystal glasses.

“Cheers, my dear. I do hope the wine fulfils my earlier promise,” he smiled, watching her with delight as she reached up to clink her glass with his in a toast. The crystal glasses produced a pleasant ringing tone in her ears as they met.

“Welcome to Frog Hall, Caroline.”

“Thank you. I’m delighted to be here. As you promised, the wine is truly lovely and has a quite sophisticated taste, which I probably couldn’t afford,” Caroline said with a smile as she gratefully accepted a refill.

“Do you really want to know? I mean, I find discussing the cost of things... erm... a bit vulgar, don’t you think?”

Caroline shrugged in response.

“Oh well, if you insist, it’s roughly £200 per bottle," Ben said, a touch irritated, as he lit a cigarette.

“Sorry, I didn’t mean to annoy you by asking. It’s just that I’ve never tasted anything like it, Ben,” Caroline grinned. "Damn, I’ve left my cigarettes in the car. Can I have another one of yours? As I said earlier, I love the aroma, and the taste is as good as it gets.”

He lit one for her and placed it between her lips.

“Look, Ben, I’ll share a little secret, for the first time in many years, I feel genuinely warm and comfortable,” Caroline said as she took a drag on her cigarette.

“I’m very pleased to hear that. I feel the same,” he said, standing and taking her hand warmly in his as he led her into the bedroom, almost unable to hide his growing excitement.

The painter sat on the balcony, sipping his wine and topping up her glass while he waited for her to return. He reflected on his certainty that he now held complete control and power over her. As a result, he had suppressed his urge to kill; she would live at least until she had played her part in drawing Meer into his web. The master of The Summer Hunt would, he was sure, be delighted with the plan that was now as clear as crystal in his mind and was excited to begin.

“No one I’ve ever been with has satisfied me like this before, Ben," Caroline said as she finally appeared. “Did I pass out or something? I just woke up feeling a bit disoriented."

“Don’t be concerned, my dear, it was just a Petite Mort moment,” replied The Painter.

“A what?”

“A French expression. Literally, a little death during orgasm.”

“Ah, not heard that expression before. I have to say your skills in that department were impressive!”

The Painter, with a tired smile, said, "Just the happy outcome of my studies in Tantric and Yoni massage."

Caroline beamed, "I’ve heard of the former but not the latter."

"Well, you'll just have to look it up, my dear. Anyway, please forgive me, but I have several urgent matters to attend to. I'll be in touch very soon. It's been a pleasure to be with you," said The Painter.

Having resisted the usual urge to kill her, he was now bored and eager for her to leave. One of his staff had brought her car from The Pale Horse Inn; if he remained in her company longer, he might end up doing something he isn't ready for.

"Of course, I understand. Thank you for everything, Ben," she said as she kissed his cheek and left.

He watched her Jaguar speed down the driveway, relieved to be rid of her. Then, he picked up his phone to tell his friend about his plans to introduce two new subjects as prey. Using Caroline's urge for revenge, he felt confident that she would agree to help him trap, drug, and transport Doctor Meer to The Chiddington Estate for participation in The Summer Hunt. After all, she was now under his control. A decision he would later regret.

• CHAPTER 33 •

Asif sat in his Mayfair penthouse with his team, all of whom had undergone Iranian training in camps spread across the Syrian deserts for several months. They were intensely loyal to him and prepared to sacrifice themselves instantly if necessary.

His No. 2, Syed Ayad, was not present; he was occupied with an assignment to explore other exit strategies that MI6 might not have uncovered from Badawi's file, an essential task in case things went awry.

The detailed, timestamped images of The Sanctuary lay on the table before them. He was pleased with his No.2, Syed Ayad, whose work had deployed the drones very effectively. He felt satisfied seeing his targets moving within the grounds. He scrutinised the close-up images of the pathologist and her children, completely unaware of their impending fate. He planned to capture her in front of her children as a final act of retribution, then kill the children before her eyes. Although they also needed to die, he intended to do so quickly to avoid unnecessary suffering.

However, she would then endure a slow and excruciating death, as he deemed fit. The very thought of it thrilled him. But he expressed his concern to those gathered that it all might have been a little too easy. Since the drinks party at Sir Chiddington's estate, his survival instincts had kicked in, raising suspicion that it was a clever ploy to trap him. Over the years, his instincts had kept him safe and unscathed, and he paid close attention to them. Accordingly, he detailed his plans with this in mind. His team, always alert, offered their opinions. Combat gear and weaponry had been laid out for inspection; everyone was pleased, ready, and eager to proceed.

• CHAPTER 34 •

After an enjoyable dinner, Katja took Cathy, Monica, and the exhausted children to the Safe Room, accompanied by Marcus and the Colonel. The latter explained to Cathy that the apartment was entirely soundproof, so neither they nor the children would be disturbed by any 'fireworks' should it come to that later. Both women were delighted with the accommodation, and Jenny was especially happy with her bedroom. Overjoyed to see her fluffy Pooh Bear waiting for her on her pillow, and in George's room, he was thrilled to find a computer all set up and ready to go. He immediately began uploading all the detailed pictures he had taken of the Bentley, then happily started playing Minecraft, his favourite game at the moment.

Marcus left the Colonel to finish the tour and slipped off to see the team in the Gun Room. He was pleased to see that the array of kit was being cleaned and checked efficiently. The SIG MCX 5.56x45mm NATO calibre weapons were to his satisfaction, along with 9mm Glock 19 sidearms, except for Willy and himself, both favouring the SIG Sauer P226 loaded with .375 rounds, although the choice of rounds wouldn't have been noticed. Willy was busy spreading out his Ghillie suit. Body armour was handed out, but Willy declined to use it for some reason; Marcus pulled one aside for himself to use later. He then made his way up to the balcony for some more coffee, joined shortly by the Colonel and Major Freddy Carr for a smoke. Chief Inspector Brinkworth was left in the Security Centre to familiarise himself with their extensive coverage of both the inside and outside of the property.

He sat comfortably in the anatomically shaped, upholstered seat, monitoring the screens, sipping gratefully on the Guatemala coffee Katja had kindly provided. In the safety of the Safe Room, the family happily watched 'Paddington Bear 2' on an enormous flat-screen TV before helping the kids with bath time and into bed. Cathy expected the children to fall asleep soon after their afternoon activities, and indeed, they were both fast asleep when she checked on them an hour later.

"I wonder what will happen. Does the Colonel think Badawi will come tonight?" said Monica.

"He feels it's likely. Come on, let's have a drink and a puff. I don't think I'll be going to bed anytime soon," smiled Cathy, trying to relax.

"Me too," said Monica. "Let's give this a try; I think it'll hit the spot," as she reached for and uncorked a bottle of Château Des Bardes Saint Emilion Grand Cru.

"This is just great," said Cathy as they sipped the rich, juicy wine, its soft vanilla notes teasing their taste buds.

"I can taste the oak," Monica said with an appreciative relish. "So, looks like we're up for the night then?" she added, lighting another cigarette, as Cathy did the same.

"Looks like it," laughed Cathy, raising her glass in a toast, trying to inwardly dismiss her growing fear for her children's safety.

***

Gibbs had reported directly to the Ground Commander that Badawi was on his way less than half an hour earlier. The Security Centre received a ping twenty minutes later from the pressure sensor embedded at the track entrance from the main road. The Ground Commander alerted everyone that the game was now in play. Willy was sweeping the tree line with his Schmidt & Bender 5-25x56 PM11 scope. The 10-round box magazine loaded with 7.62x51mm NATO rounds had one round chambered, ready to go. Movement in his peripheral vision made him swing his rifle to get a sight picture. Even with a full moon, the edge of the wood was in low light, but the scope was more than capable.

"Got four ragheads just inside the tree line. No wait, I count nine now. All dressed in black combat gear and carrying pistols, but four also have what looks like Beretta PMXs. That's a nasty bit of hardware at 900 rounds a minute," reported Willy.

Remembering that the Saudi Royal Guard Regiment had recently acquired it as their weapon of choice. "Copy that, Willy," confirmed Chief Inspector Brinkworth.

"What are they up to?" Marcus asked through his comms device.

"Don't have a clear camera image right now," said Brinkworth as he looked at the multiple security screens in front of him.

"Willy?"

"Zero all, for now. They're just sitting, probably observing and confirming that the lights have gone dark," Willy replied, amused that a barn owl suddenly landed on a branch right in front of him, gazing at him with its head tilted as if asking, What are you doing here? This is my spot, mate. Eventually, it flew away, hooting its annoyance at him.

"Yeah, we can see them now. Patient buggers, I must say," replied Brinkworth.

"So, we're now at 00:40 hours. The likely scenario is that they are now satisfied everyone is in bed and will consider acting soon," said Brinkworth.

"Affirmative, Inspector," Willy said as he checked the group's status and reported no updates via his comms.

"Hold on, there's movement. Yes, they're now moving quickly in a wide fan formation toward you. Four are heading east toward the kitchen entrance. Three are passing the entrance on the west side, and two are approaching the main entrance, attempting to get in," Willy confirmed. "It appears they're sticking to some predetermined entry points."

"Copy that, Willy. I have them clearly on screen now. The show's started, get ready. Remember, everyone, that the desired outcome is to take them alive," said the Ground Commander.

"Got the two guys in my scope now, trying to get in through the front doors but finding them locked and stepping back, way, way back. Have you got that?"

"Affirmative," Brinkworth replied.

"Wait, one of them is reaching for something on his belt. Shit, looks like a grenade. Permission to take him out, sir?"

In the split second that followed "Yes, yes, affirmative. Take him out – lethal kill authorised, he's pulled the pin," Brinkworth commanded as he watched the terrorist raise his arm back, ready to throw.

In one smooth motion, Willy, with both eyes open, stared through his scope with his right eye. He lined up his target just above the right ear and gently pressed the hair trigger with his index finger. At 600 miles per hour, the man's head exploded and fell downward, landing on the live grenade. He was dead before hitting the ground. Turning slightly, Willy adjusted his barrel and took out the other target. Milliseconds later, the grenade detonated, scattering their now shredded, lifeless bodies a few feet off the ground.

"Pretty nice shooting, Willy," Marcus said through his comms, thinking there are another two notches for Willy's belt. Although he was pretty sure that a guy like Willy wasn't counting.

Then all hell broke loose.

The Badawi team, surprised, quickly moved forward from their positions in an attack mode.

"Engage. Engage," commanded Brinkworth over the open comms.

Brinkworth's man deployed on the West Side ran forward, weapon set to rapid fire mode. But it was too late. He was only taken down by Asif's men in a merciless reply of gunfire. The medic rushed forward under fire to attend him, but found him dead.

"Freddy, four coming your way," cried Brinkworth.

Major Carr chambered a round in his Glock 19 and waited. No sweat. He'd been there many times before. They smashed through the French windows, firing multiple rounds into the back of the high-backed chair where they presumed someone was watching TV. A walking stick resting on the chair added to their belief. Managing to shatter the TV screen just as Bond was enjoying a love scene.

Major Freddy Carr raised his Glock and quickly took down two. One of the remaining terrorists spun around, firing bursts instinctively towards the Major in the corner of the room. He scored multiple hits, but fortunately only to Carr's vest. Carr staggered back from the impact and then managed to struggle to his knees, checking that his targets were neutralised. However, it was too late to stop the remaining two, who dashed into the hall of the property, shouting "Allah is Great."

On the East side, the two operatives in action managed to take out one of the three fighters as they fled toward the kitchen, the only remaining entrance available to them.

Outside the kitchen in the hall, Inspector Jacky Forsyth turned to respond to the firefight behind him in the TV room, managing to take down one. But then he found himself facing two hostile intruders crashing through the kitchen entrance. He took them out before suffering a hit to his unprotected shoulder. It was a flesh wound, but it took him down and out of the fight, at least for the moment.

In a kamikaze-like fashion, the remaining attacker ran from the doorway of the TV room towards the staircase, firing indiscriminately with his Beretta in his frantic attempt to kill anyone. He didn't notice Katja running down the staircase until it was too late. Using her Makarov pistol, she shot him down with four rapid, deadly grouped shots, shattering his breastbone and shredding his heart.

Suddenly, everything fell into deadly silence. The air was thick with the smell of gunpowder.

"According to my calculations, eight are accounted for. Where's the last one? Do you notice anything, Willy?" said Chief Inspector Brinkworth, catching his breath.

"Negative, who knows, boss. Can't see anything but bodies and fresh air," replied Willy, as he scanned the estate with the M22 binoculars he'd taken from his kit.

"Willy, take a sprint to their vehicle just in case?" commanded Brinkworth.

"On it, boss," Willy laid his rifle down, deployed the ladder, unholstered his SIG, and headed swiftly through the woods. Just in time to see it roaring away along the track to the open road, out of range.

"He's gone, boss. Don't know how I missed him, but he's managed to leg it."

It was at that moment that the Commander heard the 'ping' in the security room, confirming that the remaining member of the attack team had indeed reached the main road towards the village and was well on his way.

"Okay. Stand down," Brinkworth ordered. "Marcus, get Carter and Gibbs working on it immediately. He'll be screaming through the village any minute now. Hopefully, you'll be able to stop him or at least keep track of him, right?"

No need for that. Don't forget we've got a tracker on his vehicle, and my chap Gibbs will take it from here," explained Marcus de Vere.

"Of course, so all is not lost – good luck with that, Captain de Vere," said Brinkworth.

Marcus telephoned Carter.

"Get back to the Inn and rest. My likely plan is to take Cathy, Monica, and the children home this evening around 7-ish, so if you could have a look around the grounds of Willow Tree House before then, that would be good. I'll confirm the arrival time later, okay?

"Affirmative, boss," replied Carter, also thankful to take a breather.

"Well done, everyone. Listen up – it's over. Sadly, one of our team members is dead, and one is injured. Eight hostiles are down," said Brinkworth. "Re-group on the balcony terrace in 20. Leave the bodies and weapons exactly where they are. Keep your shell casings in place and hold onto your weapons. Turn off your Body Cams but keep them with you; I'll explain the protocols when we meet. Captain de Vere and Major Carr, you'll use facial recognition imaging on the bodies immediately. We have images of Badawi's team thanks to Gibbs, but do not move them. Unlikely that our prize is among those images but we'll wait and see. The Crime Scene Investigation Team is en route and will arrive shortly to carry out their investigation," advised Chief Inspector Johnny Brinkworth.

As Brinkworth contemplated the situation, he couldn't believe that Badawi would be so eager to be directly in the firing line of the assault. He was likely to have remained an observer, but he set the thought aside for now, nevertheless, his gut said that Badawi was on his way.

Major Carr and Marcus photographed the dead, checked their bodies for signs of life, and confirmed there were none before leaving them where they had fallen, as instructed. It was impossible to perform facial recognition on the two terrorists at the entrance of the property because there was little left of them due to the grenade's effects; therefore, DNA analysis would be needed to establish their identities. After completing their grim task, the disappointing realisation was that the Prize was not among the dead. There was no way Badawi would have been involved in the attempted entrance scenario.

"There are a few aspects in all of this that make me reconsider a few things," said Major Freddy Carr.

"Like what?" asked Johnny Brinkworth.

"Firstly, Asif's No.2, Syed Ayad, was not among the dead, suggesting he wasn't actively involved. We can now be certain of that. His face is as recognisable as Badawi's. So, why wasn't he present? Only he knows. Badawi's paranoia led him to bring in a whole team to seemingly target a defenceless woman and her children, driven by revenge. I believe that once Badawi realised he was walking into a sophisticated trap with superior weapons and skills, he fled, leaving his men as sacrificial pawns, disposable in his view. The reality is they are both out there now, plotting their next move. Badawi isn't going to surrender; revenge is deeply ingrained in his tribal mindset," Major Carr said.

"Which means that Doctor Meer and her family are still facing the same threat, but today was a game-changer for him," said Marcus. His face was grim.

"Exactly, but I believe the risk factor has now increased, particularly in terms of the urgency on his part. I mean, it's quite likely he'll ignore his usual instincts and go for the kill at the first opportunity he gets, even if it's just a straightforward drive-by hit. And then he'll clear out of the UK for good. Sadly, we suspect he has all sorts of exit routes that we remain unaware of. I mean, his profile, from our security services' perspective, is now up there with the most-wanted. Gone are the days when he thought his relationship with Section 12 offered him some kind of umbrella, as long as he covered his tracks. But, as I said, that's no longer the case," said Major Carr.

"Shit," exclaimed Marcus. "How's Inspector Forsyth?"

Shattered collar bone, but he'll survive. Medics are with him now," replied Brinkworth, relieved.

• CHAPTER 35 •

The team had all gathered on the Balcony Terrace as instructed. Scattered around with their weapons, tac-comm kits, and Body Cams, as directed, smoking and drinking the coffee that Katja had thoughtfully offered. All were waiting patiently for the Ground Commander to begin his postmortem of events.

Willy declared that the actual engagement had lasted precisely nine minutes and forty-six seconds.

"Seemed longer," commented Major Freddy Carr.

"Right, girls, I know it's well past your bedtime, but I'll get this done as quickly as I can. The Investigative Team will arrive in approximately 10 minutes. First, bloody well done. Okay, we missed The Prize, but we took out a lot of nasties. You can now remove your Tac-Comm kit. All verbal exchanges were recorded with ID tags, so no problem there. Until otherwise instructed, please keep your weapons with you for inspection. Each of us will have our Bodycams registered to our ID, allowing individual footage to be watched in real-time by the CIT team later. Keep them with you. Be ready to make and sign statements as needed. We've, of course, got all the security footage to hand, apart from the TV room, but Major Carr's head cam coverage should be enough to cover that. I know it's a bit of a bind after what we've all been through, but the sooner everyone cooperates with the CIT team, the sooner we can all go home to bed. So, stand down and wait for the team to arrive," said Chief Inspector Johnny Brinkworth, in conclusion.

Several vehicles arrived quickly up the driveway. Their teams swiftly deployed. Chief Inspector Brinkworth recognised Ducky Watson immediately as he walked towards him, hand out. They shook hands warmly. This wasn't the first time they'd faced this kind of scenario.

"Good to see you, Ducky," said Brinkworth, always amused by Watson's nickname.

"Any casualties on our side?" said Ducky.

"One dead. One injured but on the mend. We've got eight dead nasties for your people to deal with. I've detailed the protocols to everyone present and what to expect from your people. They're ready and waiting," replied Brinkworth.

"Sorry to hear we missed The Prize."

"Yeah, right, Murphy's Law again. Captain de Vere's operative, Gibbs, is, as we speak, tracking the vehicle that left the scene. Thankfully, de Vere had the foresight to set that up well before the party started," said Brinkworth.

"And the package?" asked Ducky.

“All’s well there, and they weren’t involved in the show, tucked up in the Safe Room for the duration. So, I’d like them to be on their way later in the morning under the protection of Captain de Vere. Agreeable? And in that respect, would you mind processing him first? As he, Doctor Meer, and her family are quite close, and I’m sure he’d want to get down there to bring her up to speed,” Brinkworth said.

"Affirmative, Johnny. Bring him up here. I’ve never met him, but from what I’ve heard, it’s all good,” said Ducky Watson.

“For the sake of good order, Ducky, I should mention that Captain Marcus de Vere was carrying throughout the show.”

“Did he kill anybody?”

“No,” said Chief Inspector Brinkworth, with a wry smile.

“Good news then. Under the circumstances, I don’t really give a damn, but I’m still happy he didn’t actually kill anybody, so much paperwork, right? Good call, Johnny,” said Ducky reassuringly.

Realising that Johnny had stuck his neck out a bit on that one, but nothing that could not have been dealt with without any serious kickback to cause waves.

After Marcus had undergone intensive scrutiny by the Criminal Investigative Team, completed his statement, and signed it, Ducky moved to introduce himself to Marcus. They shook hands firmly.

"Nice to finally meet you, Marcus. As I mentioned to Johnny Brinkworth earlier, your name and de Vere Security’s operations, both here, in the UAE, and elsewhere, are frequently mentioned. I don’t want to sound overly formal, but I’d like to take this chance to thank you personally, on behalf of King and Country, for your service," he said, placing his hand on Marcus's shoulder. "By the way, my family and I will visit Abu Dhabi for a vacation later this year. Would it be alright if I stopped by to say hello?"

"Thanks, you're welcome any time," said Marcus, reaching into his pocket for his business card.

"Don't need that. We know where you are," chuckled Ducky Watson.

"Yeah, I suppose you do, and you probably also know what I have for breakfast each day," laughed Marcus in response.

"Well, I wouldn't go that far. I'll leave the awareness of your nutritional needs to MI6, but take care," he said with a chuckle, moving away to oversee his people's scrutiny of the scene and their progress.

***

After his debrief, Marcus headed to the Safe Room. Although it was still very early in the morning, he did not doubt that Cathy would still be awake. The intercom buzzed, making Cathy jump.

"Yes," she replied, sounding apprehensive and nervous.

"Cathy, everything's fine, it's over, at least for now," Marcus said, hearing her long sigh of relief.

"Do you mind if I stop by while the children are still sleeping?" he asked cautiously.

"Are you kidding?"

She opened the door and threw herself into his arms, kissing him passionately with her legs wrapped around his waist. Tears of relief spilt onto his cheek. They disengaged, and he entered the room.

Marcus sat in the smoking area with Cathy and Monica, the tension of waiting clearly visible on both women's faces. Happily sipping the wine Cathy had offered as Marcus explained, in detail, everything that had happened, gulping his own down quickly.

"Any more of that?" smiled Marcus. "I can't tell you how good that tastes."

"So, he's escaped then? Is that it? Maybe he was never here, right?"

"I'm sorry, Cathy, that we didn't manage to take him out. But he was there. Gibbs followed him all the way down here. We don't know where he is now but Gibbs is following our tracker, so we'll find him. My best guess is that when it all fell apart for his team, he followed a preplanned exit strategy.

"Shit, so, you're saying that after everything we all went through, Badawi escaped?" Her hand was shaking as she refilled his glass and lit a cigarette. She and Monica had been, more or less, chain-smoking since the kids had gone down.

"So, it's not over then, is it?" said Cathy.

"No, it's not, darling, but we'll address that later," Marcus said, feeling uneasy. He reached out to Cathy and hugged her close to him but his mind was in turmoil. All he could do right now was to take care of her and the children and wait for developments.

The satellite phone buzzed, and Marcus immediately answered it.

"Yeah?"

"Got word from Gibbs, and looks like Badawi's passing through Gloucester as we speak, and I think from memory there's an airfield nearby – I'll check it out," said Carter.

"Copy that. I plan to take Cathy, Monica, and the children out later once we've had some sleep, and then, finally, home by early evening. We haven't discussed it, but after everything she's been through, my gut feeling is that she will want to be at Willow Tree House. Stand down for now, and I'll buzz you to confirm later. Are you good with that?" said Marcus.

"All's good."

Marcus terminated the call.

• CHAPTER 36 •

Asif sat grim-faced as he drove down the forest track towards the open road. He'd already accepted that his security communications must have been compromised, but was at least pleased that he'd listened to his instincts in preparing for a potential trap. The loss of his team was of no concern. Now, he pulled over to inspect his vehicle. How was his team's arrival so predictable? He soon found the answer and noted the tracking device attached above the rear offside tyre.

He decided to leave it in position. It would support his now revised exit strategy. He telephoned Syed to explain his plan and arrange a car swap. Syed would leave the Land Cruiser at Cotswold Airport as a distraction, while he made his way to Doctor Meer's home and concealed himself on the grounds for the kill. He believed his reasoning was sound, given the high likelihood that she would return to Willow Tree House at some point. He had all the time in the world – he didn't care. All that mattered was fulfilling his objective – to kill her and her children.

• CHAPTER 37 •

“Darling, let’s get some sleep. After breakfast around 11-ish, we’ll take the kids out via a side door to my car for lunch and a day out. The chaos outside should be cleared up by then. The children won’t see anything untoward, and there’s a fantastic adventure theme park nearby that they'd enjoy. By around 6-ish, we’ll all head home,” Marcus said, trying to sound reassuring.

Hours later, they had all enjoyed a wonderful day, and the children loved the theme park. Cathy, Monica, and Marcus were all on the same path towards finally relaxing.

Cathy turned to Marcus.

“Darling, would you mind if I drop the children off at Monica’s on the way? I really need some alone time tonight. Do you understand? It’s nothing against you, just how I’m feeling right now," Cathy said with a tired sigh.

"I understand, Cathy. I'll come with you to Monica's, and we'll talk in the morning," said Marcus.

"Thank you so much, darling, for understanding. I've spoken to Monica about it, and she's happy with the arrangement. The children will be delighted to spend time with her at the cottage, and she'll take them to school in the morning. Leaving me free," said Cathy with relief, eager to enjoy some time relaxing on her own away from everything – even Marcus. She felt so fortunate to have such a man beside her. And she was so happy that George and Jenny had bonded with him almost from the start. She considered herself blessed.

"It's all good, darling, don't worry," said Marcus as they hurried to their cars. The Colonel had already unlocked the barns. Marcus followed her in his Subaru Forester. As he drove, he picked up his mobile to update Carter.

"All good, boss. I'll be on the grounds of Willow Tree House within the hour and will check everything, of course – windows and doors etc., and Anna will take over the next morning. Okay?"

"Affirmative, thanks, Carter."

As he passed Cathy's car outside Monica's cottage, he blew her a kiss and made his way home to Little Manor, feeling satisfied that all was as well as it could be.

Upon arriving, he phoned her. "Darling, I'm home now. Carter is nearby and will be on the grounds very soon, so don't worry. Sleep well, talk tomorrow. Love you," Marcus said.

"Ditto, thanks for calling. I'm just going to have an early night and hope that by morning I can start to feel more relaxed about everything. It's been a rather bloody day, one way or another. But I'm glad the children enjoyed their weekend, at least, and were blissfully unaware of all the drama. I've just said goodnight to them, and both are over the moon to be with Monica. Goodnight, darling," said Cathy as she unlocked the front door of Willow Tree House, relieved to be home and safe but surprised that the alarm system didn't start bleeping on entry. She obviously forgot about setting it on leaving. But all seemed to be well.

At Little Manor, Marcus was about to get into bed when the phone rang. He answered it nervously, hoping it wasn't bad news.

"Gibbs, what's up?"

"Thought you should know, boss, I tracked the Land Cruiser to Cotswold Airport."

"And?"

"Well, I checked with flight control, and a privately owned Cessna 510 Mustang just took off minutes ago and guess what?"

"What? Get on with it, Gibbs." There was a slight irritation in Marcus's voice.

"Sorry, boss, it's owned by the same Iranian diplomat who owned the flat where Syed was staying in Chelsea some time ago. I guess it's fair to say that Asif and his No. 2 are no longer around."

"Shit. But we can't be sure, right?"

"True, but the car's here. As you know, this airport isn't under our security contracts, so when I asked to view their surveillance footage, they said I'd have to wait until tomorrow, explaining that it was their protocol."

"Okay, so be it. Nothing we can do about that now. Get some kip, we'll talk tomorrow," said Captain Marcus de Vere, wearily. He thought about ringing Cathy, but then again, nothing was forever certain in the world that he lived in – so he let it go. It could wait.

Cathy paused briefly to gaze at the beautiful painting of Fred the woodpecker. It was the cathartic moment she needed. She decided to have a nightcap – a good choice as she felt the bourbon's warmth envelop her. Moving to her bedroom, she gladly took off her clothes and turned the shower to full blast, which proved just the trick to induce sleep. It was a warm evening. She turned on the Tiffany bedside lamp, loving the organic colours that cast a warm glow over the diaphanous silk sheet as she pulled it up to cover her naked body. Her hand moved to feel the reassuring comfort of her SIG under the pillow beside her. Nevertheless, knowing that either Carter or Anna was nearby to protect if needed was a major factor in her increasing state of relaxation following the events of the day.

As she lay back, seeking the blessing of sleep to come, she recalled the time when, as a very little girl, she had been frightened by the endless, strange moaning, groaning, and creaking sounds of Willow Tree House that had often kept her awake at night. But then her dad had quickly sat down with her to gently explain that it was just the noise of the ancient timber-framed house voicing its complaints as it breathed through the changing seasons, growing older and older. From that moment on, as she grew up, she had gotten used to them, and they had never disturbed her since. However, there were two very distinct noises she had accepted as the norm over the years. But the family had never taken the time to repair the cause of these, and neither had she; it had to be said. One was the third step at the top of the stairs leading to the landing, which always creaked, and the other was the floorboard under the landing carpet that led to her and her parents' bedroom, which squeaked when stepped on.

CHAPTER 38

Cathy happily drifted into a deep, welcome sleep and didn't hear the telltale squeak of the third step on the stairs, but then she awoke at the creak on the landing outside the bedroom. Instinctively, she knew it was him and calmly reached for the SIG, which lay waiting under the pillow next to her. In one smooth movement, she loaded a round and carefully placed the pistol tightly concealed beside her thigh. The reason she felt so composed was unclear, but she was ready and confident.

The bedroom door creaked open slowly. Asif Badawi entered quietly, pleased to see her bare beneath the silk; he couldn't have hoped for more. His body responded instinctively to her sight. He quietly sat on a chair at the foot of the bed, watching her with intense desire mixed with a conflicted urge to kill. Gently, he tapped his pistol's barrel against the bedframe to intimidate her. Cathy feigned waking, striving to appear disoriented.

"Good evening, Doctor Meer. You should seriously think about upgrading your locks and security system. They're a bit outdated, but that's not the main issue now. Anyway, I digress. I can't hide how much I enjoy seeing you again and finding you exactly where I want you to be... in bed. I'll be joining you shortly. Once we've... erm... finished, I'll go and say goodbye to your children- permanently, just so you're aware," said Badawi, smiling and raising his pistol.

"It's a pity they're not here," he continued, his eyes twinkling with malicious anticipation. "I wished for you all to be together for the final act – you see, I've waited such a long time," he added, leering at her. Cathy observed Badawi's imposing stature and realised she had no chance physically against what was to come, rape and murder. She locked her eyes with his, now flashing with a clear desire for her.

Calmly, she reached slowly for the pendant around her neck. Shit, it wasn't there – a wave of panic swept over her. Only then did she realise she'd left it in the bathroom after her shower. She'd broken Carter's cardinal rule.

"Damn it," Cathy muttered to herself in frustration, realising that trying to reach for her SIG P226 would not work under his intense scrutiny.

"I need to use the bathroom first," Cathy said, stalling as she wrapped the sheer silk sheet around herself, though it did little to hide her nudity, much to his amusement.

"Sure, why not? Let's go – can't wait to see that," said Badawi, grinning. Following her with his pistol, ready.

As she entered the bathroom, she discreetly picked up the pendant she had left near the sink and squeezed it tightly. Then, to Badawi's satisfaction, she sat on the toilet, and almost as soon as she pretended to sit, she stood up abruptly and hurried to the bed, covering herself with the silk sheet.

"That's not going to protect you, bitch," said Badawi, unzipping his trousers with one hand while holding his weapon with the other. As he focused on that, Cathy's hand grasped the SIG that lay close beside her thigh – ready. Hoping against hope that Carter was nearby, otherwise it was all going to be too close to the wire.

Outside, Carter sat quietly by the little spring beneath the weeping willows – longing for the smoke he couldn't have- when he received the ping from the panic button.

Asif's intense gaze fixed on Cathy; he was sure he had her to himself, and no one was coming to rescue her.

"Well, before we begin, where are the children?"

"Screw you, Asif! You don't scare me," Cathy screamed, her eyes blazing with defiance, sounding braver than she felt. But Carter was approaching, wasn't he? She looked around wildly, thinking of different scenarios at the same time.

"Oh, but I am quite frightening, Dr Meer. I believe I hold all the cards and have the pistol, correct? I was actually a bit disappointed not to find the kids here. I even rested in their bedroom while waiting for you, playing with their toys and looking at their drawings, so sweet and innocent. Of course, I plan to kill you, but not before we have some fun first. Patience is one of my strengths. So, where are they? Start talking and stop stalling; you're on your own now. No knight in shining armour is coming on his white steed to save you this time," Asif said with a lopsided grin, enjoying the moment he had so long waited for. Now prepared, he started to approach the side of her bed slowly.

Just at that moment, the bedroom door burst open as Carter, literally, rolled in with special forces precision. In an instant, he was in a ready-to-fire stance. Badawi turned, surprised by the interruption, and aimed his pistol at Carter, but it was too late as Cathy seized the moment. Without hesitation, she sat up, grasping the SIG with a steady two-handed grip, and fired three tightly grouped shots into the centre of his chest. The impact of the rounds sent his half-naked body crashing against the bedroom wall. He managed, on reflex, to fire a stray shot, which harmlessly embedded itself in the wall above Carter's head. Badawi was dead before his body hit the floor.

Cathy registered the disbelief and shock on his face with immense pleasure and satisfaction. It was all she needed to finally feel at peace. Taking in the scene in an instant, Carter kicked Badawi's weapon away and checked the body for signs of life. There were none. He then went to comfort Cathy by her bedside, holding her now-shaking hand in his.

"I'm very sorry, ma'am. I had no idea he was waiting for you inside the house – that explains everything. He must have come straight here after the raid to hide and wait for you. I have no idea how he got in. I checked all the doors and windows earlier."

"He's dead. That's what matters most, Carter, and thank you – perfect timing," Cathy said, now fully in control again. She paused to reflect on how the bullets had affected Badawi's body, then released the magazine, pushed a round onto her palm with her thumb, and smiled.

"What is it, ma'am?

"Take a look," said Cathy, smiling.

Carter did. "Well, well, a Sig .357 round.

There you go, ma'am – that's the boss for you," grinned Carter.

"That's my man. If it came to it, he wanted me to have it in spades," smiled Cathy.

"Thank God. It's over, it's over. How are you, ma'am?" Carter said as his adrenaline started to subside, holstering his weapon.

"I'm doing well, actually better than that. Just get rid of him. I've had enough of him invading my space," she said before finally collapsing, exhausted.

Carter dragged Badawi to the entrance of the house and pulled it out of view. He immediately tried to inform Marcus, but found his line busy, then rang Major Carr, who responded instantly.

"What's up, Carter?"

"Badawi's dead, Major. I'm at Doctor Meer's place. She took him out as I burst through the bedroom door. He'd turned towards me and managed to let one go as he went down with three tightly grouped shots to his chest – bloody good shooting, I must say, given the situation."

"You mean Cathy killed him?"

"Affirmative Major. As I said, bloody good shooting considering the circumstances."

"The bedroom, you say, she's...erm...alright? If you get my drift?"

"Didn't get that far, Major. She activated her panic button, and I arrived in under twenty seconds. She's okay, except for the aftershock, which is fading as we speak. She's one amazing, cool lady," said Carter, his voice filled with genuine admiration.

"Thank goodness for that."

"To be honest, Major, I think she's more than delighted to have been the one to take him down – I'm certain in my mind that it was a catharsis moment for her. You just couldn't write this stuff. I mean, first he kills her husband, and then, six plus years later, she takes him down in spades, good and proper. I mean, you couldn't make this up, could you – talk about destiny?"

"Yeah, who would've seen that coming?"

"Where's the body?"

"She asked me to take it out of the bedroom, Major. So, I took it down to the grounds and dragged it out of sight."

"Good. Have you reached Marcus de Vere yet?"

"His line was busy, Major. Shall I try again or ring Special Branch?"

"That's a no, no. Leave Special Branch and MI5 out of this. That'll just open up a whole new can of worms – not a word to anyone – too much paperwork, mate. Got it? If nobody knows about it, then it didn't happen, right?"

"Affirmative. So, what should I do?"

"Okay, I'll deal with Marcus. And I'll deploy a 'clean-up' team as soon as I put the phone down. By lunchtime tomorrow, the house will be back exactly as it was. Nothing happened there. The body will...erm...turn up, eventually, somewhere, and Cathy's SIG will be destroyed. So, case closed. When the body's found, it will, without evidence to the contrary, be considered an assassination by party or parties unknown – end of story – no come-back, Carter. Right?"

"Got it, Major. Loud and clear."

"Okay, hand over her SIG and shell casings to the team and let them take control of the scene when they arrive. Once you've handed them over, stand down. Well done, mate, and give Cathy my regards. Are we good?"

"Affirmative Major."

"Right. Okay, one last thing – ask Cathy to call Monica and update her. I believe Doctor Meer should stay there tonight. The kids are probably already in bed and sleeping; her best option is to remain with them until morning. Marcus might want to come quickly, but I will advise him to stay calm and wait until the kids are in school. Take her home, Carter; she's had enough."

"Affirmative, Major, I'll take her straight away," said Carter, relieved. Finally, a good outcome...

• CHAPTER 39 •

Carter parked outside Monica's cottage and was about to get out to open her door for her, but Cathy raised her hand.

"Thank you, Carter, for everything. Fortunately, when I took a welcome shower, I remembered your instructions not to get the pendant wet, but then left it there," she managed a laugh as she reached across the car to squeeze his hand.

"No problem, ma'am. It's my job, but you beat me to it. I must say, I take my hat off to you. You're an exceptional lady," Carter replied, showing a rare emotional moment.

"Can I keep it?" she asked as she touched the exquisite piece of jewellery around her neck.

"Of course, ma'am, and I hope you won't need it again," said Carter, feeling slightly embarrassed, and he quickly got out of the car to open her door.

Monica stood at the entrance of her cottage to welcome her.

"I've killed him, Monica – Badawi – it is finally over."

Monica was stunned and almost speechless.

"Come here, darling Cathy," said Monica as she held her gently and wiped her tears away tenderly.

"You are an extraordinary woman. Come in and let's get you to bed, you're exhausted."

"How are my children?" Cathy asked, feeling both overwhelmed and incredibly grateful to be alive.

"Fast asleep as you should be. We all had a great evening, and they went to bed very happy without a care in the world."

"Oh, Monica, thank you so much," she said, wiping a tear from her cheek. "I need a drink even though dawn must be about to break, and then I promise I will hit the sheets,"

Later that morning, the children peeked into the bedroom, delighted to find their mother curled up, fast asleep. Monica had prepared their favourite breakfast, which Jenny and George wolfed down – eager to get to school and tell their friends all about the fun they'd had at Uncle Charlie's house in the Gloucestershire countryside at the weekend, and George had taken with him all his pictures of the Colonel's Bentley to share with his fellow enthusiasts.

***

Marcus had received a call from Monica after she'd taken the children to school, and she confirmed that Cathy was still sleeping peacefully, which was the best news he'd heard, but it didn't end there. Gibbs had also rung to confirm that he'd seen the airport's security footage, which clearly showed that Syed had left the country, which removed any further potential threat – it was, finally, over. Carter had also telephoned and had given him a step-by-step account of all that had happened at Willow Tree House in the early hours.

Marcus sat back in overwhelming relief and deep admiration for, hopefully, his wife-to-be. He walked to his car with a bounce in his step and was eager to hold the love of his life once again in his arms.

Marcus arrived to pick up Cathy for Little Manor. Both, overwhelmed by being together again, held each other for a long moment. "I've got a special surprise waiting for you at Little Manor, so let's go," Marcus said, sweeping her off her feet and carrying her to the car.

As he drove, he explained that the Ministry had issued a 'D-Notice' on the weekend's events, meaning the Government had given news editors a directive not to publish certain information for reasons of national security. As she listened to the news that morning, there was only a brief mention that a terrorist attack on a country house in southwest England had occurred but was successfully thwarted over the weekend by the country's security services, and that no civilians had been involved or injured.

Cathy felt relieved that no references to her or her family were made as she joined Marcus with a glass of bubbly on the balcony terrace, which Henry seemed to provide effortlessly, as always. They leaned back, feeling calm and content, sipping their wine and sharing a puff. Suddenly, Cathy's work phone buzzed, prompting her to answer, curious about what was coming next. Marcus observed her closely, worried, as she listened intently and then nodded in response to whoever was on the line.

“It’s my first day on call this week, darling. Sorry, I’ve got to go, but it won’t take long. I’ve been asked to give a second opinion on a body at the city morgue.”

“Can’t you take some time off? I mean, you’ve been through a lot,” Marcus said kindly. “We now know Syed has left the country, and MI5 and MI6 are listening to the chatter just to be safe. Freddy and I believe your family is no longer in danger from terrorists. Nonetheless, I want you to keep this for now. Is that okay?” Marcus asked, handing her a green Harrods bag. “Hope you don’t mind, it’s a replacement SIG Sauer P226 with a spare mag."

Cathy chuckled and said, “Honestly, it’s just what I need. I’d feel vulnerable without it, something to keep my mind occupied. Don’t worry, as I said, it won’t take long. See you later,” she added warmly, giving him a kiss before heading out. “And don’t worry, I understand about the pistol," she continued, slipping it into her bag. "By the way, where’s my surprise?”

“When you get back,” laughed Marcus, watching her drive away, his face lit up with a broad, happy grin, feeling grateful for how truly lucky he was, especially after years of loneliness. His thoughts were soon interrupted by the buzzing of his phone.

“Hi, Marcus. I’m at the airport, and I find that my Lord and Master’s not here to meet me,” said Penny, laughing.

"Oh my God, Penny, I'm really sorry, I totally forgot. It's been a crazy weekend, I'll explain later," Marcus said apologetically.

"Not to worry, I'll take a cab. See you soon."

It was her planned monthly visit. He was eager to introduce her to Cathy, recalling how excited Penny was to meet her, but that would have to wait. Marcus greeted Penny at the entrance of Little Manor with outstretched arms, ready to welcome her.

"Hi Marcus, great to see you looking well. As we arrived at your place, a stunning Bugatti sped past. Did you catch it? I think it was going over 100 mph," Penny said excitedly. Marcus was very aware of her passion for fast cars.

"Well. I didn't see it, but I certainly heard the bloody thing. He uses this stretch of road as his own private racetrack."

"So, you know him then?"

"His name is Malone. He's a neighbour from down the road at Frog Hall. He's a bit of an oddball, in my view, but I invited him to my birthday drinks the other day to be neighbourly. In my opinion, he's quite an over-the-top charm machine, and I wasn't pleased that he mainly focused his attention on Cathy."

"Jealous?"

"No," laughed Marcus. "Cathy did her best to keep clear."

"So, where is this gem of yours? I can't wait to meet her."

"On call. Dealing with a dead body somewhere, but should be back later. But I've got tremendous news!"

"You're getting married."

"How... how could you possibly know?" Marcus said, dumbfounded. "Nobody knows yet. I haven't even proposed. Cathy had to leave for a call."

"Marcus, how many years have I known you? It's written all over your face," Penny said. "Come here," she added, hugging him warmly. "I'm genuinely so happy for you, and I need to meet her as soon as possible. In the meantime, I want to see the car," Penny urged. "Can't you call him?"

"You're incorrigible, Penny. You've only just arrived, and by the way, thank you both for the birthday present – it certainly made my day special."

"Our pleasure, Commander Bond," Penny said, smiling. "Come on, Marcus, you know me and cars. Let's get going."

"Okay, Moneypenny, you win," said Marcus, accustomed to giving in to Penny's persistence to get her way, as he picked up his mobile.

"Hi Ben, it's Marcus. My No.2 just arrived from Abu Dhabi for a few days, and she's a big Bugatti fan. Can I bring her over to check out your car? I realise it's short notice, but she'll never let me hear the end of it if I don't," Marcus said, feeling a bit awkward about asking.

"No problem, Marcus. You're welcome," The Painter said.

Marcus and Penny drove up the carriage drive of Frog Hall to find Ben standing beside his 'beast', waiting for them. After the introductions, Penny looked at the car in awe.

"Oh my God, Mr Malone, this really is some impressive piece of kit. It looks like it's about to take off. If I'm correct, this baby has a power output of 1,500 HP, that's unprecedented for production vehicles, isn't it? Plus, an exceptionally high torque of 1,600 Nm between 2,000 and 6,000 rpm. Am I right?" Penny asked.

"Spot on, you know your stuff, and it's got a top speed of 261 mph, but that's just the road version. It reaches 62 mph in 2.4 seconds! Can you believe that?" said The Painter proudly, warming to Penny's passion for his car.

"Yeah. I read that somewhere. Could you just start it up for me? I'd love to hear the sound of all those horses ready to gallop!" said Penny. The sound sent waves of pleasure through her body; it was like a hundred big Harley-Davidsons starting up simultaneously.

"That's the result of the legendary and unique eight-litre W16 engine developed by them. In combination with the four new, larger turbochargers controlled by Bugatti's two-stage turbocharging, an innovation they introduced alongside numerous other technical refinements and innovations, maximum performance is constantly available and easily manageable at all speeds," said The Painter, now in his element.

"Hey, look, Marcus," as Penny opened the boot, "Even the tools are encased in stitched leather," she said appreciatively.

"There's not much space for luggage, though!" Marcus said sadly.

"It's a boy's toy, Marcus. Get real," laughed Penny.

"Look, why don't you guys come into the study, which also serves as my office. I have the car's presentation book from the manufacturer. It's in a fully illustrated format, which you might appreciate, Penny," said The Painter encouragingly.

He led them into an impressive, expansive oak-panelled room. A large sash window overlooked the gardens, soft rays of sunlight accentuated Ben's fine English solid walnut desk, bringing out its rich colour. While The Painter searched for the Bugatti Presentation Book, Marcus noticed a mahogany case resting on the desk, with a brass inlaid plaque inscribed 'H.W. Mortimer, London'.

"Do you mind, Ben?" Marcus asked, gesturing toward the case.

"Be my guest," he appeared to say, pleased by the interest.

"I seem to recall from somewhere, wasn't this company given a royal warrant by King George III?" Marcus exclaimed as he examined the pair of superb English officers' duelling pistols, admiring the perfect balance of the matched pair and the fine detail of the scroll work.

"Yes, I believe so. They're a treasured heirloom. They've been in the family for years, and note that the accessories include a ball pulling rod, original bullet mould, powder and shot measure, balls, flints, tow, turn screw, and the original 3-way powder flask," said The Painter with pride.

"So, the full shooting match then, if you'll forgive the pun," smiled Marcus, impressed.

"Must be worth a bit. Have you ever tried them out?"

"Oh yes. Had a brief fling with them some time ago. Found they performed superbly," said The Painter, relishing the memory.

He laid the illustrated Bugatti catalogue on the desk in front of Penny.

"I believe this occasion calls for a splash of pink. What are your thoughts?"

"Sounds good to me," said Penny as The Painter reached for a bottle of Louis Roederer's Cristal Rosé from a small, discreetly placed wine cooler and threw a few large chunks of ice into a conveniently positioned ice bucket in an ornate stand near the enormous desk. Then he produced three chilled Baccarate fluted crystal glasses from somewhere.

"Cheers and welcome to Frog Hall," he said, momentarily distracted by Penny's slender figure and slyly wondering what might lie beneath her elegant Chanel outfit, probably not bad for a woman of her age, but way, way too old for his tastes. Nonetheless, it was a thought-provoking possibility, *'why not,'* he thought.

"Bottoms up," said Penny, sipping her wine. "I must say, Ben, the colour and taste are truly exquisite. I'm guessing a Pinot Noir and Chardonnay blend. Am I right?" she added, holding up her glass to the gentle light coming through the arch window.

"Spot on again, matured in oak casks for about six years in their cellars," said The Painter, who was beginning to become increasingly obsessed with this woman.

"And the glasses, well, they're simply beautiful. What are they? If you don't mind me asking."

"Well, my dear, apart from having a discerning palate, you, of course, also have a discerning eye for glassware. You're holding a Baccarate Crystal Mille Nuits Flutissimo," he replied, reaching out to clink his glass with hers, completely ignoring Marcus.

"Yes, they are beautiful glasses, Ben, but is there anything else that needs saying?" said Marcus, growing irritated with Ben's constant focus on details and, in his mind, his awkward attempt to charm Penny.

"Well, as you are surely aware, Marcus, Baccarate crystal glass dates back to 1817. Examine the glass carefully. The smooth, narrow bowl contrasts with the intricacy of the bevelled stem. The detailing extends all the way down to the ridged foot. The two halves are joined by the elegant diamond-shaped centre, which is, of course, the Mille Nuits signature."

"Interesting," said Marcus, wishing he hadn't asked and couldn't wait to leave.

While Penny and Ben were heavily engrossed in all things Bugatti, Marcus sat comfortably at Ben's desk and couldn't help but admire the quality of the English furniture and the extensive library, yet remained fascinated with the pistols, testing their balance in his hand and wondering how he would fare using one in a duel. Satisfied with the Bugatti, Penny wandered off around the library, impressed by its eclectic collection of books. She came across a fine teak glass-fronted bookcase, tucked away between the rows of bookshelves, which drew her attention. She was intrigued to see twenty or more hardback editions, all by an author named J.J. Shepherd. She wondered why the collection warranted display, unaccompanied, in the fine teak case.

"May I?" she asked, glancing at the books with interest.

"So many here, Ben the author must be one of your favourites?" said Penny, intrigued. Then she noticed a framed Sunday Times review dated two years earlier.

"What's this?"

"Ah, I couldn't resist framing the news cutting critique," said Ben, more and more captivated by how her body moved with such fluidity.

"Read it out," said Marcus, attempting to sound interested.

"Okay, here goes...

'Thanatos' is the latest best-seller from the elusive J.J. Shepherd. It features more bodies per chapter than the 90s TV series 'Midsomer Murders', with his usual flair for twists and turns that keep the reader on their toes – a must-buy. Fans try their best to uncover his or her true identity, but to no avail. The author has never agreed to do book signings or public appearances, and rumour has it that even the publisher has never actually met the writer, making him a fascinating enigma.'

"Interesting," said Marcus, trying not to sound as bored as he felt. But it certainly explained Ben's wealth.

"It's you, isn't it, Mr Malone?"

"Ben, please. Yes, I confess. But mum's the word – do you promise me, my dear?" said The Painter, pleased, for some reason, to admit his authorship. Had they been on their own, he might even have made a play for her at this moment, but little did he know who he was dealing with.

Penny kept wandering around but now understood what Marcus meant about the man's unbearable efforts at charm. Sure, he was attractive until he spoke.

"Do you mind if I smoke, Ben? I notice you have discreetly placed extractor fans at each end of the room," said Marcus, beginning to tire of Ben's seemingly never-ending over-the-top attitude, and he was in no doubt about his insincerity and constant false charm.

"You're welcome, Marcus, along with anyone else for that matter," he said as he reached for one of his oval cigarettes.

"So, are you into crime fiction, Marcus?" said The Painter, also starting to tire of chatting with him and wishing he were alone with Penny.

"Not really, I don't have time. I think I've been too exposed to different aspects of the reality of crime to bother reading about it. Since I'm involved in that field, for better or worse," Marcus said cautiously.

"Ah, yes, of course you're in the security business, I forgot. So, you have an office in Maidstone as well as Abu Dhabi?"

"Yes, it's one of several scattered locations, but I must admit, the latter is among the most profitable spots. That's where Penny steps in. She manages everything for me there," said Marcus, curious about where this was heading and hoping it would end quickly.

"Actually, I only mentioned it because I have an old friend living there, Asif Badawi. Do you know him?"

Stunned, Marcus paused to suggest that he was searching his mind.

"Ah, yes, I've seen him wandering about in Abu Dhabi from time to time, come to think of it, but I never actually met him personally until I bumped into him at a drinks event at Chiddington Hall a while ago. Quite a good-looking chap, if I remember correctly. He was introduced to us by Sir James, and I seem to recall that Sir James and Mr Badawi appeared to know each other well and were both rather taken with my friend Doctor Cathy Meer at the time," Marcus said, trying hard to make light of it.

"Well, he does have a reputation for being attracted to beautiful women, a bit of a ladies' man, I understand. And, if I may say so, without offending Doctor Meer, she certainly would fit into that category without any doubt. If you know what I mean. It's a small world, Marcus."

"So, if my memory is right, you were there too?" Marcus said calmly.

"Yes, you're right, I recall now," said The Painter, somewhat surprised. "Yes, of course, but Dr Meer is a very attractive woman – how could I forget? With her uncle, as I recall. Anyway, I'm not surprised at all by Asif's interest in her," The Painter added cautiously, thinking, *'aren't we all?'*

"But such is life, don't you agree? I mean, we can't be held accountable for appreciating beauty when we encounter it, can we?"

'Touché,' thought Marcus.

They gathered around Ben's desk to savour the last sips of the excellent wine.

"Your wife?" said Penny, glancing at a framed picture of a very attractive woman resting on a shelf at the back of the library.

"Erm... no, her name's Helen, just a friend," said The Painter, inwardly shocked that he had left the bloody picture there, forgotten. At least, he had hidden his father's collection of rare obsidian blades in one of his cellars.

"Sadly, she went missing a few years ago, leaving no trace. Of course, the police looked into it but found nothing, so I hired a private detective, but he had no luck either. In fact, both she and her twin sister vanished off the face of the Earth at the same time. Very distressing, but I live in hope," said The Painter, his anxiety mounting as he noticed the attention given to the bloody photograph he should have discarded long ago, hopefully not another lapse in his concentration that he would later regret.

"Oh dear, I'm so sorry to hear that. Beautiful earrings," said Penny. "But thank you so much for everything and for your time showing me your magnificent car. But I think we'd better get back to Little Manor as I feel a touch of jet lag coming on," said Penny, sensing an inexplicable tension in the room and wishing to leave.

"Oh, by the way, Ben, didn't you have a book that you wanted to lend Dr Meer? I'd be happy to give it to her on your behalf," said Marcus, delighted to be on his way.

"Ah, yes, kind of you. But it's not just any book. It's a very rare 1st Edition and, in fact, now that I think about it, it's the only remaining copy, making it truly unique. With all due respect, I'd prefer to give it to her personally. Both of you are welcome to collect it at your convenience. Give me a ring," replied The Painter, full of lascivious anticipation at seeing her once again.

• CHAPTER 40 •

Cathy arrived back to find Henry waiting at the entrance of Little Manor to greet her – how he knew of her arrival was anyone's guess, but it was par for the course as far as he was concerned.

"Good evening, Doctor Meer. The Captain is waiting for you on the upper balcony," Henry said with a rare smile. A grin from Henry! What could it mean? Cathy wondered as she hurried up the winding staircase. Perhaps this was going to be the surprise.

As Cathy stepped onto the balcony, she was met with an array of red roses on each of the white, ornate wrought iron tables scattered across the terrace. Marcus was kneeling on one knee before her.

"Marcus, what's happening?" she laughed.

"Darling, will you marry me?" he asked, holding out an exquisite velvet ring box.

"Oh my God, darling, yes, forever. It's absolutely beautiful," she said, holding the Victorian Diamond Cluster Ring.

"It was my mother's. She would have been so happy to see you wearing it," Marcus said, fighting back a tear that threatened to fall down his cheek.

On cue, Henry arrived holding two chilled Waterford Crystal glasses of pink bubbly. "May I be the first to congratulate you both," Henry said with a slight bow.

"There's someone quite special I want you to meet. She's in my study and eager to meet you," Marcus said cheerfully as he led his surprised fiancée downstairs.

As he had predicted, both she and Penny immediately got on like a house on fire and began to chat as if they'd known each other for years, and he guessed that his name would likely come up a little in their exchanges. Wisely, he stepped back and left them to it. Henry appeared, as expected, to attend to their needs. Mentioning to Marcus, as he left, that he planned to provide luncheon in an hour.

"Great to meet you, Cathy. I've been looking forward to meeting the woman who has captured Marcus's heart. And wow, your engagement ring is stunning," Penny said as she looked at Cathy's ring.

"Thank you," Cathy said cheerfully before a shadow crossed her face and she added, "on a quick and serious note, I have to admit I was quite worried about his safety in Abu Dhabi recently. He said it was just another walk in the park, but I wasn't convinced it was as safe as he made it seem."

"First of all, Cathy, you and I have more in common than you might think. My late husband was an SAS officer killed in action many years ago, so I understand your anxiety now about Marcus's safety. He's not only my boss but also my friend. I believe the best way for you to cope with this part of his work is to realise that Marcus has had years of combat experience on the front lines with the SAS worldwide before he formed de Vere Security. He was also an active operative with E Squadron, and, from what I know of this unit, they select only the very best personnel for their international clandestine operations. You've met Major Freddy Carr, MI6; he was Marcus's boss during that period. So, in essence, they are closely linked. What I'm trying to say is that Marcus is extremely capable, especially in managing any risks that he or his team might face, so don't worry about him. He's a remarkable person who knows exactly what he's doing," Penny said reassuringly.

"Thank you very much for that. Honestly, having also lost my husband in combat, I can't help but worry a bit for Marcus. We both understand what it's like to be the wife of SF personnel," said Cathy.

"Wife, eh?" Penny chuckled with a wink.

"You got me," laughed Cathy.

"Well, let's head to the gardens and enjoy ourselves," Penny said, smiling eagerly to relax.

Marcus sat on the terrace balcony alone, sipping a glass of wine. He watched the women, arm in arm, chatting endlessly on the grounds. As he saw Cathy laugh with Penny about something, he felt grateful that she had accepted his proposal. His reverie was interrupted by the sound of a large Harley-Davidson rumbling up the winding drive, making him wonder how his 'Fat Boy' in its shed must be feeling lonely, since he hadn't been out for a ride in quite some time.

His phone buzzed.

"Gibbs, what's up?"

"For the sake of good order, I've just checked out the flat of that Iranian diplomat where Syed Ayrad was staying."

"And?"

"Well, I...erm...invited myself in to have a look around. Took the opportunity to plant some bugs and a few cameras linked to my computer, just in case some other bugger uses it in the future, now that we know Syed has fled the scene," said Gibbs, sounding pleased with himself.

"Nice work, mate. MI5 will be pleased to be made aware of a terrorist safe house."

At that moment, Marcus heard the noise of the Harley's departure as Joe stepped onto the terraced balcony.

"Morning, boss. Have you got a minute?"

"Of course. Who was that?"

"Anna. She's sorry she couldn't pop in and say hello because she's heading to a karate competition in Maidstone. She left this for you," Joe said, handing him a copy of 'The Oxford Mail' open to a story about the discovery of a body on a bench in Blackbird Leys Park, Oxford.

The police finally issued a statement confirming the identity as Mr Asif Badawi, but had no further comment, other than stating that the murder bore all the hallmarks of an assassination by an unknown party or parties.

Marcus studied the article with a wry smile.

“Interesting that we, with all our resources, only find this out now,” Marcus said, thinking what a clever bugger Freddy was.

“Thanks, Joe. I’ll handle it from here,” said Marcus, confident that without evidence, the case would go cold and those higher up would be pleased to hear it was over. And with that, the case was closed.

Cathy and Penny bounded onto the terrace, full of energy.

“Is it lunchtime yet? We’re starving,” Cathy said, hugging Marcus and giving him a peck on the cheek.

“What a surprise. Incessant talking can generate an appetite, or so I’ve heard,” laughed Marcus. “I’ve got some good news, Cathy,” said Marcus, passing the newspaper.

“Ironic, don’t you think? Badawi and his associates track you down through the press, and now he turns up dead in a newspaper article!”

Cathy’s response was a dry smile.

Henry appeared and announced that the Dover sole luncheon was ready to be served. To their delight, over lunch, both Marcus and Penny mentioned their visit to Frog Hall.

“Anything of interest?” Cathy asked with raised eyebrows.

"Just a picture of his girlfriend; she’s wearing stunning emerald earrings,” Penny said in between mouthfuls.

“That might fit,” Cathy said, puzzled.

“With what?" Penny asked.

"Oh, it might just be a coincidence, but my friend DS Tim Riley is investigating a case involving emerald earrings. In fact, it was my postmortem that identified the jewellery as a potential lead, along with a fragment of a scalpel," Cathy said slowly, her brows furrowed.

There was silence as they ate, then she added, "The murder weapon was recovered from a non-actor involved in the Parish murder. They also found that the fragment I discovered during my postmortem of Parish was an exact match."

Marcus suggested, "I'd like to meet Tim. Why not invite him over after lunch? That picture at Frog Hall seems suspiciously coincidental."

"I know Ben's a pain in the neck, maybe a bit of a sexual predator and a charm king – but a murderer?" said Cathy.

"Let's keep an open mind," Marcus suggested.

"Yeah, that works for me," Cathy agreed.

"I've spent most of my active service career relying on my instincts about people, and I have to say I think I'm quite good at it. Anyway, I'm looking forward to Tim's take on what we saw at Frog Hall," said Marcus.

"Alright, I'll give Tim a ring after we finish."

• CHAPTER 41 •

Introductions completed, Marcus, Cathy, Penny, and Tim sat on the terraced balcony overlooking the estate. Marcus and Penny detailed their visit to Frog Hall, which piqued Tim's interest. He kept nodding, growing increasingly engaged.

"Well, as you know, I'd been tasked to follow up by my boss Jordon, and I'm pleased to say that I unexpectedly received a call from a jeweller outside the net I'd initially placed, and he came up trumps. He sold the earrings to Parish, a close friend, and mentioned the name of one of Parish's girlfriends he remembered. He got the impression that she was important to him."

"Who was that?" Marcus asked.

"Possibly the key point. Her name is Helen," Tim said carefully.

"The woman in the photo, yes? The one with the earrings," Penny said.

"Yes, I believe so, based on what you've observed," Tim replied.

"Well now, there's a thing. A coincidence? I know you don't believe in those, do you, Marcus?" Cathy asked with a wink.

"Talking of jewels, Malone responded to my interest in the picture as if he'd forgotten about it. When I commented on how beautiful her earrings were, he appeared surprised and stuttered that they were a gift from her mother. But his body language showed clear signs of discomfort," Penny explained.

"You reckon he was lying?"

"Looked that way."

"Look, with everything you've said, I'm not sure what to do now, you see, my boss has pulled me off the case as of fifteen minutes ago by phone. Giving me no reasons and has assigned me to another case," said Tim.

"What? But you're almost there. Why would he do that now, for Christ's sake?" said Cathy, confused.

"Well, he's the boss, he can do what he bloody likes, but it does seem odd to me," said Tim. "I mean, as you said, now there's a reasonable link to Malone's missing girlfriend, Helen. Circumstantial, yes, but potentially damning and adds a new twist," Tim added. "And now I can't follow up – thanks to my boss. So, my hands are tied."

"Bob Brimley, as you know, Tim is the Chief Constable of Kent and a personal friend of mine. I could speak with him privately to explain our concerns about Malone. What are your thoughts?"

“Works for me, but I should inform Jordon, he’s my boss, after all,” said Tim.

“Leave him out of the loop for now. Let’s wait to hear what Brimley has to say," Marcus said earnestly. After a slight pause, he added with a subtle smile, "Malone is a big shot here, and Bob likely won’t appreciate his team storming into Frog Hall guns blazing.”

“What about a drink, anyone?” Marcus asked, attempting to lift the gloomy mood. Everyone responded with enthusiastic nods.

“And I’m off duty, so no problem,” Tim said happily.

Marcus called Henry to organise some pink.

“Malone wants to lend you a book, Cathy. Why not follow up on that and explore Frog Hall together? I believe it’s a good plan before I talk with Bob Brimley. What do you think?" Marcus said with enthusiasm.

"Yeah, why not? I’m all in," Cathy grinned mischievously. “Tell him I can’t wait to read the book about forensics,” she added with a smile. “And you can protect me, Marcus."

“Your knight in shining armour, as always,” Marcus smiled, glad to think of himself as a private detective.

• CHAPTER 42 •

Chiddington Hall

Ben Malone sat back, relaxed, in the ornate wrought-iron furniture that decorated the terrace of Chiddington Hall, overlooking the landscaped gardens. Sir James's butler, Charles, arrived with a chilled bottle of Dom Perignon Rosé 2004 and two tall, elegant Grasmere champagne fluted crystal glasses.

"Cheers – good to see you," said Sir James Chiddington happily, sipping the excellent wine. It was an 80% Chardonnay and 20% Pinot Noir blend, one of his favourites.

"Cheers," Ben said. "It's like sipping strawberries drenched in luxurious, creamy richness."

"Life's too short for anything else," his host smiled. "So, what the hell happened to Asif?"

"Who knows? But this has all the signs of a professional hit, and ignoring the media reports, I would guess MI6," said Ben.

"On UK soil, really? Isn't that unlikely? I mean, they're an offshore group. Aren't they?" said Sir James.

"Take my word for it that they are more than capable of taking him out without leaving a trace. And remember, they have all the resources to do so in a way that's completely off the grid with no comeback. No evidence. Case closed. But upon reflection, Asif mentioned an incident that happened a while ago at the Guards Club. A Major Carr took an interest in him at first glance. It might mean nothing, of course, but our friend, who, by the way, couldn't make it today, told me that Carr was a name he recognised. And he's an MI6 operative. So, maybe Carr's involved in all this. Frankly, I don't give a toss anymore; it's all academic now, water under the bridge, case closed. So let's move on," said The Painter.

"Yeah, you're right. So, as you say, let's move on. Ben, I was very pleased to hear that you potentially have two candidates for the Summer Hunt next weekend. By the way, I've, of course, given all my staff that weekend off. Tell me more about this woman, Caroline, and how you are going to get her into the mix."

"Well, after a very satisfying encounter with her, she's now fully under my control. I can tell you she's a forensic clinical psychiatrist, and I..."

"Say no more. I mean, two doctors? Ben, really? I mean, we are going to be in safe hands for sure, if you get my drift," said Sir James, amused.

"Indeed, she seeks revenge on Meer for some sexual rejection by her, and I intend to propose a solution when I see her in the next day or two," said Ben, relishing the thought.

"Details?"

"Caroline is the key to luring Meer into a situation where I can drug her and then bring both of them on Saturday morning to the Summer Hunt. I'll get her to ring Meer under the pretext of apologising and invite her to her home, and then we'll drug her. Of course, Caroline will not realise that her ultimate fate will be the same as Meer's. It might even be possible to persuade her to...erm...play with Meer before we participate, which would add a little extra spice to our satisfaction," Ben said with a smile.

"Great. A perfect scenario for our members," said Sir James with a beaming smile.

"Exactly, so I'll spend the night with Caroline to... erm... cement our relationship a little more," grinned The Painter. "And then I'll get her to ring Meer to invite her to her home, 'Pinewood Cottage,' as I said. I'll mix up some liquid ecstasy into a bottle of wine for Caroline to drink. Of course, I'll keep well out of the picture until Meer goes down, and then we'll load her into the van at the rear of the cottage and make our way here in time for fun and games before the Hunt takes off."

"Are you sure she'll play?"

"Absolutely, she's putty in my hands. She believes that The Summer Hunt will only humiliate Meer sexually and no one will get hurt – the ideal revenge scenario for Caroline."

"So, what's she look like?"

"A perfect match for Meer, slim, blond, green eyes, and truly stunning," grinned The Painter.

"Excellent, I can't wait," smirked Sir James. "But I want to take a moment to honour our late friend Asif. Over the years, he worked hard to supply us with many remarkable, young, beautiful, innocent girls as prey. Even better, most of them were merely spoiled brats from the London Club scene. They were all exceptional. What a sad loss for the sport."

Both members of the Summer Hunt raised their glasses in a toast to the late Asif Badawi.

CHAPTER 43

Chiddington Hall

Even at such an early hour, the sun was already blisteringly hot as the two members present of The Summer Hunt sat cleaning and testing their crossbows in preparation for the upcoming hunt later that day. With his staff off for the weekend, Sir James Chiddington, full of anticipation, was awaiting the arrival of Ben Malone with their prey. Two doctors for the price of one, he couldn't wait.

Pinewood Cottage – Near Chiddingstone, Kent

The stage was set. Ben Malone had borrowed Sir James's van the previous evening and left his high-profile car in exchange, better to keep a low profile, and the van was, obviously, more suitable for his plans the following morning. He drove up the impressive red-chipped carriage drive that led from the small country lane entrance and parked the van behind Caroline's property, Pinewood Cottage. It was a stunningly beautiful oak-framed three-bedroom house, aptly named, as it sat partly surrounded by a small pine forest on the outskirts of Chiddingstone village in the Kent countryside. Caroline, undoubtedly an intelligent woman, was nevertheless now under his complete sexual domination and control, as planned, since he had learnt of her close connection with the bitch doctor during their unexpected encounter at the Pale Horse. Destiny.

Reinforcing his dominance after their encounter at Frog Hall, he spent the night reliving it. Somewhere within his twisted mind, he believed it was only fair to give her pleasure before her impending death at the hands of The Summer Hunt later that day. The plan had gone smoothly. He hid in Caroline's study as she successfully persuaded Meer to come and then administered the drugged wine. They loaded Doctor Meer's unconscious body, as planned, into the van at the back of the cottage.

"I mean, you can play with her too if you want – I'd like to see that," laughed The Painter as he drove down the driveway at Pinewood Cottage towards Chiddington Hall, eager to begin the game.

"If that turns you on, Ben, I'd be happy to do it and enjoy it. She deserves it."

• CHAPTER 44 •

The early morning sunshine flooded what Captain Marcus de Vere called his Harley Stable.

"She's looking good, boss," said Joe, admiring the gleaming Fat Boy as he sauntered into the stable.

"Yeah, she's my girl and deserves the TLC. I mean, she's not only a fantastic ride but that throaty roar still never fails to fill my soul every time," laughed Marcus as his phone buzzed.

"Carter, what's up?" said Marcus, as he grabbed his phone.

"Morning, boss. Even though all threats seemed to have been resolved, I had a gut feeling that all wasn't well and decided, on a whim, to follow Dr Meer about half an hour ago to Pinewood Cottage, a property near Chiddingstone Castle. I checked the registration plates of a red E-Type Jaguar parked in the drive, and it's registered to a doctor Caroline Peterson – googled her, and it turns out she's a clinical forensic psychiatrist. Who, I guess, is a friend of Dr Meer – at least they seemed to recognise each other on Dr Meer's arrival, although Peterson was smiling, Dr Meer's body language looked decidedly uncomfortable. By the way, they could be almost twins, although Peterson has shorter blond hair. But my gut tells me that something smells off here, boss."

"I've lost count of how often your gut instincts have been correct, Carter. Go ahead!" said Marcus de Vere, with a hint of anxiety.

"Well, it's strange in that a shabby-looking, old grey van just came down the drive from the back of the property – then stopped while Peterson jumped out and locked the front door – no sign of doctor Meer. The driver's Ben Malone."

"Malone! Christ, what the hell's going on?" Marcus asked, his heartbeat rising an octave. A strong feeling of unease began to build in his mind.

"Who knows, but I'm following the van right now. The rear windows are all blacked out, so we can't be sure whether Doctor Meer's on board. If not, where is she? Her Range Rover's still in the driveway."

Marcus, nervously, caressed the fist-in-the-wind Tallboy Handlebars of his Harley Davidson, trying to process what he was hearing and what it could possibly mean.

"I'm on the saddle now, Carter. I'll check the property immediately. Keep following the van and keep me updated, thanks. I have a Bluetooth link in my helmet so we can talk in real time," said Marcus.

The uncertainty of the scenario presented caused his mind to whirl; the only satisfying plus was that whatever was going down, Carter was on top of it.

"Affirmative, boss," Carter acknowledged before signing off.

Marcus kick-started the Fat Boy, relishing the sound of the 1,800cc Milwaukee-eight 114 fuel-injected engine as it burbled away – the welcome sound, soothing his mind a little.

"Joe, pass me your Glock and a spare mag, mate."

"Sure, boss, what's up?" Joe asked as he handed over the weapon, along with a spare magazine, without hesitation. Marcus slipped into the empty shoulder holster beneath his leather riding jacket, which was decorated with biking insignia from various clubs he frequented.

"Later, Joe," said Marcus as he roared off down the drive of Little Manor and made his way to Pinewood Cottage with growing trepidation about what he might or might not find.

• CHAPTER 45 •

The van pulled into the driveway of a massive estate. Passing through the large, ornate wrought iron gates, Carter noticed, from the old brass plaque, that the van's destination was Chiddington Hall. He parked alongside the estate's walls further down from the entrance and leapt onto the roof of his car, resting his elbows on the walls, and quickly scanned the property with his binoculars. Dominating the front was a series of huge stained-glass windows. He climbed over the wall with ease and ran quietly through the scattered trees towards them.

Sir James embraced Ben Malone in a welcoming hug, whispering his pleasure at the look and figure of Caroline, as they both entered the vast stained-glass room of Chiddington Hall, which once served as the property's ballroom in earlier days.

"Welcome to Chiddington Hall, my dear – you must be Caroline," Sir James said, handing her a glass of champagne infused with liquid ecstasy.

"It's my pleasure, Sir James," Caroline said happily, delighted to see Cathy being prepared for her fate. "I can't wait for it all to begin."

"How long, Ben?" Sir James whispered.

"Oh, for Meer, it should wear off in about ten minutes or so," said The Painter gleefully.

"What about Petterson?"

"Oh, Petterson's ought to kick in soon after," said Sir James. "Can't wait to see your lovely Caroline playing with her, and then she'll find herself as the appetiser, Meer will be the main course," he chuckled. "Did you bring the handcuffs?"

"Of course, they've served me well," smirked The Painter as he bent down to secure Doctor Meer's wrists.

Caroline sat beside Cathy's sleeping body, sipping her champagne and looking forward to her ex-friends' humiliation. It was only moments before she too slipped into unconsciousness beside her.

Ben Malone grabbed Doctor Meer's handbag and yanked the stunning pendant from her neck – unaware that in doing so, he had set off the panic alarm.

Carter, hearing the alarm's ping, leaned against the surreal-looking stained-glass window and peered through it carefully.

"What's this?" The Watcher asked as Ben handed him Dr Meer's handbag.

"A pistol? A SIG Sauer P226, no less, a nice piece. God knows what she's doing with it or why?" he said, turning the weapon over in his hands.

"Who knows, who cares. As Master of the Summer Hunt, Sir James, I salute you," said The Painter, raising his glass of champagne. "Either way, both our doctors will end up in the mineshaft along with all the others after the hunt."

"Strip and handcuff Caroline, Ben," said Sir James. "But cuff them behind her head. I'm ready."

Ben Malone cuffed her wrists, his excitement mounting.

Marcus kicked the stand on his bike and approached the heavy oak front door of Pinewood Cottage, knocking with a sense of trepidation. He could hear the echo of the weighty serpent-shaped door knocker reverberate from inside the house, but when there was no answer, he peered through each window. All the doors and windows were firmly locked. Finding no sign of Cathy or any movement inside, he hurried over to her Range Rover, which revealed no further clues about her whereabouts. He then buzzed Carter, his concern mounting.

The effect of the drug had worn off some time ago, but Cathy feigned unconsciousness while, through slit eyes, she observed the scene of her captivity. And listened. Stunned to recognise the men standing drinking their champagne not far away. She'd felt Caroline's body fall unconscious beside her on the mattress. It had taken all of Cathy's self-control not to respond.

Cathy's unease grew as she secretly tried to reach her pendant, but her handcuffed wrists made it difficult. She then realised it was missing and nervously observed the threatening crossbows by the wall. From the men's conversations, it was clear they intended to violate her and Caroline and then hunt them down like prey. Nonetheless, her intuition screamed in her mind that Carter would be nearby – how, she couldn't fathom, but took solace in knowing that somehow, he would be. It was obvious to her now that Caroline had been complicit with Malone in her current predicament.

"Carter, what's happening on your end? Pinewood Cottage came up empty," Marcus asked, trying to control his angst at the appalling state of play.

The van's at Chiddington Hall Estate. It circled round to the back. I'm standing outside some large stained-glass windows, and it's not looking good.

"Go," said Marcus impatiently.

"It's bad, boss. I've got Doctor Meer and Peterson handcuffed to a mattress. They both appear to be drugged, and there are weapon-grade crossbows nearby. We need an Armed Response Team immediately."

"Shit – alright, I'll get Brimley on it."

"Not Brimley, boss – he's here clutching a bloody pistol."

"Brimley! I can't believe it. Okay, I'll be there in ten, and I'll brief Jordon and Riley to get tooled up."

"Going in, boss," Carter announced as he crashed through the glass and rolled into a firing stance, but it was too late. Brimley fired, shattering his right shoulder. Being the consummate professional, Carter rolled again, managing, through the pain, to switch his pistol to his left hand and fire a controlled three-shot response, taking out Brimley with fatal accuracy. Cathy crawled across the room and managed to pick up her pistol with her handcuffed hands.

“Are you alright, Ma’am?” Carter asked painfully as blood seeped from his injury. Through a haze of pain, he saw Malone and Sir James rush out of the room, each carrying quivers of arrows and two high-powered crossbows.

“What now?” yelled The Painter as he and Sir James hurriedly made their way to Sir James's jeep.

“Calm down. My plane is at East Haxted Farm Airfield, just half an hour away by jeep, and then we’ll disappear," Sir James said, trying to sound confident.

“I’m good,” cried Cathy as she stood unsteadily, grasping her pistol, ready to follow but freezing in place as she heard the throaty roar of Marcus’s Harley arrive.

Glock drawn, Marcus rushed in and quickly assessed the situation, worried about Cathy’s condition but relieved that she was alive.

“I’m okay, darling. Carter needs medical help, but he’s fine. Malone and Chiddington have made a run for it; catch them. We’re really all good here.”

Marcus heard the jeep speeding off and chased after it on his Harley. Not a bike built for off-road. Nevertheless, he went for it.

Cathy followed him unsteadily, calling out, "Watch out, they’re armed with crossbows," as Marcus hurriedly moved across the estate lawns.

Malone carefully raised his weapon and fired at the rapidly approaching Harley Davidson. The arrow flew harmlessly over Marcus’s head as he reached under his left shoulder to grasp the Glock and fired two warning shots in the air. Ignoring the warning, Malone waited until Marcus was about 40 yards away, steadied himself, and then raised his crossbow to fire.

The hunter was now the hunted.

Too late for Malone, as Marcus fired three closely grouped shots into his chest. Malone fell from the jeep, fatally wounded.

"Not a bad shot, mate," said Marcus to himself. Chiddington pulled over with his arms raised in surrender. Marcus looked down at Malone's body. He had hoped it wouldn't come to this; he had wanted Malone to face a long time behind bars. It wasn't to be. It was all over.

Leaving his Fat Boy where it was, Marcus got into the jeep and made Sir James drive back to the property, with no words exchanged. The Captain of the Police Armed Response Unit nodded to Marcus as Chiddington was handcuffed and taken away to the waiting Black Maria.

The ARV medic was tending to Carter's wound, and Jordon had unlocked the handcuffs on both women's wrists; everything was fine. Marcus rushed to Cathy and held her tightly in his arms, relief washing over him, not wanting to let her go. Both moved to Carter, who, even after the nasty wound, was in top form, relishing the outcome. Marcus bent down carefully to hug his old friend, and Cathy knelt to kiss and thank him for saving her life.

She couldn't help but smile as Carter sat up and responded in his typical Carter manner, saying, "No problem, ma'am." Minutes later, an ambulance arrived to take over Carter's care and transport both Cathy and Caroline to the hospital for observation.

Marcus walked Cathy to the ambulance.

"It's all over at last, darling." Cathy turned.

"Not quite yet. I heard them talk about throwing us into a mineshaft after the hunt – it's got to be on the grounds somewhere."

"So, what's next?" Marcus wondered aloud as he helped Cathy into the ambulance, giving her a warm, gentle kiss. Marcus then informs Jordon about the troubling development, prompting Jordon to make an immediate call.

Soon, the estate is swarming with police and tracker dogs.

• CHAPTER 46 •

Five Weeks Later

The Upper Terrace Balcony – Little Manor

Major Freddy Carr and Carter relaxed on the terrace balcony of Little Manor to celebrate Captain Marcus de Vere and Doctor Cathy Meer's engagement. Henry, with his typical flair, was busy pouring sparkling pink champagne into the elegant Waterford crystal glasses as they all chatted.

Monica, Jenny, and George were happily playing in the maze below. Marcus stood up to look over the balcony when he heard the throaty, bubbling roar of a motorbike approaching up the drive.

“Guess who?”

They all looked in anticipation.

"It’s just Johnny Jordon riding a bloody 1947 Indian Chief Motorcycle with a sidecar. I can’t believe it. We’re talking serious classics here,” said Marcus, smiling at his guests.

"Boys and their toys again," laughed Cathy.

"Am I right, 1,212cc Flathead 2-Cylinder, single carburettor?" Carter grinned as he tried to scratch an increasingly irritating itch under the plaster cast encasing his shoulder, but without success.

"Spot on, mate, 3-speed hand shift and 40 BHP at 4,700 rpm, a highly collectable piece of kit," laughed Marcus as Johnny Jordon entered the balcony, closely followed by Marcus's bodyguard Joe.

"You're a dark horse, Johnny, I didn't realise you were one of us. She's beautiful, mate. By the way, congratulations on your promotion to Chief Constable."

"Thanks, Marcus, and congratulations to you and Cathy – about time if you ask me," smiled the new Chief Constable of Kent, raising the Waterford lead crystal glass that had appeared in his hand by the magic of Henry.

Henry continued to hover discreetly. He had removed a bottle of the iconic Laurent Perrier Cuvee Rose Petal Robe Champagne from the rare vintage silver plate Bollinger Champagne ice bucket and stand. Ready, as ever, to pour and replenish as needed.

"Congratulations to Marcus and Cathy on their engagement," Major Freddy Carr said, raising his glass. He also offered a special toast to Cathy, saying, "With everything you've been through, you're a remarkable lady."

"I agree with that," Carter said with a grin as he lifted his long-stemmed Waterford lead crystal glass in a toast. "Here's to you, Cathy – you'll be losing your job soon, Joe. Marcus now has a very close protection operative, mate."

"What's the latest, Johnny?" Marcus asked, motioning for him to follow to a far corner of the terrace.

"Unfortunately, several bodies were recovered from an abandoned mineshaft on the estate. All but two were young women – forensic and DNA investigations have successfully identified most of them. You simply won't believe what that bastard Chiddington had framed on the wall of his study."

Marcus said grimly, "Let me guess, some sort of trophy?"

"A framed Rolling Stones T-shirt saturated with his DNA and that of Sara Grantsbury, the missing hiker, and so another nail in his coffin, he didn't even bother to wash it. Four of the young women's DNA matches those missing from a nightclub in Mayfair. One that Badawi regularly frequented at the time and was questioned by the police, but, with no evidence, walked away, yet it certainly flags him now as a previous member of The Summer Hunt."

"You mentioned that all but two were young women. What's the story there?"

"Forensic teams have identified the remains as Helen and Melissa Shore, Malone's live-in partners, with Malone's DNA present on them. Forensics have also confirmed that Malone was responsible for the murder of Nick Parish. Analysis of the lipstick he used to sign the victim's back was an exact match for that found at his home."

"So, it's all over," Marcus said gratefully.

"Not quite," Johnny Jordon said. "Syed Ayad was killed in Qatar yesterday morning. It appeared to be a professional hit. Of course, that's no loss to anyone."

"Do we know who was responsible?" Marcus asked.

"Off the record, Colonel Charlie Dankworth," Freddy Carr interrupted, his face splitting into a wide grin.

"Well, well – good old Uncle Charlie. What will happen to him?" said Marcus, mirroring Freddy's grin.

"Nothing at all. MI6 will make it all go away; his body will, no doubt, be found somewhere in circumstances similar to those of the late Badawi. I believe the Colonel felt that, although Syed had shown no obvious desire to finish what his master had begun, he still posed a potential future threat to Cathy and her family. So he stepped up to make certain, permanently."

"I heard from Penny that he was once an assassin for a clandestine MI6 unit known back then as Maximus," said Marcus inquisitively. "Is that group still active?"

"Oh, that's way beyond your pay grade, Marcus," laughed Major Freddy Carr, with a wink. "I'm sure it's ancient water under the bridge now – I mean, God forbid that MI6 would contemplate killing anyone in cold blood. We don't do that sort of stuff today, eh, Marcus? But Uncle Charlie should be taken very seriously and never underestimated."

"We invited him, didn't we, Marcus?" Cathy asked as she joined the men.

"I'll answer that, Cathy, if you don't mind, Marcus. A threat was uncovered some weeks ago against Highgrove, the country residence of King Charles. Thanks to the hot intel Marcus brought back from his mission in Abu Dhabi, we were able to thwart it. Our friend is currently chatting with the ringleader. So, he's a little busy but sends his best," chuckled Major Freddy Carr.

"So, it's truly, finally, all over now," Marcus said as Henry whispered something into his ear.

"Yes, it's all over," Major Freddy Carr said as they rejoined the group.

"Carter, I want to toast you, excellent work! Wishing you a speedy recovery, mate."

All present raised their glasses and echoed the Major's words.

"By the way, Johnny, what ultimately happened to Doctor Peterson?" Cathy asked, hesitating to use her first name.

"Doctor Peterson was arrested and charged with kidnapping, a grave offence, and she'll face a lengthy sentence behind bars."

"Good to hear," said Cathy as she slumped back in her chair, trying to make sense of everything. She had killed Badawi without hesitation or remorse. He had tried to rape and kill her and her children, all driven by revenge. But after the act, she experienced moments of reflection, questioning whether, deep down, she might have found a sense of satisfaction in her vengeance against the man who murdered her husband. She was unsure. Her thoughts were suddenly interrupted when Marcus took her hand, and his gentle touch helped her clear her mind of any further questions. Nonetheless, she had no regrets.

"Come, darling, let's party," Marcus said, noticing she was becoming quite introverted and distracted. His heart fluttering with love, he felt it was a good day, and he was committed to making sure everyone enjoyed themselves, especially his fiancée.

"Time to move on, everyone, drink up! I hear from Henry that a gourmet lunch is ready to be served at any moment," Marcus said with a broad grin as he led Cathy inside, gesturing for everyone to follow.

End...

Acknowledgements

Robert Ayling QPM MA (Oxon): (Retired Chief Constable – Kent) Thank you, Bob, for your patience and really helpful insights during the process. Forgive me for taking a few liberties here and there away from strict police procedures.

Dr Stuart Hamilton: (A working Consultant Home Office Registered Forensic Pathologist). Thank you for your guidance through the grisly matter of murder and post-mortem procedures. Any mistakes are all mine.

Sincere thanks to a former British Intelligence Officer (who will remain nameless) for his guidance concerning the raid in the Gulf. Any errors re action scenes or weapons deployed are entirely mine.

Abu Dhabi: Those familiar with the region – please excuse my 'playing' with its geography a bit.

ABOUT THE AUTHOR

Peter Roche retired early to focus on writing. He now lives in the Czech Republic with his Czech wife and eleven-year-old son and has written three children's books there. His last book, 'Little Dragon', was published in a bilingual edition in 2018. He recently completed a full-length comedy/farce stage play, 'The Naughty Monsieur Dupont', and a shorter comedy, 'The Dishwasher', which was published on June 24 in NY by 'The Westchester Review'.

Prey for Revenge is his debut novel.

www.ingramcontent.com/pod-product-compliance
Ingram Content Group UK Ltd.
Pitfield, Milton Keynes, MK11 3LW, UK
UKHW052008190226
468202UK00009B/27

9 781913 142483